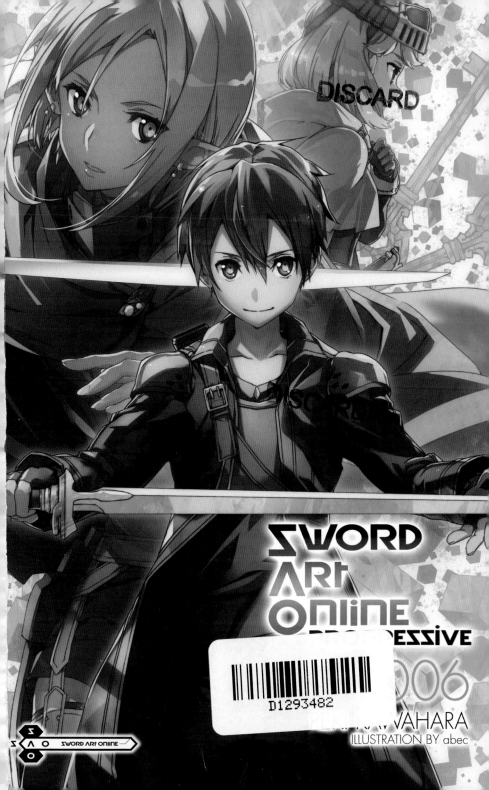

DISCARD

DISCARD

SWORD ARt OnlInE PROGRESSIVE

006

KAWAHARA

ILLUSTRATION BY abec

SWORD ARt OnlInE

"...Zzz..."

Asuna

A player trapped inside *Sword Art Online*. Without a care for her life, she throws herself into battle against monsters.

"You will be warmer if you snuggle closer."

Kizmel

A dark elf NPC who joined the party on the third floor. She was unavoidably killed in the beta test, but in the deadly full version of *Sword Art Online*, she survives and forms a powerful bond with Kirito and Asuna.

"N-no, I think I'm fine right here."

Kirito

A swordsman aiming to beat the top floor of Aincrad. He adventures as a solo player but temporarily teams up with Asuna.

Gindo

Leader of the small guild Qusack.
Uses a shortspear.

"We're going through the blelf... er, dark elf campaign right now."

"I merely wish
to speak with
that swordsman
over there."

Myia

An NPC who follows Kirito's group
around Stachion, the biggest town
on the sixth floor. But she has a
surprising identity...

The Irrational Cube
The boss of the sixth floor of Aincrad.

"N... numbers...?!"

"Evaaaade!!"

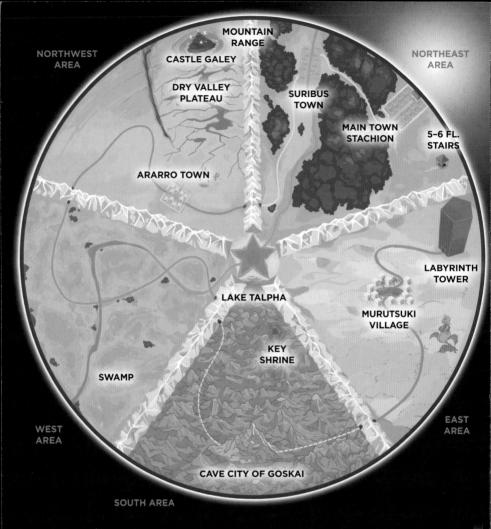

NORTHWEST AREA

MOUNTAIN RANGE

CASTLE GALEY

NORTHEAST AREA

DRY VALLEY PLATEAU

SURIBUS TOWN

MAIN TOWN STACHION

5-6 FL. STAIRS

ARARRO TOWN

LABYRINTH TOWER

LAKE TALPHA

MURUTSUKI VILLAGE

KEY SHRINE

SWAMP

WEST AREA

EAST AREA

CAVE CITY OF GOSKAI

SOUTH AREA

FLOATING CASTLE AINCRAD FLOOR DATA Aincrad

SIXTH FLOOR

Just as it was during the beta, the design theme of the sixth floor is "puzzles." In the main town of Stachion, for example, all building doors aside from the main gate are locked by a wide variety of puzzles that must be solved before the town's features are available.

The floor itself is divided by impassable mountains into five equal areas that meet at a star-shaped lake in the middle. Stachion is located in the northeast area, while the floor boss and labyrinth tower await in the southeast, just adjacent to the start but blocked by tall mountains that make direct travel impossible. Therefore, in order to reach the tower, you must proceed counterclockwise through all five areas.

Most of the northeast area around Stachion is thick forest similar to the kind found on the third floor. In the northwest area where Castle Galey is located, the ground is dry and barren. The west area is mainly comprised of swamps, the south area is a land of caves, and the east area, with the labyrinth tower, is desert. Consequently, one of the main features of the sixth floor is the sharp contrast among areas as you pass each set of mountains.

Map Illustration: Tatsuya Kurusu

SWORD ART ONLINE PROGRESSIVE

VOLUME 6

Reki Kawahara

abec

bee-pee

YEN
ON

NEW YORK

SWORD ART ONLINE PROGRESSIVE Volume 6
REKI KAWAHARA

Translation by Stephen Paul
Cover art by abec

This book is a work of fiction. Names, characters, places, and incidents are the product of
the author's imagination or are used fictitiously. Any resemblance to actual events, locales,
or persons, living or dead, is coincidental.

SWORD ART ONLINE PROGRESSIVE Volume 6
© Reki Kawahara 2018
First published in Japan in 2018 by KADOKAWA CORPORATION, Tokyo.
English translation rights arranged with KADOKAWA CORPORATION, Tokyo,
through Tuttle-Mori Agency, Inc., Tokyo.

English translation © 2019 by Yen Press, LLC

Yen On
150 West 30th Street, 19th Floor
New York, NY 10001

Visit us at yenpress.com
facebook.com/yenpress
twitter.com/yenpress
yenpress.tumblr.com
instagram.com/yenpress

First Yen On Edition: July 2019

Yen On is an imprint of Yen Press, LLC.
The Yen On name and logo are trademarks of Yen Press, LLC.

The publisher is not responsible for websites (or their content) that are not owned by the
publisher.

Library of Congress Cataloging-in-Publication Data

Names: Kawahara, Reki, author. | Paul, Stephen (Translator), translator.
Title: Sword art online progressive / Reki Kawahara; translation by Stephen Paul.
Description: First Yen On edition. | New York, NY : Yen On, 2016–
Identifiers: LCCN 2016029472 | ISBN 9780316259361 (v. 1 : pbk) |
    ISBN 9780316342179 (v. 2 : pbk) | ISBN 9780316348836 (v. 3 : pbk) |
    ISBN 9780316545426 (v. 4 : pbk) | ISBN 9781975328146 (v. 5 : pbk) |
    ISBN 9781975383336 (v. 6 : pbk)
Subjects: | CYAC: Virtual reality—Fiction. | Science fiction.
Classification: LCC PZ7.K1755 Swr 2016 | DDC [Fic]—dc23
LC record available at https://lccn.loc.gov/2016029472

ISBNs: 978-1-9753-8333-6 (paperback)
       978-1-9753-8334-3 (ebook)

10 9 8 7 6 5 4 3 2 1

LSC-C

Printed in the United States of America

"THIS MIGHT BE A GAME, BUT IT'S NOT SOMETHING YOU PLAY."

—Akihiko Kayaba, *Sword Art Online* programmer

SWORD ART ONLINE PROGRESSIVE

CANON OF THE GOLDEN RULE (END)

SIXTH FLOOR OF AINCRAD, JANUARY 2023

6

I AWOKE TO MOVEMENTS THAT WEREN'T MINE, warmth that wasn't mine, and breathing that wasn't mine.

Through cracked eyelids, I saw the faint, white-gray light of morning. Based on the color, I gauged it to be around five in the morning. Normally, I'd still be asleep at this hour, but I'd gone to bed very early and had already gotten nine hours of sleep. We were set to meet with Kizmel in the mess hall at seven, so there was still time to relax, but I decided it was better not to be lazy.

And yet, my eyes closed again. The chilly air of the early January morning versus the absolute comfort and warmth of the bed was simply an unfair fight. My partially awakened mind sank back down into the darkness.

Just thirty more minutes...No, twenty, I thought like a middle schooler on a Monday morning and then tried to turn off my brain.

But then there was a faint *"Mmh..."* and a sensation of wriggling next to me. At first, I thought I was having a dream about owning a cat, but then I realized it was neither a cat nor a dream.

My eyelids were so heavy that they felt like they'd been glued together; even though the virtual world didn't make use of your actual eyes, the way it made it impossible to focus when in a half-asleep state was oddly true to life—probably an issue between the brain and the NerveGear. I blinked repeatedly until the gray blur sharpened into a proper image.

The upper half of my field of view was dominated by a large pillow, while the bottom half was a light-brown *something*. I was resting on my right side, I could tell, and my right arm was extended forward, trapped between the brown object and the pillow.

My left arm was resting on a soft object, and my legs felt intertwined with something, as well. They were either trapping it or being entrapped themselves; it was hard to tell for sure. I blinked some more, using my free arm to try to push away the enigma stuck to my body...

"*Nnuh...*" came another murmur, from somewhere under my chin. The soft object my left hand was touching suddenly wriggled.

It wasn't a cat or any other small animal. It was a large animal, about my size—a human. A player. Specifically, it was my temporary partner, Lady Asuna. The brown object resting on my right arm was Asuna's head.

The instant the situation registered in my mind, it accelerated from a dazed state past normal attention into hyper-focus. As my mind got up to speed, I chose my course of action.

Apparently, I had offered my arm as pillow space and had my free hand holding her shoulder. I was on my right side, and Asuna was on her left, meaning that our fronts were nearly in total contact, and I couldn't tell what was going on with our legs. I moved my eyes without craning my neck to glance up at the headboard. I was firmly on the left side of the bed—meaning that I was the one violating the territorial treaty. We were only holding pinkies when we went to sleep, so during the night I had somehow advanced all the way from east to west.

"*Uyu...*"

Asuna budged again. The intervals of her activity were getting shorter, and within minutes...perhaps less than a minute, she would likely awaken. I had to retreat to my territory on the right side of the bed before that happened.

Carefully, I let go of Asuna's shoulder and let my hand hover in the air. But my right arm was still trapped between her head and the pillow, and removing it would prove difficult. Not to mention our legs, which were all tangled. At this point, the only way to free myself without disturbing Asuna would require a teleport crystal, but those only allowed for teleport to the various town teleport gates—and more importantly, they weren't available on the sixth floor.

Still, I had time to attempt it, should I believe in miracles—and I didn't have much other choice. I tried to use my left hand to lift up Asuna's head. If I could get my right arm free, I might be able to undo our legs and escape.

"Mmmh..."

The moment my fingers brushed the back of her head, Asuna grimaced. I quickly moved my hand away. She wriggled for a few more seconds, then unfolded her hand right in front of her and clenched my shirt collar.

I'm so dead.

At this point, all I could do was let my muscles go limp and wait for the fateful moment to occur.

Two hours later...

"...Why are you putting your fish on Asuna's plate, Kirito? Do you not like fish?" Kizmel asked me. We were in the dining hall.

With a sad, secretive smile, I replied, "No, I love fish," in the dry tone of a sample sentence in a language textbook.

"Then why are you giving it all away?"

"Um..."

I was at a loss for an appropriate response. Instead, Asuna stuck her fork into the fried fish I was offering her and happily explained, "Kirito did something bad, so he's paying for his crime."

"Oh...What did he do?"

"Well..." Asuna started, but before she could detail the entire incident, I interjected.

"You see, I kind of invaded Asuna's personal space…er, meaning that I got a little too physically close for her comfort," I said, to explain the English terminology of *personal space*. I got a cold glare from the fencer for my comment. Yes, the act of embracing someone in a bed was beyond the level of "violation of personal space," but if Kizmel was going to be disgusted with me, too, I might as well spend the entire day doing squats in the corner of the castle by myself.

I prayed she would understand and accept this explanation, assuming that she actually wouldn't. But to my good fortune, Kizmel nodded deeply and earnestly. "I see. It is the first time I have heard this term, but I understand your meaning. In elf society, too, it is considered to be a violation of norms to approach another too closely."

"Oh, really?" asked Asuna to my right. She set down her cup of herbal tea and wondered, "But…when you're around us, you don't seem to keep your distance, Kizmel…In the queen spider's dungeon on the third floor, you ushered us under your cape of hiding, for example."

Indeed, I recalled being rather flustered at how *much* contact there had been with her arms and legs and other body parts. The elf knight smiled wistfully and glanced at her own hands.

"…Yes, I do recall that. It would seem that, compared to other dark elves, my persi…personal space…is rather narrow. Tilnel did like to cling to me, after all…We were practically joined at the hip when we were children, so I suppose I became used to the feeling."

I could sense Asuna's eyes widening when Kizmel mentioned the name of her late sister, who had died in battle with a Forest Elven Falconer on the third floor.

Asuna and I never met Tilnel. In fact, I was under the assumption that there had never actually been a dark elf NPC in Aincrad named Tilnel. Kizmel's childhood with her beloved sister, the point at which she became a knight and Tilnel became an herbalist, and Tilnel's death during the mission to recover the sacred key…All these things had to be backstory, details invented and placed in Kizmel's memory. For one thing, elves were long-lived, so Kizmel was older than she appeared, perhaps fifty or sixty, or even older than that. Yet, the world of Aincrad itself had only been around since November 6, 2022, less than two months ago in the real world.

But after all my interactions with Kizmel, Viscount Yofilis, and even old Romolo and the camp blacksmith, that way of thinking was slowly evolving. These things seemed too rich and complex to just be simple generated memories that were implanted to define the characters and give them individuality.

In the present day of 2022—er, no, it was 2023 now, I had to remind myself—humanity had yet to develop a properly functioning AGI, or artificial general intelligence.

Artificial intelligence itself had made great strides in the five years since 2017, which was now considered the first year of the AI era. There were shogi and *go* apps you could install on your smartphone that were tougher than any pro players, programs for stock and currency trading that could perform thousands of transactions per second for efficient gains, and hospitals now had tools to automatically perform diagnostics with high-res imaging. It wouldn't be long now before we reached level 5, the point where fully automated cars were driving around on public streets.

But compared to the rapid advancements of these "narrow AI," which were focused on specific tasks, we still had a long way to go to develop a "general AI" that was capable of learning on its own and communicating on the same level as a human being. Once that level of intelligence had been achieved, the AI could then be applied to a wide variety of areas. Smart speakers were found in homes all over the world, helping with schedule management, home appliances, and information searches, but they were clearly unable to contribute meaningfully to conversation.

For one thing, AI are good at learning about things with clear outcomes—winning and losing, correct and incorrect—but struggle greatly when there is no correct answer to discern.

The concepts of winning and losing don't apply to normal conversation.

Yet, here before me, sipping her herbal tea with a pensive, thoughtful look, was a dark elf NPC in a video game—not exactly the pinnacle of cutting-edge AI development—who had never once given us a nonsense response to any statement. Perhaps that was partly because we'd been avoiding bringing up any topics that Kizmel would not understand, but even then, her ability to make conversation was essentially at a human level.

How had Argus—had Akihiko Kayaba—managed to implement such a high-functioning AI in a video game? There was only one way I could imagine: to build up an enormous text corpus of conversations between a vast number of humans and AI on specific topics and then reduce statistical noise and computational stress. That would not be easy, of course. It would be hard enough just to get hundreds of people to participate and explain what was allowed to discuss and what was off-limits. And there would be the issue of how to recruit them and how to pay them for their time and efforts.

But in a VRMMO world…

Players would generally only speak about in-game topics and quests, and who needed to pay them when they would happily log in and spend hours in the game at a time? If a thousand players spoke with AI over the course of a month, you would accumulate the kind of data that no company or researchers had ever gotten their hands on before.

Then, using that text corpus, they could have AIs talk to one another. Once actual humans were out of the picture, that conversation could be simulated much, much faster. In two months, you could simulate centuries or more of dialogue between individual AIs.

Meaning that it was possible that Kizmel and the dark elves… and forest elves, and fallen elves, and human NPCs…had all built up an actual history that started from the creation of Aincrad before *SAO* officially launched. And among them were special

AIs with conversational abilities close to a general intelligence, such as Kizmel and Viscount Yofilis.

If my imagination—no, my daydream—was even in the vicinity of the truth, then *SAO*'s AI capability was already in that "near-future" realm.

Now you had ten times as many players as in the beta, a full ten thousand in Aincrad, all trading words with AIs every day. Could that data be accumulated, refined, and polished enough to lead to the production of a crown jewel of true artificial intelligence? I certainly couldn't categorically rule it out...

"...Um, Kirito."

A poke at my elbow brought me to a rapid series of blinks.

"Hweh? Wh...what?"

"Don't *what* me. Was it that much of a shock that I took your fish? You've barely eaten a bite so far."

"Oh..."

I looked down at my plate, where I still had two pieces of fried fish after the one I'd offered to Asuna, and I hadn't even touched my salad or toast. The day's adventure was expected to be a long one, so I needed to fuel up while I could—even if the calories weren't real. I stabbed a piece of fish with my fork and shoved the whole thing in my mouth. The crisply fried portion crumbled apart, giving way to a juicy chunk of white meat. As I cleaned my plate, I couldn't help but wonder if Kizmel and her kind felt the same sensations of taste and contentment. Once I had polished off my food, I gulped down my herbal tea.

"I wasn't asking you to inhale it, you know," Asuna muttered. I leaned over and bit down on the elliptical baby tomato stuck on the end of her fork, pulling it off. "Aaah! What was that for?!"

Asuna raised her fork to swing, and I held my knife to defend against it. Kizmel only shook her head, a big-sister gesture if I'd ever seen one. Asuna noticed it and lowered her arm.

"Hey, Kizmel, can you tell us more about Tilnel?"

"Hmm...? Why, yes, of course. I shall tell you some stories on our travels today."

"Great. I can't wait to hear them." Asuna beamed, earning her a grin from the dark elf. There was no hint of shadow in her expression this time.

After our meal, Kizmel guided us to the supply station of Castle Galey. They were very generous, offering us five healing potions, five antidote potions, and a bag with rations and snacks, once per day, for free. Sadly, the antidotes were only level 1, so they couldn't counteract the level-2 paralyzing poison from Morte's Spine of Shmargor throwing picks.

The prospect of finding an antidote that was effective against the poision had me excited to hear from the storyteller that Kizmel had mentioned last night, but unfortunately, we could only meet them in the library between noon and three o'clock.

I didn't like the idea of continuing our questing without a means to neutralize the poison picks, but we would probably be fine as long as Kizmel was with us. She had a ring with magical antidote charms, and I couldn't imagine that Morte's gang would attack an elite knight whose level was so high that her color cursor must seem black. Based on the way the dagger user, aka Black Hood Number Two, had given up his main weapon to try to save Morte—or Mamoru, as he called him—they hadn't engaged in that stunt expecting to sacrifice their lives.

But that just meant that when they tried to attack us again, it would be under even more advantageous circumstances than the other night. The next time, they would do whatever it took to kill us; and they were probably working on their diabolical plan at this very moment.

I felt a fresh wave of apprehension about the idea of just waiting for them to make their next move, but I couldn't think of a way we could strike them first; and even if I did have a plan, I would need willpower on a different level than what I was working with now. For one thing, assuming we knew where their hideout was, there was no surefire method for apprehending a player in Aincrad for long periods of time. The only way to prevent them from committing any more evil would be to permanently log them out of the game.

And the only way to do that for sure at this point in time was to reduce their HP to zero. Which would bring about the death of the player in real life...

"Hey, Kirito, we're going to head out!"

"Don't make us leave you behind!"

I lifted my gaze from the tiles on the floor to the distance, where I saw the knight and fencer beckoning me toward the spring at the roots of the spirit tree.

The branches and leaves of the massive tree, which emerged from the center of the pool, glistened dazzlingly with countless droplets of dew that caught the morning sun and dripped down like golden threads. The sight of the two women against this backdrop was astonishingly beautiful.

Kizmel was Kizmel, of course, but at this point, Asuna might be stronger than me in pure fighting prowess as well. Even still, I felt a powerful urge to protect the two of them surge up from my heart as I trotted over to join them.

We were ushered out of the castle gates by the sound of the light bells and the silent gazes of the guards. After barely a minute of walking across the bridge built over the sandy valley floor, devoid of so much as a blade of grass, an unfamiliar debuff icon appeared on Kizmel's HP bar.

The symbol of a person hanging their head was the status icon for weakness, I recalled. I only suffered it once in the beta, fighting against the snake priests in the Castle of a Thousand Serpents on the tenth floor. It wiped out a large portion of my strength and agility stats, which put me in an encumbered state. Unable to run away to safety, I was killed soon after that.

Kizmel didn't look to be that bad, but I could tell in the brief time it had been that her rich, coffee-brown skin was looking noticeably paler now. Asuna called out her name in concern and tried to offer her an arm, but the knight boldly pushed her away and removed a thin cape from a pouch she kept fixed to her back.

"...I thought...that I could last longer...but this is merely a reminder that we elves are powerless without the bounty of the forest and water," she grunted, switching out her usual hiding cloak for the cape.

Like Asuna's, this cape was hooded, and it was a mysterious shade of green with silver tinting—I could even make out a pattern that looked like leaf veins. The moment she pulled the hood over her head, Kizmel's weakness icon disappeared and was replaced by a new buff icon.

"Whew..." Already the color was returning to her face. Asuna and I were so stunned by the immediate improvement that the knight gave us a proud little grin. "This cape is a special treasure that has been kept within the kingdom since before the Great Separation. It is carefully sewn together from the precious leaves of the Holy Tree, which hardly ever fall, even in midwinter... Among *all* the castles and fortresses together there are no more than ten of these capes remaining."

"Ooooh...That's fascinating," Asuna whispered, examining the cape itself. "So it's made from the leaves of the Holy Tree..."

Meanwhile, I was more curious about the effects of the new leaf icon—but I couldn't just go tapping Kizmel's cape while she was wearing it. I made a mental note to ask her permission to examine it once we got back to Castle Galey and opened my main menu to check the quest log.

We were about to tackle the main story for the "Elf War" campaign quest on the sixth floor, known as the "Agate Key." The format of the quest itself was simple—collect the key from the dungeon in the south area and return it to the castle—but the problem was that out of the five radial areas around the center of the sixth floor, we were in the northwest, meaning we'd have to get through the west area just to get to the south.

That meant getting through two of the boundary dungeons

that separated each area—the first of which was a decent challenge for a full raid party with the ALS and DKB, plus the Bro Squad for backup. Even with Kizmel, that was not going to be easy...Just in case, I checked our route there.

"Um, Kizmel, about our destination...I presume we're heading for the Key Shrine at the southernmost part of the sixth floor?"

"That is correct. I am impressed you knew the shrine was in the south," Kizmel said with marvel. Obviously, I couldn't tell her I'd been there in the beta test, so I gave her a pat answer about understanding as much with my book of Mystic Scribing. As a matter of fact, the quest log did include the location of the dungeon, so it wasn't really a lie.

"I see. Your human magical charms are powerful, indeed," the knight remarked. I walked up to show her the full map of the sixth floor, which Asuna examined from the opposite side. They traced the pathway to our destination with a finger.

"Our present location is here, and the shrine with the key is somewhere around here. That means we have to get through the passageway under the mountains both *here* and *here*...That's going to be a serious challenge if we attempt to tackle them head-on, but if there happens to be some kind of secret shortcut known only to dark elves, then..." I prompted. Asuna elbowed me in the side.

"Now, don't be tacky. I'm sorry, Kizmel, please ignore him."

"Hrmm. I do not remember hearing anything about a shortcut," the knight replied. She looked up and grinned. "But there is no need to cross the mountains at all."

"Uh...why not?"

"We can save that surprise for later. Let's head to the center lake first."

Kizmel put a hand on my back and Asuna's and pushed us onward, so I had to close my window and start walking.

The star-shaped body of water in the center of the floor was named Lake Talpha, and it would indeed cut down on travel time significantly if you could cross it. In the beta, many players did use buoyant materials in an attempt to swim across it, but the lake was home to a devastatingly powerful giant starfish monster that grabbed every person attempting to cross and dragged them down to watery graves.

That would be a thrilling bit of entertainment in a normal game, but encountering that starfish in *SAO* now was nothing short of suicide. The thought of Kizmel's intentions was troubling, but I had no choice at present other than to trust her.

The three of us crossed the stone bridge and headed into the labyrinth of canyon walls. Sandy monsters promptly began to spawn around us, but Kizmel was even stronger than when we worked with her on the sacred key quest of the fifth floor, and with ease, she dispatched the desert spiders and death worms that gave us so much trouble.

In terms of leveling efficiency, *SAO* was a lonely game in which the best way to level was going solo, but for now, there was no experience-point adjustment based on the level gap between monster and player—meaning that power leveling, where one or two over-leveled players could boost a party by taking down huge numbers of monsters by themselves, was surprisingly easy. This was exactly the present case, so I wished we could find a good high-frequency monster area and hang out for two or three hours—maybe even half a day or a full day—to gain levels. But given that we were on an important quest to recover the sacred keys, I couldn't ask Kizmel to do that. (In fact, didn't I consider that very idea on the third floor already?)

To my disappointment, we mostly avoided combat as we proceeded southward through the sandy canyons, and we reached the hills on the other end of the area by ten o'clock.

The five equal-sized areas of the sixth floor were spread out like a fan, so the closer you got to the lake in the center, the narrower the band of terrain became. About five hundred meters to our left was a sheer rocky cliff face, and if I squinted, I could see the entrance to the cave path we came through yesterday at the base of the rocks far ahead.

There was a similar rock wall on the right side, but the tunnel through that range was located toward the outer perimeter of the floor—and not visible from here. The walls would steadily close tighter and tighter until we hit star-shaped Lake Talpha at the center.

"Whew…Finally, we've made it through the dry valley," remarked Kizmel, pulling off her green hood.

"H-hey, is it safe for you to take that off yet?" I balked.

"It is. There are at least a few plants in this region, with the occasional spring of water."

But as far as I could see, the surrounding wasteland was just barren, reddish-brown ground, with the only visible plants being spiky cacti and succulents. It did not seem to be overflowing with the "bounty of forest and water," but the knight removed her cape anyway.

The debuff icon did not reappear, but even after two hours under the cape, her face still looked pale and uncomfortable. Asuna noticed it, too, and asked, "Are you sure you shouldn't keep it on until we reach the lake?"

"Yes…As I said earlier, this Greenleaf Cape is very precious. It would be a disgrace to our ancestors if I wore it where it was not necessary and damaged it in combat," Kizmel replied, folding the cape carefully and storing it in a pouch. She removed her cloak of hiding with a long exhale and put that on instead.

I opened my inventory and materialized a bottle of water for her, which she accepted gratefully. Then I retrieved two more for Asuna and me, and the three of us quenched our thirst standing in a row. For some reason, I felt like striking a pose with my left hand on my waist, but I didn't, out of fear that my companions wouldn't join in.

When the bottle was half empty, I stowed it. A player could carry as much food and water as the carrying limit would allow, but the elves didn't have fancy player inventories and had to carry around all their belongings by hand.

The same went for human NPCs, which meant that when

Morte killed Cylon, all the gold and silver coins that he dropped were stored somewhere under his robes.

I bet the lord of the town has a pretty heavy purse, I thought, which was neither here nor there, but the thought gave me pause. When Cylon died, he dropped both the golden key he stole from us and an iron key. By this logic, he either carried it around with him at all times, or he took it out of his mansion to use it. If the latter, it would only make sense that wherever Cylon intended to take Asuna and me while we were paralyzed, the iron key would be needed.

When I finished the paralysis event by myself in the beta, Pithagrus's servant and secret protégé, Theano, had saved me in the back streets of Stachion, so I didn't know where the carriage was supposed to end up. And I didn't recall any iron key being involved in the series of quests that followed. So if Morte hadn't killed Cylon, I doubted we would have seen any iron keys this time, either.

Meaning that the key I had in my inventory now was an item the game only generated when Cylon died in the middle of the quest… and that there was an alternate "dead Cylon" route to the "Curse of Stachion" quest, most likely.

Without thinking, I was scrolling through my open inventory window looking for the iron key. I had to grab my wrist with the other hand to stop it. Now was the time to focus on the "Agate Key" quest, not the "Curse of Stachion." We could return to Stachion at any time, and more importantly, if Kizmel could help us cross Lake Talpha, we could probably jump ahead of the other frontier players making their way counterclockwise around the map.

"Okay, let's go—" I started to say, but then I noticed that Asuna and Kizmel were busy with their backs to me, facing a rather large cactus. I walked over to check what they were doing and saw that they were plucking something red from between the cactus spikes and lifting it to their mouths.

"Hey! You're eating something!" I shouted. Asuna glanced at

me briefly before returning to her harvest. She was even doing it two-handed now, popping the red objects into her mouth at twice the speed.

Determined not to be left out, I circled around to the other side of the cactus and examined the base of the nearly ten-centimeter long spikes of the red object there. Gingerly, I reached in and plucked out a round fruit less than three centimeters across. When I hesitantly bit down on it, juice burst forth that was sweet and cold and sour and fizzy, numbing my mind with pleasure.

Immediately certain that the flavor was greater than even the B-rank half-fish sweet potatoes, I went in for another one, but perhaps because my hands were bigger than theirs, I couldn't pick the fruit as quickly. By the time I had pulled off a third fruit, Asuna was already rotating her way around from the other side.

She's going to eat my share! I fretted, and in my haste to grab a fourth fruit, my hand slipped and embedded itself onto a cactus spike.

"Yeow!!"

Like with the sensations of combat, it wasn't *real* pain, but I snatched my hand away out of sheer instinct anyway. Asuna took the opportunity to snatch the fruit and pop it into her mouth.

In the end, I only got about ten of the fruit by the time the entire cactus was picked clean. I looked at my two satisfied companions and grumbled. "I can't believe this. You could have told me before you started eating them…"

"Ha-ha, I am sorry for that, Kirito." Kizmel, who seemed to be in much better spirits, laughed. Perhaps the cactus fruit had some healing properties. "These Celusian Fruit have the most exquisite taste, but the flowers bloom and produce fruit only once a year. And what's more, the fruit can appear during any season, because the fruits fall just thirty minutes after they grow. So when you see them, you must eat them as quickly as you can."

"Th-thirty minutes…?" I repeated, looking out on the desert wastes. There were over a hundred cacti dotting the landscape just from what I could see, but a year would be 8,760 hours long, meaning 525,600 minutes, only thirty of which would feature any fruit on an individual cactus. The odds of actually happening across a fruiting cactus had to be devastatingly low. It wouldn't be worth wandering across the desert in search of them, no matter how tasty they were, so that might be the first and last time I would ever get the chance. I turned to my temporary partner, who still seemed to be basking in the afterglow of her meal.

"Um, Asuna?"

"Ahhh…what?"

"How many of those cactus fruits did you eat?"

"Around forty or fifty. I could go for more, though…Just give me a whole bathtub full of them."

"Hrrr…!" I moaned, swearing to myself that I would have to come back to search for them after all.

Kizmel clapped me on the shoulder. "Let us be on our way now. At this point, those pesky insect monsters will not bother us anymore."

As she said, the monsters that popped up in the hilly region mainly resembled coyotes and lizards, and neither had venom, making them much easier to dispatch. Instead, we spent the last kilometer or so listening to Kizmel tell us stories about her sister Tilnel, which had been a focus of Asuna's curiosity.

The story about how she took out a rowboat into the lake near the royal city on the ninth floor, all by herself as a child, and got lost for a full day. The story about how she put too much extract of juniper into the bath and smelled like a tree for a week. The story of how she gave Kizmel an experimental tonic during her herbalist studies that turned Kizmel's hair as green as a dryad's.

Asuna giggled at all the stories, and they reminded me of the experiences I had with my sister Suguha years ago, but I couldn't help entertaining one unsettling thought in the back of my mind. If all of Kizmel's memories of Tilnel were just "backstory," implanted memories, then they were all things that the staff of Argus, some scenario writer, had come up with originally.

But would they really give such a rich backstory to Kizmel,

who was just one of potentially countless NPCs that populated Aincrad? There seemed to be no end to the knight's stories; it was as though she recalled every single day that she had spent with her sister Tilnel. If it wasn't just special NPCs like Kizmel and Viscount Yofilis who had such richness of memory, but every single NPC in the game…it would be impossible for even a team of writers to come up with so much material.

For close to an hour we walked, Kizmel's stories entering my left ear and smoke from my overheating brain exiting the right. At last, the gap between the two mountain walls ahead reached barely half a kilometer, with the shining blue surface of the lake visible beyond.

We shared a glance, then sprinted the rest of the way until we reached the water.

"Ooooh, wow!" Asuna exclaimed, and I couldn't blame her. The sharply curved water's edge was a pure-white beach with stunningly clear water lapping at its sand. The surface was dazzling in the sunlight, the water transitioning from emerald green to cobalt blue as it deepened. Even the air seemed a bit warmer here.

Compared to the ten-kilometer diameter of the first floor, Lake Talpha was not all that big, but it was still over half a kilometer across, the far bank fading into the distance. However, the rocky walls that split the floor into five equal sections were clearly visible on the far right and left—and straight ahead of us. It was clear at a glance that this was the center where the five areas met.

"Hey, can I go in the water for just a bit?" Asuna asked. She was inching closer and closer to the sand. I was going to warn her, but Kizmel beat me to it.

"No, you must not. This lake is home to a dreadful starfish monster…I have never seen it for myself, but they say its tremendously long arms can reach the shore all the way from the depths of the lake."

Asuna immediately shrank away.

So the giant starfish, which went by the name Ophiometus, was still in place at the bottom of the lake in the release version. Now I was really curious and worried about Kizmel's plan to get to the far bank.

The knight sensed my eyes on her and smiled confidently. She pulled a new item out of her carrying pouch: a small glass bottle no bigger than her thumb. There was a pure-blue liquid inside it.

"Kirito, show me the bottom of your boot."

"O…kay," I agreed, but even in a virtual world, lifting my leg high enough for the sole of my shoe to be visible was easier said than done. I managed to get my right leg up, trying to stretch my ankle and pelvis as far as they could go, but about when I had the leg perpendicular to the ground, I lost my balance, yelped, waved my arms, and toppled onto the sandy beach.

Asuna's spontaneous laughter was stifled with a muffled *Poom!*

Embarrassed, I wanted to jump back to my feet, but Kizmel said "Perfect, that will do," and she had me lie back with my feet sticking straight up into the air, which didn't make me feel any better.

She carefully unstopped the bottle and put a single drop each on my soles. The shoes began to glow blue all over, and another unfamiliar icon lit up over my HP bar. I could guess what it meant, given the illustration of a shoe standing on water, but I waited for Kizmel to explain it anyway.

"You may stand," she said. I pulled my legs back over the position of my head, then snapped them forward to jump up to my feet in one motion. I needed to be in the best possible vantage point to witness my partner's sense of balance, after she had so kindly laughed at me falling on my butt.

Asuna shot me a glare, said "Go ahead, Kizmel," and lifted her right leg, not forward, but behind her, propping her ankle up with a hand. Of course, that was a much easier way to expose the bottom of one's foot without any awkward strain on the joints. In fact, probably nine out of ten people would do the same thing. I was both impressed and disgruntled by the idea. "No fair," I groused.

After sprinkling her own boots at the end, Kizmel put the cork back in the bottle and returned it to her pouch. Then she crossed the sand and gingerly stepped onto the clear water where it ebbed and flowed against the shore. The first few steps went through the surface, but around the fourth, a strange ripple ran across the water, and the fifth and sixth steps were clearly on top of it.

"Ooooh," Asuna and I said, marveling.

The knight turned and beckoned us forward. "Come, you two. Step slowly onto the water."

We bobbed our heads and proceeded to the lapping edge of the lake. Just to be sure, I grabbed my partner's shoulder and held her still.

"So, Kizmel, if we walk on the surface of the water, the starfish won't appear?"

"I guarantee it. However..."

"However?"

"The Droplets of Villi charm on your boots will only take effect when stepping softly. If you run or leap, you will break the surface and lose the effect. Then the starfish will notice you...so do take care not to lose your cool."

I got the feeling that last part was directed solely at me but decided it was just my imagination. The bigger question was whether or not we could entrust our lives to magic—er, a "charm"—that could lose its effect just by running. After all, Ophiometus's body never surfaced. It only sent its long, long hands up to grab players and drag them down, so it was impossible to beat by fighting. And unlike in the beta, if we died on the lake floor, we would not be respawning in Blackiron Palace in the Town of Beginnings.

I wanted to say *Kizmel, we really can't afford to die* but caught myself. That statement was just as true of NPCs like Kizmel as it was to us. Even if another dark elf with the same name and appearance was generated in the forests of the third floor after her death, it would not be the same Kizmel. How could I possibly say to her "It's all right if you die, but we're more important"?

"It's okay, Kirito," whispered Asuna, seemingly reading my mind. She reached out to grab the fingers of my right hand and murmured, "We just have to walk. And even if we do fall, I have an ace up my sleeve. Or up my pant leg."

"Your...pant leg...?"

I had no idea what the fencer was insinuating, but it didn't seem like it should be that hard to do this without running or jumping. At the very least, it should be way more manageable than maneuvering the difference between walking and jumping in a traditional video game, where the only distinction was in the exact angle your thumb tilted an analog stick.

"...Well, all right. Just be careful and keep what you're doing in mind at all times."

"Speak for yourself," she shot back, and we stepped forward. At first, our shoes just splashed the water, but soon there was buoyancy underfoot. We stood atop the water, which felt like stepping on a thick layer of rubber.

Once we reached Kizmel, who had been patiently waiting, she favored us with a reassuring smile and turned away. Then she started splashing atop the water for the far bank. We followed.

Once we'd walked about twenty meters out, Asuna said, "Oh yeah...when we fought Wythege the Hippocampus on the fourth floor, was this charm the reason that Viscount Yofilis didn't sink into the water?"

"Ohhh...But hang on, wasn't he running like crazy over the surface?"

"Asuna's guess is half correct," Kizmel said, turning her head just over her shoulder to look at us. "The liquid I dripped on the soles of our shoes is a valuable elixir that can only be made by villi—water spirits, undine maidens. But Viscount Yofilis's shoes are woven with villi hair and will never sink into the water."

"Hair...? Y-you don't mean that he killed the spirit and chopped off its hair, right...?" I asked, envisioning some tragic drama, but Kizmel vehemently shook her head.

"Never!"

A bit of water splashed at her feet, and the knight hunched her neck. Fortunately, it was not enough to break the charm itself, and she resumed quietly, "To us elves, the undines, including the villi, are just as sacred as the dryads of the forest. They are our neighbors and our protectors...If we consider cutting down a living tree or despoiling a clear brook as breaking taboo, then killing a villi herself would be calling down a curse upon all elfkind."

"I-I'm sorry, I shouldn't have suggested such a thing...But then, how did the viscount get such valuable shoes?"

Price was an unknown value in this case, but fantasy RPGs always treated equipment for feather-falling and water-walking as precious artifacts. By this point, we were near the center of the lake, and the titanic, deadly starfish lurked just a few meters below us, but I was so absorbed by this topic that I nearly forgot it as I awaited her answer.

Kizmel faced forward and shook her head again, almost imperceptibly this time. She whispered, "I do not know the details. But if rumor is to be believed...in the long-distant past, the viscount and a villi maiden...no. I should not speak of uncertain things. Please pretend you did not hear this."

Asuna, who was about a thousand times more interested than me in that sort of topic, sighed. But she did not persist—and held her silence as she walked.

I couldn't help but wonder if the blade scar on the viscount's face might have something to do with this story, but there was probably no way of ever knowing that. At the very least, Yofilis's water-walking boots were not meant to go to any player, so I could give the idea up for lost.

Up ahead, the far bank that started off hazy in the distance was coming much closer. We had maybe two hundred meters to go, and its white beach and the looming rock wall behind it were clearly visible.

Of the five areas that made up the sixth floor, the first area in the northeast, containing the main town, was forest; the second area in the northwest, containing Castle Galey, was barren wasteland;

the third area to the west was swampland; and the fourth area to the south, where we were currently heading, was designed to be caves. It was not a man-made dungeon, but a natural cavern formation, and there were few places where you could actually see the sky—or the bottom of the seventh floor, as the case may be. So it was not necessarily a fun strolling place, but it was certainly better than the western area we were skipping, with its muddy slog and deep sludge just off the beaten path.

Once we got the sacred key, we had to return to Castle Galey, but having the lake shortcut would be a huge help when it came time to tackle the floor's labyrinth, if we could make use of it. But these Droplets of Villi were clearly extremely valuable, so I couldn't just ask her for more—not when it was mere convenience's sake.

In the meantime, the far bank was growing close, and the view under the surface was clearer again, with little schools of fish swimming underfoot. At times, there were glints of what looked like coins or jewels in the sand down there, which made me want to reach in and grab them, but that was clearly a trap. I'd have to wait until we had a means of defeating the starfish first.

Our usual pattern of activity called for one of the two of us—usually me—to screw up and get into major trouble just before we reached safety, but there were no sudden splashes into the water this time. We stood on firm ground again, walked up the white beach a ways, then came to a stop with a sigh of relief.

"Well…there's a first for everything. That was rather exhilarating," the knight said.

I turned to her in surprise. "Wait, that was your first time walking across the lake, too, Kizmel?"

"But of course. I have never even set foot outside of Castle Galey here."

"Then you're saying…you don't know the location of the underground maze that holds the key…?" I asked, thinking this might be the rare occasion when we led Kizmel around instead of the reverse. But the knight took a scroll of parchment out of the long, thin case on her belt and said proudly, "I have not been there, but I know the way. See?"

I peered at the paper. It was a map of the southern area drawn in considerable detail. A red mark was placed within the twisting cave complex, and a red line indicated the route there directly from the lakeside.

"Oh, so you do have a map. So this is the lake, and this is our destination...and what's this mark for? It looks like an insect head," Asuna said, pointing at a spot near the bottom of the map.

"That's correct," Kizmel replied with a nod. "Lurking in the caverns is a giant centipede covered in rocky armor. Fortunately, we need not cross its path, but I hear tell of many humans who have wandered into its lair and paid the ultimate price."

"Sheesh...Starfish, centipedes—this place has everything. I just hope there are no millipedes or ganymedes."

I could have been a snob and pointed out that the last one was the name of a moon, not a creature, but I kept it to myself.

In the beta, there wasn't a centipede-type field boss in the southern area of the sixth floor. Instead, there was a plant boss in the labyrinth tower located in the fifth and final area, and the unbeatable starfish in the lake, but that was all I remembered.

Some of the field bosses had been changed in previous floors—like the giant tortoise boss on the fourth floor becoming a two-headed sea turtle—but there were no newly added bosses so far. The advancement group was tackling the game under that premise, so if the ALS or DKB, in their competitive haste, ran into a centipede boss in the cave that they weren't prepared for, there was the possibility for disaster lurking ahead.

"Sorry, give me a moment," I asked the two women, who were still examining the map, and went to the MESSAGES tab of my main menu. I fired off a brief message to Argo the information dealer.

WHERE'S THE FARTHEST FR NOW?

FR was shorthand for front-runner, Argo's preferred nickname for the group pushing us ahead into Aincrad. She must not have been in combat or spying, because I got a response within ten seconds.

THEY'LL BE TRYING THE DUNGEON LEADING INTO THE THIRD AREA TONIGHT. 100C, her message said, with the cost of the information indicated at the end. Fortunately, she kept a running tab for me, but the bill wasn't what made me grimace.

"Too fast," I muttered, checking the MAP tab. The lead group moved from the first area to the second yesterday afternoon, January 2, so they were moving on to the next area after just a single day.

The second area had just one small town by the name of Ararro—the dark elves' Castle Galey was meaningless if you weren't doing the "Elf War" quest—and the monsters outside of the ones in the dry valley leading to the castle weren't that tough. So I figured it wouldn't take them long, but this was still very quick. Most likely, Kibaou and Lind calculated they could take one area per day, finishing the sixth floor in just five days total. Given that we had finished the fifth floor in four days, it wasn't outrageous, but the last labyrinth tower was on a straight line if you avoided detours. This one required far more travel to reach.

At any rate, it was clear that we needed to assume the swampy third area would be finished by tomorrow afternoon, at which point the front-line group would reach this, the fourth area. I returned to Kizmel's side to examine the map; the giant centipede's lair was located a bit before Cave City of Goskai, the biggest town in the area. If the group was rushing along the path, tired after clearing out the dungeon passageway, there was a greater chance of them stumbling across the centipede's cave with little or no preparation than I wanted to admit.

I opened my window again and sent a second message to Argo. GOT INTEL ON A NEW FIELD BOSS LOCATED BEFORE GOSKAI IN THE FOURTH AREA.

GOT IT, she immediately wrote back, I'LL WIPE OUT THE COST OF YOUR LAST TIP.

That should be enough to keep the DKB and ALS from running across the centipede boss without a clue that it was coming.

However, not that I didn't trust them to hold their own, but I wanted to take part in that boss battle, too.

The real question was, could we finish up the "Castle Galey" quest by tomorrow afternoon and catch up with the group again?

"That charm of Far Scribing you humans can use is a very handy thing," said Kizmel, impressed. She'd been watching me send messages to Argo.

Asuna piped up to say, "The elves have to send scouts to hand over letters, don't you? Even with your spirit trees, that seems like a lot of hard work."

"That is right. We dark elves and forest elves have thought little of your human charms, but seeing what you are capable of doing, I suspect that your Mystic Scribing and Far Scribing alone might surpass all the magic we elves still possess."

I wasn't quite sure how to respond to her. She recognized them as a form of magic, but the player menu and instant messages were game features, and I couldn't very well explain that. Also, that human *players* could use that "magic," but NPC humans could not.

But Kizmel didn't show any further interest in the art of Far Scribing. Instead, she brought up a point I hadn't thought about in a while.

"What was it that N'ltzahh the fallen elf said on the fourth floor? When they have all the keys and open the door to the Sanctuary, the greatest magic of humankind will vanish, correct?"

"Oh...he did say that," said Asuna, her cheeks flushing a little bit. I wondered why and tried to recall the circumstances of that scene.

We had taken a gondola trip down the river out of Rovia on the fourth floor and were at the very end of the watery dungeon when the two of us overheard the Fallen having a discussion.

In addition to N'ltzahh, the masked general, there was also Eddhu, a foreman, and a woman elf who seemed to be the general's aide. The statement was from N'ltzahh to his aide, whose name I recalled being Kysarah.

Once we have all the keys and open the door to the Sanctuary, even the greatest magic left to humankind will vanish without a trace.

And in response, Kysarah had said *Of course, Excellency. The moment of our triumph grows ever closer.*

If we couldn't use our Mystic Scribing and Far Scribing anymore, that would be a huge deal. But it seemed impossible in a practical sense. Instant messages were one thing, but not being able to use the main game menu? No choosing skills, storing items away, or viewing the map—the game would be impossible to beat that way.

So did that mean the "greatest magic" N'ltzahh spoke of was something else? Something the loss of which would tie in to some great wish of the fallen elves? What kind of desire would that actually be...?

My imagination ran into a brick wall at that point. My right hand opened and clenched repeatedly in frustration. Then Asuna came marching over to me and stepped on my left foot with the toe of her boot, hard.

That sensation was the trigger that brought forth a new flood of memories. When N'ltzahh had said those things, Asuna and I had been hiding in a small wooden box, squashed and immobile. My hand had gotten stuck under Asuna's breastplate, and...

"I believe we've had enough of a rest. I'd like to finish and return to the castle while it's light out," announced Kizmel, pulling me out of my flashback. I lowered my hand and silently shook my head at Asuna. She snorted and gave me a glance that ordered me to erase that memory forever, then began walking alongside the knight. There was a tall rock face before them, with a yawning cave mouth in the center.

*Say, the harassment-prevention code didn't go off that time, either...*I thought as I hurried after them. *I wonder if she saw the window for it open when she woke up this morning?*

The majority of the cave area was not pitch-black like an interior dungeon; instead, open areas here and there allowed light in from the ceiling, and even at its gloomiest, there was still enough natural light to see by. We didn't need to carry torches or lanterns.

Fortunately, the monsters here were not insects but primarily bat and aquatic types. The most troublesome were the slimes, making their first appearance in Aincrad here. Japanese RPGs were famous for characterizing slimes as the weakest intro monsters, but that was not true in *SAO* at all. For one thing, there was no fire or ice magic in the world to effectively counter that jiggly slime body.

So we'd have to make do with our weapons. Even then, slashing and thrusting attacks were weak against the slime, with only blunt weapons having any decent effect. And for our party of three, Kizmel and I had slashing weapons, and Asuna used a thrusting weapon. Slimes were uniquely tough for us.

So…

"Aaaaargh! Jeeeez!"

Asuna made no attempt to hide her frustration as she activated the sword skill Oblique. Her rapier lit up the dim surroundings with a lightning-fast downward thrust. It struck the brown-colored Covetous Ooze on the cave floor before her.

A large hole appeared in the center of the roughly one-meter-wide slime, and while it looked as though it might be spraying apart to pieces, there wasn't much effect on its HP. When the visual effects of the skill faded, the bits of ooze squirmed back together to take their original flat, jiggly form.

I noticed that a part of it was bulging outward, so I warned Asuna, "Take evasion!"

The fencer leaped away when she was able to move, just as the bulging part of the ooze emitted a little whiplike tentacle. It tried to snake around the Chivalric Rapier but closed on air by mere centimeters when Asuna pulled her weapon back.

If it caught hold, it would yank with tremendous force, and if pulled free, the weapon would be absorbed into the slime's center mass. That made it difficult to retrieve, and the weapon suffered major durability loss in the meantime. Even I didn't know what might happen if it grabbed the player, and they were wearing, say, cloth armor.

The Covetous Ooze—so named for the way it greedily stole things—retracted its tentacle and wobbled, practically mocking Asuna.

"Grrrr! What do we do about this thing, Kirito?!" she pleaded. I glanced behind me, where a few meters away, Kizmel was dealing with two vampire bats. Her HP hadn't dropped at all, so she was probably fine on her own. I looked back to Asuna and said, at a safe volume that wouldn't call down more nearby monsters, "First, guide it into the light!"

"I...I'll try!"

Asuna slowly moved back to her right, until the jiggling ooze followed into a ring of natural light coming through a hole in the ceiling. The dirty yellow-brown body in the darkness turned a brilliant gold in the light—but that was it. It didn't take any damage from the light or seem distressed or try to run away from it.

"...Nothing happened!" Asuna wailed, so I gave her the next hint.

"Look closely at the slime's whole body while it's translucent in the sunlight!"

"Huh?! Oh...there's something there."

As sharp as ever, Asuna found what she was looking for in just two seconds of squinting. Not in the center of the ooze but along the outer edge of what constituted its "legs," there was something shiny and reflective, like an eyeball, or a fish-egg pouch, or one of those clear raindrop cakes.

"That's the slime's core! Crush that little thing with a sword skill, and you'll kill it in one blow!" I shouted. As if on cue, the ooze curled itself inward into a ball shape. It wasn't frightened, but it was tensing itself to jump high off the ground, where it spread itself out thin and wide. If it wrapped itself around your head, you'd take continuous acidic damage and start to suffocate.

But instead of backing away, Asuna used another sword skill. It was even easier to see the core with the slime's body all spread out in the sun, making it the perfect target for the single thrust skill, Streak. The tip of her rapier left a silver streak as it struck the two-centimeter-wide core. The translucent sphere resisted for a brief moment before it burst with a little popping sound.

When its HP reached zero, the slime lost its internal cohesion and flew apart into many tiny bits. They splattered against the fencer's face and body, covering her in dark-yellow jelly. She probably would have shrieked, if not for the fact that the ooze turned into little blue polygonal textures that drifted away.

Asuna stood there, rapier still outstretched, until Kizmel returned from dispatching the two bats and said cheerily, "Ah, well done, Asuna. Not many elves are skilled enough to defeat a slime with a single rapier thrust."

"...Thank you..." the young woman muttered. Were her lips twitching because some of the ooze had flown into her mouth? I was quickly becoming a master of the most freakish foods of Aincrad and wanted to ask her how it tasted, but my survival instincts told me now was not the time.

I wanted to say "Nice job!" with a smile instead but had to hold off on that, too. There were more faint sounds of jiggling and wobbling in the distance. I put a finger to my lips to hush the other two and listened closely. The unique sound of slime wriggling was getting closer and louder, but I saw no cursor around. When that happened in the beta, it was usually because...

"Above!" I shouted.

Overhead, an amorphous shape was dropping down from between thin, icicle-like stalactites on the ceiling of the cave.

Asuna noticed it belatedly and tried to jump back as she watched it fall, but she unluckily tripped over a low stalagmite that was directly behind her and fell flat on her bottom. Kizmel raised her saber to protect Asuna, but if she simply slashed at the falling slime and didn't happen to strike the core on the way through it, the liquid creature would take little damage and attack the two of them directly.

I lifted up my sword on pure instinct to queue up the sword

skill Sonic Leap. I would jump up at as hard an angle as the system would allow and strike the falling slime with it. Because it was just off the hole in the ceiling, the slime didn't catch the sun, and it only looked like a dark smudge. There was no way to tell where the core was at this point.

But I kept my eyes as wide as I could and smashed the amorphous creature with my Sword of Eventide +3. Normally, I would take the power boost of adding my own swing to the system's auto-assistance, but this time, I purposefully slowed it down just enough to keep the sword skill from fumbling.

When the blade cut through the sticky substance, I felt it catching on the denser little orb. Promptly, I stopped pulling back and let it follow through, hearing the burst of the core shattering. The slime's HP were gone in an instant, the creature obliterated before I could even read its name on the cursor. I'd get a good taste of its flavor if I caught some flying jelly in my mouth, but a sudden premonition told me to block my face with my arm. When I landed, all the pieces were disintegrating into blue light.

It was quite an impressive feat, if I said so myself, so I turned with a flourish and asked, "Are you two all right?" like a manga character.

For some reason, Asuna glared at me balefully from the floor.

"It...It got in my mouth again."

"...What'd it taste like?" I asked, unable to fight my curiosity this time. She said that the bits of Covetous Ooze tasted "hellishly sour, like sour plums pickled in lemon juice." The second one dropped an item called Ooze Jelly, but I wasn't the biggest fan of sour flavors and decided to let it sit in my inventory to rot.

As soon as Asuna was back on her feet, she pressed me for answers. "Kirito, I'm going to set aside the fact that you could have *started* by telling me slimes have cores—and how to find them. When you cut the second one, there was no light shining on the slime. Did you just hit the core by getting lucky?"

"No way. I don't have that kind of actual luck." *Even if I did, I would have used it all up getting these two particular party members, putting me well into the red to do so*—a thought I kept to myself, of course.

"Natural light is the best way to find a slime's core, like you just did," I explained, "but it also works with torches or lanterns in very dark environments. But once you've hunted enough slimes to get the hang of it, you learn how to find the core from other light sources, too."

"Other light...?" she repeated skeptically. But Kizmel suddenly clapped her hands in epiphany. "Oh, of course! You can use the flashing of your sword technique to illuminate the core."

"Correct!" I said, giving her a round of applause. But then I paused. It was a known fact that NPCs could use sword skills—but should I talk about the "extracurricular" tricks involved in this case? Kizmel's expression of excitement and anticipation sealed the matter, however. Asuna, meanwhile, looked skeptical.

"What? Sword skills give you less than a second between flashing and landing on the target...Can you really find a slime's core in that amount of time?"

"Well, it comes down to experience...and slowing down the sword skill. Slimes aren't very mobile, so if you slow the skill down as much as you can, it gives you more time to spot the core."

"Slow it down..." Asuna muttered with equal parts wonder and exasperation. She dropped her rapier back into its sheath. "I'll admit...I think that technique's incredible, but it's going to take me quite a while to learn it, so for now, I'll count on you to take care of all the slimes in the dark."

"Uh...s-sure thing," I said, the only thing I *could* say.

Kizmel added, "Don't worry, I will learn this skill as well."

"Y-yeah...I'm looking forward to that," I said, *also* the only thing I could say.

After that, we saw not just the dark-yellow Covetous Ooze but blue slimes, red slimes, and even some familiar-looking black slimes. As she proclaimed, within three battles, Kizmel had effectively grasped the trick of the so-called skill-lighting ability. From that point on, we didn't have much trouble reaching the entrance to the dungeon, deep inside the cave, before lunch.

If possible, I was hoping to make the slight extra walk to the Cave City of Goskai not too far off in order to eat and recover supplies, but Kizmel wouldn't want to venture into a human city, I assumed, and if any players were there on the forest elf faction of the quest, they would see Kizmel's cursor transcend red straight into black.

So we sat down at the entrance to the dungeon, partaking in some of the rations we got from Castle Galey. To my surprise, the baked treat full of nuts and dried fruit was fantastically good. Even Asuna, the snooty gourmet, seemed satisfied. Our spirit recovered, we then plunged into the dungeon, tearing deeper and deeper into it, and fighting an abruptly different set of monsters—until just after one o'clock, when we ran into an obstacle I never imagined I would see.

"Huh...? This was a dungeon the elves built ages ago, right?" Asuna murmured as she stared up at the thing. Kizmel's head bobbed in agreement.

"That is correct. According to legend, in the olden days just after the Great Separation, the six keys were split across six floors and placed within six different labyrinths to keep them hidden and safe."

"Then why would *that* be there...?"

".........I do not know."

Kizmel stepped forward and reached up to the square stone panel that blocked the great doors before us, to touch the numbered pieces lined up on it.

It was clearly a 15 puzzle—except that, in this case, they were lined up six by six, so it was actually a 35 puzzle. At any rate, it was one of those cursed puzzles found everywhere in Stachion.

Kizmel carefully clicked the tile next to the open space and turned back to me. "This...is not anything made by the dark elves, or the forest elves, either, I believe. Count Galeyon said nothing about there being such a contraption in this labyrinth, either."

"No...this one was created by humankind," I said, which made Kizmel wince.

"What...? Meaning, some human snuck into this labyrinth before us and placed this device upon the door? Does that mean...the key's already been taken out...?"

"N-no, no, not necessarily. Besides, this puz—this seal might not have been literally placed by the human who snuck in here..."

"What does that mean?" Kizmel asked suspiciously. Asuna and I explained—with difficulty, because we couldn't explain that these were all "quests" in a "game"—the murder mystery in Stachion, and the ensuing puzzle curse it had spawned.

The elf knight was silent for several moments when we were done and finally said, "So the curse of this human lord being murdered ten years ago has spilled out of the town of Stachion and has produced this number puzzle on the door of this distant labyrinth?"

"Yep...that's the only way to describe it at this point. Not that I think old Pithagrus has any reason to curse an elf maze, specifically."

"You never know. Curses are truly terrifying and unpredictable things. Especially when they are curses set by the dead...The dark elves have a number of stories about those unfortunate enough to have come into contact with curses unrelated to them. To say nothing of the famous tale of how the wicked dragon Shmargor came under the Holy Tree's curse and tormented the humans who did nothing to it."

"Ah yes...You do have a point..."

In a sense, the entire floating castle of Aincrad was like the curse of the mad genius, Akihiko Kayaba. And we were the ones unfairly trapped inside it...although, as a beta tester as well, I suppose it was inevitable that I would become a victim.

There was no point lamenting my plight at this point, however.

All I could do was trust that I would one day beat this deadly game—and keep moving forward each day toward that goal.

Asuna's gaze was distant, suggesting to me that she was thinking much the same thing. Kizmel gave the two of us a glance, then turned to the door again and said, "If this puzzle is the work of a curse, then I suppose no sword can destroy it."

"Huh…? Oh y-yeah, it's indestructible."

"Then we shall have to solve it," the knight said simply.

I rushed to ask her, "H-hey, do dark elves solve puzzles, too?"

"Hmm? Well…as children, we solve picture-matching boards and tangle rings, but I have never seen a puzzle of numbers like this. Are we meant to reorder the boards in numerical order?"

"Yes, starting from the top left and moving in rows," I explained, though on the inside, I was starting to panic.

One of these sliding puzzles with fifteen pieces was hard enough if you didn't know the trick, but this one had thirty-five to deal with. I figured it would be too tough for Kizmel at her first shot—and that was without knowing if NPCs had the AI power to solve puzzles like this. From what I recalled, N × N grid puzzles like this one were called NP-hard problems in computational theory, meaning that normal computers found it difficult to compute the lowest number of moves possible.

"Kizmel, maybe I should…" I started to say, but then my mouth hung open.

After just three seconds of staring at the randomly placed numbers, Kizmel was now tearing through them. The rapid clicking of tiles sliding into place filled the dark corridor, and before my eyes, the thirty-five tiles began to line up in order from the top left. To our shock, soon the thirty-fifth and final tile snapped into place.

The entire stone board momentarily glowed, and the door behind it slowly rumbled open. Kizmel looked over her shoulder at us and grinned.

"Ah, I see now. Your human puzzles are quite refreshing."

* * *

It was virtually a direct path through once the door was open, with hardly any monsters inside, so we reached the final room quickly. It was the same key-dungeon boss as on the fifth floor, a headless dullahan, but much stronger. Fortunately, we'd leveled up, too, and Kizmel's presence was positively unfair, so while we did make use of the healing potions from Castle Galey, the fight was won with little difficulty.

In the rear of the boss chamber was a stately little shrine. Resting on the altar in the middle of it was a pitch-black object—the Agate Key. Recovering it was pretty much the end of the mission. There was no teleportation in *SAO* aside from the gates and crystals, so without a means of fast travel, we had no choice but to return to Castle Galey on foot. It helped to know that this just meant more time together with Kizmel.

We returned to the entrance of the dungeon in half the time and made our way out of the caves altogether, avoiding slimes wherever we could. At last, the brilliant blue of Lake Talpha greeted us back. After a brief break on the monster-less beach, we walked back across the lake and returned to the northwest area.

There were no fallen elf ambushes on the road back this time across the wasteland—but no fruiting cacti, either. Kizmel sheltered herself under the Holy Tree cape again, and we protected her through the dusty canyon. By the time the great gate of Castle Galey came into view again, the bottom of the floor above us was dyed the colors of sunset.

As we walked through the gate, accompanied by the ringing of bells, I checked the time in my game window. It was 4:20 PM. Sadly, we'd missed the period that the old storyteller would be in the library, but for a major floor-spanning quest like that, it was very good time. I stretched, feeling the pleasant ache of fatigue, and Kizmel slapped me on the back with a smile.

"Nice work today…but there's more of it yet to do. We must deliver the key we recovered to Count Galeyon."

"Oh…yes, that's right," I said, but in all honesty, I wasn't in the mood to rush off to see the count just now, and I didn't think Asuna was, either. Once we delivered the key and completed the quest, Kizmel was probably going to use that spirit tree to leave for the seventh floor this time.

The royal city where the dark elf queen lived was on the ninth floor. That was where the "Elf War" questline would reach its grand finale. It felt like such a long way to go when we started the quest on the third floor, but here we were, about to cross the halfway point.

After the campaign was over, I had no idea what would happen to Kizmel and us. Perhaps we could see her whenever we went back to the royal city, or perhaps not. But at the very least, I felt certain we would never fight side by side with her again. Kizmel was just too strong for me to optimistically imagine that we would be allowed to take her along on totally unrelated quests and grinding sessions.

"Um…Kizmel," Asuna said, speaking in my stead, "when we give the count the key, are you going to leave for the next floor?"

She was a hundred times more honest with herself than I was. The elf knight appeared to be holding something back—or so it seemed to me, trick of the eyes or not—but put on her usual pleasant smile soon enough.

"That's a good question…It depends on the determination of the priests sent from the royal city. Most likely, I will be ordered to deliver the four keys to the fortress on the seventh floor."

"I see…It's a very important mission, after all…" Asuna murmured, looking up at the spirit tree ahead of us. Then she turned to the knight, took a big step forward, and asked in hushed tones, "But in that case, why does it have to be *just* you who goes around gathering these keys? We've gotten four of the six back…Why can't the knights from the castle or those darn priests themselves go and get the last two?"

"I don't think of this mission as being difficult or unpleasant." Kizmel grinned. She stroked Asuna's chestnut-brown hair lovingly, like an older sister would. "As Her Majesty's knight, I have a duty to uphold, and I have you two helping me...Sometimes I wish it was not six keys, but ten or twenty instead."

"......Kizmel..."

Asuna hunched over, looking ready to cry. Kizmel moved her hand to the girl's back and beckoned me over with the other. She offered quietly, "Also, in the background of this mission are a host of troublesome political calculations and squabbles. As I told you a while ago, my Pagoda Knights Brigade, the palace security Sandalwood Knights Brigade, and the heavily armored Trifoliate Knights Brigade are often at odds...Our leadership, especially, has always been competitive with one another. When the word came that the forest elves were going after the hidden keys, there was considerable argument over which brigade should respond..."

"And they weren't trying to foist off the responsibility on one another, but just the opposite, of course," I conjectured.

Kizmel nodded seriously. "That is correct. It has been over a century since knights of Lyusula left the castle for a practical mission, rather than training...and against the forest elves of Kales'Oh, no less. The three brigades fought for the honor of this duty, and ultimately, it was given solely to the Pagoda Knights Brigade, for our light armor and fleet movement. A vanguard of sixty was sent down to the third floor, but there is no dark elf fortress there. We were to build a camp for our base and scout the labyrinth that contained the key. There was not supposed to be any combat..."

She exhaled heavily. I knew where the story went from that point and wanted to tell her she didn't need to bother, but I was too late to interrupt.

"...But on our first scouting mission, which split the vanguard into two groups, we suffered a forest elf ambush. The scout group was virtually wiped out by an attack from the rear, and that was when Tilnel lost her life. The commander of the vanguard requested more members from the brigade's headquarters, of course...but the request was refused. They probably knew that if it was revealed that the group freshly descended to the third floor was already half gone, the other brigades would swoop in to steal our glory..."

"No...! You fought as hard as you could! They can't just..." Asuna started to shout. Kizmel glanced around and led us to a bench placed along the wall of the castle. She sat between Asuna and me, crossed her fingers over her stomach, and looked up at the spirit tree looming over the open courtyard.

"We fought hard..." she repeated peacefully. "That is correct. But fighting hard, by itself, is not enough when you are the queen's knight. When you fight, you must win...so I do not curse our headquarters for refusing our request. If anything, I am grateful that they allowed me the opportunity to regain my honor."

But Asuna didn't seem fully convinced by that answer. She balled her fists where they rested atop her knees, and her head pointed downward.

"...But...that doesn't mean...you need to do this...all on your own..."

"Asuna, it is true that I alone am on the mission to retrieve the keys, but that is not because the other knights are sitting around, doing nothing. The vanguard's commander put together a new plan to complete our mission with a much smaller number. About ten knights would take turns harrying the forest elves and drawing their attention; meanwhile, one knight skilled in stealthy matters would get the keys from the labyrinths...I nominated myself for the retrieval. Tilnel and I played tag and hide-and-seek in our youth, so I am confident in my sneaking."

I wonder, when elves play tag, and they envision "it" as being a monster, what do they think of? Probably an ogre type... I considered this briefly before snapping back to attention.

I remembered how Kizmel said she elected to do the mission alone, when we stood before Tilnel's makeshift grave at the third-floor camp. Diversion, infiltration—it was a very skillful plan, I was sure, but one that exposed Kizmel to great danger. She got the key on the third floor safely, but the elite Forest Elven

Hallowed Knight gave chase, and they nearly killed one another in the ensuing duel.

Before her sister's grave, Kizmel told me she took on that mission expecting that she could very well die. That a part of her might have even wanted to.

But looking at her peaceful smile in profile now, I could no longer see the deep sadness I witnessed in that lonely moment. I turned to the left, looking past the knight to my partner, who was still clenching her fists.

"Asuna, Kizmel's mission is a very tough one. But she's *not* doing it alone…She's got us helping her out."

"Yes, that's right. That's exactly right," Kizmel said, nodding deeply. She caressed Asuna's head. "Since you and Kirito began helping me, I have never thought of this mission as a painful one, and I have no intention of dying without completing my task. We'll recover all six keys and go to the palace on the ninth floor together…I think you will like it, Asuna."

"………Yeah," she squeaked, quiet but firm, placing her head on Kizmel's shoulder.

We sat there on the bench in silence, watching as the color of sunlight reflecting off the floor above grew darker and deeper with the approach of the night.

7

WITH OUR REPORT TO COUNT GALEYON, THE "AGATE Key" quest was over. Asuna and I received a huge amount of experience, and as on the fourth floor, we had our choice of item rewards.

That was fantastic, of course, but what made us even happier was learning that Kizmel was given a full day of downtime. She could do whatever she wanted tomorrow, January 4, and she didn't need to go to the seventh floor until the morning of the fifth. I was still worried about the front-line group reaching the south area by tomorrow afternoon, but I did pass along the info about that new centipede boss through Argo, so I didn't think there was any danger of them fighting it unprepared.

We had to take part in the labyrinth tower and floor-boss fight, of course, but if Kizmel gave us more of those Droplets of Villi, we could go straight from the second area to the fifth one. And if not, we could still probably catch up with the group using the normal route in about half a day, assuming the pathway dungeons had been cleared out. I said as much to Asuna after we returned to the room on the third floor of the west wing, and we agreed that we would spend tomorrow taking it easy.

When we returned to the hallway to meet Kizmel, we went to the basement bath to wash off the imaginary sweat and grime of the day. In order to avoid repeating yesterday's tragedy, we agreed beforehand to keep each half of the bathing area separate between the sexes. But hearing the two women chatting and laughing on the other side of the spirit tree's roots did not make the process any easier for me.

When we were done bathing, we relaxed in the waiting area for a while before heading to the dining hall. The main course today was grilled fish. Not only did it not have the strangely spiced sauce that the game's human cooks liked to use, the fish's skin was crispy and fragrant, and I had to go ask for seconds.

We enjoyed some tea after the meal, chatting and reminiscing about the events of the fourth and fifth floor. I left the dining hall feeling extremely satisfied. Kizmel left briefly to return the Greenleaf Cape to the treasure repository she'd borrowed it from, so Asuna and I decided to explore the castle a bit. We started walking toward the east wing, which we hadn't seen yet in our time here.

Just then, there was a bell ringing in the darkened courtyard. We stopped, noting with muted interest that they still rang the bells after bathing and dinnertime...and then I recalled that this was not actually a time for zoning out.

Hadn't Kizmel said that the bell only rang when the south gate opened...? And as a basic rule, the dark elves in the castle did not leave it. The bell was alerting us to the fact that players aside from ourselves had shown up at Castle Galey.

Asuna figured it out at the same time I did. We shared a look, then dashed to a window. When we looked down at the courtyard, pressed against the glass, we saw that the mammoth gates were indeed very slowly opening.

My first thought was that this visitor was Morte or the dagger user, or even both at once. Castle Galey was outside the safe-haven zone, so nothing would stop them from coming in with criminal orange cursors. All they needed to open the gates were the same Sigil of Lyusula rings that we had. Last night, I surmised that it would be difficult for them to get through the dark elf side of the campaign in time, but there was no absolute evidence of that.

"We need to figure out who just showed up," Asuna murmured, her voice tense.

I pushed away my brief moment of indecision and said, "Yes, let's go down. Make sure you're geared up."

"Got it."

We turned and started running for the stairs, both opening our game menus. We switched from my indoor wear to my usual combat gear and equipped our beloved weapons. I barely registered the steps as we flew down to the first floor of the west wing. Rather than the main doors to the castle, we rushed to a side door at the end of the hallway and opened it a crack to peer out into the courtyard.

The bell was still ringing, but the front door was already in the process of closing. If the visitor had already vanished into the spacious castle, it would be very difficult to find them.

But even then, we could probably ask the soldiers near the door what the player looked like. I steeled my courage and went into the open, heading toward them along the sheer wall cut into the rock.

After about five steps, Asuna reached out and grabbed my collar. I let out a strangled yelp and came to a stop.

"Wh-what was that for?" I whispered.

"Look, Kirito," she whispered back, pointing in the direction of the courtyard's spirit tree, rather than the gate. As soon as I looked that way, I blinked. There were four people gathered around the spirit tree's spring, their backs toward us. Their cursors were the very same green as ours.

Based on their number, it probably wasn't Morte's group. And for one thing, Morte and I had an official duel on the third floor, so our names would display for each other, making one of those four cursors read MORTE—but all I could see were HP bars and guild tags.

Kibaou's Aincrad Liberation Squad had a tag of a gray sword and shield on a green background. Lind's Dragon Knights Brigade used a silver dragon on a blue field. But this guild tag was neither of those; it was an unfamiliar mark like the letter Q in gold against a black background.

"...Have you seen that insignia before, Kirito?" Asuna whispered. I shook my head.

"No. Do you...? Well, I guess you wouldn't have asked if you did."

She did not reply, but I sensed her head bobbing. The system had confirmed that Morte was not among the four, and it didn't seem likely to me that the PK group led by the man in the black poncho would form a guild and register it with such a distinct, memorable logo—but it wasn't confirmed yet that the two things were unrelated. This castle was not a safe haven, so we had to be careful at all times.

I was standing there, plastered against the rough rock face, wondering what to do now, when Asuna whispered, "Hey. Let's say that some humans...er, players get into a fight inside the castle, and their cursors go orange. How do you suppose the dark elves would react? Would they ignore it, or..."

"Ummm..."

I didn't have an immediate answer to that one. The reason that orange (criminal) players couldn't get into human towns with the Anti-Criminal Code active wasn't because of some magical barrier that repelled anyone who was evil. It was because you'd get attacked by tremendously powerful NPC guards. In the beta, there were people who intentionally went orange, then stepped into town so they could try to fight and defeat the guardians. They called themselves Guardlers—apparently that was short for Guard Killers—but unlike the sudokers in Stachion, from what I heard, no one had succeeded by the end of the beta test.

Most likely, the dark elf soldiers in Castle Galey were not as unfairly powerful as the guardians of the peace in player towns, but I felt like they would not simply ignore humans running around with swords inside their castle, either. I could say for certain that if those four players attacked us, Kizmel at the least would come to our aid, and if she ordered them to, the castle guards would get involved, too.

I condensed all that logic into a simple "I don't think they'd ignore the entire thing."

Asuna agreed. "Exactly. So let's just talk to them."

"Yeah…I guess that's the only real choice," I admitted. Unless we simply left the castle altogether, there was no way we could lurk around the place without being spotted, and we had still too much to do around here.

We walked away from the darkness of the wall, ready to draw our swords if need be, toward the four players who still gazed at the spring water before them. Neither of us was particularly trying to hide our footsteps, but even within ten meters, none of the players with their backs to us reacted at all. They were probably too engrossed in their conversation.

"…You'd better not. You'll get yelled at."

"Yeah, but I at least wanna try it once. Nobody's ever confirmed if the blelfs are the only ones who can teleport from the spirit trees."

"Fine, test it out, but if you vanish, we're not going after you."

"If the guards get mad, we're running and leaving you behind."

It sounded like the group was three men and one woman. Based on the content of their conversation, they were definitely running the campaign quest on the dark elf side. The term *blelf* was a mystery to me, though.

We stopped two meters behind them, and they still didn't notice, so I sent Asuna a telepathic message to take it away and took a half step back. Her look went from exasperated to ultra-sociable before she called out pleasantly, "Good evening!"

The group of four was shocked, whirling around on the spot, but no one reached for their weapons. They all stared at Asuna for about five seconds, stunned, before their eyes traveled a bit higher. That was probably a sign that they were examining her color cursor. Then they looked at her again for three seconds, before finally noticing me over her shoulder.

The first to speak was the woman, who used a large scimitar and smallish buckler.

"G...good evening. I'm sorry—you startled us."

"Oh no. I apologize for shouting like that out of nowhere," Asuna said with a smile, and the apprehension in the other party's faces instantly vanished. If I had spoken to them instead, it would have taken ten times as long to get them to soften up.

"Wow, you really got me jumpy. I never expected to actually see another player here."

That was the small man with the two-handed sword who talked about wanting to test the spirit tree's teleportation earlier. Now he was rubbing his breastplate instead. Next to him was a tall and skinny fellow with a glaive, who shrugged.

"Of course there will be players here. The castle's public."

Last was a man with the odd combination of a tower shield thick as a metal slab and a slender shortspear. He had a stubby beard and an affable smile as he offered his hand.

"Hi there. We're in a guild called Qusack. We're going through the blelf...er, dark elf campaign right now."

So apparently, *blelf* was their nickname for dark elves. As Asuna and I shook the shield man's hand, I idly wondered what their nickname for the forest elves was.

Then came the introductions. The scimitar woman, who seemed smart and sensible, was Lazuli. The lackadaisical guy with the two-handed sword was Temuo. The rather sharp, tall glaive user was Highston. Lastly, the hardy and bold shield bearer was Gindo.

I didn't recognize any of their names—or the Qusack guild. Neither did Asuna.

There were eight thousand players currently trapped on this floating fortress, so of course nobody could memorize the names of them all. In fact, I probably knew less than a hundred players by name. If we'd crossed paths at one of the main towns on another floor, I wouldn't think twice about them, but Castle Galey was the wild frontier as of January 3. They had to beat many of those nasty poisonous monsters in the canyon on the way here, and they didn't even have a full six-person party. They had to be pretty close to us in level—so how was it possible that I'd never even seen them before?

I almost wanted to be rude and ask if they definitely weren't NPCs. But another glance at their cursors revealed pristine green. While I was on the mean streak, I glanced at their armor and attempted to price it all. Two had light metal armor, and the other two had heavy; and they all had the deep, rich shine of expensive quality. And despite just having come through a deadly map to get here, their gear looked fresh and unharmed, outside of Lazuli's and Gindo's shields.

Perhaps they were players who didn't burst out of the gate when the game started two months ago but had the talent to catch up to the front-line players afterward. If so, that was a heartening thought. *It seemed likely that the ALS would recruit them before too long*, I thought.

"Are you two doing the elf quest on your own?" asked Lazuli, the scimitar girl, stepping forward. Her dark-green hair was tied into a ponytail, and her proud features and husky but piercing voice gave her an air of vitality and activity.

I gave Asuna another *Take it away!* psychic message. She looked at me sidelong before smiling again and replying, "Yes, that's right. We just got to this castle yesterday, in fact."

"Um…does that mean you're in the advancing group?"

"W-well, technically…" Asuna shrugged.

Lazuli's big eyes got even bigger. "Wow, I've never met one of them before! And you're so pretty! I can't believe it."

There was nothing but honest surprise and delight in her voice, but for just a brief moment, the three men behind her shared an uncomfortable look.

What was that about? I wondered instantly, but I couldn't read their minds from their expressions alone. After constantly being around Asuna for so long, I was only just now starting to understand the way she thought about things…possibly.

Asuna would have noticed the men's reaction, too, but she continued speaking with Lazuli without betraying any hint of suspicion. She talked about how we were part of the front-line group, but not in any guild, and Lazuli mentioned that the Qusack four only left the Town of Beginnings four weeks ago. At that point, Asuna suggested we continue talking in the dining hall.

The hungry adventurers immediately agreed, and we headed through the entrance hall of Castle Galey to the second floor. Kizmel's task at the treasure repository would be done by now, but I didn't see her in the dining hall. In all honesty, I couldn't anticipate what might happen when she interacted with players other than us, so I decided it wasn't worth searching for her. The six of us sat down at a table by a window.

A steward came over, so Asuna and I just asked for tea, while Gindo's group ordered the meal course plus bread—and they got seconds of the fish, too. Only Highston the glaive user stuck to his one plate. When he finished first, there was an apologetic look on his gaunt face. "You'll have to excuse them. We're broke as a general rule, so now that we're here at the dark elf base, and the food is free, they can't help themselves."

Temuo, whose head was shaved like a high school baseball player's, chomped down on a fish headfirst and butted Highston on the shoulder. "Don't act all smooth and in control in front of the pretty girl! In the fifth-floor elf village, you were double fisting those skewers!"

"And you had *three* in each hand!"

They were a jolly bunch. But once again, something about them seemed off to me. Highston said they were broke, but they had very expensive equipment. And if they had the skill to get this far—and assuming they weren't pouring their funds into sketchy items or gambling—they should at least have enough col to spend on decent food.

But obviously, I wasn't going to pry into the financial situation of a guild I'd just met, so I sat back and sipped my tea. Then, with the most effortlessly natural smile and tone of voice imaginable, Asuna asked, "So how do you all know each other?"

Considering that she was like a prickly hedgehog when we first met at Tolbana on the first floor, Asuna's transformed into quite the pleasant socialite...

The thought sent a little snort out through my nose, rippling the liquid in my teacup. Sensing my thoughts, the fencer gently stepped on the top of my left foot, sending a very clear signal not to say anything out of line.

Unaware that this act of intimidation was happening under the table, the four exchanged another look, including Lazuli this time. Gindo the bearded dandy—though of a different sort than Okotan from the ALS—wiped his mouth politely with a napkin before responding.

"We met in the Town of Beginnings. But we never planned to actually leave the town at first...We were more like an information-exchange fraternity."

"Information exchange...?" Asuna repeated.

Gindo could sense the suspicion in her voice and explained, "I know this will sound pathetic to you, given your place in the game, but the 'waiters' back in the Town of Beginnings who choose to stay safe until the game is beaten still get hungry and sleepy every day. You won't die without food here, of course, and you can sleep on the street, but everyone wants a hot meal and soft bed. That means you need money for food and lodging each day."

This was true. And though I hadn't been back to the first floor in quite a while, I knew that it was much harder than it sounded. The quickest way to earn col was to beat monsters. *SAO* wasn't the kind of game that said "Bugs and animals wouldn't be carrying gold coins!" so even the weakling worms and boars right outside the Town of Beginnings dropped a few col. Kill ten a day, and you could afford a decent meal and a place to sleep—but even against boars, there was no way to eliminate the possibility of an accident happening.

Focus too much on one monster, and you might miss the sound of another one popping into existence nearby and end up linking the two in combat. Through repetition of little mistakes or lapses in judgment like this, one gained knowledge, experience, and ultimately, strength. But in this world, you had only one life that could pay the price of a mistake. Most likely, the majority of the two thousand players who'd already dropped out of the deadly game did so not far from the Town of Beginnings. And according to Argo's rough calculations, that included a few hundred beta testers. One mistake, one accident leading to panic, was all it took to deplete your hit points, no matter how much you knew about the game...

"...But we didn't earn our money by going out into the wilderness and beating mobs. As a matter of fact, there are lots of quests in the Town of Beginnings if you look for them," Gindo said.

It was my turn to repeat his words. "Quests?"

"Yes. Of course, we couldn't mess with the ones like 'Go out of town and get this thingy' or 'Beat X number of monsters,' but within the city, you can do stuff like errands, finding lost objects, and even some rare ones like housecleaning and pet walking..."

"Oh, right, right!" said Lazuli, who was picking at the side of pickled veggies that came with the grilled fish. "The one where you had to clean up the hoarder house? That was a tough one... There were piles and piles of items all throughout the house, and you had to separate them into these huge wooden boxes out in the yard. You had to sort every last item perfectly to beat the quest, and lots of them you couldn't really tell if they were toys, or practical items, or..."

"Did you know that if you pilfer the coins and jewels and stuff that pop up in those piles, you get locked in the basement of that mansion for like half a day?" Temuo added.

Highston sighed. "Only you would attempt something like that."

The bickering made Asuna giggle. Their erstwhile leader, Gindo, smiled wryly and spread his hands. "The point is, there are lots of quests that give you safe earnings. But since they don't endanger your life, they're all tedious instead. We started running into each other so much at the various quest spots that we naturally got to trading information."

"That's right. At first, I tried to keep my distance from this fishy old guy," said Lazuli, pointing her fork at Gindo. He whined, "I'm not that old…"

Although his looks and manner were completely different, I saw a similarity in Gindo's gestures to the scimitar-wielding man named Klein whom I'd spent a few hours hunting boars with on the first day of the game.

He'd stayed behind in the Town of Beginnings to be with his friends. Was he hard at work leveling up now, so he could reach the frontier? Or was he staying put to focus on his safety? His name was still in my friends list, so I could write him a message whenever I wanted, but the last two months had passed without any communication between us. I suppose I felt guilty about abandoning him and chose not to draw attention to it by reaching out now.

Mentally speaking, the Town of Beginnings felt endlessly distant, but with a teleportation gate, it was, in fact, just a step away. If we had an opportunity to go to Stachion, maybe it would be nice to visit the bottom floor again.

Just then, Lazuli said, "Still, as a general rule, there's no downside to the rewards when doing quests as a group. If you work together, you get it done quicker, and you can use the extra time to search for Japanese books to read. Pretty soon, our little info-trading group became a cooperative strategy group."

"Oh, I see…" murmured Asuna, who was satisfied with that answer. She lifted the toe of her boot off my foot under the table.

It seemed perfectly natural that people would work together to clear out city quests in the Town of Beginnings, but this was Castle Galey, right on the frontier. There was a huge mental leap involved in going from a group that banded together to avoid the danger of fighting monsters to an official in-game guild—meaning they completed the tricky and dangerous guild quest on the third floor—with fancy gear that could knock out the scorpions in that dusty canyon on the way to this castle.

Highston sensed my suspicion and turned to look me square in the face, his long purplish hair waving.

"...Now that we've gotten to this part of the story, we might as well see it through to the end. When we started the group, we were making pretty solid income for a while...However, the Town of Beginnings might be big, but it doesn't have an endless supply of quests. Some are daily quests that can only be done once a day, but when the word got around about them, so many people tried them that you had to wait half a day just to be able to undertake them..."

"Oh...that makes sense," I said.

Gindo the bearded dandy picked it up from there. "The city quests got picked clean before the first floor was cleared out, so we were in trouble. Uh, not that I'm criticizing you folks in the front-line group—just the opposite. We're very grateful for your hard work, and we feel bad that you're doing all of this for our benefit. We couldn't even imagine trying what you do, clearing out labyrinths and beating floor bosses..."

"Huh? That's not true, though," I said, a bit more blunt than I probably needed to be. "You appear to have some high-grade gear, and if you can get to this place, then I would imagine you can fight in the labyrinth towers without too much trouble..."

I wanted to ask them if they'd help out by joining the raid group, but all four suddenly began shaking their heads.

"No, no, no way—we can't. We're not like that..." Lazuli started to protest, but Gindo cut her off.

"Let's explain it in order. So, um...I told you how the quests in the Town of Beginnings ran dry. Well, at that point, we had some decent savings, so we weren't going to go hungry anytime soon... but even staying at the cheapest inn, that wallet was eventually going to empty out. So the four of us talked it over and weighed two options: Ration our money for as long as it can go in the safety of town? Or blow it all out to buy gear and potions—and leave the town?"

"Huh…?"

If you had that option, you should've just picked it from the start, I thought, before I realized something.

"Oh, right. If you beat quests, you get more than just money. You get experience points."

"'Zackly," said Temuo, fish tail sticking out of his mouth. He worked his lips to pull the rest of it inside and crunched away with a smile. "By the time we beat all the interior quests in the Town of Beginnings, we were all at level five."

"Fi…?" I gaped. Asuna and I shared a look.

I left the town at level one after Akihiko Kayaba's tutorial speech, but I remembered that when I got the Anneal Blade at the town of Horunka, I was still only level four. A team of four level-five players with good gear would need a disastrous anti-miracle to lose to the worm and boars around the starting town.

But the thing about MMORPGs was that the possibility of disaster was always present. For players who'd stayed in the safety of town for nearly a month to finally leave that safe zone, there had to be some other motive that pushed them along.

"We did feel reassured that our levels were higher…but the reason I argued we should go out into the world was a simpler one than that," said Highston shyly, holding his teacup with both hands. "I just wanted to do more quests…*SAO*'s quests tend to be detailed, but many also feel like they were written by a child. You just can't tell what's going to happen in them. It feels like the moments when we're thinking hard about the clue that will solve the riddle, or running around town looking for that one missing item, are the only moments when we can actually forget we're playing a game that's trying to kill us…"

"Huh?! Is that seriously what you were thinking?!" Lazuli yelped, grumpily bopping Highston on the shoulder. The scowl turned into a grin very soon, though. "You should have just said that instead! Then we wouldn't have had to argue and argue over it for all those hours."

"Yeah. We all knew you were the biggest quest lover of the bunch already," Temuo pointed out. Highston flushed and tried to argue that he wasn't that obsessed.

Gindo smirked again at the way his companions bickered and got the discussion back on track. "Anyway...we decided to use just about all of our col to buy gear and went out of town. First, we went through all the extermination and harvesting quests that we couldn't do before, then we all got to level 6 and earned a new skill slot. At that point, I even started to think that at the rate we were going, we'd catch up to the top group before too long..."

Suddenly, the smile left his lips, and he clenched his hands into fists. "We finished all the quests in Horunka and Medai with ease, then tried to take a shortcut through the swamp to Tolbana. In the week since leaving town, we thought we'd gotten good at fighting, and the kobolds around there were easy enough, so we got cocky. We came across a group of three kobolds in the swamp and didn't realize that one was new to us..."

"Was it a Swamp Kobold Trapper?" I asked.

Gindo looked surprised but nodded. "Yes, I believe that was the name. At the time, I used a one-handed sword, but the snare the kobold threw tangled up my blade, and it fell into the swamp... I tried to pick it up, but while I was reaching in the muck for it, another kobold attacked me..."

"You didn't read the strategy guide?" Asuna asked, her voice just a little bit harder than before. "I'm pretty sure it was being distributed for free in Medai by that point."

"Oh...uh..."

Gindo turned uncomfortably to look at his friends, then sighed. "We made use of it when leaving the Town of Beginnings, of course. It's just, those guides are mainly about monsters and items, and their quest info is limited to the big ones and the combat ones... We were proud—arrogant, even—about having completed all the quests in the Town of Beginnings. We began thinking that we knew more than the book did, so we only flipped briefly through the updated version in Medai. And when we read it closely afterward, we saw that it had a full breakdown of the Swamp Kobold Trapper and warnings about the danger it posed..."

"..."

I opened my mouth to say something but realized I didn't know what I would actually say. The contents of Argo's strategy guides naturally skewed toward safety information. That was the reason she made and distributed them in the first place, and she was going to need a full writing staff to actually cover all the quests that didn't have the potential to be deadly.

"...At the time, I was close to dying, and Temuo and Lazuli were in the yellow, too," Gindo said, head downcast with shame. "I was in a full-blown panic. I just wanted to run away, but it was a swamp, so running was hard...All I knew was that I was going to die. We ran and ran like people possessed and finally threw them off, but at that point, our spirit was broken..."

I'd been fighting at the front line of player progress since *SAO* officially launched, but the number of times I'd felt the Grim Reaper reaching for my neck was surprisingly few. But I understood exactly what he meant when he spoke of broken spirits. I still felt a vivid chill run down my spine when I recalled that moment fighting Asterios the Taurus King on the second floor, when I'd been paralyzed after his lightning attack, helpless to do anything but to look up at the approaching boss.

The fact that I didn't drop out of the advancing group and hide in the safety of town after that was probably because I was with Asuna, I supposed. She would say something like *"I'd rather die than give up,"* and I couldn't possibly leave her to her own devices and return to the Town of Beginnings.

I imagined that these four had probably stuck through it because of their personal bonds.

Meanwhile, Gindo continued, "When we returned to Medai, battered and broken, there were about ten players in the town square shouting about something. When we asked what happened, they said that the first-floor boss had been beaten while we were out adventuring. That was exciting and wonderful, and we were grateful to the players who did it, but we honestly felt conflicted."

Gindo sighed, and the close-shaven Temuo stepped in. "It's like, there we were, defeated and miserable, and then we hear that news? It just pointed out how unfit we were...Like, I played in a youth baseball league until middle school..."

"Huh?!" I yelped. Only half of that was surprise that he was *actually* a baseball player like I'd imagined, and the other half was that he willingly divulged real-world details about himself to strangers. Temuo seemed surprised by the reaction, but Highston shook his head in annoyance.

"We always tell you, don't dredge up talk of the outside."

"So what? I can talk about my own life if I want to. Right?" he asked, turning to me for validation. I awkwardly agreed.

"Er, uh, yeah."

"See, in baseball, it's really easy to tell when you're outclassed. It's true of all sports, of course...but there's always at least one guy on your team that you realize you'll never be better than, and when you play in a tournament, you find monsters that even *he* can't overcome in competition. Only the people who keep at it and don't let that discourage them will reach the top, but I couldn't hack it. When I heard the boss was beaten, I remembered that feeling again. That feeling of being in the stands at the park, yelling myself hoarse, and sensing just how *far away* it all felt..."

He trailed off, his eyes gazing into space. It was like he was watching the heat haze over the baseball field in midsummer.

As someone who was actually present at the battle against Illfang the Kobold Lord, the first-floor boss, I should've said something, but I couldn't find the words. Temuo was talking about being outclassed and feeling like we were so distant, but I didn't share that sensation at all. The only thing that defined the current front-line group was a successful sprint off the starting line, nothing else. None of the floor bosses had been easy. When they were in Medai marveling at our victory over Illfang, we were mourning the loss of Diavel, our raid party leader.

"So...why didn't you go back to town after that?" Asuna asked, wasting no breath.

Temuo blinked a few times at how direct her question was.

"Well, if I had to use a single word, I guess it was...stubbornness?" He looked to his sides, where Lazuli, Highston, and Gindo all nodded. "We knew that we weren't going to get into the frontier group...but we were still stubborn in thinking that we knew more about quests than anyone else. So we said to ourselves, before we give up and run back to the safe zone, let's test out how far we can get with quests alone."

"Q-quests alone...?" I asked, while next to me, Asuna gasped. "Oh! Does that mean the Q from Qusack is for...?"

"Yep! Very astute, Asuna!" Lazuli remarked, snapping her fingers.

At this, thinking he was being called, the dark elf steward rushed over to the table, much to Lazuli's panic. But Asuna took the opportunity to order some honey ale, and as the waiter left, Highston took over the explanation.

"You're correct—the Q is short for *quest*. And *sack* came from our baseball-playing friend here, to refer to the sacks of gold we would come away with."

Asuna burst into cute laughter, and I added a stifled gurgle of my own that was much less cute. Since all the guilds we knew had cool, flashy names like Dragon Knights Brigade and Legend Braves, the sheer simple honesty of Qusack being short for *questing for sacks* had tickled our funny bones.

The honey ale was conveniently brought out at that moment, and I took a swig of the sweet, refreshing liquid to quench my thirst. "I see...I'll be honest, I thought you folks were a little fishy at first, but the riddles are being answered for me. So the reason your gear is so good, despite you being broke, is because it's all quest rewards."

And the reason you looked so uncomfortable when we admitted we were in the front-line group was because you felt guilty about dropping out, I mentally added. But something in the way Gindo tugged his short beard told me he understood my meaning.

"Yes, that's right. You tend to get more experience than money for quests...and between all the rewards with a selection of loot to take, you can assemble a pretty good set. Unfortunately, you need to go hunting to get those sacks of coins, though."

"Now that you mention it, that's true," I admitted. But there was still one question on my mind. For being a quest-focused guild, how was it that they seemed so fresh and clean even after reaching Castle Galey? The giant insects and arthropods in the barren canyons outside were about the toughest of the generic monsters you could find at this point.

"So...you're telling me...that you started the dark elf faction of the "Elf War" campaign quest on the third floor, and you came here to Castle Galey to continue the hidden key quests?" I wondered.

The four members of Qusack nodded. "That's right. Didn't you? Have you already recovered the key from this floor?" Highston asked. I glanced at Asuna before replying.

"Yeah, we just got back from finishing it. If you'd like, we can tell you the main points to watch out for."

"That would be much appreciated." He smiled, inclining his head. Then he turned toward the water.

"But I suppose the random mobs along the path were tougher than the actual riddle solving...Did you have trouble with the giant bugs on the way to the castle?" I asked, a very smooth leading question by my standards. My partner saw through this attempt, though, and cleared her throat uncomfortably. The four were as straightforward as their guild name suggested, though; none appeared skeptical of my question.

"Oh, we just left the attacking to our escort and focused on guarding the whole time..." Gindo said, which didn't immediately make sense to me.

"...E-escort? You hired another player...?"

"Oh no. We don't have the money for that. I mean the dark elf NPC...Don't you have one, too?" he asked. I glanced at Asuna again.

The first thought in my head at "dark elf NPC" was Kizmel, but she wasn't our guard or escort, and we didn't reunite with her until we arrived at Castle Galey. Or did that mean they had their own "Kizmel"? Like us, did they manage to beat the Forest Elven Hallowed Knight in the Forest of Wavering Mists, avoiding Kizmel's death and giving them a companion...?

I glanced around the dining hall but saw no one that fit the bill. Perhaps they had already broken up the party at the time they arrived, but that might mean that our Kizmel in the treasure repository might run across *their* Kizmel somewhere in the castle. I couldn't imagine what would happen if that came to pass.

Asuna filled in the silence I was leaving. She asked hoarsely, "What is...your escort's name...?"

"Name?" repeated Gindo, taken aback. He looked at his companions. "You guys know that blelf's name...?"

The other three shook their heads. Lazuli said, "The cursor just says Dark Elf Scout. Wouldn't that be the name?"

Now it was our turn to glance at one another. Kizmel was a knight, not a scout. Her official title was Dark Elven Royal Guard. That made it much less likely that Qusack's escort was another Kizmel, but I had to be sure.

"By the way, what's the gender of your escort...?"

"A man. He's a real dick," said Temuo. Both Asuna and I exhaled.

Upon further inquiry, we learned that, as initially designed, their entry event to the quest featured the dark elf and forest elf both dying. The four managed to complete the camp commander's quests somehow, but at the final mission on the third floor, "Retrieving the Key," they were given a Dark Elven Scout to serve as their escort and fifth party member. Apparently, he vanished at the entrance of human towns, then reappeared when they left them.

If they undertook unrelated quests or hunted in any one spot, he would disappear again. He was exceedingly cold, as befitted a dark elf, and did not engage in any kind of personal or small talk.

When I did the "Elf War" campaign quest in the beta as a solo player, I didn't get an escort; what they were experiencing was probably a support measure added to the official release, but if that elf was anywhere near as strong as Kizmel, I could see how these four quest-centric players had gotten to Castle Galey without any damage.

But at the same time, I sensed danger. This questline continued to the ninth floor. That scout escort would vanish there when the quest was over. Would they be able to keep up after that point without someone to do the heavy damage for them?

I wondered these things and more as I sipped at my honey ale but decided that it wasn't really my business. They'd done their other quests outside of the elf campaign without a bodyguard, and Asuna and I certainly received a great amount of tactical and emotional benefit from Kizmel's presence. Given that the scout was just a simple bodyguard NPC to them, Qusack might find it easier to move on when the campaign was done without losing motivation.

"...Gosh, look at the time," Gindo said, rousing me from my thoughts. The plates on the table had been cleaned off, and Temuo and Lazuli looked sleepy. Gindo closed his window, got to his feet, and patted Temuo on the head.

"Kirito, Asuna, it was a pleasure to chat with you. We're going to get our quest from the lord of the castle, so we'll take our leave for today..."

"No, thank you for letting us take up your time," said Asuna, getting up from her chair. I inclined my head, too. We agreed to meet up again in the morning and watched the four of them leave the hall.

When the doors closed and their cursors vanished from view, I gave my temporary party member a look. After a long few seconds, Asuna muttered, "I guess there are also people like them up near the front line, too."

"I never considered the possibility of a quest-focused guild… Even without grinding for levels, you can get this far on quest loot alone, I guess."

"Not that we do that much grinding, either," she pointed out.

"That's true."

A lull followed, and eventually, we exhaled simultaneously. It was a good thing that more players were becoming focused on leaving the towns and reaching the frontier—and being quest-centric opened up new possibilities for that. Our meeting with Gindo's group was a welcome development—but there was something in my chest that itched about it and refused to go away.

Perhaps it was just some infantile irritation that others had intruded on our supposed private relaxation time around the castle with Kizmel. Castle Galey was a public location, so all players had the right to visit. In *SAO*, as in any MMORPG, it was a classic violation of manners to "claim" a public space and refuse others the right to be there.

As fellow members of the dark elf faction of this questline, this was actually a place for us to trade useful information. I told myself to stop being childish and selfish—and to follow Asuna's example in the way she had cordially interacted with Qusack. And yet…

"…Earlier, I said I wasn't a fan of instances. Now I take that back," my partner said out of the blue. I stared at her.

"Wh…why?"

"Because! Anyway, where has Kizmel gone off to?" she snapped, clearly trying to change the subject and looking around the dining hall for no good reason. Virtually all the other dark elves had continued on their way, and of course, Kizmel wasn't here.

"M…maybe she went back to her room…"

"Well, we should go back, too, then."

"Y-yeah, good idea."

The fencer promptly strode away, and as I followed her, I wondered if I would ever fully understand the way her mind worked…

No, I decided with a sigh, that day would probably never come.

8

WHEN WE OPENED THE DOOR TO OUR GUEST ROOM on the third floor of the west wing, intent on changing clothes before we visited Kizmel's chamber, both Asuna and I exclaimed with surprise. The slender elf knight was already sitting on the sofa in our room.

"What are you doing here, Kizmel?" asked Asuna, trotting over to her.

The knight lifted a narrow glass in her right hand. "I was waiting for you, of course. Have you finished talking with the new visitors?"

"Huh? You knew we were meeting with other play...I mean, other human warriors?" I asked, which brought a little curl of a smile to her lips.

"But of course. I kept my distance, not wanting to interfere."

"You wouldn't have been a bother at all..."

Despite my reassurance, however, it was indeed a good thing for us that Kizmel had been considerate. Kizmel was far more human in her mannerisms and intelligence than other dark elves—and certainly more than the generic Dark Elf Scout accompanying Qusack. I couldn't imagine how they might react to her, and it wasn't clear what effect it would have on her to interact with players who might speak openly about the fact that this world was just a VR game.

In the online RPGs I played before *SAO*, I was not good at actual role-playing. But somehow, it had become natural for me to assume the role of a "human swordsman traveling across Aincrad" when interacting with the dark elves—a development that filled me with a mild wonder.

Kizmel waved at us to sit. "Did you finish speaking with the new visitors?"

"Yes, they said they were going to visit with the master of the castle," Asuna explained. The knight placed a new glass before her and poured a pale-golden liquid from the bottle on the table. When she did the same for me, I noticed a refreshing, familiar scent wafting up. It must have been that moontear wine that her sister Tilnel loved.

We shared a toast, and I took a sip of the rather strong alcohol—that couldn't *actually* get you drunk—before saying, "I think those four will be leaving the castle in the morning to go to the shrine in the south, so we won't see them until the evening. It's your valuable day off tomorrow, so we should find our own useful task to—"

Softly and suddenly, Asuna jabbed me with her elbow. I looked at her in bewilderment before I realized what I'd just done.

The four members of Qusack were going south tomorrow to retrieve the Agate Key from the shrine. The same key that we'd just brought back today.

This set of six hidden keys that would open the mysterious Sanctuary device, which the dark elf legends held would destroy Aincrad, and which the forest elves believed would return it to the earth, would not exist in duplicate. As far as Kizmel knew, we had gone from the third to the sixth floor and, through great trials, had managed to collect four of these precious, one-of-a-kind keys.

But within the game system, there were as many secret keys as there were players undertaking the "Elf War" questline. At this moment, Qusack was receiving a request from Count Galeyon to recover the Agate Key. What if they left tomorrow and returned after finishing the quest—and Kizmel witnessed them carrying a new copy of the key? It could very well happen.

What if she asked us why the four of them were going to that very same shrine? If NPCs in this game had such advanced AI, shouldn't they be programmed with the ability to integrate that information and take it all in stride?

"I see…It is much to ask of you humans, I know," Kizmel murmured. She drank down the last of her wine. I picked up the bottle automatically and reached out to pour her another glass, then cautiously asked, "Uh…do you know the reason they're going to the shrine, Kizmel?"

"To retrieve the hidden key, of course."

"…"

Asuna and I stared at the dark elf, who seemed unbothered by the knowledge. When she noticed us staring, she looked a bit curious, then smiled. "Ah…so you did not know, then."

"D-didn't know what?" Asuna asked quietly.

Kizmel's smile turned a bit apologetic. "The commanding officer of the vanguard force explained that he was using knights to confuse and mislead the forest elves, did he not? We are arranging a similar thing for the duty of retrieving the keys."

"Wh…what does that mean?"

"Even after *we* recovered the keys from the shrines, other knights and scouts have headed to the same shrines, carrying false keys mocked up by our priests to our camps and fortresses. If any humans pledge assistance along the way, we accept it. This is all to mislead the forest elves, remember…"

"…"

Asuna and I had no words. The existence of fake keys itself was a surprise, but even more than that…

"But then…wouldn't that expose those decoy knights and soldiers to danger…?" I asked, stunned.

Kizmel looked down. "That is correct. More than a few knights have been attacked by the forest elves, and I understand some have lost their lives."

"But...why do you need to go to such lengths?!" Asuna demanded, leaning forward. The knight placed a gentle hand on her shoulder.

"Because that is how serious a duty it is to retrieve the sealed keys, and the mentality one needs to undertake the mission. Failure is unacceptable. Now the history and knowledge of the collected peoples of Lyusula, Kales'Oh, humankind, and dwarfkind are contained within this floating castle, and should it collapse, all will be lost...along with many, many lives. We cannot allow ruin to come to the things that the priestess of yore gave her precious life to protect. I believe that Her Majesty the queen wants the six keys so she can keep the Sanctuary door shut forever..."

Kizmel stopped there, but my mind was half-occupied with other things. After Asuna and I interfered in the battle between Kizmel and the Forest Elven Hallowed Knight back on the third floor, the duels between dark and forest elves had continued without end. This was only natural, as it was the event that entered a player into the "Elf War" campaign quest, but if Kizmel's explanation was taken at face value, it suggested that the elves undertook even this unavoidable matter of the story's convenience at the risk of their own lives.

But had the designer of this quest, some writer at Argus, really considered this angle when designing it? It was common sense that in an MMORPG, the same events occurred for each player; anything less wouldn't be fair. When seen from inside the game world, it would look like the same character was dying and coming back to life, over and over, but no player was going to complain about this being illogical. That little girl from my Anneal Blade quest, for example, spent an eternity getting sick and being cured, back and forth.

Was it really the game's designers who created these secondary elements like fake keys and decoy knights, in order to protect the integrity of the worldview and the game mechanics under the hood? Or was it something else, like the very world itself...?

"What is it, Kirito?"

I looked up when I heard my name and met eyes with Kizmel, who had been equally lost in thought.

"N-nothing...just thinking about things..."

"I understand how you feel. Sometimes even I wonder if the four keys we are carrying around are the real thing or not."

"Uh...for real?" I asked, accidentally slipping into some real-world slang, but that saying had clearly been absorbed into Kizmel's vocabulary at this point, and she paid it no mind.

"Yes, for real. It would have been real because we took it from the shrine, but once it has been placed in the vault of a fortress or castle, there is no telling if the priests might have switched it out..."

"Ah, I see..."

So it's potentially true that both our keys and Qusack's keys are fakes...Or maybe the story holds that they're both real...? I wondered, once again lost in questions that had no answer.

Next to me, Asuna asked, "If you're going to the length of creating false keys to distract the forest elves, wouldn't it be a bad thing to have the keys, real or fake, collected in the same place? I mean, Yofel Castle got attacked..."

"Yes, there is a logic to what you say," agreed Kizmel, who looked up at the ceiling.

The guest chamber at Yofel Castle had huge windows that afforded a view of the outside, but Castle Galey was carved right into the rock, so the windows were only on the hallway side. They compensated with plenty of interior lights; in addition to the wall-hanging lamps that the inns in Stachion and Suribus had, there was an elaborate candelabra hanging from the ceiling like a chandelier, its little fires flickering.

"We assumed that Yofel Castle would never be attacked. The forest elves on the fourth floor had only a few small boats, and we couldn't have imagined they would team up with the fallen elves...If you had not warned us, we would not have prepared for the attack in time. Even with Viscount Yofilis's power, the castle might have been lost. But..."

Kizmel looked back at us and gave a reassuring smile. "Even with the wicked cleverness of the Fallen, it is impossible for them to attack Castle Galey with a huge army. As you saw for yourselves, I could not take ten steps outside of this place without the Greenleaf Cape. The forest elves will have some kind of similar cloak, but surely in only small numbers…And that cape was sewn from the leaves of the Holy Tree; there shall never be another of its kind. Even the boar warriors of the forest elves would not dream of attacking this castle with no more than ten, at risk of losing all the treasures handed down since the Great Separation."

"What about the fallen elves? Is it possible that they have something similar?" Asuna persisted, but Kizmel again shook her head.

"Have you forgotten? The Fallen were cursed by the Holy Tree. If they should put on the cape made of its leaves, they would be burned to ash…or something similar, if not to such an extreme. The pain and scarring would be intense, regardless."

"Oh…y-you're right," Asuna said, sticking out her tongue to show how forgetful she was. Kizmel chuckled back, but her mirth did not last for very long. She folded her arms in a thinking pose.

"But as Asuna says…keeping the keys in one place for too long is only inviting needless risk, perhaps. There is a spirit tree here at the castle, so I suppose I shall have to give up my day of rest and continue as soon as the morning arrives…"

Whaaat? I was going to shout, but Asuna was quicker.

"No!" She practically flew over the low table to Kizmel's side and grabbed the knight's hands in her own. "I'm sorry that I caused you to worry. I understand now that this castle is safe. Just stay with us tomorrow! I've been thinking about what we would do!"

Kizmel's dark-purple eyes blinked several times, and then—how many times had I seen this by now?—gave the gentle smile of an older girl to her younger sister.

"All right. Then I will leave in two days, as originally planned. What shall we do tomorrow?"

"It's still a .secret. I'll announce it in the morning, so look

forward to the surprise," Asuna said with a grin. I, however, felt a bit unnerved by that.

Minutes later, the slender wine bottle was empty, and Kizmel slumped against the back of the sofa. "Whew...I believe I am a bit intoxicated."

I examined her face, but the coffee-brown skin was not any different from usual, and I couldn't anticipate what would happen to an AI if it got drunk. Asuna looked worried, however, and asked, "Are you all right? Can you get back to your room?"

"Ha-ha, I am not so drunk that I cannot stand. But..." she said, pausing to look at us in turn, "the room I've been given is too large for one person. Do you mind if I sleep on this long couch tonight?"

"Wha—?!" I yelped out of reflex, but in fact, Asuna and I had no reason to refuse her. I was going to tell her it was perfectly all right, of course, until I realized something: In a situation with two women and one man, it seemed clear which one of the three should take the sofa.

"Uh, in that case, you can sleep in the bedroom with Asuna, Kizmel. I'll sleep on the sofa instead."

But the knight arched her back and shook her head. "No. This is your room...I cannot force you out of your bedchamber, Kirito. I would rather return to my room, in that case."

She started to get to her feet, but Asuna grabbed the end of her thin tunic. Asuna was still in her sulky begging mood. She grumbled and glanced at the bedroom door. "That bed...can fit three people, right?"

"Huh?!" I yelped again, unable to help myself.

But Kizmel was very rational about it. "Oh, I do believe you are right."

"B-but that only leaves about half a meter of space between each person..." I argued, before wondering if dark elves understood the measurement systems of the real world.

Kizmel just shrugged her shoulders. "It is not much different from when the three of us shared that tent at the camp on the third floor. Or do you not want to sleep in the same bed as me, Kirito?"

"Th-that's not what I'm saying." It was the only answer I could give to that question. The knight grinned mischievously.

"Then, there is no problem."

We still had to figure out the issue of how we would arrange ourselves in the bed, and the consensus was that Kizmel would take the middle, with Asuna on the left and me on the right. I'd been worried about the space, but Asuna and Kizmel huddled closer, leaving me with a bit less than a meter of space to work with.

I got into the bed after them and kept my body as straight as an arrow, just far enough from the edge that I wouldn't fall over. With our arrangement, at least I wouldn't repeat the catastrophe from this morning, but there was still the possibility that I would wake up clinging to Kizmel somehow. And I was pretty sure that the anti-harassment code for inappropriate contact with an NPC skipped over the stage where the victim hit the button on a pop-up window and simply auto-transported the offender when the warning period ran out. I didn't want to wake up in a cell, so it didn't hurt to keep as far away as I could...

"If you sleep on the edge like that, you'll fall out of the bed, Kirito," said a whisper in the deep darkness. A hand wriggled through the blanket and grabbed my right arm. I reluctantly scooted a bit closer, at which point my fingertips brushed some part of Kizmel.

"You will be warmer if you snuggle closer."

"N-no, I think I'm fine right here."

"You should not be at an age where you are bashful about this sort of thing..."

Does she mean I'm too grown up? Or I'm too much of a child? I wondered, but Kizmel did not elaborate. If Asuna wasn't interrupting this whispered conversation, then it was a sure sign she was already asleep.

On the other hand, it was true that the temperature improved quite a bit from just that much movement, and I felt very drowsy. I closed my eyes and let out a long, slow breath.

When I was a child, I found it very difficult to sleep anywhere but my own bed. I had trouble falling asleep on the outdoor school field trips in elementary school and even on family vacations.

It had been the same when I first came to this world. More than a few times, I ended up farming a single spot overnight because I couldn't get to sleep anyway. But at some point, it just stopped happening. Regardless of the fact that I slept in a different place virtually every night, I could be fast asleep within ten minutes of getting under the covers.

I wondered idly if it was because I'd gotten used to the experience of sleeping in a virtual world, but then I realized that wasn't true. I hadn't found it easy to fall asleep until I started working with Asuna. *There was more trouble in my life this way than when I was solo*, I thought, which made this strange…Or perhaps it was that in exchange for all the extra troubles and considerations, I was receiving something else that counterbalanced all that.

As I drifted off into into slumber, I hoped that it was the same way for Asuna and Kizmel.

The night of January 3 passed in silence…

…or so I thought.

A forceful alarm woke me, stabbing deep into my brain. Without opening my eyes, I felt for my game window and turned off the alarm that only I could hear.

My eyelids rose to see that the room was still dark. Before I entered the bedroom, I had set an alarm for two o'clock, so of course it was dark, but now I felt like I shouldn't have bothered. I focused on the sounds of the room and heard only peaceful slumber from Kizmel and Asuna, which made me want to go back into that pleasant warmth, too. It was willpower alone that forced my eyes to stay open.

Once I had maintained thirty continuous seconds of wakefulness, the temptation of sleep subsided. Careful not to wake the two women, I snuck out of bed and into the living room.

It occurred to me as I crept along that, to a dark elf, an alarm that only I could hear would fall under their category of "human charms." Still, I carefully opened the door and went out into the hallway. I was 50 percent certain that Kizmel at least would detect my movement, but it seemed that I had pulled it off. I opened my window again and equipped my long coat and sword.

There were no humanoid figures on either side of the curving hallway. No guard was likely to scold me if they spotted me, but just in case, I stayed quiet as I headed to the staircase in the center of the west wing.

When the bell rang early in the evening, I had plunged down these stairs, but this time, I was slow and deliberate in climbing them. As I remembered from the beta, the stairs continued past the fourth floor, which was the highest in the castle. Eventually, they ended in a small door. I turned the knob and pushed it open. Fresh, chilly air instantly surrounded me.

The doorway led out onto the roof of the castle's west wing. There was no man-made light here, but the moonlight coming from the outer aperture of Aincrad was just enough to keep the dark at bay.

Then again, the exterior of the staircase corridor itself was about the only feature of note on the vast roof anyway. In a single-player RPG, you'd expect to find a chest or two in a secluded location like this, but here, there wasn't even so much as a pebble to pick up.

Unlike the polished castle walls, the surface here was rough and pockmarked. I walked along the exterior that bordered the courtyard. There were parapets barely a third of a meter tall, but they weren't going to prevent anyone from falling. It was a good twenty meters down to the paving stones below, so a headfirst fall could prove fatal.

I made sure I was alone, just in case, then leaned over to stare into the courtyard at scenery that was the polar opposite of its daytime setting. Countless little torch lights cast the huge spirit tree in alternating navy blue and orange, and the dew that hung and dripped from its leaves and branches shone like liquid fire. Pairs of guards marched slowly around it, like a vision from some fantastical dream.

After a moment of entranced viewing, I snapped back to attention and examined every part of the courtyard I could see—nothing was amiss. The bells hadn't rung, so that meant no one had entered the castle, NPC or player, but I still had to check to make sure, before I allowed myself to step back from the edge.

When I turned around, I looked at the exterior of the castle instead.

Galey was a castle that had been carved into the walls of a previously extant circular stone hollow, so the outer edges were surrounded by sheer natural cliffs. Even from the roof, it was nearly ten meters to get to the top, so despite the Sword of Eventide's agility bonus, I couldn't quite race up the cliff.

But since the beta, I'd always wondered what exactly might be found beyond this rock face. I was sure that the castle gates on the south side were impregnable, but until I saw it for myself, I had trouble ruling out intruders coming from atop the cliffs. I needed to make sure the possibility of a forest elf invasion was no more than zero.

I pulled my gaze away from the cliff wall and began walking to the right. Up ahead loomed the three-part gabled roof of the castle's center building, which was one floor taller than either of the wings. The angle was steep but not vertical like the cliffs.

The peak of the roof reached the edge of the cliff, so my thinking back in the beta was that I could just climb that structure instead. But no matter how I tried back then, I always slipped and fell back down after about three meters. However, my stats were better now, and my boots were higher quality, with good grip. I came to a stop about twenty meters from the gabled roof, envisioned the course I would take, and began to sprint.

With about five meters to go, I hit max speed. Under the roof was the forbidden fifth floor of the central building, which probably included the count's private chambers, so there was a possibility I could get myself in major trouble, but that was something to worry about later. A massive jump got me to the midsection of the roof, and from there, I began to Wall-Run diagonally up the seventy-degree slope. I felt my soles slipping at the fifth step, and they gave way a few centimeters by the seventh, but I managed two more steps before jumping again.

If I grunted with effort, it might wake up Count Galeyon just under the roof, so I had to make do with silent emphasis, stretching as far as I could reach. My fingertips grasped the lip of the cliff, and I let the momentum boost me and scrabbled for all I was worth.

I was prepared to be met by an invisible purple barrier set up by the system itself, but it did not happen. I managed to pull myself up the wall and rolled over onto my back, panting for several long moments. What I'd just done didn't—as far as I knew—expend a single calorie of energy from my actual physical body, but when you worked your avatar to its physical limit, there was always a period of heavy breathing afterward.

But in just a matter of seconds, the feeling passed, and I slowly sat up.

All that I saw before me was flat. I doubted the designers had cut corners here, but the only thing ahead was rough, flat rock, with hardly any features or change in elevation. I stood up and kicked the ground. It was very tough—at the very least, it seemed like I didn't have to worry about slipping through some polygonal crack and clipping into another dimension.

In other words, it could support the weight of hundreds of soldiers. Kizmel claimed that the elves couldn't move through the dusty canyon outside of Castle Galey without capes made of leaves from the Holy Tree, but there was no guarantee that this held true for the top of this cliff, too. I needed to ascertain if there was any other way up here aside from the roof of the castle.

After a brief survey, I started walking directly north. There wasn't a single monster or even a cactus on top of the flat mountain, so I used the massive pillar supporting the next floor of Aincrad in the far distance as a landmark, utilizing nothing but moonlight for illumination.

Asuna liked high places, and I figured she would enjoy the barren terrain, but there was a good reason for not bringing her. Truth be told, I still didn't entirely trust the members of Qusack. It was true that if you beat all the many, many quests so far, you would earn as much XP as if you were efficiently farming monsters, and you would get high-spec gear as quest rewards. With a powerful, ever-present dark elf soldier around as a bodyguard, it wasn't unthinkable that the four would reach this castle, even without much battle experience.

But it still didn't answer the question of *why* they would do this.

Their claimed reason for leaving the safe haven was to earn money for food and lodging—in other words, to make their waiting time in the Town of Beginnings as pleasant as possible. Apparently, they were surprised to learn how strong they were and temporarily hoped they could reach the advancing group, but that dream ended after the disaster with the Swamp Kobold Trapper.

So that led to being quest-centric, forming a guild based around "making sacks with quests"…That all made sense. What bothered me was the timing of their arrival here at the frontier of player progress.

At present, the only people farther ahead than us were the ALS and DKB, proceeding on the counterclockwise route around the floor toward its end, with the Bro Squad and Argo the info broker accompanying them. There was no good intel out yet on the monsters and tricky terrain of this slice of the sixth floor, and even with a powerful NPC accompanying them, the risk of death was greater than zero. If I were in their position, I would stay one floor down from the front-line group at a minimum and only engage in quests when I had plenty of help from Argo's strategy guides. The "Elf War" campaign quest wasn't some race to be first anyway.

So there had to be some other reason for their rush to reach Castle Galey. Perhaps someone had hired them to do something. Perhaps someone who wished to do us harm. In other words, I couldn't rule out the suspicion that Qusack had some connection to Morte's PK gang.

There was a 99 percent chance I was overthinking it, but coming right on the heels of that paralysis-attack incident, I swore never to be caught unawares again. If Qusack was connected to or manipulated by Morte, they would search for alternate routes into the castle. And the first thing to come to mind would be crossing the cliff that formed the back half of the castle. As the historical battles of Ichi-no-Tani and Itsukushima had shown, the best traditional means of ambush was to come down a cliff… or maybe I was just being dramatic.

I strode across the desolate rock, my eyes carefully combing the area for information. Still, no people or monsters to be seen. If I did a full perimeter lap and encountered no one, I'd have to give the members of Qusack a silent apology the next time I saw them.

"Wha—? *Yow!*"

The next moment, I let out an actual yelp and struggled to pull back the leg I had extended. My balance rocked, and I windmilled my arms, trying to catch air. There was no ground beneath my extended foot. Blended perfectly in color between the rocky ground and the background was an abrupt cliff, as sharp and clean as if cut by a knife. The drop was over thirty meters, it looked like.

With the help of the air expelled from my lungs, I managed to pull my center of gravity backward and plopped onto my butt.

When my heart stopped pounding, I crawled forward and timidly peered over the edge. The cliff was so sheer it was practically an overhang that continued all the way to the ground below. No player or forest elf could climb that surface. It was impossible.

I backed up, still on all fours, and only stood once I was a safe distance from the cliff. I opened my window and checked the map to find that the distance between my present location and the outer aperture of Aincrad was not much more than two hundred meters. This was the northern tip of the rocky mountain.

It was nearly three in the morning now, but I had to find out how far this cliff went. I took a bottle of water out of my inventory for a quick swig, then started walking east. Though I was keeping a safe distance from the edge, in the darkness of predawn night, it was very hard to tell where the line was. I wished I had a lantern for light, but if any other players were on top of the mountain, they would certainly see it—there was no cover at all on the plateau's surface.

The trudging continued, with maximum care given to the ground around me. Occasionally, I approached the edge and peered over but never saw any change in the angle. I started to wonder if I was just overthinking things with regard to a forest elf ambush or a sinister Qusack angle—until about fifteen minutes later, when—

I saw something I absolutely did not expect to see.

It was not a protrusion from the rock floor, but a hollow. A descending staircase, cut right down into the stone without any structure overhead, like something from an early RPG. There was faint flickering of firelight coming from farther down the stairs.

"..."

I stopped for two seconds before my brain started running again, and then I silently got down on one knee. A little touch on the edge of the stairs told me that, like the castle itself, they were carved straight down into the rock. The chisel-mark texture was very similar to the castle's, but I couldn't yet be sure that it was also done by dark elves.

If there just so happened to be someone hostile down there, and they were dangerous enough that I died in the fight, there was no

way I could ever apologize to Asuna and Kizmel for my foolish-
ness. For both figurative and literal reasons, of course.

Sadly, I knew I ought to avoid danger for now and go back to
speak with the women. But when I stood up to leave, I sensed an
olfactory input that was out of place.

It wasn't a nasty smell. Just the opposite, in fact. It smelled like
spices, onion, and fatty meat cooking. There was nothing else I
could compare it to—it smelled like a good old hamburg steak.

"........."

For three seconds, my mind went haywire. My stomach curled
up, and saliva flooded my mouth. Only when it threatened to
drool out of my lips did I come to my senses.

There on my knees, I considered the situation: If what awaited
at the bottom of the stairs was some kind of ogre that lured prey
with the smell of a steak so that it could kill and eat them, then
going down there to my death would make me a world-class idiot.
But…but what if there was some tiny chance that this staircase
was an invitation from the hamburg steak fairy, who only appeared
one time a year? After all, there were cacti that only fruited for
thirty minutes out of an entire year, so couldn't this miracle happen as well?

I clenched my fists for about ten seconds and finally came to a
decision.

*Asuna, Kizmel, I'm sorry. Even knowing this might be a trap…I
believe that I was meant to walk down these stairs.*

Then I got to my feet and took a step down into the narrow
stairway. The opening was a square barely over half a meter to
a side, so just from taking three steps down, my stomach hit
the ceiling side of the opening. *It seemed like the opening to a
stairway should be a rectangle*, I thought, grumbling, and leaned
backward so I could essentially slide down the steps. Only when
I was about twenty steps down did it finally end in a hallway tall
enough for me to stand—and even then, my head nearly touched
the ceiling, and I was not particularly tall.

This space, too, was narrow enough that it was almost impossible for two people to squeeze past each other, so at least I knew I wasn't going to get attacked by an ogre or giant in here. There was no light source in the passage, but the red flicker of flame reflected from the curve about ten meters ahead, and the smell of cooking meat was getting stronger. I stepped lightly and slowly onward.

When I reached the right turn, I stuck to the corner and peered around for just a moment before pulling my head back.

"......?"

I played back the still image in my mind like I'd caught it on film, but it was confusing.

At the end of the hallway was a room about three meters to a side. In the middle was a small table and chair. The right wall was wooden shelves, and the left wall featured a small door. On the far wall was a black cylinder that looked like a heating stove, in front of which stood someone in a black robe who was peering into the frying pan on top. The pan, clearly, was the source of the sizzling sound and tempting smell, but sadly, I couldn't make out the contents.

The black-robed figure had its back to me, so I couldn't tell if it was human, elf, or some other demihuman monster like a goblin or orc. At the very least, it was shorter than me, so it couldn't be some man-eating ogre. I peered around the corner again, this time looking long enough that the figure's color cursor came into focus.

Surprisingly, the black robe seemed made of a very fine material like velvet. Unruly curls of gray, almost white hair ran down their back, and on their head, there was a pointed hat of the same material as the robe. The cursor floating above it was yellow: an NPC. The figure's name was BOUHROUM: DARK ELVEN ANECDOTIST. I couldn't make out how to say their name, and I had no idea what an anecdotist was, but I could definitely tell they were a dark elf. So they weren't going to just attack me out of the blue...probably.

I steeled my nerves and rounded the corner, passing through the open hallway and into the room.

"…G-good evening," I called out, and the robed dark elf instantly leaped over a third of a meter into the air, its curly hair flying upward as it spun around to face me.

"Wh…wh-wh-who goes there?!" demanded the elf, who was revealed to be, in human terms, an elderly man of at least eighty years, with his skinny, wrinkled face framed by a small pair of rounded spectacles. But of course, there were those character- istic long, pointy elf ears protruding from the curls, so in fact, he could be hundreds of years old. There was a silver beard that hung from his chin nearly down to the floor.

Of all the people I'd met in Aincrad, this was clearly the closest to the classic visual representation of a wizard. But it also struck me for another reason—a slight feeling of déjà vu…like I had met this fellow somewhere before, perhaps. But I would never forget someone so distinctive.

At the very least, the old fellow did not recognize me. His tiny eyes bulged behind the glasses, and his lengthy beard quivered as he shouted, "B…boy! You're a human, aren't you?! How did you get into my secret chamber?!"

"How…? Th-the normal way, down the stairs…" I said, point- ing to the hallway I'd just walked down. The old man raised a fist.

"You fool, that is not an entrance!"

"Huh? Then…what is it?"

"It is my chimney vent! And besides, that is the bald mountain top up there, where even birds do not dare to cross! How did you climb up there?!"

"W-well…" I stammered, thinking I would probably be in trou- ble if I told him the truth. Then again, I was clearly already in trouble with him, so what was the difference? "I climbed up the roof of the central castle building…"

"……"

Now both the man's eyes and his bearded mouth hung round

and open, an expression that lasted for over three seconds before he finally emitted a strange burst of noise.

"*Ka-hya! Ka-hya-hya-hya*…You are telling me…that a young human boy climbed his way…up the roof of little Melan's bedchamber…?"

Apparently, the *ka-hya* sound was his laughter. He lowered his raised fist and stroked his beard with the other hand. In a softer voice, the old man continued, "I see, I see. So the human swordsman who's been helping with the key collection must be you. I understand now that you are not a thief, but what would bring you to climb the mountain in the dead of night like this?"

"Well, uh…I was out for a night stroll, you know…a little night mountain climbing…and I wondered what the top of the cliff was like. I wandered around until I found your stairs—er, your vent—and smelled something nice coming out of it…"

"*Hwaaaaa!*" the old man screamed, and now it was my turn to jump. But he wasn't angry, and his AI hadn't just gone haywire, apparently. He spun back around with tremendous speed and grabbed the handle of the frying pan barehanded. "*Yeowwww!*"

He transferred the hot pan to the table and blew on his now-reddened palm. It was all so sudden and alarming that I didn't know what to do—until I saw what was sizzling in the middle of the pan.

It was an elliptical slab of minced meat, about fifteen centimeters long and seared to a beautiful brown. This was a perfect hamburg steak, the likes of which I'd never seen in Aincrad before.

The old man noticed my gaze and ceased blowing on his hand so he could exclaim, "Wh-what do you want? It's not for you! This is my one delight a month, and I haven't many left to enjoy! Why, you nearly caused me to char it black."

"………Hrng…"

If the food was one of the whitefish or chicken dishes that the elves so often served in their camps and castles, I would have won my saving roll against temptation and claimed "I didn't say I wanted to eat it."

But this was hamburg steak. It wasn't my number-one favorite dish in the world, but without curry or ramen in Aincrad, the sheer impact of that smell and appearance was nothing short of explosive. The mental image of a knife sinking into it and producing a rush of meat juice from inside crowded out every other thought in my brain.

If only there was some way to get this stubborn old man to give up half his steak...even a third! My mind was working as fast as when Morte attacked, when I was struck by a humble inspiration. I sucked in a sharp breath.

The old man used what looked like a wooden spatula to transfer the hamburg steak to a metal plate. As calmly as I possibly could, given the circumstances, I asked, "Are you...just having that?"

"...What do you mean?" asked the old man suspiciously, moving the plate away from me.

"Oh, the human custom would state that such a delicious meat dish cannot be eaten simply on its own. Only with a side of bread or mixed vegetables can the flavor of the meat be truly appreciated."

"Hah!" the old man mocked, waving his free hand. "I grew tired of vegetables over a hundred years ago. It's bad enough that the cooks at this castle try to feed me leafy greens and fruit every day, because 'it'll make you live longer'...To put that rubbish on my plate would be to ruin my precious fricatelle."

Fr-fricatelle?

I just barely contained my impulse to ask him how that differed from a hamburg steak. As long as it looked and tasted like one, it didn't matter what the elves called it. Instead, I waved my hand to call up my game window. The old man clearly hadn't seen much of the human Art of Mystic Scribing, as he reacted with curiosity, but I promptly found what I was looking for and pulled it out of my inventory.

"Then...what about this?"

In my fingers I held a long, elliptical vivid-purple object. It was the last of the sweet potatoes dropped by those half-fish monsters. A regular potato was the best match for this hamburg steak, but I didn't have any, and this would do fine anyway.

"...What is that?" asked the dark elf elder, who had apparently lived centuries without seeing such a thing. His gray brows drooped in concentration. I rounded the table to show him.

"It's a sweet potato you can find on the fourth floor. If you crisp this up in that frying pan, it'll go great with your hamb...your fricatelle, I bet."

If Asuna were here, she'd use her ample vocabulary and knack for lyrical expression to charm—er, convince—more than a few stubborn old men to try it out, but it had been my decision not to wake her up first. The man still looked suspicious, and he lifted his spectacles to get a better look.

"A sweet potato, you say? It has a strange color..."

"Th-the inside will be the proper shade. It'll be hot and sweet and creamy," I said, like I was some kind of pitchman for a roasted sweet potato cart. The old man glanced back and forth between my face and the potato and, at last, cleared his throat.

"*Ahem-hem*...Well, I suppose I can try it out. If it is as good as you say, I will even give you half of my fricatelle. The potato will go entirely to me, however."

That seemed like an abuse of privilege, but I'd eaten a number of Ichthyoid Potatoes, so I could let it slide this time.

The old man took the potato, then placed the frying pan back on the stove, still slick with the juice and fat of the meat. In the right corner was a tiny kitchen area, and he went there to slice the sweet potato into pieces less than two centimeters wide. Then he dropped the pieces into the pan, which had begun crackling again. Soon, a sweet scent filled the air.

He peered into the pan, murmuring and exclaiming to himself, and I watched with more than a little consternation. You didn't need the Cooking skill to employ primitive methods like thrusting them into an open fire, but it seemed like frying one up in a pan with oil required some amount of expertise. Assuming he had made the steaming hamburg meat out of ingredient items, it appeared he would have to possess the Cooking skill.

A minute later, the old man lifted his plate and used a long meat fork to transfer the potatoes one by one. The circles of sweet potato, fried and golden, looked perfectly cooked.

"H-how is it?" I asked eagerly, forgetting my manners. He glared at me out of the corner of his eye.

"I would tell you, if I had *eaten* a bite yet. Now, then…"

He switched to a normal fork and popped one of the smaller pieces of sweet potato into his mouth. He chewed it for a good long time, swallowed, and groaned.

"Ooooohhhh."

"H-how is it?" I repeated.

This time, the old fellow looked me straight in the eye and said, "It's not bad."

"Not…bad…"

It seemed like the deal was off, but if so, I felt that I now had the right to eat all the sweet potato he rejected. Until he said—

"But it would *really* be terrific with a dab of butter on top."

"B-butter…?"

At first, I was surprised. *There's butter in Aincrad?* But before my eyes, the old man pulled a small jar off the shelf on the right. He placed it heavily on the table and said, "Well, don't just stand there like an idiot. Sit down, human boy."

"Uh…y-yes sir." I sat down on the other little stool at the table, and the old man set another metal plate in front of me.

"You win, boy. Enjoy half the fricatelle…and, out of my great magnanimity, these two pieces of potato."

Before I could say a word, he sliced the jumbo steak in two and transferred one half, juices flowing outward, onto my plate. Then he set two pieces of sweet potato next to it, dumped the rest onto his own plate, and sat across from me. After that, he pulled the jar closer and stuck a small knife inside, scooping out a heap of a creamy white substance that he dropped on the potato slices. I did the same when he passed the jar to me.

The metal plates must have had some kind of heat-retaining magic on them. I didn't have the vocabulary to express the devastating sight of rapidly melting butter on top of fried sweet potato, right next to a hot, juicy hamburg steak. It was time to turn off my brain and indulge. I lifted my knife in one hand and fork in the other and declared, "Let's dig in!"

Across the table, the old man had cut a large piece of meat loose and was lifting it to his mouth. He chewed a few times, popped in a piece of buttered potato, chewed some more, then put on an expression of bliss and moaned, "Hwhoaaaa…"

Instantly, I had another blast of déjà vu.

I had definitely seen this old man before. It wasn't in the last two months trapped in Aincrad, but before that…Yet, that was obviously impossible. I didn't know any ancient dark elves in real life. So where…?

"Ah…aaaah!" I shouted, rising out of my seat. It earned me a suspicious look from the man.

"What is it, boy? Why aren't you eating?"

"I will, I will—but before that…Sir, are you the master of Meditation…?"

"Hrmm?" the old man grunted, raising just one eyebrow and glaring at me. "Boy, you know who I am? Yes, I am the greatest storyteller of Lyusula and a master in the art of meditation, Bouhroum the great sage. Have we met before?"

We have! In the beta test! I exclaimed in my head. My mouth flapped pointlessly.

Over the month-long beta test, the only Extra Skill we found was Meditation. It was a hidden skill that only appeared as a choice when certain conditions were fulfilled, much like the martial arts skill earned through the rock-breaking lessons on the second floor. In fact, Argo the info dealer found martial arts in the beta, too, but it was right as the test was ending, so the info didn't get around.

Therefore, Meditation was the only hidden skill I earned in the beta, but I remember it being so finicky that I didn't have much use for it. The appearance, voice, and speaking style of the NPC with the Meditation training quest were identical to this steak-cooking old man. Only his clothes and long ears were different.

The Meditation NPC in the beta was a human elder in a simple brown tunic. He did not live in a cave near Castle Galey but in a little shack deep in the swampy western area of the sixth floor. His attitude was mostly grumpy, and I did not recall him having any special love of hamburg steak.

But right during the moment I unlocked the Meditation skill, the old man gave me a satisfied smile that was absolutely identical to the smile I saw on the dark elf elder as he savored the marriage of steak and buttered sweet potato. That was what kicked open the door to my memory. Yes…this Bouhroum (who pronounced it *Booh-room*) was the same figure as the Meditation NPC from the beta, just placed within a different setting and context. I had to choose my words carefully now.

"…No, I haven't met you, but I've heard the rumors…"

"Aha. So word of my skill and fame has reached even the human towns? *Ka-hya-hya-hya…*" he cackled, then stuck another piece of meat in his mouth, looking positively intoxicated. I realized that I needed to eat my portion, too, and stuck my knife into the end of the half of steak on my plate. The seared surface was resilient, but the inside was light and perfectly cooked. The moment I cut through it, meaty juices oozed out, exuding a spicy scent.

Anticipation caused the muscles on the inside of my mouth to tighten, and I lifted my first bite of hamburg steak in over two months to my mouth. I gave Asuna a silent apology, swore that I would take her here when we got the chance, and opened my mouth wide.

Just then, the man said, "I should ask just in case, boy. Do you wish to understand the meditative arts?"

"Huh…?" I stared, mouth open wide. To my surprise, there was a golden ? over his head. The symbol of a new quest, though Bouhroum himself could not see it.

"Uh, w-well…" I stammered, despite the bite of meat two centimeters away from my mouth occupying the majority of my thoughts.

If I answered no, I would probably never get another chance to earn the Meditation skill. By coincidence, I'd reached level 20 just two days ago, and I had an open skill slot. But the Meditation skill was of questionable benefit—you had to assume a funky, Zen-like pose for a certain time to receive a continual healing buff and a negative status resistance buff. The shared opinion among beta testers was that there were better skills you could use a valuable skill slot on.

It was possible that the effects of Meditation had been buffed for the official launch, so I could just go ahead and take it, then remove it from the skill slot if it didn't work out. But remembering how long and arduous the martial arts training period was kept me from saying yes.

"Uh, ah, hmm," I groaned, hoping to delay my answer so I could at least eat my steak. This was admittedly rather optimistic of me.

"If you wish to train in it, boy, you must not eat that fricatelle."

"Huh? Wh…why not?"

"Because that is your training—in the arts of Awakening, the special Meditation technique."

"A…Awakening…?"

I'd never heard the term before. For a moment, I actually forgot about the meat on my fork.

A straightforward interpretation of what he meant was that in the advancement tree for the Meditation skill, there was a higher ability called Awakening. But the Meditation NPC in the beta made no mention of it. I had no idea what it did. Besides…

"Isn't that something you can't train unless you already have the ski…the art of Meditation?" I asked.

Bouhroum took a third bite of his hamburg sleak and smiled. "A very intuitive youth, you are. That is correct, of course…but the conditions to train in the art of Awakening involve solving a mystery in the castle library and discovering the existence of this little room. You managed to find me here—although it was through the ceiling vent—so you have fulfilled the requirements."

"…"

My eyes traveled from Bouhroum's face to the small door on the left wall. "You mean…on the other side of that door is the library of Castle Galey?"

"Correct."

I suppose I could just leave that way, then, I thought, trying to avoid facing the challenge before me: the juicy hunk of meat hanging on the end of my fork.

If I accepted old Bouhroum's words at face value, the moment I stuck this hamburg into my mouth, I would no longer be able to acquire the mysterious Awakening skill. A rational player would find a single dish of food to be far outweighed by the opportunity to gain an ultrarare skill, which probably even Argo didn't know about yet. But in reality, the allure of that meat just centimeters away from my mouth, its appearance, smell, and supposed flavor—it was just too much to resist. This might be my only chance at getting the Awakening skill, but I'd also gotten this hamburg steak after some tricky negotiation, and I might not ever get to eat this again, either.

What should I do…? What should I do?

I clenched my jaw. My fork hand trembled. I was trapped in a tug-of-war between my brain and my stomach. Across the table, Bouhroum was stuffing hot meat and buttered sweet potatoes into his mouth and muttering provocations like "Ooooh, ahhh—it's so good." I stared at my hamburg steak again and, with all the willpower I possessed, lowered my right hand.

When I'd first started to lift it to my mouth, I had given a silent promise to the sleeping Asuna that I would bring her here one day. That was a promise dependent on having more opportunities to eat this food. I couldn't make a choice that would permanently take that option off the table.

Over five-plus agonizing seconds, I lowered my fork to the

plate, breathing heavily, and asked the old man, "Before I train in the art of Awakening…can I at least eat the potatoes?"

"You may not," he said mercilessly, then scooped the last bits of hamburg steak and buttered sweet potatoes into his mouth. His face went slack, and he moaned, "Ohhh, it's the best…"

I waited for him to chew and swallow before I said, "Old man…I mean, Mr. Bouhroum, please teach me the ways of Awakening."

Abruptly, the *?* symbol floating over his head turned to *!*, indicating that I had accepted the quest. Bouhroum pulled a handkerchief out of his robe and carefully wiped his beard before stating imperiously, "Very well. But the training will not be easy. I have lived a very long life, but I can count the number of people who passed the trials and mastered Awakening on my two hands…and none were human."

"T…trials? Not a training period?"

If it was something like *Go to this place and defeat so-and-so monster*, that would actually be preferable. In fact, I prayed he would say as much.

The old man stroked his silver whiskers into place and said cryptically, "It is training, and it is a trial. First, straighten your back."

"Huh? Uh…okay." I sat up atop the round stool. This time, his robe produced a short staff, which he used to tap the metal plate before me.

There was indeed magic upon that plate, because the cooling meat suddenly began to sizzle again. The scent of fat, spices, and butter wafted up, rich and thick, attempting to reawaken the appetite I was keeping at bay.

"What you must do, for the next three hours…is cast aside your distractions and maintain the tranquility of your heart. If you can do this, boy, then you will stand at the entrance to the path of Awakening."

"…Tr-tranquility of my heart…?"

Faced with a baffling trial, I glanced back and forth from the steak-loving old man to the old man's beloved steak.

It did sound like an appropriate training method for a meditative skill, but how was he supposed to determine whether or not my mind was filled with worldly thoughts and distractions? It wasn't really that hard to avoid moving your body or facial muscles in Aincrad. You could maintain the same avatar posture for hours on end without getting dead leg or a sore back, and unless you found a truly bizarre position, the hidden Fatigue stat rarely ever came into play. I'd never intentionally frozen in place for three hours, but I felt like I could do it, if need be.

Whatever the actual effect on the skill was, the unlocking conditions for an advanced Extra Skill couldn't be easier than martial arts. I had to assume that Bouhroum had some means of detecting if I was distracted by something. Or more accurately, that the *SAO* system itself, through Bouhroum, had that ability.

At that point, I realized something.

The NerveGear over my head in the real world was monitoring my brain's electrical activity in close detail at all times. So my brain waves should be radically different between periods of intense concentration and periods of lazy distraction, and the system—and thus Bouhroum—could tell the difference that way. If I wanted to earn the Awakening skill, I couldn't just hold my avatar still. I needed to exhibit true mental concentration. For three whole hours. With a sizzling steak under my nose.

The Awakening skill was intriguing, to be sure, but as a teenager more interested in food than the opposite sex, I couldn't imagine myself keeping focus for that long…

No, wait.

Couldn't I just use the situation to my advantage and focus on nothing but the hamburg steak instead? The NerveGear might be cutting-edge technology, but it couldn't actually tell the content of my thoughts. Think about nothing but a steak for three hours straight? I could do that.

"…All right. Begin the clock whenever you want."

It was after three o'clock in the morning. By the time I finished my training, it would be after six, but if I sprinted, I could get back to the room before Asuna and Kizmel woke up.

As I prepared by taking a deep breath, the old man removed a new item from his robe and set it on the table. It was a large hourglass with a wooden frame. It looked essentially the same as the real-world item, except that all the sand was contained in the upper chamber, and not a single grain was falling.

"Very good. Then we will now begin your training in the arts of Awakening. Begin!"

Bouhroum tapped the hourglass with his staff, causing mysterious green sand to silently spill into the lower chamber. I began to stare voraciously at the hamburg steak. It was perpetually heated by the magical plate, but its juiciness hadn't dried up in the least. The meat along the cut shone brilliantly, and the juice flowing out of it mixed with the melted butter on the sliced potatoes, forming a bewitching marbled puddle on the plate. I wanted to set aside the knife and just stab the whole thing with my fork in one go. I could see myself slicing a roll in half and turning it into a hamburger, too. In that case, I would throw on some barbecue sauce, or even better, spicy-sweet teriyaki mixed with mayo. Oh, how I wanted it, wanted it, wanted it……

"*Kaaaaah!*" Bouhroum suddenly screamed, smacking me hard on the shoulder with the short staff. "You fool!! You've gone and drowned yourself in impure thoughts!! Start over!!"

"Huh…? You could tell what I was thinking…?"

"Do not mock the great sage Bouhroum! Your head was full of crass, greedy desire for the fricatelle!"

"Urgh…O-okay, you got me…" I said, drooping my head. The old man snorted.

"Will you give up, then?"

"No…I'll keep going."

"Aha. Very well." He tapped the hourglass again, and the small amount of sand instantly returned to the upper chamber. "And now, once again…begin!"

With a third swing of the staff, I closed my eyes.

So Bouhroum, as an extension of the *SAO* system and the Nerve-Gear, had better perception than I counted on. If my plan to think *only* of hamburg steak wasn't going to work, that made the difficulty much higher, but I still had to challenge the task of extreme meditation.

I would shut out all sensory information and relax my mind. Fortunately, spacing out was a skill of mine. I let my mind expand in the darkness, thinking nothing, but not sleeping, just becoming empty, empty...What a wonderful smell, though...and the tempting sizzling sound. I could use this sound as a morning alarm...Oh, what a smell...How I could go for a teri-mayo burger right about now......

"*Kaaaaah!*"

Whap! He hit my shoulder a bit harder than before. I yelped. "Ow!"

"That was exactly the same as the last time, boy!" I opened my eyes to see Bouhroum with his staff raised overhead. "Your first attempt was ten seconds, and your second was twenty! You will never reach three straight hours at this rate!"

"Hmmmm..."

Naturally, even with my eyes closed, I could not shut out the sound and smell of the steak. If anything, they were even stronger. My hunger was rising, too—it was not going to be easy at all to maintain an empty mind.

"Will you continue?" the old man asked, his look dismissive. I grumbled.

I knew the moment my hamburg-focused plan failed that my chances were slim, but I hated the idea of giving up now. Upon fresh consideration, the act of continuing a perfect lack of thought for three whole hours was impossibly hard for a video-game quest. Perhaps there was some strategy here, a trick that could be employed to make it easier.

Bouhroum had said to "...cast aside your distractions and maintain the tranquility of your heart." I felt like the key was in the interpretation of tranquility. Keeping your thoughts focused was not tranquil if the content of that focus was wanting to eat hamburg steak. So if I could fix my mind on a target that did not involve desire or agitation, perhaps I would clear the requirements.

Something I could imagine in detail but that brought peace rather than agitation.

The first thing that came to mind was my sword. Its appearance, texture, and weight were already etched into my mind. A sword was a tool of combat, of course, but when I was feeling down or worried, clutching the entire scabbard relaxed me for some strange reason, and when I was ready to stand and fight again, the vitality to do so came flooding upward. All the players trapped in this world who hoped to beat the game felt the same way to a greater or lesser extent: One's weapon offered mental support.

But I wasn't sure if I could really maintain a state of tranquility for three straight hours, just thinking about my sword. The worst would be if I hung in there for an hour or two, then lost my grip. If I had to start over with a three-hour countdown, I definitely wouldn't be able to get through it, and I could easily imagine Asuna waking up and sending me messages.

It had to be something with a stronger attachment than just my sword—and with more vivid memories attached. For one thing, it had been a while since I had one of my lonely nights against an inn wall or tree trunk, clutching my sword with both arms to keep the anxiety away. That was because...

"Ah..." I gasped.

However Bouhroum interpreted that, he then taunted, "What do you say? Are you giving up? If you do, you may eat that fricatelle."

"No...I'm doing this," I announced, telling myself that this would be the final attempt.

"Very good. Now...begin!"

He tapped the hourglass with the staff, and the recharged green sand began to fall again in silence. I closed my eyes, tilted my head just a bit downward, and opened the door to my memories.

A silver meteor split the darkness of the screen that was my mind.

It wasn't a real meteor. It was the shining light of a sword skill finishing off a dangerous Ruin Kobold Trooper deep in the first-floor labyrinth. The basic rapier thrust, Linear...executed by a fencer whose name at the time I didn't even know.

The first thing I had said to the fencer, who slumped back against the wall after defeating the heavily armed kobold, was *A little bit overkill, if you ask me.* Not the most elegant or poetic of sentiments. When she failed to understand my meaning, I explained the concept of overkilling, and the fencer replied brusquely *Is there a problem with doing too much damage?*

That was how I had first met Asuna, my current ongoing game partner.

At the time, Asuna kept her hood on all the time, even when eating. She held her conversation to a minimum, and she never smiled. The first time she showed me anything resembling a smile was...yes, it was when we had beaten Illfang the Kobold Lord, boss of the first floor. I had left the boss chamber first to go activate the second-floor teleport gate, and she came chasing after me.

She said that for the first time, she'd found something she wanted to do in this world. When I asked her what that was, she just smiled and said it was a secret. That had been on December 4...and today was January 4. A full month had passed, but that smile was still the same, burned into my memory.

Somehow, I'd forgotten all about the sound and smell of the hamburg...and moreover, that I was in the midst of a trial for the Awakening skill. Instead, I simply relived the route that Asuna and I had traveled together since then in minute detail.

On the second floor, Asuna's Wind Fleuret got swept into a weapon-upgrading scam, which took a lot of work to unravel. On the third floor, we met Kizmel and went on an adventure for a secret key. On the fourth floor, we engaged in water battles riding a canoe we dubbed the *Tilnel*. On the fifth floor, we tackled the boss in a tiny group so as to avoid all-out war between the ALS and DKB. Throughout all that time, both Asuna and I had found many more occasions to smile than before, it seemed to me.

Nothing had changed about this deadly place, where "game over" was forever, and it was hard to hold much hope for the future when we'd only reached the sixth floor out of a hundred total, but nevertheless, the two of us—and sometimes three, with Kizmel—worked our hardest to survive each day.

We nearly died many times. I'd trembled with rage, been devastated by despair...but I kept walking forward through it all, and that had to be thanks to Asuna's presence.

I knew that this arrangement, our partnership, was not meant to last forever. We met in extreme circumstances, and we must have sensed something in each other that made us choose to fight together. If we had never gotten involved in *SAO* and passed each other on the street somewhere, neither Asuna nor I would have stopped or given it a second thought.

For now, I didn't know how our temporary partnership was going to end. But that moment would come, whether we broke up our duo or not. Either our HP would reach zero, and the Nerve-Gear would fry our brains, or we'd beat the deadly game and be returned to the real world...So as long as we kept fighting at the front line, one of those endings would inevitably come.

So I didn't want to give a name to whatever emotion I felt toward the player named Asuna. My role as a former beta tester was to tell her everything I could and keep fighting by her side when that was no longer necessary. Asuna had much, much greater ability and potential than I did. She could be a true leader, more so than the DKB's Lind, the ALS's Kibaou, and even Diavel the Knight himself. Perhaps the entire meaning of my presence here in this prison world was to ensure Asuna survived until that grand moment.

On the other hand, I didn't think of myself as a simple shield or disposable pawn. I had received many things from Asuna in return. Every last thing I saw with my eyes closed like this—even her puffed-up sulking face, and the feeling of an elbow in my ribs—was a brilliant entry into my memory and gave me the strength to continue living.

Until I became trapped in here—really, until I met Asuna—I thought that dealing with other people was nothing but a bother. I didn't try to make friends at school; I put up walls between myself and my parents and sister; and I only sought out a trifling substitute for human interaction online.

But the truth was, I'd been built up as a person by the parents who raised me for fourteen years, the sister who looked up to me despite my disdain, and all the other people I'd met in life. Every human being gave something to others and received something in return. Even Morte and his friends, in the act of trying to kill Asuna and me, were no exception.

I didn't know what reason they had for going after us. Morte, the dagger user I suspected was Joe from the ALS, and the man in the black poncho who was their leader…They might have their own motives, their own sympathies, even their own kind of justice.

But when I had decided to use Rage Spike on Morte, that choice of mine was to kill him in order to protect Asuna. Technically, the Sword of Eventide's accuracy bonus kicked in and struck his heart, and even knowing that the continual piercing damage would kill Morte within seconds, I did not attempt to pull it loose.

I only had two hands, and I could not save every last player. Whatever the PK gang's reason for trying to kill Asuna, I would strike back as many times as necessary. I would do anything to protect that gentle smile I saw on the back of my eyelids, pointed at me…

"…Very well. That is enough," said a voice, but I could not open my eyes right in that moment.

But when I recognized whose voice it was and recalled the situation, I lifted my downcast face. It didn't seem like three hours had passed at all, but the green sand of the hourglass was entirely filling the bottom chamber.

"Is...the training over?" I asked, my throat hoarse, as I looked to the robed old man across the table.

"Hmph...I am willing to lower my requirements and admit that you have passed the hurdle to learn the Awakening arts. I suppose, for a human boy, there is only one thing more precious than a fresh-cooked fricatelle."

He made it sound as if he could tell exactly what I was thinking, but I stopped myself from asking to confirm this suspicion. It would be beyond uncomfortable to hear him spell out my innermost thoughts in detail.

Later, I realized that when I restated my desire to fight against Morte's gang, my mental state had been drifting further and further away from tranquility. So perhaps the fact that the old man did not yell "*Kaaaah!*" was a sign that he really was observing my thoughts.

But at this point, the rebound of having thought exclusively about one thing for three hours meant my mind was half-unresponsive. I watched dully as the golden *!* above the old man's head vanished, but as I started to get up from the stool, I realized that the hamburg steak on the metal plate was still hot.

"Um...since the training is over, can I—?"

But before I could say "*eat this,*" Bouhroum quickly yanked the plate back and snapped, "No! If you eat this now, your training will be for naught!"

"Whaaat...? Really?"

Extra Skills were still a part of the game system, so once you had it in your skill tree, there shouldn't be any way that eating a steak would cause it to disappear. But after how forcefully the old wise man stated it, I couldn't really argue.

I stood up, vowing to myself that sometime in the future, I would bring Asuna here and eat that damn hamburg. As I stood, Bouhroum sat, sticking his knife into the plate of meat he'd just taken from me. "Now, get going! And if you ever want to visit again, use the proper entrance, rather than my ceiling vent!"

"Yeah, yeah," I grumbled, looking at the door on the left wall, which I assumed was the "proper entrance" he was talking about. Going through that door should put me in Castle Galey's library. It was probably a shorter trip back to the room that way, but I still had business to conduct on the top of the rocky mountain.

"Well, I guess I'll come back sometime. Thanks for everything, Bouhroum," I said.

The sage sent me along with a warm "And next time, bring three of those sweet potatoes—no, four."

I left the little room, headed up the cramped stairs—er, vent—in the southern hallway, and returned to the flat mountaintop. According to my game window, the time was six fifteen in the morning. The sky through the aperture of Aincrad was violet now, with red rays arriving from the east. I sucked in a deep breath of chilly air, hoping to kick-start my fuzzy mind.

It really was an odd experience. Like it had all been a strange fairy tale…but when I turned back to look, that square entrance was still there on the rusty-red rock face.

I shook my head slowly, then switched my window to the skill tab. On the left side, it indicated five skill slots, four of which were occupied by one-handed swords, martial arts, Search, and Hiding. Their proficiency, in that order, was 168, 97, 142, and 117. Martial arts was lowest because I used it only in a complementary way, but Hiding was the next lowest because, thanks to my partner, the number of times I needed to use it was lower than on my own.

Briefly, I considered removing it from the slot but didn't go through with it. Just moments ago when unlocking the Awakening skill, I had reminded myself that my partnership with Asuna wouldn't last forever. When I returned to being a solo player, I was going to need that Hiding skill.

My first line of business was to check out what that unlocked higher Extra Skill actually did. Asuna and Kizmel could awaken at any time. I needed to wrap this up and rush back into the castle, but surely I could just do this first. I sorted my list of skills by unlock date.

As soon as I saw the skill at the top of the list, I let out a yelping "Fwah...?"

What I found there was not Awakening, as Bouhroum had mentioned so many times, but the old skill from the beta, Meditation, which I...hadn't really used all that much.

"Wh-what's going on here...?"

I felt like crawling back down the vent to ask the great sage to his face, but sadly, I didn't have the time. I craned my neck back and forth, debating whether to slot it or not, and eventually went ahead and dragged the Meditation icon to the left. When I dropped it in the fifth slot, I gasped again.

"Hngwah...?!"

There should have been the number 0 next to the skill to indicate proficiency, but it was rising with incredible speed instead. In a blink, it was over 100, then 200, without slowing down. 300, 400...and only at 450 did its pace begin to slow, with the tens and single digits still rotating, until it at last came to a stop exactly at 500.

After three seconds of no thought at all, I rubbed the number with my fingertip, just in case. It did not magically vanish, of course.

Proficiency, 500.

I'd been using one-handed swords every single day for hours on end over two months straight, and it was only at 168. And unlike weapon skills, which rolled a small chance for ticking upward with each attack, the Meditation skill only received proficiency when you assumed a Zen pose for close to a minute until the buff kicked in. I couldn't even imagine how much Zen meditation you needed to do to get it to a preposterous number like 500.

I forced my stiff finger to tap the skill name for a detailed pop-up. It was in the mod screen that I found the source of this strange phenomenon. In the oddly simplistic mod tree, there was a small AWAKENING note next to where it said PROFICIENCY: 500.

"...So Awakening wasn't the name of a different skill, it was just a mod for the Meditation skill…?" I muttered, looking toward the vent. Only in my imagination did old Bouhroum actually pop his head out of the opening and yell, "*That's right!*"

A mod—short for "skill modifier"—was a special effect that applied once a skill's proficiency reached a certain level. There were other terms for this concept in other games, like *perk* or *extension*, but they all meant the same thing. It was a major feature, as the decision of which mod to use could have a drastically different effect on how the skill worked for the player.

For example, when I reached proficiency 50 with the one-handed sword skill, I chose Shorten Sword Skill Cooldown I, and at 100, I picked Quick Change. I hadn't used my 150 choice yet, but I was probably leaning toward Increase Critical Hit Chance I. But one of those "crittlers" who obsessed over landing critical hits would probably use up all three mod selections on Increase Critical Hit Chance I, Increase Critical Hit Chance II, and Increase Critical Hit Chance III. In this sense, skill mods could encourage vastly different playstyles, even among players using the same type of weapon.

Pretty much all the other skills had mod selections at proficiency 50, too. Martial arts, which was classified as an Extra Skill, was no exception. I powered it up right after gaining it during a period of collecting upgrade materials and selected Relax Equipment Conditions, a crucial mod that gave me the ability to activate martial arts skills with an open hand or legs, even when I had a weapon equipped in my dominant hand.

But according to the skill tree, there was no mod selection option for Meditation until you reached proficiency 500. In other words, because I passed Bouhroum's trial and earned the Awakening mod right off the bat, the game system most likely ensured this was possible by instantly raising my Meditation proficiency to 500.

It seemed ridiculous, but there was no other interpretation. Wondering what sort of effect a mod that required such a high proficiency would offer, I tapped the Awakening label and read the explanatory text that appeared.

Focuses concentration to the extreme and draws out hidden strength.

"What the hell is this?!" I shouted, all alone on the empty rock.

It said nothing about the actual concrete effect. I figured I would just go ahead and use the skill, but there was no USE button. That meant it wasn't an active mod like Quick Change but a passive one that conferred its effect just by having it unlocked. The problem was that not only did I not know what that effect was, there wasn't even a new buff icon next to my HP bar that might tell me. All I knew was that now I couldn't take Meditation out of my fifth skill slot. It wasn't locked there by the system, of course, but I had a feeling that as soon as I took it out, that 500 proficiency would go back to 0, and I would lose the Awakening mod, too.

Perhaps if I sat down to meditate and activated the Meditation skill, the effect of the Awakening mod would kick in automatically, but I didn't have the time to sit around messing with that. Instead, I closed the window, trying to suppress my irritation. It was around the time that Asuna might send me a message, but I had to finish the job I'd been doing before I returned to the castle.

I glanced around the mountaintop, which was much brighter now, confirmed that there were no other figures or monsters in the vicinity, and started running along the sheer cliff just to the west.

Since I didn't have to worry about where I stepped like I had in the middle of the night, I was able to sprint at full speed. After a minute, the ground vanished up ahead of me. I put on the brakes so I could look straight down the cliff. All I saw were the grand carved castle gates. That meant Castle Galey was surrounded on all sides by sheer vertical cliffs that even a mountain goat couldn't climb, and it was impossible to get inside except through the gates. It seemed impossible for the forest elves to come over the mountain in a sneak attack.

With that concern ruled out, I exhaled in relief. That hadn't eliminated the possibility that Qusack might be aligned some-how with Morte's gang, but if they could only get in through the front gate, then as long as I heard the bell first, there was no worry about waking up to find an intruder with a knife over my bed. We'd probably see the group of four again in the dining hall, so the next time we met, I could get them to clear up the issue of why they came to the frontier so early.

Just as I stretched and began to ponder how I should get back to the room, a breezy sound effect and its icon alerted me to an incoming instant message. I hunched my shoulder guiltily and tapped the icon, bringing up a simple question from my current partner: WHERE ARE YOU?

A second later, I replied MORNING WALK, BE RIGHT BACK. A glance around showed that I was currently atop the mountain connected to the east side of Castle Galey's gate. But our guest room was in the west wing, so there was no direct route back. I'd have to circle around the cylindrical mountain, go back down the triangular roof of the center building, and onto the rooftops again...

As I pondered this, my eyes traveled down the sheer cliffside again. Atop the thick gate was a walkway with parapets, which a single dark elf guard was patrolling now. The drop from where I stood to the walkway was about six meters, impossible to scale barehanded—but a jump I could handle with my current stats.

Of course, if a sudden gust caught me, and I missed my land-ing, I could plummet to the ground far below to my instant death. Pointless challenges like this were verboten now in a game where death was real, but for some reason, I got the feeling that it was a good idea to test whether or not you could get from the mountain to the gate walkway while I had the chance. I lined myself up just right for the attempt.

When the guard was heading farther in the other direction, I jumped. The walkway was close to two meters wide, so out-side of an emergency, I didn't think my judgment would be off. I kept my arms wide to maintain balance and landed smack in the middle of it.

I didn't suffer any damage, but I couldn't prevent the sound, and the guard heading the other way whirled around. He raced over, long spear at the ready, so I quickly held up my left hand with the sigil ring on it.

I wasn't sure if that was going to do anything, but at any rate, the guard lowered the spear and asked suspiciously, "What are you doing here?"

"I'm, uh...on a walk," I said, repeating my excuse to Asuna, and the guard seemed to buy it.

"I see. You are free to walk about the castle, but do not impede our official duties. This gate is the key to Castle Galey's defense, and we cannot allow the tiniest mouse to sneak in under our noses."

"I—I understand, of course," I said, then asked, "Um...has any foe ever attacked the castle before?"

"If by foe you mean the forest elves, never. The elves shrivel and weaken when traveling across those dried sands," the guard said, pointing south of the gate. I saw how the canyon, bordered by cliffs much lower than the one I'd just been atop, continued along for hundreds of meters, with a bridge of stone that crossed the piles of white sand on the canyon floor. A new question suddenly occurred to me.

I turned to the guard and asked, "In that case...who lined up those stone platforms? Wouldn't the dark elves who constructed this castle in the distant past have trouble working in the canyon, too?"

"Ah, you are correct," he said, turning around to look at the huge spirit tree that loomed over the inner courtyard of the castle. "Human swordsman, do you know why that spirit tree has been living for centuries upon centuries?"

"Because it's sucking up the hot water bubbling up from the earth, right?"

"So you have done your homework," the guard noted with satisfaction, his shining black helmet bobbing. He pointed at the spring around the roots of the tree. "In the distant past, there was a project to create an aqueduct from the spring that would travel out of the castle so that more trees could be planted. The idea was that if trees could take root in that dusty canyon, we might be able to venture outside the castle. But after just a hundred meters of a channel from the castle, the spring appeared ready to dry up, and the project was hastily canceled. The stone looks like a pathway, but as a matter of fact, it is the remnant of that ancient aqueduct."

"Ohhh…I had no idea…" I said, noting to myself that though the hamburg steak had become a "fricatelle," they still used real-world distance units. "Thank you for teaching me all these things."

"It is no matter. In return, I ask only that you offer your protection to your knight."

"Well, of course," I said, leaving his side. I descended the stairs on the west side of the walkway—this entrance being properly rectangular, thankfully—and proceeded to the courtyard, where I raced for the door to the west wing.

I dashed up the nearest staircase and flew into the third-floor guest room, where I met the gaze of the two women sitting on the sofa. The moment I smelled the fragrant scent of tea wafting up from the cups on the table, my stomach grumbled a complaint over the lack of hamburg steak in it. But now was not the time for that.

"H-hey…good morning, Asuna, Kizmel," I said with an utterly natural and pleasant smile. The fencer glared up at me. In a tone of voice notably cooler than usual, she asked, "Did you enjoy your morning walk?"

"Uh, it was…cold. And I got hungry."

"I'm not surprised. It's January."

I could tell she was quite displeased. Fortunately for me, the dark elf knight threw me a bone.

"*Hee-hee*…Don't be so cross, Asuna. It's in the nature of boys his age to simply get up and wander off."

Boys seemed like a mean word to use, but when I considered that I'd turned fourteen only two months earlier, I might as well be a baby to the long-lived elves. And from that perspective, my partner didn't seem to be that different in age, still a child herself. But she turned to Kizmel with the smuggest look I'd ever seen and said, "If he was going on a walk, he could have at least left a note. He's not a *child*."

"Gosh, I'm really sorry about this," I said, bowing with my hands pressed together. At last, Asuna's expression softened. She turned to me and looked me square in the face this time.

"When I woke up and realized you weren't in the room, I was worried. You haven't forgotten that we're outside the safe zone, right?"

The fact that she used the video-game term *safe zone* in front of Kizmel and didn't even realize she did it told me that her concern was real. I put on a serious look and told her the truth—if only half of it.

"Sorry, but I was really curious about something, so I went inspecting the mountain around the castle."

"Oh...?" Kizmel murmured, more interested in what I had to say than in the safe-zone term. She lowered her teacup to the table. "You climbed the outer ring of the castle? How?"

"Um...I raced from the roof here up over the lord's bedroom..."

Kizmel's reaction was much the same as Bouhroum's. Her eyes bulged briefly, then she chuckled in a way that I rarely ever heard from her.

"I see...then you are a more mischievous lad than I took you for, Kirito. Even Tilnel the tomboy never carried out such a bold plan, even if she had thought of it."

"No, really, it wasn't that special..."

"I don't think she was complimenting you," Asuna snapped. My eyes swiveled back to Kizmel, who was composing herself after all the chuckles.

"And...what were you looking for on the outer ring?"

"I wasn't looking for anything specifically..."

I decided that I wasn't going to tell them what I *did* find, the storyteller's secret hideout, and stuck to my original mission. "I was just wondering…if the forest elves might climb over that mountain to attack the castle."

"Ahhh…I see. I had never considered that possibility…"

"Well, it ended up being wasted effort. The mountain, that 'outer ring,' has a drop of over thirty meters straight down, and no human or elf could possibly climb it. So I think we can rest easy with that knowledge today," I announced.

Asuna blinked several times. "Kirito…you went up there to inspect the mountain, just for today's sake?"

"Well, I guess that's true…"

"I see," she murmured, then smiled. "Well, in that case, I forgive your unapproved leave of absence. Now, let's go get some breakfast."

"Yes, I agree. And you are the one deciding what we shall do today, Asuna?" Kizmel confirmed, getting to her feet.

Asuna patted her on the back. "Of course! Look forward to it!"

All I could hope as I followed them out of the room was that we weren't going to spend the day doing a full tour of various baths.

We enjoyed a healthy but fulfilling breakfast of green salad made with basil-like plants from the courtyard, an omelet mixed with crushed nuts, a yogurt-y substance with sliced fruit inside, and thin, crispy toast. But Asuna did not unveil her schedule for the day as we ate. She really wanted to draw out the suspense until right before we left.

After the meal, we had tea and went back and forth about ideas ("I bet we're doing such and such over at blah-blah-blah." "*Bzzt*, wrong again.") until, eventually, the four members of Qusack appeared in the dining hall. They were plodding sleepily along.

When they noticed us and shuffled over, I was inwardly alarmed. Unlike last night, this time, we had Kizmel at the table. But it would be unnatural to get up and leave, and we couldn't simply shoo them away.

As I waited, praying they wouldn't start talking about in-game systems, Gindo's group sat down right at the table next to us. After a few moments, I said good morning and introduced Kizmel as "the dark elf knight adventuring with us."

Fortunately, Temuo, who seemed the most likely to flip out over this situation, was half-asleep at the moment, and the introductions went by without extra comment. Kizmel had told us about the decoys and fake keys last night, so I thought we'd be safe if the topic of today's quest came up in conversation, but just in case, I decided to bring up a different topic to start things off.

To kill two birds with one stone, I asked Qusack why they came up to the front-line region so suddenly, when there was very little information surrounding it at this point.

Highston's answer didn't sound fishy in the least, but it stunned Asuna and me nonetheless.

"Well, the truth is, we expected to take another three days or so on Stachion's series of quests. But we had to call that off for an unexpected reason…"

"What happened?"

"Wait, you guys don't know? The central figure of the quest, Lord Cylon, just up and vanished. It was the night of the first, I think…Ask any servant at the mansion, and none know where he went, and there's no hint about it in the quest log. We just didn't know what else to do but move on."

9

AFTER SEEING OFF QUSACK ON THEIR QUEST TO recover the Agate Key, Asuna and I shared a silent look for a good five seconds.

"......Is the reason Cylon vanished...because Morte's group killed him...?"

"......He said it happened the night of the first. It matches the time of Morte and the dagger user's ambush. But...is that even possible...? I would assume that *our* Cylon is dead, but *everyone's* Cylon is still alive and well at the mansion..." I muttered.

Kizmel looked over, curious. "What are you talking about?"

"Oh, it's a quest we were doing in Stachion...Or, er, when we say quest, that's just a human word, like *request* or *duty*..." I explained, before launching into a brief explanation of the Curse of Stachion.

A murder that took place ten years ago and a missing golden cube. Lord Cylon hired us to find it, and he made us search an abandoned home in the nearby town of Suribus. The lord himself showed up there and paralyzed us—but while on the ride back, loaded into his carriage, Cylon was abruptly, shockingly murdered...

By the end, Kizmel's brows were low. She murmured, "So you went through all of that before arriving here...And the ones who killed this lord were the brigands who attacked you? You claim they had the poison needles of the Fallen..."

"That's right."

"Then this cannot be overlooked. Asuna," she said, turning to her right toward the fencer, "I am very eager to learn how you planned for us to spend my day of rest, but should we not investigate this first? To find out how to use the two keys you have acquired."

"Wh...what?" Asuna blurted out. We were both wide-eyed at this.

I'd been concerned about the "Curse of Stachion" questline, since we'd left it hanging, and I wasn't against the idea of taking this time to move it further along, but if Kizmel was going to join us, she'd have to set foot inside the town of Stachion. I opened and closed my mouth several times before I figured out what to ask the knight.

"Well...your presence with us would give us the strength of a thousand, but are you sure you want to go walking into a human town...?"

"It is not as if an elf fails to draw breath within the town limits, correct? I have never been within one, but there are more than a few stories of my comrades sneaking into towns out of curiosity or for some secret mission or another. And before the Great Separation, it was common for humans and nonhumans to come and go from one another's villages. If I wear a hood, they might not even notice my long ears."

"Th-that may be true, but..."

Even with your ears hidden, they'll see the NPC cursor that says DARK ELF ROYAL GUARD, I thought, sending my partner a look. For some reason, though, Asuna beamed at Kizmel.

"Yeah, let's go! As a matter of fact, I was planning to give you a tour of Stachion today, Kizmel."

"Wh-whaaat?!" I yelled. "That was your plan...?"

"Technically, the teleport gate in Stachion. The elves' spirit trees only start at the third floor, right? So I figured that neither

Kizmel nor the other dark elves have ever seen the first or second floor of Aincrad," she said, turning to the woman.

"That is correct. Some elves have explored the Pillar of the Heavens towers that connect the floors vertically, but only from the third floor upward. As far as I know, not a single elf has set foot on the first two floors since ancient times. I will be able to boast to my relatives and comrades on the ninth floor that I passed through a human gate to the first floor. I can even tell Tilnel, whenever we are fated to meet again..."

Smile never breaking, Asuna reached out and brushed the knight's back with her hand. I, too, felt a bit teary over this, but I couldn't stop myself from considering the logistics of it all.

There were hundreds of NPCs in Stachion, and the players weren't going to go inspecting the cursor name of every last NPC that wandered through the streets. But that didn't clear up all of my concerns. Could an NPC even travel through a teleport gate? Of all the main towns I'd been through in the game, I had never once seen an NPC use the gates.

What if the three of us walked through the gate, but Kizmel failed to travel and was left behind? Well, then Asuna and I could just go right back. But more seriously...what if some system error caused Kizmel alone, or even all three of us, to be sent to some random coordinates? In a worst-case scenario, perhaps Kizmel herself could be entirely deleted from the system. I couldn't rule out that possibility.

"No...wait."

A sudden idea came to mind, and I opened my window over the table. In my message inbox, I still had an instant message I received outside the cave in the fourth area yesterday. I tapped it and used the REPLY button to send a new question.

WHAT HAPPENS IF YOU GO THROUGH A TELEPORTER WITH AN NPC IN THE PARTY?

It took Argo the informant no more than thirty seconds to send a reply to this abbreviated query.

A QUEST NPC GETS REMOVED FROM THE PARTY. GUARD NPCS

YOU'RE HIRING WITH MONEY STICK WITH YOU. 100c—AND AS A
BONUS, FR ARE IN THE MIDDLE OF THE THIRD AREA.

So I'd run up my tab again, but at least I got the information
I wanted. In the larger towns were guard barracks and facilities
of that sort, where you could hire bodyguard NPCs for a certain
amount of col per hour. I'd never made use of the service and
had hardly ever seen parties with such NPCs, either, so I simply didn't know what happened to those guards when you went
through a teleport gate.

Asuna and I weren't paying Kizmel for her companionship, of
course, but our quest for the hidden key on the sixth floor was
already finished. At this moment, Kizmel was accompanying us
of her own will, so it was hard to tell which of Argo's two outcomes this fell under.

At the very least, it seemed that the system was prepared for the
possibility of NPCs stepping into teleport gates, and we wouldn't
have any accidents with being teleported to random variables or
Kizmel becoming corrupted and deleted. I looked up and interrupted the women, who were now talking about the ninth floor.

"I'm thinking that Kizmel can use the teleport gate, too. So
with that settled, let's get going. It'll take a while for us to get to
Stachion from here..."

"Indeed. I am ready to leave at any time."

"Me too!"

With my female companions on board, I leaped to my feet and
stuffed the last bit of Asuna's toast into my mouth, chewing as
I walked. I heard a complaint about my poor manners over my
shoulder and hunched my neck downward. Both Kizmel and the
elf women at the nearby table giggled.

I expected that the trip from Castle Galey to Stachion would take
at least four hours, no matter how we traveled. Even avoiding battle wherever possible in the open, the dungeon that separated the
first and second areas was a straight shot with nowhere to hide.
The thick forest that covered the center of the first area was an

unmapped zone, so we'd have to swing far west to travel through Suribus instead.

But ultimately, despite taking ten minutes for Kizmel to receive approval to borrow the Greenleaf Cape again, we ended up nearly halving the four-hour time I expected.

The primary reason was that Kizmel gave us the Droplets of Villi again, allowing us to walk over the lake to the first area, rather than going through the tunnel dungeon. The second reason was that when we approached the forest of the first area, Kizmel regained her energy with extra to spare, proclaiming that we would go directly through the woods and then guiding us the whole way. We even found a small ruin deep in the forest, beat its boss, and got some treasure—if not for that, it might have only taken an hour and a half, not two. And the third reason, of course, was having Kizmel's tremendous fighting ability on our side.

When the trees started thinning out, and brilliant-white Stachion appeared in the distance, Asuna marveled, "Wow, straight ahead...How did you know the way without a map, Kizmel?"

"You should not underestimate my ability, Asuna. We elves are never lost in a forest."

"That's incredible!" she said with delight. On my own, I wondered cynically if she was accessing the game's map data. Right on cue, a scene from yesterday's adventure replayed in my mind:

In that dungeon housing the Agate Key in the fourth area, we'd been faced with a sliding puzzle with thirty-five tiles—and Kizmel had solved the entire thing in a minimum number of moves without even taking much time to think about it.

This was not something you could explain away as "the brainpower of an AI." Traditional computers attempting to solve NP-hard problems like $N \times N$ grid puzzles in the most efficient number of moves required a vast amount of CPU power. On the other hand, the *SAO* system itself generated that puzzle for the dungeon door, so the system, at least, had to know the quickest solution. What if Kizmel, without being conscious of it, accessed the system's stored solution? The same way that elves could travel the forest without getting lost because they had the map data there at their fingertips.

Deep in thought, I followed the two women out of the forest, my head tilting left and right. There was an open field before us, slightly brown in the winter chill, beyond which lay Stachion with its odd stepped layout.

Kizmel stretched in the soft sunlight and lowered the hood of her navy-blue cloak—the precious Greenleaf Cape long ago stashed away in her pouch. Then she swept the back of her cloak around the front and tied a rope around the Pagoda Royal Knights emblem so no one could tell she was a dark elf by appearance alone.

Asuna pulled her own dark-red hood up, which made me want to join in, but I thought a group of three all hiding their faces would be suspicious. The main group was out fighting giant frogs and water bugs in the distant swampland of the third area, so it was unlikely we would run across anyone we knew in Stachion at this hour.

We cut straight across the field, eventually meeting up with the main path, and paused just south of the town limits when Kizmel stopped to gaze up at the white-colored town. "It is beautiful..." she murmured, "but what an odd place..."

Asuna and I were used to it by now, but it was indeed true that Stachion and its uniform construction of fifteen-centimeter blocks was very strange.

"Are all large human towns built this way?"

"N-no! It's only this town that's especially weird," Asuna quickly explained. "Remember when we told you about the golden cube disappearing from the town lord's mansion? This entire town is constructed of blocks of wood and stone cut to the exact dimensions of that cube."

"Ah..."

"But let's not stand around and chat here," Asuna said. "I'm hungry."

Thanks to Kizmel's help with the shortcuts, it wasn't even ten o'clock yet, but I felt a little hungry, too. I was just thinking that it would be nice to show Kizmel what human-style cakes were all about before we got to tackling the curse quest in honest.

I was a bit nervous walking through the gate, but nothing about Kizmel changed after the SAFE HAVEN sign appeared in my vision as we crossed the boundary. She didn't seem to see the same visual marker as us. I recalled that she must have snuck into Zumfut on the third floor, too.

There were more than a few players on the wide main street of town, but most were just tourists coming up from the lower floors to check it out. As I expected, nobody stopped to examine Kizmel's yellow cursor. Relieved and relaxed, I suggested, "Should we stop for some tea nearby? We can spend the rest of the morning investigating the lord's disappearance, and then we can take the teleport gate down after noon."

"Agreed!"

"I believe that will be acceptable," Kizmel added.

So I steered us toward a restaurant with an ample sweets menu not far from the southern gate. We turned west off the main road and down a smaller one. After a while, Kizmel came to a stop and rubbed one of the dark-brown wood blocks used for the buildings.

"...You cut the trees down to this size and then stack them up again...Humans do the strangest things..."

Asuna and I shared a look. The elves—dark elves, forest elves, even the fallen elves—would never cut down a living tree. If they used any wood in their buildings and furniture, it would only come from trees that had fallen at the end of their life span.

In that sense, the lower part of Stachion on the south side was perhaps the biggest waste of wood in any major human town. Maybe this wasn't the best place to have chosen as a destination. But despite my concern, Kizmel just gave us a glance and blinked in surprise.

"Oh, I am not complaining," she said, smiling. "Elves have their way of life, as do humans. The old me...in fact, all dark elves, since the long distant past, have scorned other races as foolish and below us, but since meeting you, and accompanying you at times, I have learned that humankind possesses many virtues as well. For one thing, we first met when you saved my life from the forest elf who was about to defeat me. I suppose having my life saved by humans is bound to change my mind..."

Asuna and I shared another glance, then looked bashful. When we saw the two elf knights fighting in the woods, the biggest reason that I chose Kizmel over the Forest Elven Hallowed Knight was because it was what I did in the beta. I just picked the familiar route.

So why did I choose her in the beta? At the time, I wasn't a solo player but was hanging around in a four-person party of strangers, so it wasn't my decision alone, but no one else had protested, and I seem to remember that we reached the consensus in just a matter of seconds.

Perhaps it was because the other three were also guys, and Kizmel was a beautiful older woman. But it was often the case in other games and novels that the dark elves were antagonists. The forest elf looked every bit the heroic, shining knight, and we could have cast our allegiance with him for that reason.

Had I felt something in that moment, *besides* the fact that Kizmel was a woman?

"Um, Kizmel," Asuna mumbled, stepping closer to the knight, "the truth is, when we stepped in to help you on the third floor..."

I briefly panicked, unsure of what she was about to say, but there was no chance to step in or hear the rest—because Kizmel grabbed Asuna's shoulders and pulled her closer, while looking over *my* shoulder and shouting, "Who goes there?!"

The tone of alarm in her voice made me spin around to look.

There was no one in the three-meter-wide street. We weren't in the shopping area, so the only buildings lining the road were homes with their doors shut tight. I looked about but saw no hint of green, yellow, or even (impossible in this place) orange cursors...

But just then, a small silhouette practically melted out of the shadows of a building. It was dressed in a full gray hooded cloak, hiding its identity. The cursor over its head was yellow, indicating an NPC.

Kizmel promptly grabbed the hilt of her saber, and I reached backward for the sword over my shoulder. However, the figure shook its head and, just loud enough to hear, said, "I mean you no harm."

The voice belonged to a very young girl—and it was familiar somehow.

Where had I heard it, I wondered…but could not arrive at an answer. The name under the cursor was Myia, but that did not immediately ring a bell for me, either…

Kizmel repeated her question. "Who are you? Why were you following us?"

She had her own black hood pulled low, so in clothing, the two looked very similar, except for the issue of height. Kizmel was a fair bit taller than me, but the gray-cloaked woman across from us seemed more the size of a child.

"I merely wish to speak with that swordsman over there," the NPC said, pointing at my face with a skinny hand.

"Huh…? Me?"

"Sir Swordsman, do you have one of these?" she said, opening her hand to reveal a small key hanging from a little string. Now, *this* item I recognized.

"Kirito, isn't that…?" Asuna whispered, and I nodded. I opened up my inventory and materialized the same item that I'd just gotten three days earlier. It was the iron key, one of two that dropped when Morte killed Cylon.

I lifted the key up, which also was strung on a little loop, closed my game window, and let it dangle like the NPC girl was doing.

Then something very strange happened. The completely ordinary gray key began to thrum with a faint ringing, vibrating gently. Across from me, the NPC's key was exhibiting the same reaction.

"...Who are you? And what does that key do...?" I asked. The gray-cloaked NPC stashed away the key and approached. Kizmel kept her hand on the hilt of the saber but did not draw it.

"As long as we have these keys, we are not safe, even in town. Let's go somewhere else," said the NPC named Myia. I shared a look with Asuna and Kizmel. We couldn't discount the possibility of a trap. But we had come to this town to investigate the mystery of Cylon's two keys, and here was a major clue, so there was no point backing away now.

"All right," said Asuna. "Where should we go, then?"

The NPC nodded, glanced around, and whispered, "Follow me." We followed the cloaked woman to the western end of the south half of Stachion, where the construction was the most dense. She used yet another key, one colored bronze, to open the door to a small house there, ushered us inside, then peered around outside to make sure the coast was clear before shutting and locking the door again.

There was a living room at the end of a short hallway. Despite it having just passed ten in the morning, it was quite dark inside. The shutters were down over the largest window, so the sunlight could only get in through the few smaller windows around the room. The NPC lit a lamp hanging on the wall, then turned around to apologize.

"I'm sorry that I can't open the window for you. Hang on, I'll put on some tea," she said, heading for the kitchen, but Asuna pulled her back.

"No, there's no need. Please, tell us what you have to say."

"...Oh. I see."

The NPC paused, then motioned to the sofa in the middle of the living room, so the three of us sat down on it. She took an armchair across from us and lowered her hood.

Asuna gasped. I felt stunned, too. Based on her height, I assumed the woman was very young, but seeing her features in the light now, she was actually just a child—perhaps no more than ten years old. Just in case, I glanced at the ears under her neatly bobbed blond hair, but she was not an elf.

"My name is *Mee-a*," she said, and all of a sudden, I understood how the name *Myia* was meant to be pronounced. It was a simple name but somehow mysterious.

"I am Kizmel, a knight," said the elf, who kept her hood on. Asuna and I followed her lead.

"I'm Kirito...a swordsman, I guess."

"And I am Asuna. I'm a swordswoman."

"Kizmel, Kirito...and Asuna. Do I have that right?" she asked, using the familiar NPC routine for checking pronunciation. She looked right at me with grayish-green eyes. "Kirito, the iron key that you possess came from Lord Cylon of Stachion, correct?"

"Y...yes," I agreed, then realized I might be creating a dangerous mistaken impression. "Oh, b-but I didn't take it from him by force. Technically, I, uh...picked it up off the ground..." I stammered.

Asuna calmly asked, "Myia, do you...know what happened to Cylon?"

"......Yes." The girl nodded, her long-lashed eyes downcast. "I heard from Terro, the gardener at the mansion. Cylon...my father was attacked by brigands outside of town three nights ago and died..."

...Gardener?

...Father?

The two words collided in my brain, and it took a while for them to fall into the proper places.

The only ones who knew Cylon was dead were me, Asuna, Kizmel, Morte and the dagger user, and the large NPC man who served Cylon. That would mean the large man who rode off in the carriage was the gardener named Terro.

That was all well and good...but the girl also called Cylon her father. Taken at face value, it would mean she was the daughter of the late lord.

The morning after Morte's attack, Asuna asked me if Cylon had any family, and I said that I didn't recall any wife or children at his mansion. I had never seen Cylon's family in the beta or this time around, but that wasn't proof that Cylon had no family at all.

"Myia...you're Cylon's daughter?" Asuna asked, getting to the root of everything I was thinking. Myia acknowledged she was. Asuna hesitated for a brief moment before she offered, "I...I'm sorry, Myia. We were present when those brigands attacked your father. In fact, the truth is, the bandits were after Kirito and me. Cylon was just a victim..."

I felt as though my head were splitting in two. Myia was an NPC, and the conversations with her had to be a part of the "Curse of Stachion" quest. But Morte killed Cylon, and he was a player—it was a spontaneous event, not a programmed step of the quest's story. How was it that in just three days, it had been incorporated into the quest scenario? I was certain that after we saw Cylon die, another identical Cylon would pop up in Stachion, so that the quest proceeded for all other players regardless...

"You don't need to apologize for that," Myia said, mature beyond her years. I lifted my head. "I heard about everything from Terro. How Father gave you poison and abducted you...and was going to lock you in the maze beneath the mansion, forcing you to perform the duty, no, the atonement he was meant to bear..."

"Atonement..." I repeated without realizing it. Myia turned her mysterious green eyes on me. I summoned my courage and asked the NPC girl, "Do you know...what your father did...?"

"......Yes," Myia said, looking down. "Mother told me everything the other day."

"M-Mother...?" I parroted back again. Myia's mother would have to be Cylon's wife, I assumed, when Asuna jabbed my arm with her elbow. The shock helped my synapses finally fire properly. I had already explained, to Asuna no less, that Cylon had a lover ten years ago.

"Um...Does that mean your mother is the previous lord's app...I mean, servant...?" I said, nearly saying the word *apprentice* by mistake, based on my knowledge from the beta. Fortunately, Myia didn't seem to notice or find it suspicious.

"Yes," she said, "my mother's name is Theano, and I've heard that she served Pithagrus, the previous lord of Stachion, until ten years ago."

Theano.

I met her four months ago, during the *SAO* beta test. But she left a strong impression, and if I closed my eyes, I could summon the image of her handsome face right away. If I tried, I could see some of those details in Myia's features, too.

In the "Curse of Stachion" quest, on the correct route—well, at this point there was no telling what was correct, so let's call it the beta route—I was paralyzed by Cylon in the house in Suribus, stuffed in a bag and taken back to Stachion, then saved in the backstreets by none other than Theano.

She was once a servant at the lord's mansion, a puzzle expert who earned Pithagrus's admiration, as well as a skilled fighter with the sword. One night ten years ago, she witnessed a furious Cylon bludgeon Pithagrus to death with a golden cube.

She should have told a guard at once, but after much anguish, Theano decided to keep her silence. This was because Cylon was also her lover, and while Cylon killed Pithagrus for not naming him as the successor, in fact, Pithagrus's plan was to name the next lord of the town the person he was secretly training: Theano. When Cylon left the room, she slipped in and took the bloody cube, then locked it in the deepest part of the Dungeon of Trials beneath the mansion. She then placed the key to open the dungeon in the hideout in Suribus and quit her job as servant.

Theano hoped that Cylon would regret his sin and reveal all that he had done to her. Only then did she plan to tell Cylon where to find the key. But Cylon claimed the body, whose face was crushed beyond recognition, belonged to a nameless traveler and that it was Pithagrus who killed the traveler. The result was a curse of puzzles that befell Stachion—and was steadily expanding beyond the town to this day.

In the beta test, Theano and I snuck into the mansion, convinced Cylon to see the error of his ways, and used the golden key to go into the dungeon beneath the building. The three of us completed many puzzles and blazed through the astral-type monsters that shouldn't have appeared there, until we reached the end of the dungeon. There, we beat Pithagrus's vengeful ghost in a puzzle battle, retrieved the cube, purified it with holy water, then offered it to the grave of the traveler (actually Pithagrus). Then his ghost appeared again and forgave Cylon, bringing the story full circle.

But this time, Cylon couldn't atone for his sin and undo the curse, because he got killed by Morte the PKer. This event, which should have only affected the quest for Asuna and me, somehow now applied to all players. Cylon had seemingly vanished off the face of Aincrad altogether.

There was no longer a way to complete the quest in the same order of events that I used in the beta. I had the golden key in my possession, so we might be able to get into the dungeon and retrieve the cube, but would that alone undo Pithagrus's curse? And why weren't we being visited by the crucial Theano herself, but by her daughter Myia?

"Theano...Where is your mother now...?" I asked gingerly. The girl's lips pursed, and she shook her head. She pulled the iron key out of her shirt and stared at it.

"...I don't know. The morning after she learned that Father had been killed, she left a note and this key behind and vanished."

"What did the note say?"

"It had an apology to me, the truth of the traveler's murder at the mansion ten years ago, and a reminder to visit Barro if she never came back..."

"Who's Barro...?" I asked, thinking that name sounded familiar, too. To my surprise, it was Asuna rather than Myia who answered.

"The gardener at the mansion at the time Theano worked there. Remember, we talked to him three days ago?"

"Oh y-yeah..." I mumbled.

Myia nodded and explained, "Barro is the father of Terro, who tends the gardens now. Ten years ago, my father killed Pithagrus, the previous lord...although he made it sound as though a traveler was killed, and Pithagrus went missing. After that, many of the servants left their jobs there, including my mother and Barro. But Terro was having trouble learning his words, and they said he wouldn't be able to support himself in town, so my father, the new lord Cylon, agreed to take him in."

"...Oh, I see..." I said, recalling the silence and obedience of the large man who showed up at the secret hideout. It seemed like perhaps Cylon wasn't utterly evil to his core after all. I sighed.

A heavy silence settled upon the scene. It was broken by the soft voice of Kizmel.

"Myia. You said that as long as we had the key, we were not safe in town. Why is that?"

That was a curious point, it was true, but more interesting and nerve-wracking to me was that two NPCs were interacting in a way that could not have been pre-scripted into the story. I wondered if they would actually hold a logical conversation, when...

"The night that Mother left this key and letter behind, a thief broke into the house where we lived for years, right near the town square. I was awoken by the sound and went into the living room, where a brigand dressed in black was holding this key and drew his dagger to attack when he saw me...I managed to fight him off and take back the key, but I realized it was dangerous to remain in the house, and so I moved here as soon as I could."

"Oh? Whose house is this?"

"My father's. This is where Lord Cylon lived before he went to dwell in the mansion as Lord Pithagrus's apprentice. My father never returned, but my mother would bring me here to clean the place every once in a while."

"I see," Kizmel said, crossing her arms. "So the brigand does not know about this house yet."

Next to her, I hummed to myself. *I see. So this is the original home of Cylon. If we look around, we might find some clues to—no, wait. Before that. Didn't Myia say something odd?*

"W-wait just a moment, Myia. You said that a thief with a dagger came to steal your key…Did you fight him off by yourself?" Asuna asked while I was trying to recall just what she had said.

But yes, that was the part. Myia had said she had fought him off, but how could a girl of only ten years or so do such a thing?

With new eyes, I stared at the bob-haired girl. Even with the gray cloak on, it was clear at a glance that she was incredibly thin. Resting atop her knees, her hands looked like a doll's. Could she even swing a knife, much less a sword?

Myia nodded to Asuna and said, without changing expression, "Yes, from a very young age, my mother…"

But we didn't get to hear the end of that. There was a loud, hard crash, and a small window at the back end of the living room shattered.

"What was that?!" I shouted, rising to my feet. Bouncing our way along the ground was a black sphere. As soon as she saw the baseball-sized object, Kizmel shouted, "Everyone, hold your breath!"

I sucked in as much air as my lungs could handle and closed my mouth. The ball split in two and began to emit a thick purple smoke.

Not more poison gas! I swore in my head, drawing the Sword of Eventide +3 from my back. I didn't know what kind of poison it was, but no events of this nature were going to end with just the gas.

At my side, Asuna had her window open, materializing a masklike object. The leather-made item was the gas mask that Cylon dropped when he died. I thought she was going to put it on herself, but instead, she leaped over the table and stuck it over Myia's face.

More glass broke. This time, the large double windows shattered, shutters and all, and two dark figures leaped into the room. They tumbled smoothly over the floor and popped to their feet, drawing short, curved blades in unison. The cursors above their heads were yellow, the text reading UNKNOWN BURGLAR. They were NPCs, not players.

As soon as the blades pointed our way glinted like razors, I finally remembered that we were inside town. This was a quest-event battle (I assumed), but this house was within the Anti-Criminal-Code safe haven of town. No monsters could get inside the zone, and players' HP were protected from harm and would not lose a single pixel, no matter what. That was one of the ironclad rules of *SAO*, as I understood it.

But wait...

A player attacking a player was a crime, but would it be a crime if an NPC acting according to the story attacked a player? I'd never experienced this for myself. Was it possible that if a story battle occurred within town, the safety code might not actually protect us?

I wanted to shout to Asuna and Myia to get back, but I couldn't do that with my breath held. The purple smoke, half-translucent, was already up to face level, and as soon as I breathed it in, I was going to suffer some kind of debuff. If the code didn't work, and I took continuous damage, for example, I could chug potions to stay safe, but if this was paralyzing poison again, I had no means of counteracting it. I gave a hand signal, hoping the message got across, and held up my sword.

Just to my right was Kizmel, saber drawn. She had that ultra-rare antidote ring on, but that didn't mean much in the midst of a gas.

The black-clad attackers had their faces entirely wrapped in cloth, plus they had gas masks on that were different from Cylon's, hiding their features from view. They held up their gleaming curved blades—but failed to attack.

They simply didn't need to: We would run out of breath in just thirty or forty seconds.

In other words, we had to eliminate our enemies in that time frame.

Kizmel and I made the briefest of eye contact before charging together. The black-masked burglars leaped, too, a split-second later.

The instant our blades crossed, the enemy cursors turned to brilliant red. Even for me, at level 20, the color looked dark. The power they exhibited was about the same as the deadly Forest Elven Inferior Knight at Yofel Castle on the fourth floor.

I gritted my teeth and pushed hard against the enemy, but my breath was already running out. Sparks were flying from Kizmel's saber where she pushed, too, but even the elite knight's arm strength was not enough to bowl back this foe. We had to break the stalemate somehow, before the poison got us......

"Kirito, Kizmel, pull inward!" shouted a brave-yet-young voice from behind us. I leaned to my right and saw a bright-red flash shoot past my left side.

Kra-ka-kam! went a series of shocks, and the brigand in black flew backward, bearing three damage-effect lines on his chest. A moment later, Kizmel's opponent suffered the same fate and slammed against the far wall.

It was Asuna who had helped Kizmel out, and my own rescuer was...Myia. Like Asuna, she used the three-part rapier thrust skill, Triangular.

Stunned, I looked down at the masked girl and her short but fancy-looking rapier. But not for long—we couldn't let this opportunity pass. Kizmel and I bounded forward to deliver the finishing blows to our tumbling foes.

But the burglars each put a hand to their waists, pulled something from their belts, and threw. I just managed to deflect it with my sword, but they used the opportunity to stand and essentially backflip out through the broken window.

Their footsteps rapidly scurried away. *You're not going anywhere!* I thought, leaping through the window to the backyard. With fresh air finally flooding into my lungs, I swept through the

wooden gate and looked left and right, but there were no people in the midday back alley—and no red cursors.

"...They got away," said a voice behind me. I spun around to see the dark elf knight looking severe. I nodded to her and went back into the yard, pulling the wooden gate shut.

"They were pretty tough—and speedy, too," I said. "It's a good thing you were with us, Kizmel. Of course, I'm sorry—you didn't sign up for all this."

But she did not change her expression. "That might not be entirely true."

"Huh...?"

The Curse of Stachion was an incident that happened entirely between humans and had no relation to the elves at all, I wanted to protest—until Kizmel thrust a long, narrow object toward my face. It looked like the throwing picks the burglars threw as they escaped, but when my gaze brought it into focus, my jaw dropped.

Held between her fingers was a wicked poison needle with a spiral hexagonal shape: a Spine of Shmargor.

At first, I wondered if the masked attackers were none other than Morte and his dagger-using friend. But that was impossible, of course. Their cursors were as yellow as Kizmel's before they turned red, and if they were players, they would turn orange, rather than red.

But then, who were they...?

"I recognized the thin crescent blades they used," she said softly. "Those are the weapons of the Fallen's assassins."

"......You mean the fallen elves?" I asked, perhaps unnecessarily.

The elf knight arched an eyebrow. "Gather your wits, Kirito. Have you ever heard of fallen goblins or fallen orcs in Aincrad?"

Actually, I would prefer those, I thought to myself. "Er...right. Of course. But...what are fallen elves doing here? The elves have nothing to do with this que...this incident..."

"Yes, indeed. It's possible I was followed leaving Castle Galey, but in that case, they could have attacked us in the wilderness or forest at any time, rather than waiting until we entered this human town," Kizmel pointed out.

She was absolutely right about that. Which meant the target was...

I spun around, just as Asuna and Myia emerged from the back door to the right of the broken windows. Asuna was in maximum alert mode, surveying the area with her Chivalric Rapier in hand, while Myia still wore her gas mask. The rapier she'd used to execute a Triangular was now encased in its sheath, hung on the inside of her gray cloak.

The girl trotted over, remarkably calm in the immediate aftermath of the dramatic attack. She seemed to have heard the conversation between Kizmel and me, and when she spoke, her voice was muffled by the mask, but not enough to be indecipherable.

"They were dressed the exact same way as the thieves who snuck into my house two days ago. Like the last time, I think they were after my mother's key."

"...I...I see..."

In other words, this girl of no more than ten fought off not typical burglars, but fallen elf spies or assassins of some kind, all by herself. After witnessing how her sword skill was just as sharp as Asuna's...I still had a hard time buying it. She couldn't be more than a year or two older than poor sickly Agatha, whose quest I completed to earn the Anneal Blade back on the first floor.

But something was more important right now than solving that mystery. I took the iron key out of my waist pouch and held it up at the height of Myia's leather gas mask. The key around her neck reacted, the two resonating faintly.

I asked, "Myia, what are these keys? Do you know where they're supposed to be used...?"

"No," she said, shaking her head. "All my mother's letter said was that it was a memento of her time with Father, so she wanted me to take good care of it. If she knew that dangerous people would come after it, I don't think she would have left it in my care."

"I see…"

This appeared to suggest that we wouldn't know the truth until we found the missing Theano. Kizmel bent down and said to the girl, "Myia, how did you find us? You were following us before I detected you in the alley, weren't you?"

"Yes…I'm sorry for having done that, but I wanted to make sure you weren't with the burglars…"

"No, I am not blaming you," Kizmel said kindly. "It only makes sense that you would do this, considering the circumstances."

The girl in the gas mask nodded and pressed her tiny hand over her chest. "The key my mother left me and the key that Kirito holds, belonging to my father, are drawn to each other. Even when separated by great distances, they always vibrate faintly, trying to point to the other."

"Huh? Really…?"

I shifted the height and angle of the key I held to point directly at the key hanging from Myia's neck. Indeed, the key vibrated subtly at the end of its string. Myia twitched, feeling the same sensation from her key.

So the keys used vibration to indicate direction and sound resonance to indicate distance to each other. Once you knew that, it wouldn't be hard to find us, even in the crowded, complex interior of Stachion. Still, that didn't answer the question of what locks these keys were meant to open—and why the unrelated fallen elves would want to steal them.

As I stared at the fine detail of the key Cylon left behind, Asuna, who still had a hand on Myia's shoulder, seemed to figure something out. "Say, Kirito…does the golden key we found at the hideout in Suribus react to the iron key at all?"

"Huh? Oh, I don't know…"

I opened my window and pulled the golden key out of the KEY ITEMS tab and checked my quest log, too, just in case, but the latest hint hadn't updated yet: LORD CYLON OF STACHION HAS BEEN KILLED BY THIEVES. YOU MUST FIND THE RIGHT PLACE TO USE THE KEYS HE LEFT BEHIND.

Ignoring the question of who actually wrote that synopsis, I closed the window and hung the iron key from my right hand. The golden key didn't have a string, so I held it directly in my left hand and pointed them at each other, moving them closer and farther apart, but they produced no vibration or sounds.

But on closer inspection, they were very similar outside of the color. The keys in Aincrad were all old-fashioned ward-lock keys, in keeping with the medieval fantasy style, so while they all kind of looked alike, I could see many shared elements in the head design and teeth of these keys.

"Is that...?" prompted a soft voice, and I looked up from my examination. Myia had taken a step forward and was looking closely at the golden key through her mask. "Is that golden key the same one that my mother took from the mansion ten years ago?"

"Uh...yes, I think so. We found it at Pithagrus's hideout in the town of Suribus."

"Then maybe," Myia said, looking briefly gloomy, "maybe my mother went to search for that key."

"Huh...?" I grunted.

But Asuna seemed to understand. "Yes, I think that's possible. Terro the gardener was following Cylon's orders, but while he knew he was supposed to paralyze us and locked us in the dungeon beneath the mansion, I don't think he actually knew the purpose of that mission. So I don't think that he would've been able to explain what happened to the golden key to Theano..."

"Yes, when Terro visited the night before Mother disappeared, I was there, too. But he didn't mention anything about a key."

"So...did Theano go to the hideout in Suribus? But the basement dungeon won't open without this key, so she would have known the key was removed. After Cylon was killed, only the brigands and our group could have the key...so has she been searching for us for the past three days...?" I wondered.

Kizmel said, "No, that is not probable. The one with the golden key would likely have an iron key, and Theano knew that the two iron keys reacted, so if she wanted to find the current holder, she wouldn't leave her own iron key at home like that."

"Oh...yeah. Good point..."

Trying to find the other keyholder without bringing her own key would be like trying to find the seven somethingballs without the so-and-so radar. So where was Theano, then...?

"Think carefully, Kirito," Kizmel said, like a big sister or teacher. I gaped. "Huh? About what?"

"A key does nothing on its own. For a key to be stolen, there must be a place where it is used."

"Oh...I—I get it now," I mumbled, looking to the northern sky. Over the roofs of the wood-block houses lining the little alley, the chalk-white mansion could be seen at the far north end of town.

After she heard the story from Terro, Theano must have deduced that the purpose of the brigands who attacked Cylon was to steal the golden key. Of course, Morte's real aim was not the key, but our lives; yet, there was no way Theano could have known that.

If she was looking for the brigands who stole the golden key, she wouldn't need the iron key, and in the low probability that different people had the golden and iron keys, it would be a waste of time. More importantly, as Kizmel said, a far better choice would be to stake out the place *where* the brigands would need to use that key.

When we fought together in the beta, Theano was a clever and patient warrior. It was quite possible that she was hiding out near the entrance to the basement dungeon for the thieves to arrive. Unfortunately, that was the biggest waste of time of them all. *I* still had the golden key, and Morte's gang seemed to have no interest in keys or cubes.

"...If Theano's at the mansion, we should go find her and explain the situation..." I suggested. Kizmel and Asuna agreed, but Myia said nothing.

A few seconds later, her masked face rose, and as quietly as was still audible, she said, "Kirito, Asuna...My father deceived you, poisoned and abducted you, and hoped to force a dangerous duty upon you. Evil acts only beget more evil…It was divine punishment when he was attacked and killed by those brigands. If my mother is trying to avenge his death, you have no obligation to help her. I only wanted to warn you of the danger around…so why are you going to these lengths?"

"Um…well…"

Her question was perfectly reasonable, but I had no answer. Theano had saved me—but only in the beta test. She didn't know my name or face in this version of the world, so she had no reason to help avenge the death of Cylon, who had paralyzed Asuna and me and stuffed us into sacks. The "Curse of Stachion" quest was still ongoing, of course, but Myia wouldn't understand what that was, and I was rapidly losing interest in whatever the "correct" route for this quest was.

I just didn't know how to actually explain all this. But luckily, instead, Asuna circled around Myia's front and bent down. "It's not about logic or reason. You tried to warn us about the danger we were in. If you're in trouble, too, then of course we'll help. You're worried about your mother, aren't you?"

"……"

Myia said nothing for many seconds, before finally nodding her head.

"…Yes. Um…thank you, Asuna, Kirito, and Kizmel."

"It is no matter. I have my own meaningful connection to those ones who attacked us, too," said Kizmel with a smile. Then she asked, "But, Myia, how long are you going to continue wearing that mask? The poison is long gone."

"Oh…uhhh…" Myia lifted her hands up to the side of the mask before turning to look at Asuna. "Um, do you mind if I borrow this mask just a bit longer?"

"Huh…? It's all right, of course. But isn't it stuffy?"

"I'm fine. I feel more secure when I have this on."

"Oh…"

Asuna looked skeptical still—but then she froze. I understood what she was thinking. The gas mask Myia had on belonged to Cylon. They'd been apart for ten years—possibly she had never actually met him—but now the young girl was able to smell her father in that mask. If it put her at peace, how could we demand she take it off? Even if it meant the pretty young swordgirl's looks were diminished.

My partner straightened up again and put her hand on Myia's back. "In that case, let's go to the lord's mansion together. I bet we'll find your mother there."

"Okay!" Myia said brightly.

Just then, a fourth HP bar appeared under the three already present in the upper-left corner of my view. When I saw the little number next to the name MYIA, I very nearly shouted *"Whuzmeen?!"*—an abbreviation of "What does that mean?"

Currently, my level was 20, and Asuna's was 19. After splitting off on the fifth floor, Kizmel passed us to reach 21—and Myia's level was 23.

Kizmel was an elite-class NPC whose stats were higher than other NPCs or monsters of her same level, so the comparison wasn't direct, but at the very least, this meant Myia had battle power to match Kizmel's.

I'm glad she didn't suspect me of killing Cylon, I thought. *In fact, at this rate, we're going to end up with more NPCs than party members soon.*

Feeling a bit awkward and self-conscious, I trudged through the gate into the alley.

10

UNFORTUNATELY, WE DID NOT FIND THEANO UNDER-
neath the lord's mansion.

And she was not the only one we missed. There was something
else—not a person but an object—that was incredibly important
but gone from the building.

Because Lord Cylon was dead—or missing, as the official word
went for now—most of the servants were gone, and the mansion
greeted us in a desolately quiet state. Our party of four headed
first to the entrance of the dungeon on the second basement floor,
but Theano was not there, and the marble door was shut tight, so
we went outside to look for Terro the gardener.

When we found him in the corner of the yard, Terro refused
to answer any of our questions, claiming he didn't know or
understand—and it wasn't clear if he even remembered Asuna
and me or not. But when Myia, still wearing the gas mask,
demanded he explain what he was hiding, the big man spilled
the beans at once.

The day after Cylon's death—the morning of January 2—
Theano showed up out of nowhere and got Terro to help her
open the secret back door to the underground maze. This time, I
did not hold back from shouting "Th'ellman?!"—a contraction of
"What the hell, man?"

A back door. If that existed, then the key to get into the dungeon was completely pointless. Cylon could have just gone in there and whisked out the golden cube himself. I was so stunned that I fell into a sitting position with my arms around my knees.

Asuna knelt down to whisper in my ear, "Don't dungeons usually have some hidden passageway or door in the very last room that you can use to get out?"

The fencer hadn't really played an RPG before being trapped in *SAO*, so if even she was calling me out with basic knowledge like this, I had to suck it up. And upon closer reflection, only a person who had been through the dungeon before would know about the secret back door, and given that this was under the mansion, that would leave only Pithagrus and Theano; and the former was dead. I'd been through it in the beta, but I recalled being teleported back to the entrance after I got the golden cube.

Thinking back on it, there were very frequent uses of teleportation in the beta outside of teleport gates and activation of the anti-harassment code—but it seemed like nearly all of them were removed in the final release. Including, of course, teleporting to Blackiron Palace when you died.

It was with this in mind that I stood up, composed myself, and allowed Terro to lead us to the dungeon's back door. The large man used his considerable strength to shift the entire base of a stone statue in a corner of the yard, revealing a staircase below. The four of us filed through into the final chamber of the dungeon, bypassing all the puzzles and ghosts and boss monsters in the process.

As I expected, there was no sign of a bloodied golden cube or Myia's mother, Theano. We left the mansion without much to show for it and came to a stop about ten meters from its stately gates. Silence dominated the group.

"...Shall we just find a quiet place where we can reexamine the situation?" Asuna suggested, to Kizmel's and Myia's agreement. I was with them, of course, but I knew that two players and two NPCs, three of us hooded, would attract attention, and we'd already been attacked inside a locked house, so there probably wasn't anywhere safe to go inside the town.

"...You know, maybe the open terrace seats along the main road with all its traffic are less likely to get us attacked..." I proposed, thinking we should just accept the visibility and focus on safety.

But before Asuna could say anything, it was Kizmel who said, "Do you—and Myia—still have any reason to be in this town?"

"Huh...?" Asuna and I shared a look, then went back to Kizmel. We did have plans here. After we did what we could about the quest, we were going to use Stachion's teleport gate to visit the first floor and show Kizmel the Town of Beginnings. But in this situation, we'd have to be prepared for an attack while sightseeing—and was it right to drag Myia along with us?

"Well...um..." I stammered, which was all Kizmel needed to hear. I could see her smiling under the deep hood.

She turned to my partner and said, "Asuna, I am very touched to learn that you planned many things for us to do together. But I cannot ignore Myia and her Fallen attackers and go on a sightseeing vacation. The old me might not have cared at all about the squabbles of humankind...but much as you two saved me, now I wish to save Myia."

Asuna closed her eyes slowly and opened them again with a smile that was breathtakingly gentle, even loving. "Our plans can wait. We have all the time in the world. I can set up something else once we've solved all these problems. And both Kirito and I aren't in any mood to abandon Myia, either."

She rested her hand on Myia's shoulder. I was sure that Asuna had seen the girl's level, but she didn't seem to be viewing the situation through that particular lens. And for Myia's part, she didn't hold her own considerable skill in any kind of high esteem.

She bowed deeply to us. "Thank you...I cannot imagine where my mother is now or what she is doing. Please, I would appreciate your help."

"But of course," Kizmel said at once, before looking to me. "Now, I have a suggestion...Why don't we take Myia back to the castle? There is no concern of the Fallen attacking her there, and we will find plenty of places to relax and speak openly."

"Whaaat?!" I yelped.

But it was true: If the Anti-Criminal Code wasn't going to help us now, then no place could be safer for us than Castle Galey. The only issue was whether Myia would agree to leave her home of Stachion and travel that far...

So I explained about Castle Galey to Myia. Behind the ports of the gas mask, her eyes were big and sparkling. In a rush, the words came tumbling out.

"Of course I want to go see an elf castle."

We left Stachion, taking the short route back through the woods, and used the rapidly dwindling stock of Droplets of Villi on our soles to cross Lake Talpha. While crossing the wasteland of the second area north, we found another fruiting cactus and took a short break to pick it clean. Myia took off her mask for the first time in hours to eat and exclaimed that she had never tasted such delicious fruit before. Kizmel proudly explained to her that a cactus fruited for only thirty minutes throughout an entire year.

The giant scorpions of the canyon area were as tough as always, but we made quick work of them with the addition of not one, but two high-powered NPCs. The gamer in me wanted to just hang out and farm for half a day, but my conscience got the better of me, and I knew it wasn't right to use a ten-year-old girl as a power-leveling tool. Still, with what we earned in the south-area dungeon yesterday and the reward bonus for the "Agate Key" quest, I got to level 21, and Asuna reached level 20. Kizmel and Myia gave us both a round of applause when it happened.

A few minutes after one o'clock, we reached the canyon just before Castle Galey.

"Ooooh...!" Myia marveled at the massive castle in the distance.

She hadn't been out of Stachion in ten years, so the wonder of seeing the stately dark elf building had to be far beyond when I first saw Kawagoe Castle in the real world. For that matter, Kawagoe Castle didn't even have any towers, so its profile was much less impressive.

A little while ago, I would have agonized over the question of "What does a sense of wonder really mean to an NPC?" but my view of NPCs (of AIs in general) had been updated many times in recent days. I couldn't just assume that only Kizmel and Viscount Yofilis were special NPCs above the rest.

As we approached the castle over the stone bridge that was apparently once an aqueduct, the bells began ringing, and the heavy gates started to open. Only then did it occur to me that Myia was a human and had not accepted any dark elf quests, but the guards did not seem interested in accosting her, perhaps because of Kizmel's presence. I made a mental note to ask about getting the girl another one of the sigil rings as we trotted through the half-open gates.

Myia exclaimed again as she looked up at the vast branches of the spirit tree and the looming castle behind it. Castle Galey ran in an arc along the curved cliff, which had to be a delightful change from Stachion and all its relentless straight angles. Once this was all done, we could take her to see Karluin on the fifth floor, Yofel Castle on the fourth, and Zumfut on the third. Meanwhile, Kizmel lowered the hood of the Greenleaf Cape and said, "Shall we speak in your room, Asuna? Or in the dining hall?"

The fencer lowered her own hood and said, "The bath."

I knew I didn't have the right to refuse her, and my only hope in getting out of it was little Myia, who happily accepted, so I had no choice but to follow the three women. We used the west-wing stairs to go underground and arrived at the changing rooms for men and women. Sulking, I decided that I wouldn't wear a pair of swim trunks for defense, just to spite them, and headed into the hot spring for the indented part below the spirit tree's hanging roots.

Once I sank into the cloudy hot water up to my shoulders, I

accidentally let out a wheeze of exhilaration. I hated to admit it, but after marching to Stachion and back, and all the fighting in that dusty canyon valley, a good soak in a hot bath was like nothing else. I leaned back against the spring roots and closed my eyes, letting my mind relax and expand. In the real world, falling asleep in a hot bath put you at risk of dehydration or drowning. But in the virtual world…well, if you fell asleep and went under the water here, you'd probably wind up in a drowning status and lose some HP. And yet, it was impossible to resist the pleasure of all my muscles relaxing amid the pleasant, musky plant smell…

"I wonder if he's still back in there," said a voice not too far away, but I was nearly 70 percent of the way to being asleep and didn't react in the moment.

"He must have various things to prepare," said a different voice.

Then the first voice said, "I can't imagine what *he* would possibly need to get ready…But anyway, let's wait for him near the roots. Yesterday, I found a dent in them that was almost shaped like an easy chair…"

Suddenly, something soft rested itself on top of me. No amount of serenity could prevent me from reacting to this, however. "Hwhoa—?!"

It took over two minutes to defuse the crisis that ensued after that.

"I could have sworn that we had a deal to stay on opposite sides of the center line," said a voice so cross that I could practically visualize the puff of steam coming off it.

Without hope of winning, I argued, "But I thought that seat position was just about at the border line…"

"No! You were nearly four centimeters on the women's side of the bath!" Asuna claimed. She was sitting right in the little cocoon space she stole from me, with Myia resting on her lap. Kizmel sat on a thick root nearby, but the steam from the bath here was so thick that I couldn't even see their silhouettes. The only reason I knew where the ladies were was from the green and yellow cursors.

"And for one thing, if you're already in the water, you should at least let us know. When you're hiding in this spot the way you were, of course I'm going to assume you have something devious in mind," Asuna continued, still grumpy.

Myia innocently chimed in, "I thought you and Kirito were either brother and sister or boyfriend and girlfriend."

"W...well, you're wrong! He's just a party mem...er, a partner, or a sidekick, or an attendant, or what have you!" Asuna protested with fantastic awkwardness.

Idly, I wondered if Myia thought I was the older brother or Asuna was the older sister. Given the price of the NerveGear and the difficulty of buying a copy of *SAO* at launch, it seemed unlikely that Asuna was any less than fourteen years old, and her wide knowledge and general bossiness gave her an older-sister air. But every now and then, she showed a glimpse of childishness that made it much harder to tell. In any case, *attendant* was a cruel word to use. Maybe *sidekick* really was a better fit...

My thoughts were really going free-form when I was brought back to attention by Kizmel's vivid, delighted voice rippling the surface of the water. "Ha-ha-ha...I have been around you for quite a while, and even I have trouble ascertaining the particular nature of your connection. You seem to act with one mind in battle, but you fight three times a day. That was the second, by the way."

"What? No, we've only fought the one time."

"You were angry at Kirito for coming back to the room after taking a walk this morning, weren't you?"

"Oh, that wasn't a fight. I was just giving him a warning."

If you're going to break it down that way, I can't even remember being angry or upset at Asuna, so none of these count as a fight. Of course, part of that is because I'm the one who's always making a mess of things.

At any rate, if I kept listening to them talk, my nerves were going to sweat me into a dry sponge, so I cleared my throat and called out from the other side of the roots. "So, uh, shall we talk about what to do?"

There was a little splash, and I was keenly aware of three people concentrating on my presence.

"I suppose so. But I do feel like there aren't many hard facts that we can go off of..." Asuna said, so I decided to go ahead and list off what we knew, which I'd been arranging and mulling over in my head on the trip to the castle.

"Let's look at it in chronological order. First off, ten years ago, before the incident started: Stachion's lord was Pithagrus, the genius and so-called puzzle king, while his primary apprentice Cylon and serving woman Theano lived at his mansion. At that time, Cylon and Theano were lovers..."

"I wonder if Pithagrus was aware of that," Asuna murmured.

"No..." Myia piped up, "Mother didn't speak often of her time living at the lord's mansion, but she did say that no one else there knew about her and my father."

"Ah, I see..."

"And just before the incident, I'm guessing, Theano became pregnant with Myia," I said, trying to be as mature as possible for a middle-school boy talking about the concept of pregnancy. But that statement made me wonder, on a whim, how the game system handled the concept of babies and birth. Then I changed my mind, realizing that NPCs wouldn't go off and create children of their own accord. After all, this murder case from ten years ago wasn't some actual event that happened in Aincrad; it was just a series of memories given to these NPCs to build the story for the player...I thought. I was pretty sure.

I cleared my throat and continued, "So...one day ten years ago, Pithagrus tells Cylon that he is choosing another apprentice to be his successor, and in a rage, Cylon beats Pithagrus to death with the golden cube that is the symbol of the town lord. Theano, who witnessed it, couldn't bring herself to publicly accuse Cylon, her lover and the father of her unborn child, of murder. While Cylon was out of the room, she snuck in and removed the golden cube and golden key. She locked the cube in the dungeon beneath the mansion, and she hid the key in Pithagrus's secret second home in a nearby town. Then she left her job at the mansion."

I'd explained this all to Asuna on multiple occasions, but I had beta knowledge that might have been filling in gaps where details had changed in the final release. Myia did not correct me at any point, however, which told me that I had the broad details correct.

"After Pithagrus was killed, one cursed puzzle appeared in the town of Stachion each day. Theano went back to her original home, focused on raising Myia, and waited for Cylon to come to her and admit his crime. But Cylon invented a fictional traveler who had been killed, took the position of lord, and asked any adventurer who came to the mansion to seek the golden cube. After ten years, Asuna and I came along and went to the separate home in Suribus on Cylon's request, where we found the golden key."

That made it sound like we were just that much better than anyone else who tried, but it was inevitable, because that was just how the story of the quest was set up. The problem was the next part.

"...Then Cylon appeared, paralyzed us with poison gas, stole the key, and had Terro help take us back to Stachion. But on the road there, thieves attacked and killed Cylon. Terro fled to Stachion alone, visited Theano's house, and explained what had happened. The next morning, Theano left Myia a note and the iron key she always kept on her, went into the dungeon below the mansion via a secret back door, took the golden cube, and vanished. That same night, a burglar got into Myia's house, trying to steal the iron key, but failed...I think I have all that correct," I finished.

From across the steamy water, I heard Asuna groan. "Hrrrmmm... Putting it all together raises more questions than it answers, I feel. Mostly about Theano...I just don't understand why she would leave the iron key at her house. Cylon and Theano lived apart for ten years, but they kept the keys that were their remembrance of the relationship for all of those years. I would assume it was something very precious to Theano…"

"Ha-ha. You have the most romantic opinions, Asuna." Kizmel chuckled, drawing a hurried defense from Asuna.

"I—I don't mean it that way. I'm just being realistic and rational about it…"

Personally, I was more concerned about the way Kizmel had actually used the English word *romantic*—probably an example of Asuna's vocabulary infecting her own—but it was a reasonable question. Given that the keys attracted each other and could lead Cylon's killer right to the other, it was much too dangerous to leave it behind with Myia. And now they had come for the key twice. Myia might have received Theano's excellent sword training, but that didn't seem like a good reason to expose your own young daughter to danger.

"Speaking of which," I prompted across the wall of roots, "where is your mother's key now, Myia?"

"It's right around my neck," she said.

"Oh, that's good."

I exhaled. It was impossible for the fallen elves to sneak into this castle, but it was also a bit scary to think about it being left unattended in the changing room.

"And where is your key, Kirito?" she asked.

I was going to say it was "*in my inventory*" but realized I couldn't do that. "It's, uh, in my book of Mystic Scribing."

That was the elvish term for it, but fortunately, Myia seemed to understand. "Oh, you mean that ancient charm that only adventurers can use."

Ooooh, I see, I thought. Then another thought occurred to me, and I asked the girl, "Say, is it all right with you that I'm holding that key? That was Cylon, your father's key, so shouldn't you have both…?"

"No," she said without an instant of hesitation. "If it's not too much trouble, I want you to have it. I think there is a reason there were two keys and that each of my parents kept one. I feel it is best to keep them from being too close, until we discover the proper use for them."

"Oh...okay."

For a ten-year-old, she had a very good head on her shoulders. But was it appropriate to think about an NPC on those terms?

Just then, there was the sound of squirting water—quite literal, I was certain—and Asuna said, "So if we don't know where to use the two keys, and we don't know why Theano took the golden cube out of the mansion, then we're kind of stuck. I have no idea where we should go and what we should do next."

"About that," said Kizmel, who finally broke her silence. Her voice echoed softly off the rocks. "Why don't we show the keys to the storyteller? It is clear they are under some magical charm. I am not an expert, but the storyteller might be able to tell us something. And if I am not mistaken, Kirito and Asuna, you wanted to ask the elder how to defend against the evil dragon's poison, yes?"

Once we were done in the hot spring and met up in the lounge room, it was two o'clock. The four of us downed glasses of cold water together, then headed for the library on the third floor of the castle's east wing. As I walked behind our guide, Kizmel, and Myia, who had put her gas mask on again, I found myself filled with both excitement and worry.

If we got new information on the iron keys, it could propel us forward on this stalled quest. But I was fairly certain that the storyteller Kizmel mentioned was none other than Bouhroum, the eccentric old man I met in the outer mountain ring early this morning. I didn't dislike the steak-loving old coot, but I still didn't know how to use the Awakening skill—not actually a skill but a modification for the Meditation skill—that I'd worked so hard to get, and he didn't give me a single bite of hamburg steak, either. I had a hard time imagining him giving us honest answers about the keys. And on top of that, how should I act around him when we met him in the library?

"Hey, Kirito," said Asuna quietly into my ear. I quickly looked in her direction.

"Wh...what's up?"

"When do you think Qusack will return?"

"Oh..."

Until she said that, I had completely forgotten about the other group of players. My eyes wandered for a moment. "Um...they said they were going for the 'Agate Key' quest today, so it might be as late as this eve...no, wait. They can't take the shortcut across Lake Talpha, so they have to go from the northwest area where we are, counterclockwise, through the west and then south. That's a long journey...I'm guessing they'll spend the night at Goskai on the southern end, then be back by tomorrow afternoon."

"I see. So they won't happen across Myia until that point."

At last, I understood what Asuna was worried about. We were able to explain Kizmel's presence because she was our bodyguard NPC for the "Elf War" questline. But it was clearly abnormal for a human NPC to be hanging out in Castle Galey. I could easily imagine, given his status as an expert on quests, that Gindo would ask all sorts of questions to satisfy his curiosity.

"Hmm...Well, I suppose we ought to come up with some kind of story that seems natural enough..." I muttered.

But Asuna frowned. "I don't want to lie to people who are really taking their quests seriously, but if they find out that the 'Curse of Stachion' quest is still ongoing, they'll definitely be curious about it."

"And if things get messy, they might end up targeted by the fallen elves, too. The Unknown Burglars in Stachion were definitely tougher than the fallen elf soldiers we've dealt with in the 'Elf War' campaign quest, and if they use paralysis needles, they're even deadlier. Depending on the circumstances, we might want to leave the castle before they return tomorrow..."

On the other hand, we needed a destination before we left.

Without any idea about Theano's current whereabouts or goal, our only hope was old Bouhroum's knowledge and item appraisal.

A moment later, Kizmel spun around, her long cape twirling. "This is the library. The storyteller should be within..."

She opened the heavy door there, on the left side of the hallway. A scent came flooding out of the doorway, like dried plant matter but not unpleasant at all.

Beyond the threshold was a very spacious room filled with huge bookshelves that stretched all the way to the ceiling. I'd been imagining a library like the kind in school, but the crimson carpets running along the aisles and the huge oil paintings on the walls were even more posh than the decorations in Pithagrus's secret home. I reached out to one of the polished and heavily decorated bookshelves in order to remove one of the leather-bound books, but as usual, the contents belonged to a text from some European country and were completely illegible to me.

I put the book back and hurried after Kizmel. We did a one-eighty around one aisle and found a small room-sized open space ahead with a table, sofa, and large resting chair. The space seemed empty at first, but as we approached, I noticed that the easy chair, which was pointed toward the far wall, was making an odd noise.

Kizmel and Myia came to a stop, so I went past them to get a view of what was in the chair. Peacefully asleep was an old man with a black robe, black hat, long white beard, and little round glasses on his nose: none other than Bouhroum, the self-styled sage.

"Well...it would seem the storyteller is resting now. So what should we do...?" Kizmel wondered, looking troubled. I gave her a glance, then grabbed the backrest of the easy chair and began to hurtle it back and forth.

"Whaaaa—?! What is it?! What's happening?!" shouted the old man instantly, leaping upward. He then saw me, his glasses askew, and shouted again. "Y-you! The potato boy! Why are you here?! I already told you—you can't have any of my fricatelle!"

An NPC, sleeping on the job. Disappointed, I told him, "I'm not 'potato boy'—my name is Kirito. And I'm not here to eat any fricatelle."

"Hrmm...?" The old man hummed, fixing his glasses. He looked around and finally noticed Kizmel, Asuna, and Myia standing behind me. He leaped immediately to his nimble feet, rubbing his long beard into place and clearing his throat.

"Ahem! *Ahhh*-hem! Beautiful knight of Lyusula and human swordswoman, how may this old man help you?"

Wow, that's not the welcome I received, I couldn't help but notice. Since the women were too stunned to respond, I decided to pick up the mantle instead.

"We came because we need your help with something, Grandpa Bouhroum. I was hoping you could tell us a few things."

I explained our early-morning meeting in as abbreviated a form as possible, glossing over the secret chamber and hamburg steak, then went into my game inventory to pull out one of the iron keys. I dangled it before the old man's eyes and asked, "Gramps, do you know what this key goes to?"

"Hmm...?" Bouhroum took the key, scrutinized it closely, then tilted his pointed hat to the right. "Well, now...it appears to have an odd charm placed upon it, but I do not recognize it."

"L-look closer. You're our only hope now, Gramps...I mean, Master Sage."

"Ah, so you only suck up to me with the 'Master Sage' routine when you need something," the old man muttered, resting in the easy chair again. He glanced at the women, who still looked stunned, and gestured to the sofa with a wrinkled hand. "Ah, forgive me for keeping you standing. Please, young ladies, have a seat. There is tea and some cups on that table, boy, so go and do the thing."

I decided to swallow my complaint and went to the table. If I had to grind it from whole leaves, it would be beyond my means, but fortunately, the large glass pot was already full of reddish-brown liquid. I set the four cups on the silver tray and carefully poured out the tea, then took it over to the low table.

I put one cup each before the women on the three-cushion couch and started lifting the fourth one to my lips when a hand stretched from the easy chair and snatched it away. The old man sipped the tea noisily and looked up from the dangling key to my face.

"You have another one just like this, don't you?" he gruffed.

"Uh, yeah...How did you know?"

I almost wanted to remark that I thought he was just some steak-loving old coot. Over on the couch, Myia silently pulled the other key from her shirt and held it out, only silence emanating from her gas mask. The old man took it and let it hang so he could inspect it.

"Hrmm, hrmm..."

Bouhroum returned his teacup to the table and moved the key closer to mine. A high-pitched ringing echoed off the high library ceiling, and each time the keys were directly facing each other, they shook as if alive. The old man pushed the keys even closer together.

You know, I don't think we ever actually stuck the keys together. Which is funny, because usually these things don't take their true form until you combine them...

No sooner had the thought occurred to me than there came a silver flash and a *bzak!!* sound. The keys hurtled out of our hands and struck a wall and bookshelf.

Neither I nor any of the women could react in the moment. The only sound came from Bouhroum himself.

"*Fwaaah?!*"

"Hey, you were the one who did it!" I shouted, going to look for the key that flew out of my hand. I saw it hit the wall and bounce off, but after that...It was probably around the tea table in the corner...

"Ah...found it." The string had snagged around the tall teapot. The other key flew toward the bookshelf, and Asuna got up to retrieve it from between shelves. She gave it back to Myia, and then, having apparently adjusted to Bouhroum's personality, finally addressed him in her usual way.

"Mr. Bouhroum…what just happened? It looked like the keys repulsed each other…"

"Ah yes…That is because they did. There is a powerful charm placed upon the keys that prevents them from making contact."

"Placed upon…?" I asked. "In other words, it didn't already exist until someone cast the charm on the keys?"

"Well, obviously," he said, about three times ruder to me than he had been to Asuna.

Undeterred, I pressed, "Who would do such a thing? And why?"

"How would you expect me to know that?" he snorted, infuriated.

Next, it was Kizmel's turn: "But, Storyteller, you are said to be one of greatest minds in all of Lyusula. Do you not have any deductions, any hunches? We will take any clue we can get at this point."

"I can certainly do that much," Bouhroum admitted. He glared at the key in my hand. "From what I can see, those two keys were originally meant to be combined before use. The head and teeth of the keys are carved to align perfectly."

"Huh? Really…?"

I looked back and forth from my key to Myia's, but I couldn't tell from their appearance. And I couldn't test it, because they would hurtle away from each other. But I also couldn't imagine that the self-styled sage would just make something up off the top of his head, so I assumed that my hunch that they combined to take their true form was actually not far off the mark.

In that case, if we could undo the charm on the keys and combine them, we might gain some new clue or bit of information.

"Undo the charm, Gramps," I said promptly. He glared at me.

"It is not that simple. I just told you it was a *powerful* charm…I suspect that only the one who placed this charm can undo its effect."

"Aww...then tell us who put the—"

"*Kaaaah!*" he snapped, the familiar noise I heard multiple times during my Awakening training. Without getting out of the chair, he brandished a fist at me. "Just because I am a great and wise sage does not mean I know everything! I've told you all that I know about those keys!"

Or that you know anything, I snapped from the safety of my innermost thoughts. Once again, I considered the keys. Even Bouhroum's wisdom did not bring us much new insight, but on the other hand...without Morte's interference in killing Cylon, this was not an item that was officially meant to fall into player hands. So I couldn't complain too much about a lack of explanation.

Hopefully, the old man could at least live up to his billing with the other topic we wanted to hear about—but that remained to be seen. I grabbed Asuna's half-finished tea, downed the rest, and broached the second topic.

"By the way, Gramps...we'd like to ask you about a wicked dragon by the name of Shmargor..."

Ten minutes later, I left the library alone. Asuna, Kizmel, and Myia remained behind to train under the old man.

Our mission to ask about a means to counteract the fallen elves' poisoned needles was a success, if in a different form than what I expected. Bouhroum did not know how to craft the Platinum Shield that the ancient hero Selm supposedly used to protect against Shmargor's spikes, but he was able to suggest a substitute means of knowing. It was, in fact, through using the Meditation skill.

Training for Meditation was not as difficult as breaking the rock for martial arts. All you had to do was hold the pose that activated the skill for one continuous hour. In the beta, the sitting place was atop a pillar no more than fifteen centimeters wide, so it was difficult to get the hang of it.

But this time, when the ladies suggested learning the skill,

Bouhroum's method of training was to stay still for an hour atop some soft, poofy cushions on the floor. I couldn't help but yell about that one. But there was no point ranting about how *"the beta was different."* I wanted to observe this alternate training, but Asuna kicked me out of the room, claiming that it was embarrassing to have me watching.

Certainly, holding a Zen-like meditative pose wasn't exactly glamorous or cute, but if you wanted to use it in battle, you had to do that pose, regardless of location. I told her she needed to get used to the idea of people watching, but she shut me down and booted me out of the library.

At least I knew, given the cushy setting, that all three of them should pass the test on the first try. It seemed unprecedented that NPCs could pick up Extra Skills, but the bar for surprising me had risen considerably over the last few days. Nothing was going to truly shock me anymore unless you told me that, say, Kizmel and Myia were actually being controlled by human players.

But enough about that. I shook my head to clear it and headed for the windows on the southern side of the hallway. It was still before three o'clock, meaning the sunlight filling Castle Galey's courtyard was growing just a faint tint of gold, but there was still time until sunset. I wanted to put this extra hour to good use, but I didn't want to go grinding outside the castle, in case Asuna noticed my HP bar going down, and she got distracted by it.

"So my options are…nap or a snack…"

Three seconds later, I settled on snack. My store of sweet treats was rather lonely, but I could probably find something good if I went to the dining hall.

I walked west down the hall and went to the second floor of the center building. The dining hall was quite empty, because it wasn't mealtime, but when I sat down in a sofa along the wall, a servant approached at once. I asked for the dessert lineup, then selected a chestnut-and-walnut tart and an herbal tea.

The tart was a luxurious one, with sweet boiled chestnuts, fragrant cooked walnuts, and a heap of smooth sweet cream, and it quickly vanished into my virtual stomach. I sipped the sour tea and was considering ordering another tart when a strong desire to sleep hit me like a ton of bricks.

Suddenly, I recalled that I'd forced myself awake at two in the morning, went exploring around the rim of the castle, and completed Bouhroum's Awakening training in his little hidden room. Then I marched all the way to Stachion and returned not long after. After that hard schedule, it was no wonder that sitting on a comfortable couch and eating a piece of cake made me sleepy. I tried to resist, but the weight on my eyelids accelerated with each blink.

There would be another thirty…no, forty minutes until their Meditation training was over. Surely I was allowed to get a bit of a nap until then. If this was a restaurant in the real world, a stern waitress would be by to ask if I wanted anything else, but certainly the dark elf stewards would be nice enough to let me sleep……

Clang…clang…clang.

The sharp sound of the bell pulled me out of my comfortable slumber.

I tensed up at first, then realized it was just Qusack returning from their quest. I imagined it would have been tomorrow, but maybe they'd just rushed through the steps without any stops or side-questing along the way.

There I sat, pondering that idea with my eyes closed, half-asleep—when suddenly the speed and intensity of the ringing jumped in pitch: *Clang-clang-clang-clang-clang!!*

11

I LEAPED UP FROM THE SOFA AND SPRINTED ACROSS the dining hall to the door, almost entirely on autopilot.

The chilly air of the hallway helped to banish the last lingering embrace of sleep. I pounced toward the window across the hall and stared through the glass down into the courtyard.

The first thing I saw was the wide-open gates of the castle. The flickering white flashes I saw intermittently coming from there were definitely the visual effects of a battle.

I pushed open the window, hardly thinking about what I was doing, and the sound of sharp clanging and shouts rose in volume. The servants gathered at the doorway behind me shrieked.

Fighting at the inside of the gates were the familiar dark elf castle guards against a group of black-clad warriors with similar features but who sported distinctive face-covering masks. I squinted, focusing on the group, and saw a bright-red cursor appear with the subtitle FALLEN ELVEN WARRIOR.

Fallen elves!

I had an inkling it was them when I first saw them, but to have it spelled out officially by the system made the shock bigger. They'd led small ambushes and sneak attacks in the wilderness and dungeons before, but no large-scale assaults like this. They'd kept to the shadows in the background of the struggle between forest and dark elves. So why would they lead a head-on invasion of Castle Galey, perhaps the best-defended of the dark elf strong-holds? How had they gotten the guards to open the gates? And I thought the elves weren't supposed to be capable of getting through that barren valley without help...

The questions came hard and fast, but they weren't going to answer themselves if I just stood here and watched. I had to make a decision about what to do.

For the moment, the invasion seemed to be contained between the castle gates and the spirit tree's pool, but more and more fallen elves were pouring through the open gates by the moment. There had to be twenty at this point, possibly thirty. More guards were rushing forth from the palace to defend it, of course, but the Fallen seemed more powerful individually. I had a feeling that relying upon the guards to defend the castle might not be a winning strategy.

But my highest priority at this moment was the lives of Asuna, Kizmel, and Myia.

Working backward from that conclusion, I supposed we should try to escape the castle while the guards were still holding back the fallen elves. On the other hand, proud knight Kizmel would never flee and abandon her comrades, and Asuna would surely want to fight at Kizmel's side.

In any case, the first step was to regroup with them in the library. I pulled away from the window and began to run.

"Ah...!" I heard myself gasp.

The dark elf guards fighting at the courtyard line of defense fal-tered, three of them dropping at once. Their cursors showed their HP at still over half full. I was stunned, until I noticed a certain ominous icon blinking below the bars. Paralysis.

Some distance away, along the side walls of the castle, a num-ber of enemy elves labeled FALLEN ELVEN SCOUTS were throwing something at the guards. I couldn't see it from here, but I under-stood instinctually that it was those poison needles again.

The dark elf guards had metal armor on, but it was not full plate. Much of their arms and legs was uncovered, making for easy targets. The hole in the defensive line reformed with new guards, and the collapsed members were pulled back to safety, but it was clear that if too many more got paralyzed, the line would quickly crumble.

To regroup with Asuna or to rush to the aid of the guards? I myself was paralyzed with indecision for a moment, until at last I sucked in a sharp breath and broke into action.

I opened my window and plopped down onto the ground of the hallway. First, I sent a brief (possibly unnecessary) message to Asuna to FINISH THE TRAINING, then folded my legs into the Zen lotus position. In real Zen meditation, I was supposed to form an elliptical sigil with my hands, but in this world, I simply had to stretch out all my fingers and place my palms atop my upturned feet. This was the activation pose of the Meditation skill.

In the beta, you had to hold this pose for sixty whole seconds before the buff would take effect. Since there was no way to make that kind of time once battle started, it was quickly labeled a worthless skill, but now I had it leveled up to 500. That probably lowered the pre-activation time.

Please let me be right about that! I prayed. The system didn't respond, of course, but by the time I silently counted to twenty, an icon that I hadn't seen in several months appeared on my HP gauge. It was the silhouette of a person in a Zen pose: the Meditation buff.

If I was to take Bouhroum at his word, this buff could nullify level-2 paralyzing poison. If it didn't, that would be very bad news for me, but if I stood here and watched, the same thing would happen anyway. All I could do was trust the old man and act.

I undid the lotus position, stood up, and commanded the servants behind me, "Go to the storeroom and bring all the healing and antidote potions you can to the courtyard!"

Most of the servants shrank back toward the dining hall, looking terrified, but the oldest-looking of them all said bravely, "I understand. Come, you lot, let's go!" and lifted up her long skirt to run for the east wing. Her younger coworkers, properly chastised, shared a brief look before rushing after her.

I started running without a backward glance. I would have loved to jump down into the courtyard from the window, but the Fallen scouts would spot me. I wanted to get at least *one* by surprise.

I sprinted for the end of the west wing, sending a second message to Asuna in the meantime. Make sire all three of yuo have Med buff before going down to cortyard, I sent, too quickly to bother correcting my typos. Based on the present time, it had been about fifty-five minutes since they began Meditation training.

If the training was over the moment the bell started clamoring, then none of these instructions mattered, but the fact that there had been no response was a sign that the training still continued—I assumed. I had a feeling that the matter of whether Asuna's group gained the Meditation skill or not, and whether they could utilize it in time for the fight or not, would be the key to victory or defeat.

On I rushed from the main building to the west wing, leaping down the stairs ten at a time, when all of a sudden I heard a memory of my partner's voice in my head:

You're not going to rush off without a word to me again! You must be within my sight for all twenty-four hours. Is that understood?!

That had been three days ago...after we talked with the DKB officers in the inn room in Stachion. I'd kept to her command since then, excepting only unavoidable situations like the hot spring's changing room, but I'd assumed Castle Galey was safe and apparently let down my guard. Asuna told me not to watch them training, but there were all those bookcases in the library. I could have just waited around the corner of one.

And right during that lax hour, as if specifically timed, the fallen elves attacked. It was a coincidence, of course, but it felt like a sign. I picked up speed, trying to outrun my foreboding, and blazed through to the side door at the end of the west wing's first floor.

I had to put on the brakes, as satisfying as it would have been to kick down the door and rush through it. Instead, I opened it just a bit to check for the presence of nearby enemies. Because the side door was quite close to the interior wall, if I went out and headed along the wall, I should reach the scouts throwing the poisoned needles soon. But it was only half-past three in the afternoon, and there was little darkness that would hide my presence.

I couldn't wait until nightfall for cover, obviously. I just had to draw my blade and head out into the open.

A wall of sound met me there, swords clashing and bellows of combat and rage. I hunched against the noise and ran along the wall to my right.

The round hollow that entirely swallowed Castle Galey was a bit over two hundred meters across, and the spring that fed the spirit tree in the middle of its grounds was about thirty meters wide, so that made about eighty meters from the castle wall to the hot spring. The defensive line of the castle guards had already been pushed back over half of the way. If they managed to break into the castle, it would be very difficult to prevent the Fallen from reaching the treasure room on the fourth floor of the main castle building, where the four sacred keys were currently held.

We had to stop them in the courtyard. And eliminating the Fallen Scouts throwing their paralyzing needles was paramount.

As soon as I saw the first scout ahead of me, I went from staying low and quiet to a full-on spring. The scout sensed me and turned, wearing a mask with only holes for the eyes. He pulled a black pick from his belt and wound his arm back.

When I saw the glint of the throwing needle, a memory of three nights ago flashed back in my head. The feeling of being helpless on the ground, unable to move a finger, staring up at the horrifying sight of Morte approaching, became a liquid colder than ice that shot through my veins.

But I gritted my teeth, withstanding the fear, and readied my Sword of Eventide on high.

The Fallen Scout's hand blurred. A Spine of Shmargor coated with level-2 paralyzing poison rushed for my chest, whistling faintly. It was too late to dodge or defend.

If my Meditation buff didn't protect against this paralysis, I was going to land helpless on the ground in the midst of a chaotic battle.

There was a light impact below my left collarbone. A dark blot appeared out of the lower corner of my eye. But I cut off my sense of touch and sight, focusing my entire mind on the sword in my hand.

The blade shone blue. The invisible hand of system assistance pushed my body.

No paralysis!

"Go!" I shouted, the word trapped behind closed lips, and I activated the four-part slash skill, Vertical Square.

The scout's eyes widened just a bit when he realized I wasn't paralyzed. He reached behind his waist for a dagger, but it was too late. My first blow struck the scout's left shoulder, leaving a shining vertical line in the air.

In a single moment, my sword bounced back upward, completing slashes straight down and straight up, leaving parallel visual effects from head to toe. These three slashes took down nearly 60 percent of the scout's HP.

Then my sword returned to its original position and arched farther, nearly to my back, before unleashing the devastating fourth strike. Once again, I felt the hilt of the Sword of Eventide trembling in the palm of my hand. But rather than fighting against the sword's will, I added a boost of force to its adjusted course.

Zumm! The elf-upgraded blade dug itself heavily into the Fallen Scout's breast. The weak-point critical blow obliterated his remaining 40 percent. The completed square of blue light flashed brighter and dispersed, and a moment later, the scout's body shattered into countless pieces, too.

I'd killed over ten fallen elves since the start of the "Elf War" campaign quest. It was a simple matter, of course, as I had to do it to finish the quests—or so I had always assumed, but that probably still counted as a kind of murder.

Regardless, I couldn't stop now. I was helping the dark elves, and I had to protect Asuna, Kizmel, and Myia from harm. Asuna treated the NPCs as even more human than I did, and she wouldn't hesitate at all to fight against the Fallen.

Through the polygons melting into the air, I saw the other two Fallen Elven Scouts throwing their needles at the guards from the other side of the castle gates. I couldn't imagine that they hadn't noticed my attack, but for now, they prioritized helping their comrades fighting farther in.

For just an instant, I glanced left and saw that there were now slightly more red cursors for Fallen Elven Warriors than yellow cursors for the castle guards.

"…?!"

Before my gaze could return to the two scouts, I noticed something and squinted.

The fallen elf combatants, dressed all in black and fighting with their backs to me, had something odd tucked into their sword belts. They were narrow rods with brilliant-green shards of something tied to the top…No, those were not artificially fashioned objects. They were tree branches.

The branches were about a third of a meter in length with leaves on the end, as though broken off of any nearby tree. I wouldn't think twice of any player carrying the same thing around.

But the fact that these were fallen elves changed the situation. They, like all elves, could not harm living trees. I remembered General N'ltzahh saying as much in the submerged dungeon on the fourth floor, where the fallen elves were secretly buying lumber from humans. *Eons since we were removed from the blessing of the Holy Tree, yet, we are still bound by the taboos of the elven race.*

The secret of how the Fallen had moved through the canyons was probably—no, definitely—contained in those branches. However they had circumvented the taboo, they seemed to be protected by a kind of personal barrier cast forth by the branches. Which meant their next likely move was…

"Gaaah!"

A scream from the courtyard distracted me. A dark elf guard at the front line of combat collapsed on the ground, struck down by a Fallen Elven Warrior's curved blade. Before his companions could reach out to him, his body turned to blue shards and vanished.

"Damn...!" I swore, banishing the mystery of the branches from my head. Our first priority was to turn back the tide of battle. My Meditation buff would eventually wear off. I had to eliminate the other two scouts before it did.

I switched my sword to my left hand and pulled out the paralyzing needle stuck under my collarbone. It was still usable, so I wound up and threw it at one of the scouts located near the right-gate tower.

Until I used Meditation in my fifth skill slot, I'd been considering putting Throwing Knives in there. Thankfully, even without it active, the needle still managed to land in the left leg of the scout, who was a nice stationary target. He didn't seem to have any paralysis defense himself, and he collapsed without a sound after a green border appeared around his cursor. The other one rushed to give his partner a potion, but I was already charging at full speed again.

The last scout gave up on curing his partner and readied a dagger. I gave him a simple high slice. He evaded with a backstep rather than guarding it, but I was expecting that. When I froze briefly following my big swing, the scout deftly darted forward and whipped his dagger at me.

This fierce blow was a fair bit sharper than any I'd seen from the Fallen thus far, but I was already lunging into his range so I could pull off Flash Blow, the basic Martial Art skill I used against Morte.

The dagger grazed my right shoulder while my left fist slammed into his side. The NPC and monster algorithms, whether intended or not, had a habit of responding just a bit slower to sudden use of a different type of attack skill.

"Oogh…"

Flash Blow's damage wasn't much to speak of, but the scout grunted and froze. This would be my chance to use a sword skill…but instead, I reached around the scout's back with my free hand. As I expected, my fingers brushed what felt like a tree branch. I grabbed it and pulled it out of his belt.

I didn't expect this to cause the fallen elf to immediately collapse. After all, we were in the courtyard beneath the spirit tree's protection. They wouldn't need the branch unless they went back out the gate.

But the scout's eyes bulged behind the mask, and he shouted hoarsely, "Give it back!"

Before he could scramble and lunge for it, I held the tip of the Sword of Eventide to the elf's throat and demanded, "How did you get this branch?!"

"…That is nothing you need to know, human!" the elf spat, lowering his weapon in favor of dialogue. There were fires of hatred in his eyes. "And what business does *your kind* have in this fight?! The enmity between elves has nothing to do with humankind!!"

"'Your kind…?'" I repeated, sensing something off about this. I glanced around—but the only figure nearby was the third scout, paralyzed. Asuna and Myia had not joined the battle.

The scout clicked his tongue, angry that he had apparently spoken too much. He leaped backward to get away from the tip of my sword and readied his dagger again. Sensing that I wouldn't get any more information out of him, I held the branch high in my free hand. The moment his gaze traveled upward to follow it, I tossed it to the side and lunged.

The scout looked back, but it was enough to delay his reaction. I took advantage by using the close-range three-hit skill Sharp Nail. Three slashes of red light, like the claws of a fierce beast, glowed on the scout's chest, and he flew backward, slamming against the castle wall. When he bounced back to me, I added the single-strike Horizontal.

His torso cut in two, the scout silently came to an unnatural stop in midair and dispersed. I turned around as the shards enveloped me and ran.

The paralyzed scout had another branch behind his back, too. The paralysis status wasn't wearing off anytime soon, but the eye that was visible from this angle speared me with a look sharper than any throwing needle.

He would eventually recover, so I couldn't just leave this Scout untouched. If I simply pierced him through the heart while he was immobile, the continual piercing damage would be enough to kill him.

Instead, I stopped myself from raising my sword any farther. Perhaps it was a pointless fixation, perhaps even a harmful emotion, but I just couldn't bring myself to execute a helpless enemy like it was some kind of insect.

The scout had pockets for throwing needles on either side of his leather belt, and there were nearly ten Spines of Shmargor still inside them. I removed them all, stuck them in my own carrying pouch, took away his branch and black dagger, and tossed them into my inventory. I also found the other branch I'd tossed—and turned to inspect the battle.

The paralyzing needle sabotage was over, but the defensive line was pushed back to barely fifteen meters from the hot spring. If the guards fell into the water, the line would collapse, and the enemy could rush through. Once that happened, they could be at the castle entrance in moments.

There were about twenty-five Fallen Elven Warriors in combat and not even twenty castle guards fighting them back. About ten were paralyzed and dragged to the rear, and there were no more guards rushing out of the castle.

This was the full combat force of Castle Galey, because, sadly, I didn't expect that Count Galeyon himself would come rushing down to turn the tide of battle.

A few seconds later, I had the lay of the battle and pulled the paralyzing needles out of my pouch, intent on making good use of them. There were nine needles, plus the two I recovered from Morte and the two that the Fallen who attacked Myia's home left behind, for thirteen in total. If I could knock out ten warriors with those, we could turn this battle around. I aimed for the back of the closest target and threw.

The needle landed right on target, in the gap between armor pieces. The warrior froze for a moment...then continued swinging his scimitar as though nothing had just happened.

"Wha...?"

I held my breath, then noticed an unfamiliar icon on the warrior's HP bar. It looked like a black leaf; perhaps it was a paralysis resistance buff. I supposed that with all the needles the scouts were throwing from behind, a few might hit their own side. So it would make sense for them to have some kind of safety measure against that...but it also felt like a very clever strategy, almost *too* clever for NPCs.

And for another thing, I still didn't know how the fallen elves had gotten through the gates.

I was sleeping in the dining hall when the bell woke me up. But I recalled first hearing the normal tolling for the opening of the gates; only after a few moments did it turn into a rapid alarm bell. Did that mean the guards had opened the gates for someone who was allowed in, and then the Fallen rushed through? But there was no place to hide in the long, dusty canyon leading up to the gates. If dozens of enemies were running from the start of the canyon, there would still be time to let the guest in and close the gates before they arrived.

There was only one possibility.

Whoever got the gates to open was in cahoots with the Fallen... and at this moment, there was only one group of players this far along in the "Elf War" campaign quest: Qusack. If they went into the castle and took over the tower-gate room, they could ensure the gate remained open long enough for the fallen elves to arrive.

"...Is that really it...?" I asked myself, unable to believe it. I turned and raced to the nearby gate tower and opened the metal-reinforced door. I thrust my sword into the open space, but there was no one inside. If the dark elf who would have been here was murdered, there was no way for me to search for evidence.

I looked up to see that the tower chamber was packed with gears and weights and such over my head. On the wall straight ahead was a wooden lever that I yanked with all my strength.

With a heavy rumble, the gears overhead began to turn. That should at least close the gate and ensure that any potential Fallen reinforcements outside couldn't get in. I was worried about where Qusack might have gone, but the battle in the courtyard was the most pressing matter at the moment.

I leaped out of the tower and raced for the line of battle. If the paralyzing needles weren't going to work on those Fallen Elven Warriors, my trusty sword would have to do.

"Raaaaah!!"

I roared, power surging from deep in my gut, giving up my back-attack advantage. Three nearby enemies turned around and closed the gap. I hurtled into the middle of them, getting as close as I possibly could before activating the sword skill Horizontal Square. It didn't do as much damage to a single target as Vertical Square did, but it had a better accuracy and wider range.

The sequence of four horizontal slashes hit all three warriors, taking two-thirds of their health and hurling them backward. If I could use this newly learned skill over and over, I could probably take them all down, but it sadly had a cooldown timer to match its considerable strength, and I wouldn't be able to use it again for a bit. I would have to make full use of all the sword skills I'd learned so far. There were over twenty foes here, and if I got surrounded, I was instantly dead meat.

Two more enemies noticed my presence behind them. I used the long-range jumping attack Sonic Leap on one of them. That warrior guarded the attack, but his scimitar was weaker than the Sword of Eventide, and he faltered, unable to withstand the full brunt of my charge.

The instant that hateful post-skill delay let up, I used the martial arts kick Water Moon on the faltering warrior. My instinct measured the distance of the other enemy behind me—I spun and activated the two-part Horizontal Arc. The slashes left a sideways V in the warrior's chest. He flew through the air with a grunt.

It was too bad that I couldn't deliver him a finishing blow, but if I spent too much time on one foe, I would get surrounded. The three knocked down by my Horizontal Square were getting up now, I noticed, and so I used the low-to-the-ground charging attack Rage Spike on one of them.

My sliding dash was so close to the ground that it practically army crawled. The warrior tried to use the basic scimitar skill Reaver to fight back. If it hit me, not only would my skill fail, but I'd be put in a mild-stun status. So I twisted as I ran, trying to escape the path of the Reaver. On the other hand, if I strayed too far from the right motion, I would automatically fumble my sword skill. The pale-blue shine coating my sword flickered, letting me know that the technique was in danger of running out.

"Jyaaa!" the warrior roared, swinging down his blade that glowed a sinister orange. The sharp tip grazed my chest, taking away about 5 percent of my HP with it—but in return, my sword severed his left leg from the base. The warrior's remaining HP were gone, and his slender form crumbled like fine glass.

The beautiful, horrendous sound effect seemed to draw the attention of all the other Fallen fighting in the vast courtyard. One especially large one in the center of the fighting, who seemed to be the commanding officer, pointed his scimitar—more like a long saber—and shouted, "Get rid of that impediment first! Surround him on four sides and crush him!"

Instantly, four virtually unharmed warriors peeled off the line and came rushing for me. That opened a hole in their line, of course, but the Fallen still had the higher number.

One of the guards shouted "Protect the swordsman!" but it would be difficult for them to break through the Fallen line even with the hole. I had to deal with these four by myself—in fact, if I could just get through this oncoming rush, it would turn the numbers in our favor and make victory a possibility.

The fallen elves slid smoothly around me on either side. I still couldn't use Horizontal Square, my one good wide-range attack, so I backed off, looking for the right target to strike, but they were all dressed in matching black gear and hoods, with about the same remaining HP, so it was impossible to choose an obvious answer.

Behind the four, the warriors whose HP I'd halved were now retreating to the wall and drinking what appeared to be healing potions. If they got back to full health, and the four surrounding me turned to eight, it would be difficult to even escape, much less wipe them out.

The worst mistake to make in this situation was to be too hasty in knocking down the enemy numbers and to stop moving. As with monsters, the common wisdom was to keep moving, avoid being surrounded, and grind down the enemy HP, bit by bit. If this happened in a dungeon, other players might get mad, because you could easily build a "mob train" by drawing the attention of more and more monsters, but manners didn't mean anything here.

"…!!"

I sucked in a sharp breath and pounced off the stone ground, sprinting after the target I chose on pure instinct. The enemy raised his scimitar diagonally in a defensive position, while the other three rushed to get behind me. Their reaction speed and teamwork were much better than monsters', though one should expect that much.

The only plus, for whatever it was worth, was that none of the Fallen Elven Warriors had heavy gear or shields. Such fighters were very difficult to break down, but these ones only had metal light armor and their curved swords, which meant I could get past their defenses.

I charged straight ahead, sword hanging from my right hand. The warrior's eyes seemed to waver, losing their nerve. Perhaps he intended to defend my first blow, but charging without an attacking stance was introducing an element of uncertainty to the AI's algorithm.

When I was two meters away, the warrior finally entered an attacking stance. I accelerated as best I could and thrust out my open hand with my fingers formed in the shape of a capital C. I made sure to let the enemy's scimitar slip through that narrow gap and dispelled the primal fear of losing my fingers as I clenched down hard.

There was a silver flash in my hand, and I felt my grip and the warrior's sword become fused into one. I yanked the weapon out of the enemy's hand and flipped it around to grasp the hilt. This was the weapon-snatching skill, Empty Wheel, which I acquired when my martial arts skill reached a proficiency of 100, right in the middle of this very battle. Naturally, it was my first time using it, and if I hadn't ponied up the dough for Argo's info on martial arts, I might not have realized I had it available until the battle was over.

"How dare you, knave?!" snarled the warrior, who lunged for his weapon. I swiped at his arm with the Sword of Eventide and scored a severed part bonus. The warrior moaned, clutching his partially missing arm. I kicked him over and spun around.

The other three warriors showed no sign of slowing down after seeing my weapon-snatching trick.

"Shyaaa!"

I blocked a black-traced diagonal slash with the scimitar in my off-hand. The sparks of that impact splashed off my face as I slammed my sword into his side.

Sensing another attack to my right, I used the sword to block a horizontal strike. The warrior faltered, and I slashed at his neck with the scimitar I'd captured, then rushed through the gap between the two.

As long as I had the Sword of Eventide in my right hand and the fallen elf scimitar in my left, I was in an irregular equipping state, which meant I couldn't use any sword skills. But in a one-on-four battle, I didn't want to use any major skills that might lead to a significant movement delay afterward. On the contrary, having a sword in each hand gave me more options for defense.

I couldn't help but think that if I was going to go to these lengths, I could've just kept a shield around for my Quick Change mod, but I was still just good enough to block the quick, light slashes of the Fallen with a sword. Plus, I just felt like it suited me, having two swords so I could pull off a block-and-counter move with either hand.

Spinning around, I told myself that if I got through this fight, I should seriously think about practicing with two swords.

I found the unharmed fourth warrior in front of me, with two more damaged but fairly healthy warriors coming behind him. The one whose scimitar I stole rushed back toward his healing comrades, perhaps to borrow a weapon.

According to their cursors, their HP was already healed back up close to 70 percent. There was maybe a minute left until they were fully healed—I had to beat these three before then. But could I do that without sword skills? I'd already shown them everything I had.

It wasn't a question of whether I *could* do it or not. I just had to *do it.*

Standing still would only get me surrounded, so I focused on the warrior on the right and charged. They must have learned from my tendency to attack the sides, however, as they changed directions, too, to ensure that they were always coming head-on. But if I kept turning to the right, eventually I would get trapped against the castle wall.

Do I pull back? No, I don't have the time. I have to go straight through, into the melee, and hope I find the route to victory...

I was just about to launch into an all-or-nothing gamble when I heard a voice.

∗   ∗   ∗

"Kirito, watch out!!"

For an instant, I thought I was just hearing things. But my body reacted on instinct, hurtling me to the left.

Crimson red shone past my eyes.

The brightest visual effect I'd seen yet barreled down on the Fallen Elven Warriors from behind with breathtaking speed. There was a silhouette in the midst of that light that I couldn't make out from the brightness. The very air roared, and the stones beneath my feet trembled.

The three warriors turning to follow me noticed the abnormality and spun around. But by then, the red light was upon them.

"N'wah!" shouted the center warrior, lifting his scimitar. The other two took similar guarding positions.

Kabooom! With an explosive eruption, the center warrior rose high in the air. The two at his sides were thrown flat on the ground, and one tumbled all the way to my feet. Out of sheer reflex, I struck him with my right-hand sword, whittling away the last bit of his red HP bar.

I looked up through the exploding blue particles to see the intruder, blowing past like a runaway freight train, come to a stop in a whirlwind of dust about six or seven meters away.

A red hooded cape. A pleated skirt of the same color. Long, chestnut-brown hair. I didn't need to check her cursor to know that this was Asuna, my temporary partner.

But what sword skill was that just now…? I didn't recall any charging attacks that flashy in the Rapier category. The force and range of it were off the charts in comparison to her favorite, Shooting Star…

"Huh…?!"

The instant I saw it through the dissipating cloud of dust, I gasped.

The weapon Asuna had in her hands was not the Chivalric Rapier she used but an enormous lance that looked to be at least

two meters long. It had a dark-green leather grip, the body itself was a brilliant silver, and there was fanciful decoration around the base. It was clearly quite an excellent weapon based on the design, but my question was not where she got it, but how she was able to wield it so well.

At present, there were four skills involved with handling spear-type weapons. One-handed spears, two-handed spears, one-handed lances, and two-handed lances. Out of those, two-handed spears were the most typical. There were few spear users overall, but I could name Cuchulainn of the Legend Braves; Okotan the halberdier and Hokkai Ikura the trident user from the ALS; and Qusack's Highston, who used a glaive. All of those landed under the two-handed spear skill. There were even fewer one-handed spear users—aside from Schinkenspeck of the ALS, I could only think of one or two in the front-line group.

But the Lance skill was far rarer in the wild than even those. I had never yet seen a player on the frontier using a lance.

The reason for this was the small selection of weapons and how difficult they were to use. The only things that operated under the Lance skill were lances and guard lances, which had a larger hilt—both of which could only thrust. Not only were they difficult to wield in battle, but whether solo, in a party, or in a raid, there were no situations where a lance was crucial. So in the present *SAO*, where there was no room for picking hobby skills, they were a waste of a good slot...in my opinion.

"Why...? Where...? What...?"

That was all I managed to get out of my mouth from the rapid series of questions: *Why do you have that? Where did you get it? What is going on with your skills?* But Asuna seemed to catch the general gist of my shock, and when her long delay wore off, she turned to me and shouted, "I'll explain later! Watch my back!"

Indeed, with a two-handed lance that was longer than she was tall, turning around would be difficult. I rushed up toward her, then remembered that two of the three warriors she'd bowled over were still alive.

But I didn't need to finish them off.

I heard two crystalline ruptures behind my back, nearly in unison. Looking over my left shoulder through a cloud of texture shards, I saw Kizmel with her saber and Myia with a rapier.

"Sorry for being late, Kirito!" Kizmel shouted, while Myia nodded her head, still covered in that leather mask. The side door to the east wing was in the distance behind them, so they must have come from that direction. I assumed the skill training had gone well, because I could see the Meditation buff on their HP bars.

I'd cleaned up the three Fallen Elven Scouts who'd been throwing their paralyzing needles with abandon, but I couldn't guarantee that none of the remaining swordfighters had their own supply of needles. For the rest of this battle—and every other potential fight against the fallen elves—we had to have defensive measures against paralysis.

But these powerful allies coming to our aid at least made this an even fight. If Asuna could drive one or two of those heavy-charge attacks into more clumps of enemies, we'd win. I just had to watch my partner's back in the meantime.

"How many more seconds on the cooldown, Asuna?!" I yelled, sword in each hand.

Over my shoulder, I heard her say, "A hundred!"

"Got it!"

Twenty seconds had passed since her charge, so that meant the cooldown on the skill was two minutes, which was reasonable for a huge attack like that one. The guards should be able to hold out that long, plus five or six waitresses from the castle were coming out and giving potions to the paralyzed and injured guards who weren't fighting anymore. Sadly, their medicine didn't seem capable of instantly curing level-2 paralysis, but as long as we could hold the line where it was now, they would eventually recover.

"Coming from the south, Kirito!"

Kizmel's voice snapped me back to attention, where four Fallen Elven Warriors who'd been healing up were heading this way, though their HP was only at 70 percent or so. The one whose

scimitar I'd stolen was also there, with a borrowed dagger, bringing up the rear.

"Kizmel, Myia, swing around from the sides! Kirito, handle the
foes coming from the north!" Asuna directed. The elf knight and
girl warrior rushed off. After watching them go, I turned around
and saw two Fallen Elven Warriors peel off from the battle in
front of the hot spring pool and race toward us. They were working with the five to the south in an attempt at a pincer attack.

It was seven on four, but I knew we couldn't lose. Whittling
down the enemy numbers meant that the defensive line was
steadily recovering strength and pushing back.

"Stay out of this, humans!!"

Two warriors leaped at us, their voices full of rage. I blocked
their perfectly timed slashes with each of my swords. Yellow
sparks burned my eyes, and jolts ran from my elbows to my
shoulders, but I summoned all the strength in my body to resist
that pressure. I promised to watch Asuna's back, and I would not
give a single step.

As soon as I sensed that I'd withstood the full force of the
swings, I used the martial arts leg skill Water Moon, which was
the only skill I could use while holding two one-handed swords.
One of the warriors I kicked in the stomach stumbled but held
his ground, while the other flew off his feet and crashed to the
dirt.

On a sudden inspiration, I jammed the scimitar into the earth,
undoing the irregular wielding status, and used my longsword to
activate the Vertical Square sword skill, which had just cleared its
cooldown period. The warrior before me took all four slices and
exploded after being thrown to the ground.

When I could move again, I pulled out the scimitar and performed a series of consecutive swings on the other warrior as he
rose to his feet.

Of course, back in the beta, there had been players who tried
dual wielding one-handed swords. A major counterweight to the
drawback of being unable to use sword skills was the fact that

magical bonuses from both weapons would still apply. So if, for example, I somehow had two copies of my Sword of Eventide, I would receive a +14 bonus to agility, giving me a huge upgrade in mobility.

But as far as I knew, by the final day of the beta test, not a single player had emerged as a master of the art of fighting with two swords. I'd tried it out, but I found the experience of a sword in each hand to be jarring, like each half of my body was its own independent being.

Ultimately, the common understanding in the beta was that, at best, you could use one sword to defend while using the other to attack, and at that point, you might as well use a shield instead. And on the front line in the finished game, I had never seen anyone using two swords—if you excluded Argo, whose claws were really two weapons in one. Even in the case of claws, you would only be able to use them both within the confines of a sword skill.

But in this moment, I had unleashed a string of five or six swings before I finally realized that I was executing those forbidden simultaneous attacks. Immediately, I was plagued by that dissociative feeling again, and I accidentally dropped the scimitar from my left hand.

Fortunately, the last swing was enough to reduce the warrior's HP to zero. On instinct, I turned my face away from the exploding blue shards.

That made a total of six fallen elves I'd killed since the start of the battle. I would think nothing of killing demihuman monsters like kobolds and ichthyoids by the dozen, but in this case, I felt a kind of strange pressure weighing on me. I shook my head, dispelling the feelings of both dissociation and faint guilt, and looked to the south.

Asuna was just about to activate a new sword skill. Her two-handed lance, glowing green, plunged toward the five fallen elves whom Kizmel and Myia had maneuvered into one tight bunch. It wasn't as powerful as her earlier charge, but her tremendous reach and sharp point pierced the Fallen anyway. Then she pulled the spear back and darted it forward again. One more time…a three-part attack.

Once the last metallic sound finished echoing, three of the five fallen elves were down and bursting apart. The power was devastating; in a one-on-one fight, the nimble fallen elves would be a formidable enemy, but in a large group-on-group battle, when you had the option of trapping your enemy, no weapon could be more effective, it suddenly seemed to me.

But there was no way she'd learned a two-handed spear skill since the start of the battle. Based on the power and number of sword skills she was using, her proficiency with it had to be at least 100. And now that I thought of it, when we were talking about gained skills the other day, Asuna had said something odd…

That brief thought was interrupted by a new bursting sound. With blindingly quick attacks, Kizmel and Myia dispatched the remaining two foes. The warrior whose scimitar I stole never had the chance to use the dagger he borrowed. He had turned into fragments of data and been deleted.

We had defeated all seven of the warriors who peeled off to attempt that pincer attack. I turned back to count the number of living enemies, and a fresh bellow rang across the open courtyard.

"Sulaaaaaa!!"

I panicked at first, but this was not a fresh new batch of enemies, nor was it more guards coming to the rescue. The dozen-plus dark elf guards holding a desperate defense in front of the spirit tree's spring had all raised a yell together. I could see now that the numbers were roughly equal in the battle of the defensive line—and if you added the guards getting healed in the back, we actually had more. The Fallen commander bellowed to rally his warriors, too, but none responded in kind.

"Okay, let's beat that commander and break their…" I started saying to Asuna when something whizzed past my eyes. Then another…and another.

"Wha…?" Kizmel gasped and pointed into the sky.

When I followed her finger, I lost all speech.

Against the backdrop of the golden-blue base of the floor of Aincrad above us, countless little flakes spun and danced through the air. They were...leaves. The leaves of the spirit tree, which stood over the courtyard, were withering and falling off the branch.

I automatically reached out and grabbed one before it hit the ground. It was light brown and desiccated, and it crumbled in my fingers before melting into thin air.

I looked up again and stared closer at the tree itself, thirty or so meters above. There was no change to its trunk at this moment, but the leaves continued falling from its branches in all directions.

This couldn't be a natural phenomenon. It was January, too late in the season for the leaves to fall, and the spirit tree had never withered because it received constant life from the hot spring at its roots for centuries...

It was then that my eyes gaped, and I had a terrible premonition.

It couldn't be a coincidence that the fallen elves were attacking right as the leaves started falling off the spirit tree. If all the leaves fell, the "protection of the spirit tree," as Kizmel called it, would be lost, and Castle Galey would be the same as the dusty canyon outside its walls. A weakness debuff would affect all the dark elves in the castle, and the guards would obviously be unable to fight. But the fallen elves had those fresh-cut branches on their belts and could keep going.

That had been their plan all along. And the most likely way they could harm the spirit tree was...

"Kizmel, do you have your Greenleaf Cape?!" I shouted.

The knight looked back at me, startled out of her shock, but shook her head. "No...I returned it to the treasure room. Oh! If the spirit tree withers, then..."

"Right, that's what they're after. Here, Kizmel, take this," I said and, as quickly as possible, opened my window and took out the branch I had removed from the Fallen Elven Scout. Kizmel had noticed that the Fallen were wearing these things, and she looked slightly evasive.

"Did they cut those branches off of living trees…? But how…?"

"I don't know. But this is the only option you have…If all the spirit tree's leaves fall, I don't think the guards will be able to fight anymore."

I pressed the leafy branch into the knight's hand, then turned to Asuna with her huge lance and Myia in her gas mask. I couldn't help but feel very worried about Asuna being here. But Kizmel wouldn't abandon her comrades, and in any case, Asuna would not run away.

"Just hang in there…I'll be right back!"

"Where are you going, Kirito…?!"

"Underground!" I shouted as I ran off.

In moments, I was at full speed, racing through the falling leaves. The guards had paused when the abnormal phenomenon started and were starting to fight again, but the leaves would be gone within three minutes. There were still fifteen Fallen Elven Warriors, including their commander, and even with the three women present, it would be tough to eliminate them all within three minutes. I had to stop the withering of the spirit tree before then.

I readied my sword above my right shoulder, hoping to add at least one blow before I left. I steadied my aim, hearing the start-up sound of the sword skill, and activated Sonic Leap. It scored a clean hit on the back of a warrior standing apart from his group, sending him tumbling. I grabbed the branch from his belt.

"Aim for the branches on the Fallen's backs!" I shouted to the guards—and so that the Fallen would hear me, too—and rushed past the fighting toward the front entrance of the castle. No doubt it would be difficult to aim for the branches on the enemy's backs in the midst of battle, but at the very least, it should put some mental pressure on the Fallen. If they lost those branches, they would be just as susceptible to weakness when the spirit tree died.

I reached the entryway in seconds and handed over the branch I just stole to the waitresses helping the injured and paralyzed right next to the door. "If the spirit tree withers, gather everyone close around that branch!"

The range of the branch's effect would be very short, I was certain, but still enough to make a difference. Once the waitresses nodded, stunned, I rushed inside.

The first-floor entry hall was empty. Most likely, Count Galeyon and the high priests were barricading themselves up on the top floor. I didn't think they were going to hear out some human wanderer the way that Viscount Yofilis did, and if the tree withered, the count would be just as helpless as the rest of them anyway.

The stairs down to the underground hot spring were a little ways down the west wing hallway. I curved to the left and was speeding up again when I heard a familiar voice.

"Hey! Boy! Slow down!"

"…?!"

I went into a double-footed brake and looked up in the direction of the voice. On the second-floor terrace of the stairs in the atrium-style entry hall was a figure in a black robe, hands waving wildly.

"G…Gramps?! What do you want? There's no time for…"

But Bouhroum, the self-styled "great sage," cut me off with a desperate "I know that! I suspect the Fallen have dumped poison in the spring, and I know you're going down there! But you cannot fix it by yourself!"

"Th-then what can we do…?"

"Pour this into the spring!" he said, tossing something that looked like it was made of glass from the terrace.

If this was a quest with a proper storyline, then failing to catch the object would immediately fail the quest, I knew, so I dropped my sword and used both hands to catch the ball of glass.

It turned out to be a round-bottomed flask about ten centimeters across. There was a cork plugged tight into its short neck, and it was full of a deep-green liquid. Based on appearances, it was very poisonous.

I wanted to ask him if this was really safe, but there wasn't a second to waste. Deciding to take the word of the sage for properly training Asuna and the others in the Meditation skill, I picked up my sword and made to leave.

"All right, I'll do it!"

"Very good, boy!"

With that, I resumed running. A downward staircase appeared on the right side of the hall, and I practically tumbled down the steps to the basement. I had to be as cautious as possible while running down the hallway with its reddish lamps. The Fallen could be lurking anywhere from this point on.

At the end of the curving corridor was the large door to the underground hot spring. White steam wafted out from the open door.

"Ooh…"

I covered my mouth with my sword hand on instinct. Before, it had only smelled like spring water, but now there was an unpleasant odor mixed in. Something like drying mud—a musty, moldy smell.

I stopped at the entrance, listening closely before I entered. There was no one in the spacious lounge area, but the stench was sharper here. If the smell was coming from the pool the spirit tree's roots drank from, there wasn't a moment to waste. I threw open the far door, raced through the empty changing room, and went into the great subterranean dome…

"…!!"

I clenched my jaw when I saw it.

The pure, milky-white water of the spring was tainted and black. Thick, sticky bubbles rose to the surface, emitting a gray miasma when they burst. The roots hanging from the domed ceiling were nearly four-fifths black, no doubt due to sucking up the polluted water. If I didn't purify that water now, that centuries-old tree was going to die within a minute.

But I couldn't move forward.

Ahead of me on the stone tile walkway, near the lip of the water, stood a man.

He wore full-metal armor, a shortspear in his right hand, and a tower shield in his left. His face was aged, and his chin sported a short beard.

It was the leader of Qusack, Gindo.

The spearman eyed me warily.

"Get out of the way," I said.

But Gindo just pointed his large shield in my direction and rasped, "No…I can't move until those roots have completely rotted away."

That made it essentially certain that Gindo had dumped the poison into the hot spring. But the color cursor over his head was green. So whoever went into the gate room of the tower and either killed or drove out the dark elf guard so that the gate would stay open, it wasn't him. It must have been one of his three other companions.

In any case, Qusack had me fooled entirely. Bitter regret and sour hate flooded my mouth. "Are you…*helping* the fallen elves? Or are you part of that PK gang…?"

Whatever I expected out of Gindo, it wasn't this. "No way…neither! I…we didn't even know that people were PKing in Aincrad. So I…I never suspected him of…"

"…Him? Who…?"

But I didn't have time to keep talking. There wasn't a second to waste. In the courtyard just above us, Asuna, Kizmel, Myia, and the guards were fighting desperately to save the castle. From what I could see on their HP bars, they hadn't lost too much, but if the spirit tree died, and the guards could no longer fight, my party members would be in grave danger.

"…I don't have time to talk with you. If you don't move now," I said, lifting my sword and pointing it at the man who stood five meters away, "I will move you by force."

If I attacked Gindo, who had a green cursor, mine would turn orange. But I would do the alignment recovery quest as many times as it took to keep Asuna and the others alive.

In response, Gindo adjusted his tower shield, which stood over one meter tall. He wasn't going to budge until that tree had withered up. It wouldn't be easy to break through his defense, but if it came down to it, I could use a series of sword skills to smash the shield...

An idea popped into my head, and I looked at the sword in my right hand.

I returned it to the sheath over my back without a word, opened my window, and put the flask in my inventory. When he saw me barehanded, Gindo let a flash of uncertainty cross his face that I did not miss.

Instantly, I was flying. Gindo frantically tried to raise his short-spear, but I jumped to the right, hunching into the blind spot his large shield created. Then I darted forward again, putting both hands on the shield and pushing with all my might.

Within the Anti-Criminal Code zone, even the strongest player could not force other players or NPCs out of their personal space. The action of planting your feet in place fixed your personal coordinates and made the game treat you like any other immovable object.

But outside the safe-haven area, that system did not apply. And even I did not know where the line between simply pushing a person and committing a crime lay. If you pushed someone off a high ledge and caused fall damage, you would definitely turn orange, but this seemed safe to me...

"Yaaaah!"

I bellowed, summoning all the power from my gut, and pushed on the heavily armored warrior, whose gear had to be twice the weight of my own. Out of a difference of strength or simple surprise, Gindo faltered backward and couldn't recover, sliding bit by bit. He put up a brief moment of resistance at the lip of the walkway, then fell back first into the filthy black water.

A huge plume of liquid shot up, and then Gindo's face emerged from the water.

"Bwah!"

He spat and flailed his hands, but because of the weight of his plate armor and tower shield, he couldn't keep himself afloat. Fortunately (I supposed), the blackened water was smelly but apparently not poisonous to players, because no debuff icon appeared on his cursor. Belatedly, I realized that if his HP ended up going down, I could have gone criminal, but at least for now, I wasn't suffering any alignment loss.

I ran my fingers across my open window and materialized the flask I'd just placed in it. Quickly, I popped the cork out and poured the green liquid into the hot water.

White smoke practically exploded out of the water where it landed, causing me to turn my face away. Gindo's struggling figure was engulfed in the smoky steam. The reaction quickly spread across the vast pool of water, painting white over my entire field of view.

It reminded me of a prank I played as a kid with my little sister Suguha, when we dumped a huge block of dry ice into the bathwater.

"…I hope you know what you're talking about, Gramps," I muttered.

There was no response, of course, but a few seconds later, the first change I noticed was not in the sight of the spring, but the smell. The stench hanging thick in the dome rapidly began to reverse, replaced by a fresh, woody smell, like a forest after the rain. Eventually, the white cloud dispersed, allowing me to see once again.

Within moments, the poisonous swamp of the hot spring underwent a dramatic transformation. The greenish water was now clear again, the paved stone floor crisply visible, and the nasty smell was completely gone. The bundles of hanging roots from the ceiling were still blackened at the top, but even that was slowly fading. It seemed that we had avoided the nightmare scenario of the spirit tree withering away completely.

I checked the HP bars of my party members again and, satisfied they were still holding out at around 70 percent, breathed a sigh of relief. A dark elf victory was surely guaranteed at this point, but with other players involved, there was no telling what might happen next. I had to return to the courtyard and help eliminate the Fallen.

I turned on my heel, then paused and looked back to Gindo, who was no longer struggling. The heavy warrior, resting on his knees in the water, turned his face up toward mine, and at the bare minimum of volume needed to be audible, muttered, "Now...they're all going to die."

"What...? Who is?" I asked.

His face was sunken, like the soul had drained out of it, with just a touch of anger and despair.

"Who do you think? My friends. Lazuli, Temuo, Highston... They've been given poison. They're being held prisoner."

12

BY THE TIME I GOT BACK TO THE COURTYARD OF Castle Galey, there were only three Fallen Elven Warriors left. Unsurprisingly, one was the commander with the long saber. The actual surprise was who I saw them fighting *with*.

Decked out in shining silver armor and a blue cape, swinging a slender longsword, was none other than the master of the castle, Count Melan Gus Galeyon. He'd lost nearly 20 percent of his health, and his swinging was rusty, but the Fallen commander was down in the red, and I wasn't worried about a comeback. The other two enemies were surrounded by guards. The majority of the spirit tree's leaves had fallen from overhead, but at least the damage had stopped.

A quick scan of the courtyard showed me that Asuna, Kizmel, and Myia were helping the servants tend to the wounded. I also saw Bouhroum nearby.

When I rushed over, the sage was as self-important as ever. "It's good to see you know how to follow directions, boy. I had to break into little Melan's bedchamber to rouse him from his hiding place and shame him into joining the battle."

I watched the old man cackle, then looked to Count Galeyon fighting bravely—and back. "Actually...since you're wiser and greater than the master of the castle, I have a request of you..."

"Hmm? And what would that be?" Bouhroum asked suspiciously.

I leaned over to his long ear, partially hidden behind his white whiskers, and whispered, "Give me the four keys you're keeping in the treasure room."

"Wha...?!" the old man started to shout, until I covered his open mouth with my hand.

"Please! My friends...er, more like some acquaintances, are in mortal danger. I'll give them back once I've saved them!"

In the moment, I completely forgot that the old man in front of me was an NPC.

If I had been thinking straight, I would know that an NPC acting along rules laid out for him would never assist in an act of thievery. But the last few days, the actions and statements of the NPCs we'd met didn't have that same sense of programming. There was something too human about the way they acted.

Count Galeyon, who was fighting the commander of the Fallen now, had seemed like nothing more than a quest-giving NPC when we first met him, reciting canned lines as directed. But watching him now, the way he fought awkwardly but with hints of desperation, painted a vivid portrait of a man with a pampered upbringing doing his best to live up to his lordly role, inexperienced at combat but spurred on by his stern elderly teacher. Earlier, I had thought that Kizmel and Viscount Yofilis were the only special NPCs I'd met, but after Bouhroum and Myia, it began to feel as though *all* the NPCs living in Aincrad were actually like that.

Bouhroum answered my plea with a fierce glare and a grumble. "Hrrrmmmm..."

"Look, I know it's a crazy request. But it's the only way..."

"Hmm. Very well, then."

Huh?!

It was that simple, apparently. He glanced at Asuna, who was feeding a guard a potion, and muttered, "The lance I lent to that young lady came from the treasure room, too. Wait right here."

Bouhroum turned, black robes twirling, and began running for the front entrance. Gindo had been watching from the shadow of the massive door and pulled his face back in a hurry, but the old man paid him no mind and disappeared into the castle.

Just then, there was a great cheer across the courtyard. Count Galeyon had defeated the enemy commander. At last, the two remaining warriors threw down their scimitars and surrendered.

We had successfully avoided the collapse of Castle Galey, but the fight wasn't over yet. The unnamed man who had abducted three members of Qusack and threatened the remaining one into opening the gates needed to be dealt with, once and for all.

I took a deep, slow breath, let it out, and headed toward Asuna to explain the situation to the others in my party.

Five minutes later, I was rushing quickly through the dusty canyon outside Castle Galey with Asuna, Kizmel, and Myia in tow.

Thirty meters ahead was Gindo, lighter now that he had removed his tower shield and plate armor. I warned him that he'd be in great danger if the monsters attacked him while alone, and therefore he shouldn't run, but his pace was clearly picking up. The giant arthropods that populated the canyon used vibration for targeting more than sight, so you could avoid them by being quiet and careful, but he was beyond caring about that.

I understood how he felt, but if he drew the attention of monsters, we'd have to step in to save him, and that would cause trouble if the enemy saw us. I didn't see anyone scouting out up ahead, but there were dozens of little hollows and shadows that a player could be hiding in.

"...By the way, whatever happened with that dark elf escort that Qusack had around?" Asuna wondered.

I repeated what Gindo had told me. "He died in battle when they got attacked by monsters in this canyon, apparently... That's when an unfamiliar man showed up and saved them, according to him, but I'm betting that he rounded up those monsters and set them on Qusack in the first place."

"Is this the same man who killed Myia's father and tried to kill you and Asuna?" Kizmel asked.

Without thinking, I put a hand on Myia's shoulder and nodded. "Technically, I'm thinking of the boss of the people who killed Cylon. Asuna and I call him the man in the black poncho. He usually doesn't fight for himself but plots in secret and sets people and groups against one another."

"Ah...He sounds like one of the demons of the ancient myths."

"D...demons?"

That reminded me that I still hadn't seen any real demonic-type monsters yet in Aincrad. I glanced over at Kizmel, and she nodded and continued, "Deep underground in the earth of old, there was a subterranean realm where wicked demons and devils were said to live. Occasionally, they would rise to the surface, disguising themselves as beautiful humans and elves, and, by taking the places of nobles or military leaders, would then sow discord among the innocent."

"Yikes...that sounds exactly like the black-poncho man," Asuna, on my left, remarked with disgust. "I...I hope he's not a *real* demon..."

I couldn't tell if she was talking about the man in the black poncho being not a player but an NPC from some long-dormant demon race of Aincrad, or if she was suggesting he might be a real-life demon wearing a NerveGear and logging in to *SAO*. Obviously, I wasn't going to ask, so I focused on Gindo's back far ahead of us.

"Once we pull that poncho's hood off, we'll know," I said, half-joking.

To my surprise, Myia nodded and said, "When I was little, Mother read me a story that had a demon in it. I think that if he has pointy horns on his head, he is a demon."

It sounded like an innocuous comment, but she was talking about the boss of the people who killed her father. And I had to repay him for sticking a knife to my back in the streets of Karluin. It was tough enough just trying to beat these floors; we didn't need to deal with a bunch of PKers trying to stir up trouble on top of that. If the man in the black poncho had kidnapped the rest of Qusack on his own, then this would be the perfect chance to settle the score with him—once the other three were safe, of course.

"Whether demon or human, he's a dangerous foe. I'm looking forward to your help, Myia, even though I know you're tired." I patted her on the shoulder and let go. The little girl in the gas mask nodded, as did Kizmel and Asuna.

In all honesty, what I really wanted to do was take Asuna aside and ask her about the two-handed lance skill, but it was hard to talk about game systems in front of the NPCs. When I came back from the hot spring to the courtyard, there was no sign of the giant lance that Bouhroum had supposedly taken from the treasure repository, but I bet it was in Asuna's inventory, so there would be another chance to ask. Everything could wait until we'd rescued Lazuli, Temuo, and Highston.

According to Gindo, after the swarm of monsters attacked and the dark elf bodyguard died, a cloud of odd-smelling smoke had swept through, along with a voice that said "This way." They ran in that direction to escape, where they saw a "handsome player with a charming smile," who then guided them to a cave at the end of the canyon. Once they'd relaxed, knowing they were safe, the man had handed them potions, which paralyzed them.

Then he dragged Gindo out of the cave, and with the same smile, told him the conditions he needed to fulfill to recover his guildmates. Gindo would return to Castle Galey alone and poison the underground hot spring. Then, once all the dark elves in the castle died, he could return. Alternately, if the fallen elves all died in the attack, he could steal the four sacred keys from the treasure chamber during the chaos of the battle and deliver them to the cave. Only when one of those conditions was fulfilled would his friends be returned to him alive…

When Gindo finished explaining the situation, my first thought—recollection, really—was of the former blacksmith and chakram user of the Legend Braves, Nezha.

He had described the man in the black poncho who brought the upgrade-scam idea to the Legend Braves as a movie star–beautiful man with a pleasant smile. I'd never seen his face myself, but it seemed obvious that Gindo's "handsome player with a charming smile" was the same person. How charismatic did this guy have to be to get so many players to drop their guard around him?

Maybe he really was a de—

But I had to stop myself from thinking that. Whether demon or human, if he had an HP bar, he could be defeated. I had hesitated when I fought Morte, but I wouldn't make that mistake twice. I'd killed six fallen elves in the battle at Castle Galey, even knowing that there was no fundamental difference between their lives and the lives of players in this world.

Up ahead, Gindo pointed his shortspear upward and changed course. That was the signal that the destination was close. It had only been ten minutes since leaving the castle, and even avoiding battle, we hadn't covered much more than half a kilometer. A giant scorpion plodded along the right side of the ravine, so we snuck past it, hugging the left wall, and came to a stop at the branching path Gindo had gone down.

We peered in, hunched together, and saw that the path came to an end just twenty meters or so in, with a yawning cave mouth in the middle of the rock face. That would be where the other members were held captive. Gindo opened his window outside the entrance, equipped his plate armor and shield, and started walking in.

If the man in the black poncho or his friends were near the cave's entrance, he was supposed to raise his spear to point up again, but it was still dangling toward the ground. Our plan was for Gindo to exchange the four keys for his companions, and once the other three emerged safely from the cave, we would charge inside. The cave was a dead end, too, so we didn't have to worry about the poncho man escaping.

It was possible that the black assassin would take the keys and immediately break his promise, but if so, we would rush in immediately. Gindo was registered in our party now, so I could see his HP in real-time, and given his defensive focus, even an enemy over level 20 couldn't kill him in a single instant.

Gindo slowly approached the cave. As soon as he crossed the threshold between orange sunset-lit sand and the shadow from the tall cliffs, the spearman sank into dark gray.

"...Hey, Kirito," murmured Asuna to calm her nerves as she crouched below me, "I've been wondering...it's the fallen elves who want the hidden keys, and the man in the black poncho is helping them with that, right?"

"Hmm...I suppose so. He shouldn't have any particular interest in the warfare between the two groups of elves. Maybe in exchange for helping the Fallen, he and his buddies have been getting those daggers and paralyzing needles?"

"But the fallen elves who attacked at Myia's house in Stachion were after the iron keys that you and she carry. They're only related to Stachion's curse, so why would the Fallen want them? You don't think those iron keys are the two remaining sacred keys, do you?"

"No...that can't be the case," said Kizmel, who was practically leaning onto my back to peer down the canyon tributary. "The Ruby Key and Adamantine Key are safely contained in the shrines on the seventh and eighth floors. No human would know the location of the shrines or what to do with the keys should they find them."

"Yeah...good point," I said, choosing not to point out that the first half of her statement was definitely untrue. Any player who beat the "Elf War" campaign quest in the beta would know where the seventh- and eighth-floor shrines were—like me.

But the two iron keys had been in the possession of Myia's mother, Theano, and Lord Cylon, not players, and only elves could go up floors while the labyrinth tower of the sixth floor was still unconquered. So if the keys Myia and I had were not the sacred keys, but the fallen elves wanted them for some reason, that meant...

Just then, Myia piped up from below Asuna. "Oh…look, everyone…"

I returned my attention to the back of the canyon. Gindo still wasn't in the cave; for some reason, he was standing still a few meters from the entrance. Either he'd spotted something, or…

But the premonition I felt was immediately disproved—a familiar bunch of faces emerged from the darkness of the cave.

The ponytailed woman was Lazuli. The shaved-headed one was Temuo, and the long-haired one was Highston. Their weapons were taken away, but their armor was the same. The awkward wobbling in their steps wasn't an effect of the paralyzing poison but probably a mental thing.

I was relieved at first that the other three were safe, but then I became very suspicious.

Gindo hadn't given the man in the black poncho the four keys yet. Why were the hostages released? Were the keys just an excuse, and all he really wanted was the gate of Castle Galey opened?

But the fallen elves were defeated, and the spirit tree had just barely survived. Nearly ten of the guards had perished, but I doubt that was the extent of what he wanted to achieve.

It didn't add up, but at least the rest of Qusack were safe. Gindo tossed his shield aside and rushed to them, taking their hands. After rejoicing in their reunion, he turned and waved to us.

"…I suppose there's no reason to hide anymore," Asuna said. I agreed and straightened up. Once Myia had stood up from the gravel, we headed into the branching path. At the end of the little ravine, Gindo greeted us with a teary smile.

"Thank you…thank you so much. Because of you, we're all alive and well."

"No…we didn't do anything…" I said, scratching my head.

Highston, who looked a bit on the pale side but had nearly full HP, said, "The man who poisoned us left the cave about five minutes ago. I think he knew you guys were trailing Gin, and he ran off. So you see, it *is* thanks to you."

"…Well, if he knew we were following, that's a problem in

itself," I muttered, looking around. Five minutes was a tricky amount of time—enough to cover a good distance at a sprint, but at walking speed, he might still be close. Then again, the cave and the branching path were a dead end, so if he'd taken a leisurely exit, we would have seen him.

"Did it seem like the black-poncho man got a message before he left?" Asuna asked. Lazuli shook her head.

"No, he was totally quiet after he took Gin out, and he pricked us with these poison needle things every now and then...then, a little while ago, he just stood up and left the cave. When the paralysis wore off, and we stepped out, there was Gin..."

"......Oh..."

But there was still suspicion in Asuna's features. Kizmel and Myia were looking around a slight distance away, as if they didn't feel entirely safe. If the black-poncho man was using his Hiding skill nearby, it *should* be impossible for him to sneak up on us in this place without drawing attention, but there were no sure things in this world.

Meanwhile, Gindo seemed totally relieved and relaxed. He walked over to me, blinking rapidly, and bowed. "I owe you all so much for this. This experience has been a painful lesson...We weren't ready for the front line yet. We'll go back to the fifth floor, finish up the quests that are left, and build ourselves up from scratch again...Oh, right. You can have these back."

He opened his window and produced a small leather bag. I peered inside and saw the green, blue, yellow, and black sacred keys.

"All accounted f..."

I paused. If he had switched the keys out for fakes in his inventory, there was no way for me to discern the difference. I couldn't rule out the possibility that they were aligned with the man in the black poncho and that this was all a big act to steal the keys from us.

"...Um, hang on. Sorry, can I just check something?" I asked, but Gindo didn't seem upset at all.

"Sure, of course."

"Okay..." I said, then beckoned Kizmel over and showed her the bag. "Can you check to see if these are the real keys or not?"

"I can do this, but as I said earlier—" the knight began with a shrug—when just to our left, the sand erupted upward from the ground.

"...?!"

I leaped back to see the reddish-brown sand being sucked up into a little vortex. A whirlwind? But I'd never seen that happen in these canyons before...

The moment I saw the dull shine in the midst of the two-meter-tall sandstorm, I shouted "Defense!!" and pulled out my Sword of Eventide, gripping it with both hands.

I held the sword in front of me and positioned Asuna behind my back; at my side, Kizmel drew her saber and took position in front of Myia. The members of Qusack were farther away—all I could do was hope that Gindo used his huge shield to protect his friends.

The sand whirlwind split top and bottom without a sound, and crimson light shot forth.

It was a sword skill. A rotating area attack—the scimitar's Treble Scythe...except, it wasn't.

No, this was the heavy area attack of the Katana skill, Tsumujiguruma.

Deep, almost unprecedented shock shattered what few thoughts I could manage. I held my sword in both hands but couldn't brace myself. Sparks burst before my eyes, an incredible jolt ran from my wrists through my shoulders, and my back collided with Asuna as we flew a good six meters and sprawled onto the gravel.

I rolled several times and managed to stop on my knees. I'd guarded the attack itself but still lost about 20 percent health, and on the ground nearby, Asuna was down 10 percent. Kizmel managed to stay on her feet, but she'd been pushed back a good distance in her defensive position, and Myia had fallen onto her bottom behind her.

A glance over my left shoulder showed me that Qusack had fallen back but was otherwise fine...except that the top quarter of Gindo's tower shield was gone.

Ahead, the sand had fallen back to earth, revealing our attacker. It was *not* the man in the black poncho.

The figure's body was thinner than Kizmel and wrapped in studded dark-gray leather. A hood of the same color covered shoulder to head, but the figure was clearly feminine. Her weapon, outstretched after the swing, was indeed a katana. It was only the second time I had seen that rare weapon type in the launch version, after the huge *nodachi* used by the first-floor boss, Illfang the Kobold Lord.

The attacker straightened up from her deep kneeling position with feathery lightness and pulled the hood off with her free hand. Ash-gray hair fell over her forehead, shining brilliantly in the setting sun.

Her bangs were longer on the left side from my perspective, hiding nearly half her face but not her stunning beauty. I searched for her color cursor.

It was...a blackish-red the color of dried blood. Her name was *Kysarah: Fallen Elven Adjutant.*

I recognized that name. It was the woman elf who had been with Fallen General N'ltzahh when we saw him in the submerged dungeon on the fourth floor. And it was only at this point that I realized I'd left one big mystery unsolved until now.

Gindo had fallen into the black-poncho man's trap with his companions held hostage and returned to Castle Galey alone as ordered. The guards had opened the gate for him without skepticism, because he had the sigil ring. That was the moment the ordinary gate bell had woken me up in the dining hall. I recalled that it turned into the rapid warning bell barely ten seconds after that.

It was impossible for a whole battalion of fallen elves to race all the way through the canyon to the castle gate in ten seconds. As I initially supposed, someone must have passed through the gate with Gindo and killed the dark elf in the gate room. But that person never made an appearance during the battle, leaving me guessing to the end.

Now I knew that this katana-wielding woman was the one who had attacked the gate room. I didn't know why she hadn't taken part in the battle in the courtyard, but it was quite possible that if she had, the Fallen would have won.

The elf looked around with bluish-purple eyes like ice in darkness, then stuck the end of her black katana into the sand nearby. When she raised it again, it lifted up the leather bag that fell from my left hand when we were attacked. She flipped it up into the air and caught it, four sacred keys still contained within.

"……Thirty of my brethren died so I could gain these…"

The voice that came from her thin lips contained a sweetness in the midst of its harsh bite. The moment she heard that, Kizmel recovered from her frozen shock and brandished her saber.

"You…you're General N'ltzahh's aide, Kysarah the Ransacker!" she shouted. "Return that bag to the ground! It is not meant to be touched by the likes of you!"

But Kysarah did not bat an eyelash. She fixed Kizmel with that icy gaze and answered in a flat affect, "Knight of Lyusula, I am afraid I do not know your name. And I will not be returning the keys…They are necessary for the sake of our great desire."

"Then I will force you to return them…by my sword!" Kizmel said, already charging. In my head, I knew I should be attacking at this same moment, but my avatar wouldn't listen to me.

Kizmel's attack was tremendous, worthy of the title of royal guard. It wasn't a sword skill, yet the tip of the saber as it cut through virtual air shone silver, and the breeze it created brushed my face, many meters away.

Claaang! There was a nasty ringing, along with a sound like metal screaming.

"…!"

I heard Asuna gasp into my left ear. The moment Kysarah lifted her katana with one easy motion to block the attack, a crack ran

down the length of Kizmel's saber blade. It was a sign that a weapon's durability was just about to run out.

Kizmel floated backward, gnashing her teeth. She still had the saber at the ready, but one more good blow would easily shatter it.

Kysarah, meanwhile, lowered her katana with nary a care and stuck the bag of keys into her waist pouch. Her gaze traveled from Kizmel to Asuna and me, then to the members of Qusack. At the foot of her knee-high boots, another little dust devil kicked up... and then she moved with alarming speed, stopping right next to Gindo's group.

"Aaah! Aaaaaaah!" screamed Temuo. Kysarah grabbed him by the back collar of his breastplate with her free hand and easily hoisted him up. He swung his arms around, struggling to break free, but went absolutely still the moment she pressed the tip of her katana to his throat.

"...I can kill you all right now, but I do not have a taste for murdering children, and my branch is about to run out of life."

Belatedly, I realized that Kysarah had one of those tree branches behind her back, too. If I could steal that, then Kysarah would suffer the weakness debuff and be unable to move, since she did not have a Greenleaf Cape like Kizmel did.

But I also couldn't move with the katana at Temuo's neck. If he were a player of Kysarah's level, his HP couldn't be reduced to zero in a single instant, even if she attacked a vital point. But based on the strength of the katana, which nearly destroyed Kizmel's saber in one hit, and the fact that to my level-21 eyes, her cursor was nearly black, she might indeed be able to inflict an instantly fatal blow.

"Among you, there are two other keys, not sacred but made of iron, that fit together as one," Kysarah said, still dangling Temuo in the air. It took me an extra second to understand what she meant. My shoulders twitched inadvertently, and Kysarah turned her visible blue-purple eye right on me. "You will give them to me, too. For every ten seconds that I do not have them, I will kill one of your acquaintances."

Temuo promptly struggled again, and Lazuli uttered a quick scream. Highston, who was sitting on his knees in the sandy gravel, looked from Kysarah to me and back and said in a tremulous falsetto, "This...this is a forced event from the "Elf War" quest, right?! Someone's...someone's gonna save us, right?!"

I wanted to believe so. But I was pretty sure—no, dead sure—that this attack did not have anything to do with the proper story scenario of the campaign. It was an irregular outcome as a result of the black-poncho man and his PK gang making contact with the elves. It was an incident.

...Seven...Eight.

When the count inside my head reached nine, I bolted to my feet. "All right. I'll give you the keys."

Once I said so, I realized that Kysarah was an NPC, and she might carry out the ten-second limit in a very literal sense. If she didn't receive the keys within ten seconds and have their ownership transferred to her in the system, she might slaughter Temuo without mercy...At least, if this were a fully scripted event.

But ten seconds had already passed by the time I told her I'd give her the keys, and she merely nodded and didn't move her katana. Convinced anew that this was not some pre-scripted event, I moved as quickly as I could in pulling the iron key out of storage anyway.

I tossed it into the sand at Kysarah's feet, and another one flew forward from behind me, sticking into the surface near the first. That was the key Myia got from her mother. The keys faced each other at a distance of about a third of a meter, ringing and reverberating.

Kysarah glanced down, then tossed Temuo toward his friends with one hand. Gindo opened his arms but failed to catch the man, and they crashed backward onto the ground. There was no HP loss, fortunately.

The fallen elf crouched, all interest in her hostage lost, and reached out for the closer of the two keys. Suddenly, I was keenly aware of the weight of the sword in my right hand.

If Kysarah picked up the two keys with one hand, there would be a repelling reaction between them, like we saw in the castle library, and they would forcefully hurl each other apart. That would be our only chance at a counterattack. I could hit her with every blow of a Vertical Square and not take her out, but if I could get one good blow in and throw her off-balance, there should be a chance to steal the branch from her backside.

Kysarah scooped up the first key. I adjusted my center of gravity just a bit forward.

Right at that moment, someone grabbed my ankle.

"...?!"

I spun around and looked directly into Asuna's wide eyes. She didn't say a word or make any other kind of gesture, but it was very clear that my temporary partner was warning me not to move.

I looked forward again. As I expected, Kysarah had picked up one key and was reaching with the same hand for the other. The resonating ring grew much louder, but the fallen elf paid it no heed and grabbed the second key, too.

Bzak!! That odd sound happened again, and a silver light shot from Kysarah's hand—but the two keys did not fly in opposite directions. Kysarah squeezed them tightly in her palm, as though she had been expecting that to happen.

Her ash-gray hair rippled with the force of the light shooting between her fingers. The bangs that covered the right side of her face were pushed away briefly, too, enough that I could see for the first time that she had a small eyepatch over her right eye, but my mind snapped right back to that hand.

Her lips clamped shut, Kysarah continued to clench the two keys together with astonishing force. In the meantime, she had her katana pointed toward us, so there was no chance for us to sneak attack her.

Eventually, there was a larger sparking sound, and the silver light faded and went out.

Kysarah rose to her feet, holding what was now a single iron key. She hadn't fused them together physically from sheer hand strength, of course; as Bouhroum said, the teeth and heads of the two keys were meant to align perfectly.

"I had heard that there was a strange charm placed upon them..." she muttered, tossing the key into the bag with the four others. Then she straightened out her disheveled hair and turned to us. "Now my business here is done. Human warriors..."

She paused then, her slender brows twitching just the tiniest bit.

"Do not involve yourself in elf matters any further. Let *them* be the only ones to bring trouble into this," she huffed, placing the black katana into the sheath on her left hip and spreading her arms. The wind whipped up from her feet and formed a little sand whirlwind that swallowed her whole.

I turned my face away from the stinging wind for just a second, and the swirling dispersed, dropping the sand to the ground. The katana-wielding fallen elf was gone.

"...I think we're giving up on the elf quest. If that sort of stuff is going to happen farther down the line, I can't imagine us getting all the way to the end," Gindo said.

And with that, the members of Qusack left for the exit of the dusty ravine. They were going to use the teleport gate in Stachion to go back to the fifth floor, where they would discuss their plans for the future, they explained. Temuo, Lazuli, and Highston had lost their weapons to the man in the black poncho, but they said they had backup weapons in their inventories, so they could get safely back to town.

As for me, I wanted to apologize to Qusack for suspecting them of being aligned with the fallen elves during the battle to defend Castle Galey. I was hoping to exchange more info with them and didn't want to say goodbye just yet, but Lazuli said, "Thank you for saving us. We'll find a way to make it up to you once things have settled down," so I had a feeling we'd meet again.

Once the four were out of sight, I walked over to Kizmel, looked her in the face up close, and bowed deeply. "I'm sorry, Kizmel. You did all that work to gather the keys..."

But that was all I was able to get out. Kizmel bent over at the waist, too, and said gravely, "Kirito, Asuna, forgive me. It was my job to keep you two safe..."

Our heads brushed together, and we awkwardly snapped upright again. Asuna giggled.

"There's nothing for you to apologize about, Kizmel. Besides, I don't think you came up inferior to that fallen elf. She just had a much fancier weapon than you."

Kizmel looked up and grimaced. "The official swords of the Pagoda Royal Knights are not cheap trinkets...but mine nearly broke from trading a single blow with her. That comes down to the inferiority of my technique."

"Don't say that," I reassured. "I wasn't able to attack her, either."

Then it was Asuna's turn to look apologetic. "Sorry about grabbing your ankle, Kirito. You were waiting for a chance to strike back, weren't you?"

"Oh...Actually, you made the right choice. I was going to leap at Kysarah the moment she picked up the keys, but it was like she knew they were going to push each other apart...so if I'd jumped in, she would have sliced me up instead."

"I see...But how did she undo that charm on the keys anyway? Bouhroum said it was a powerful bit of magic, and only the person who placed it could undo it," wondered Asuna.

Her answer came from Myia, who took off her gas mask at last to drink some water. Once she was done and put the cap on the canteen again, the girl said, "It looked to me like she simply crushed the charm out of existence with sheer strength alone."

"B-but if that's true...this is just getting ridiculous," I said, then suddenly hunched my neck and realized I owed the girl an apology. "Oh, right...I guess that wasn't very nice of me. I gave away the key your mother kept safe for so long, just to save some people I know..."

"If you hadn't done that, I'm certain she would have killed me, too," she replied with a calmness beyond her years, only to then pull the gas mask back over her little face. With her voice a bit muffled now, she continued, "Plus, based on the way she spoke, I think what she really wanted was the first thing, the...sacred keys? The keys she got from you and me were more incidental, it seemed. Maybe someone just asked her for them."

"Oh, I got that feeling, too..." said Asuna. She rested her hands on Myia's thin shoulders from behind.

I frowned, wondering who might have asked for such a thing. But before I could come up with any potential answers, the incoming instant message icon popped up. It was from Argo. And it read...

DKB and ALS just fought centipede boss in south area. It was a tough fight until an NPC woman rushed in and beat the boss. She had a golden box in her left hand, and when she raised it up, the centipede's armor turned into little blocks and crumbled apart. Lin-Kiba have no idea what it means, either. Information wanted.

".........Huh?"

Kizmel and Myia glanced over at me, wondering what I was yelping about.

"Oh, er, it's just...I got some weird information from an instant...er, my Art of Far Scribing..."

"You did? From whom?" wondered Asuna, who left Myia's side and came over to see. I switched the window to make it visible to party members and pondered what this meant.

A "golden box" might possibly be the golden cube that had been removed from the lord's mansion in Stachion. Would that make the NPC who barged into the fight Myia's mother, Theano? What did it mean that she held up the cube, and the centipede's armor crumbled? The golden cube was just supposed to be a quest item that signified the master of the town and not have any intrinsic power of its own. Plus, what was Argo doing with this Lin-Kiba business? If Lind and Kibaou found out about that, they'd be furious...

At that point, having lost my train of thought down a side alley, I glanced over at Asuna. My partner lifted her head, and we shared a look for a couple seconds before nodding together.

As I closed my window, Asuna turned to Myia and said, "You know...I think we might have found Theano."

"What...?!" The girl's back went straight as an arrow, and she took a step toward Asuna. "Wh-where...? Where is my mother?!"

"Well...supposedly she was seen in the caves in the southern area..."

"Southern...area?" the girl asked, confusion radiating through her mask. Only then did I recall that the girl had never been out of Stachion. Asuna crouched down and drew a simple map in the sand.

"See, this is how the sixth floor, which is where we are, is split into five areas...There's a star-shaped lake in the middle, and the south area, or fourth area, is right here. We're in the northwest area, so it's all the way on the other side..."

"But...that's so far away. What is my mother doing there...?" Myia mourned. In fact, the straight-line distance from Castle Galey to the Cave City of Goskai in the south area was only a little over five kilometers. In the real world, that would be the distance from the center of Kawagoe City to the center of neighboring Sayama—but I didn't think Myia or even Asuna would understand what I meant by that.

To the people who essentially spent their entire lives where they were programmed to stay, however, the place on the other side of the map might as well be another country. In fact, the first time I left the Town of Beginnings, the labyrinth tower felt like it was across the entire world from me.

"...I don't know what Theano's ultimate purpose is," I said, "but based on her actions, it seems like she's trying to take the golden cube she removed from the mansion to some other place."

Asuna nodded. "I agree...and I doubt the south area is her destination."

"It is probably the Pillar of the Heavens," said Kizmel, her first words in quite some time. The other three of us focused on her.

"Do you know something, Kizmel?"

"Not specifically...When I visited Stachion with you, a memory came to my mind. Though I have not seen it myself, I understand that the Pillar of the Heavens on this floor is built of those same stacked cubes of rock."

"*Oh, that reminds me,*" I nearly said out loud, only stopping myself at the last moment. In the beta, I'd gone up the labyrinth tower of the sixth floor, of course, but I couldn't explain that to Kizmel and Myia. I did recall the tower's exterior incorporating blocks that were similar to Stachion's.

"Which means...we should probably hurry. I don't know what Theano means to do at the tower, but there will be a fearsome guardian beast there," Asuna noted, throwing me a knowing glance.

I nodded. "Yeah...good idea. But...hang on, let me check something."

My window was still open, so I typed a response at the speed of light to Argo, feeling Myia's fascinated gaze on my skin the whole time. It occurred to me only just then that human NPCs couldn't use an inventory or menu window, either, but obviously, I couldn't explain that to her.

The info broker was waiting for my response and had a new message for me in less than a minute.

NPC RAN NORTHEAST THROUGH THE CAVE WITHOUT A WORD AFTER BOSS DIED. LIN-KIBA EACH SUSPECT SHE WAS AN NPC FROM THE OTHER'S QUEST. ONCE FR REFUEL IN GOSKAI, THEY'LL PROBABLY HEAD STRAIGHT TO FIFTH AREA.

That one sent me grumbling. On the third and fifth floors, the PK agitators had set Lind's DKB and Kibaou's ALS against each other, but this time, the one making them paranoid about each other was Theano—a person from *my* quest. We couldn't let the matter go unaddressed, both to set Myia at ease and to ensure there wasn't needless discord between the two big guilds.

I let Argo know I'd tell her more in person and closed my window. After another bit of eye contact with Asuna, I crouched down to speak to Myia.

"It sounds like your mother is heading for the fifth area, after all. We're going to rush after her, but..."

I wanted to tell her that she should go back to Stachion and wait, but Myia exhibited an extremely curious reaction for an NPC: She cut me off.

"No, I want to go with you. If my mother is doing something dangerous, I cannot simply stay at home and wait."

The girl had already lost her father. If she was this insistent, I really couldn't stop her. Not to mention that Myia was a higher level than me or Asuna.

"...All right," I said, straightening up again.

"I would like to as well," said Kizmel with a crestfallen tone, "but I must report to the storyteller and castle lord that I allowed the fallen elves to steal the four sacred keys. My sword is damaged, too..."

"But...aren't they going to blame you for that, Kizmel? It was our fault that the keys were stolen, so we should be the ones to go..." Asuna said, looking nervous.

"Yeah," I piped up. "I'll go and make a proper apology to old Bouhroum and Count Galeyon..."

But the knight just smiled. "Do not worry. I am one of the queen's own Pagoda Royal Knights. Only Her Majesty and the knight commander have the right to formally rebuke me. The priests might complain, but the simple truth of the matter is that I could not match Kysarah the Ransacker...I shall have to focus myself anew and regain the keys myself."

"...Oh...But when you do, we're going to be fighting at your side," Asuna proclaimed, grabbing Kizmel's right hand with both of hers and squeezing. I walked up to the knight and shared a firm handshake with her.

"Kizmel, tell old man Bouhroum that I'm going to go back and apologize to him. And if you want, until your sword gets fixed, take this...You might not like it, since it's an enemy blade, but..."

I had pulled out a weapon from my inventory for this purpose: the Elven Stout Sword I received from fighting the forest elf captain on the fourth floor. Even in its base, non-upgraded state, it was nearly as strong as my old Anneal Blade +8.

"Ooooh…" Kizmel murmured as she took it and pulled the mirrorlike blade out of the silver-decorated sheath.

Unfortunately, I immediately regretted my action. Kizmel's long saber was in the Curved Blade category, and the Stout Sword was under the one-handed sword skill. Using a weapon with a skill you hadn't learned meant you couldn't make use of its stats, nor any of its sword skills, of course.

But Kizmel just smiled, slid the sword back into the sheath, and said, "It is a good sword, and I will gladly use it. The forest elves may be our longtime foes, but their blacksmiths' work is undeniable… And also…"

For a moment, it seemed like she was going to say something more, but the knight just shook her head and hung the Stout Sword from her side instead of the cracked saber. She put that weapon over her back, then reached into her pouch.

"It is not much of a trade, but you may have this from me."

She handed me a small bottle that was carved like a crystal. It was only the size of a thumb, but I knew it contained something unfathomably valuable, and so I stared her straight in the face. "Are…are you sure? Isn't this a great dark elf treasure…?"

"If not for you and Asuna and Myia, the Fallen would control Castle Galey at this moment, and all the contents of the treasure chamber would be lost. In that sense, this is a meager reward… and with it, you can cross the lake directly rather than taking the long left path, correct?"

She was right, of course. Going the normal route from the second area to the labyrinth tower in the fifth area would take nearly an entire day, even avoiding combat with monsters. In order to catch up to Theano, who was already in the fourth area, the Drops of Villi in this bottle were not just useful, they were vital.

"…Thanks. This will really help us," I said, accepting the gift.

Kizmel stepped back and looked at Asuna and Myia. "I suspect that once I finish reporting to the lord of the castle…I will be moving to the seventh floor. We shall part ways for a time, but I believe I will see you again soon enough."

"Yes, of course!" Asuna said, embracing Kizmel. Myia reached up a small hand for a shake. The four of us walked to the exit of the dead-end canyon and went our separate ways, waving all the while.

Several times after we started walking south, I turned around to look and saw that Kizmel's back was hidden against the reddish cliffs as she returned to Castle Galey. Within a minute, the knight's HP bar silently vanished from the upper-left corner of my view.

13

WE GOT THROUGH THE DRY CANYON WITH A MINIMUM of battle and crossed the wasteland without being tempted by any sudden cactus fruiting, eventually reaching the bank of Lake Talpha before it got dark.

It was after five thirty in the afternoon, and the navy-blue lake shone and flickered with the light of the flame-like setting sun. Myia stood at the edge of the water, lifted her gas mask up, and exclaimed in wonder:

"Wow...I've never seen so much water in my life. Is this the ocean...?"

Asuna stood behind Myia—she seemed to like that position—and held her shoulders as she said, "This is Talpha...It's a lake, Myia. An ocean is much, much bigger...hundreds and thousands of times bigger than this."

"Thousands of times...? Bigger than this entire floor of the castle...?"

"Yeah, that's right...The real ocean is something you can only see down on the earth that's far below Aincrad, I suppose..."

As they chatted, I popped open the bottle Kizmel gave me, lifted my foot behind me rather than in front this time, and carefully dripped it onto the soles of my boots. Once the buff was active, I approached the girls and performed the same process.

The level of the bottle was much lower than the first time I saw it used, but it looked like we still had a few doses left.

I put the little bottle back in my inventory and carefully stepped into the water. After a few strides, I felt the familiar pushback on my soles, and the surface of the lake began to behave like a layer of rubber.

Behind me, Asuna and Myia were slowly following, holding hands. We had to explain the threat of the giant starfish Ophiometus that lurked in the depths of the lake, so there was definitely an element of fear in Myia's uncertain steps. But because she was so small and light, I figured she was in less danger of breaking through the surface by stepping roughly. Asuna and I were about the same height, and I couldn't be sure which of us had heavier equipment, but that sort of thing was hard to ask a person about.

The topic of personal questions reminded me that I still hadn't asked her about the mystery of the two-handed lance skill. This seemed like a good opportunity to chat, since there wasn't anything else to do but walk, but the memory of Asuna charging with that lance was so shocking and vivid, I was finding it difficult to broach the topic. I silently promised myself *Next time* and focused on the sensations in my feet instead.

When going to the fourth area to retrieve the hidden key, we went almost directly south, but going to the fifth area meant cutting across the lake to the southeast. The far bank was shrouded in fog and hard to see, so I made sure my map was open as we walked. It wasn't much more than a kilometer, but being forced into a slow sneaking walk meant it took time. The reddish light of the sunset on the base of the floor above us passed with shocking speed, and dark-blue dusk soon followed.

Suddenly, the winds blowing across the lake grew colder, and I hunched my shoulders. The chill rising from my feet began to tickle the back of my nose. Then another chill, something entirely unrelated to the cold, assaulted my body.

Oh no.

I need to sneeze.

I came to a stop, covering my mouth in an attempt to make the itchiness subside, but it was only getting stronger. My lungs filled on their own as I sucked in mouthfuls of air. I couldn't take it. I couldn't resist.

"...Ehh-shoo!"

Having my mouth covered killed some of the sound, but I couldn't stop my body from jerking. My weight pressing against the water broke the heightened surface tension, and my right foot loudly plunked through the top of the lake. Naturally, I tried to force my left foot down stronger to push myself up, but that, too, sank. But right before I was sure I would topple fully into the water, I felt my outstretched arms pulled on either side. I looked up to see Asuna with my right hand and Myia with my left, the two trying to hold me up.

"Slowly! Slowly pull your feet up!" Asuna ordered. I relaxed my muscles as best I could, balancing my weight evenly between my left foot and my hands, then carefully extracted my right foot from the water, resting it on the surface again and exhaling.

"Th-thanks, you saved..."

But before I could fully thank her, Asuna thrust out her hand.

"Shh! Do you hear that...?"

I clamped my mouth shut and focused my attention—on what felt like a deep bubbling sound rumbling up from the center of the lake. I looked over, terrified at what I would find, and saw large bubbles rising and popping here and there over the water.

"What...? Just from *that*...?" I groaned. All I did was break through the surface for a second!

But the bubbles didn't stop. The water wasn't translucent with the setting sun shining off it, but I could sense something unfathomably huge rising up from the bottom of the lake.

Eventually, about thirty meters away, three cursors appeared on the surface in a row. The name displayed on all of them was TENTACLE OF OPHIOMETUS. Their color was a deep red, if not as dark as Kysarah's. They were located approximately in the center of our route, and whether we turned back or pushed on, there would be no escape at our walking speed across the water.

I was almost about to get desperate and suggest letting the tentacles grab us so they would drag us down to the starfish's mouth where we might stand a chance at a last counterattack—when Asuna shouted, "Kirito, Myia, let's run!"

"B-but if we run, won't it break the effect of the Drops of Villi...?" I stammered.

"Shorten your strides and put out your left foot before the right starts sinking! With the buff the drops confer, you should be able to pull it off!"

It sounded like something a ninja would do, but before I could complain, she was pushing me onward. I had to stick out my right foot before I toppled over, and although it felt like I was going to break through again, I made sure not to try pulling back but quickly took a step with my left foot before the resistance completely broke. Then my right foot, then left, right, left...My first few steps were awkward, but once I got the idea of quick steps at high speed, I soon realized that I was running across the water.

"Whoa...this actually works," I murmured, trotting quickly. Soon Myia passed me on the left side. She almost seemed to be having fun, making crisp little *spak-spak-spak-spak* sounds as she went, probably because she got better resistance being lighter. On my right, Asuna followed with a smooth, gliding run. She seemed very practiced at this somehow—and then I recalled something she had said yesterday: "If the starfish does show up, I have an ace up my pant leg."

She was probably referring to this running technique, but the only reason I was able to just barely pull it off at my first attempt was because of the protection of the Droplets of Villi. I could easily imagine myself sinking before my third step without the buff. The same would be true for Asuna, so how did she come up with this ninja-like technique?

These thoughts only used a tenth of my brain, though. Six parts went to the control of my legs, and the remaining three were focused on the watery sounds behind us. I couldn't stop to ascertain the nature of the splashing, but it was very easy to imagine those starfish tentacles breaching the surface and chasing after us. I got the feeling that they were drawing closer, but we didn't have any other recourse than to keep running as fast as we could.

After one, two, then three bands of mist hovering over the lake, the beach of the far bank, orange in the sunset, came into view. It looked to be about a hundred meters to the part of the land that jutted farthest into the lake.

"Nrraaaaah!" I bellowed, shuffling along the top of the water as close to the red zone as I could manage. Normally, I ran with long, leaping strides, so this kind of running was hellishly alien to me, but if I took steps any longer than this, I wouldn't be able to safely pull them back above the water in time.

I bet that Argo would be good at this sort of thing. Maybe I should bump up my AGI a bit, too, I thought as I sped across the remaining distance and reached the bank two seconds behind Myia. I kept my scampering speed even after it was sand beneath my boots and waddled onward as I slowed my pace.

Only when the ground underfoot turned from beach sand to grass did I finally come to a stop, panting. When I turned around, there were three red cursors floating about ten meters onto land past the water's edge. Writhing like snakes beneath the cursors were dark-gray tentacles. Their ends were extremely sharp, but they widened to about a third of a meter across where they went back into the water. How wide they were at the base, and the total span of the body, were too frightening to consider, and I had no interest in finding out.

The tentacles waved through empty air for ten seconds, frustrated, before giving up and slithering back into the water. The cursors trailed away into the body of the lake and vanished, at which point I finally let out the breath I'd been holding.

At my sides, Myia and Asuna were staring at the water in silence. The beach faced west, so the sun shining through the aperture at the far side of the floor blazed red against the surface of the lake. It was a beautiful sight, even when you considered that there was a monstrous giant starfish lurking just underneath it.

As I gazed upon the sunset of January 4, I suddenly felt a powerful fatigue.

After all, I'd started at two AM, gotten up to explore the outer rim of Castle Galey, gained the Awakening skill while being taunted by Bouhroum's steak, then gone to Stachion in the morning, met Myia, gotten attacked by fallen elves, returned to the castle in the afternoon, started to nap but was awakened by a major Fallen invasion, fought that off, then went out to rescue the Qusack hostages, lost our sacred keys and iron keys to Kysarah, split off from Kizmel with barely a moment to reflect on it, crossed Lake Talpha, ran away from a giant starfish, and here we were. That might be a record for the most I'd ever experienced in a single day since the game's official launch.

My batteries were pretty much drained, and I was more than ready to eat my fill at a fancier-than-usual inn and dive into bed, but that wasn't in the cards. If Myia's mother, Theano, was heading for the labyrinth tower, our only chance to catch her was while she was moving across the map. If she entered the intricate dungeon inside the tower, it would be very hard to find her.

"...Ready for just a bit more?" I asked the two girls. Asuna and Myia spun to face me.

"Of course. I'm perfectly ready," said Asuna.

"I'm good, too," said Myia in her gas mask. "I can still go."

That ruled out any possibility that I could plead for a break. "Then let's head for the nearest town. This area's basically just a straight shot down the road, so that's what Theano and the front-running group will travel down."

When I turned my back on the lake, I was faced with a new sea: one of sand.

The five distinct areas of the sixth floor, separated by tall, jutting rock formations, were each wildly different. The first (northeast) area, which contained the main town of the floor, featured forests and fields. The second (northwest) area, which contained Castle

Galey, was a rocky, arid wasteland. The third (southwest) area, which we skipped, was swampland. The fourth (south) area, with the dungeon containing the elves' sacred key, was themed after caves, and the fifth (southeast) area, where we stood now, was desert.

It was a classic RPG terrain theme, but facing a real desert in a VRMMO presentation, I was stunned at the overwhelming scale of it. Massive sand dunes stretched as far as the eye could see, and there were no landmarks to define the distance. There were even heat mirages that served as visual traps, appearing like an oasis but vanishing just before you reached it. On top of all that, the far distance was blurred out by a wind-and-dust effect that meant we couldn't even see the labyrinth tower until we were within a hundred meters of it.

Worst of all, the handy map screen on my window was given the same treatment as the Forest of Wavering Mists on the third floor, graying out sections at random. The only thing you could trust was the narrow redbrick road that ran through the desert, visible only at certain sections.

Even the little bit of grass we were standing on faded out within ten or fifteen meters, transitioning into sand that was of a different texture than the stuff at the lakeside. A lonely trail that looked ready to fade away in the wind stretched onward.

"...And we just follow that path?" Asuna asked.

I nodded. "Yep, that *should* lead us to the final resting point of this floor, the village of Murutsuki."

"Any bosses out there?"

"If you're coming from the fourth area, there's a carnivorous plant–type boss right before Murutsuki, but from our direction, it *should* be all clear."

"I'm hearing a lot of shoulds," she noted drily, which elicited a giggle from Myia.

"Kirito, have you been to this desert before?"

"Yeah..." I said automatically, before reconsidering and holding myself to the bare minimum of an answer, lest I start telling Myia about the beta test. "Just once before, a long time ago. I...*should* remember where the village was, at least."

"Then let's go and leave a trail of breadcrumbs, in case we get lost," the girl said, presumably joking—until I realized she wasn't. It made me wonder if Theano had read her fairy tales like that one.

"Hmm. Well, I think in a desert, the wind would blow the bread crumbs away. As long as we don't lose sight of the brick road, we should be fine. And if we get lost, we can always come back here."

"Then I'll make sure we're always on the path!" Myia said, starting to walk and forcing Asuna and me to catch up. My partner leaned over to me and whispered, "You seem to be surprisingly adept at dealing with little girls."

"Wh-what...? I'm ultra-bad at it! Just as bad as girls my age and older girls, too."

"...Uh-huh," said the fencer, pulling away with a look that might have been exasperation or possibly pity.

After just five minutes of walking in the desert, Lake Talpha was out of sight behind the huge sand dunes. All that I saw over my shoulder was faded-purple sky and dark-red sun, and ahead of us and to the sides, everything was shrouded in a sandy haze, with even the pillars of the outer perimeter hidden from sight. I could make out the rocky floor above us, but the details were fuzzy.

Even our trusty brick road was covered by sand or crumbled away in parts. Now and then, desert monsters like lizards and snakes attacked from the nearby sands. If you had to look for a positive feature, at least this place was without the "blessing of the green," like the wasteland area, so there shouldn't be any danger of a fallen elf attack...except for those darn branches they had. Then again, after Kysarah took the iron keys away from us, maybe we didn't need to worry about them bothering us anymore.

Still, I kept my guard up as we walked. After about thirty

minutes with Myia in the lead, we arrived at Murutsuki just as the last rays of light vanished behind us.

It wasn't a big place at all, but it did have a large oasis spring in the center of town, with palm trees and cycads spreading their long, narrow leaves along the edge of the clear, crisp water. The buildings were made of sand-colored stone with the same rough texture as Castle Galey, but without any kind of ornamentation whatsoever. The short main street was lit with simple fires, and there were sad, lonely strings playing from somewhere.

"This kind of Arabian-sounding instrument..." I whispered to my partner. "I remember wanting to look up what it's called back in the beta."

Asuna inclined her head briefly. "I'm pretty sure it's...an oud."

"Oh...well," I said, impressed at her worldly knowledge. I lowered my voice further. "If I don't forget by the time we beat this game, I'll have to look that up when we get back."

"Since you're here, why don't you try practicing with it?"

"I, uh, I don't think the Musical Instrument skill is going to be of much use here..." I said, shaking my head. This actually seemed like the perfect time to bring up the two-handed lance skill, but before I could broach the topic, Myia turned back from up ahead and called out to us.

"There's a...very strange horse over there!"

She was pointing at one of the palm trees on the north end of the spring, where a large four-legged creature with brown shaggy fur was tied up. I recognized its distinctive back and curved neck from the real world—pictures and videos, if not personal experience.

"That's not a horse, Myia. It's a camel," said Asuna, walking up to the girl and pointing at the animal's back. "See those big humps on its back? If it has one, it's called a dromedary. If it has two, it's a camel."

"But that camel has more than that."

"Huh?"

Asuna and I looked closer and saw that the camel indeed had three humps on its back. It wasn't a shock to me, because I'd seen it in the beta. But Asuna just paused, and a bit awkwardly, she said, "That's…called a three-humped camel…"

"*Frmphs!*" went the sound that escaped my throat. Asuna shot me a nasty glare, then trotted off with Myia to get a closer look.

Upon closer examination, while the center area of Murutsuki was smaller than the courtyard of Castle Galey, they were similar in layout. In the center was the natural spring, about twenty-five meters across, with palm trees lining the edge. Along the outer edge of the doughnut-shaped plaza were shops, inns, and restaurants.

Theano would surely pass through this plaza on her way to the labyrinth tower, so as long as we took a seat on an open terrace along the north side, where the path began again, we wouldn't miss her. The oud-playing NPC was on the south side of the spring, so I couldn't see them, but the distance made for just the right volume for dinner background music.

As I pondered what to eat, I gazed out at the row of buildings. The restaurants I could see—really more like fancy food carts—were only two. One was kebab-like roasted meat, while the other served a soup that resembled curry. There were few restaurants that served curry in the game, so in the beta, more than a few players made the trek from Stachion to distant Murutsuki, but I found it a bit underwhelming. For one thing, there was no rice on the menu. The Arab-style curry with Aincrad's traditional flatbread was fine, but as a growing teenage boy, I just wanted a huge dollop on top of a steaming mound of white rice. So tonight it would be kebabs.

"Hey, I'm gonna order some food now," I called out to the camel watchers.

"Okay," they said, waving. That meant I was in charge of the order. I turned away, determined to put every meat dish on the table. No space to waste on measly salads or steamed vegetables!

I had gone about three steps, clutching my empty belly, when a short player came tearing across the open area from the south and darted to the counter of the kebab shop. Once I saw the green cursor, I hurried to stand next to them.

"Hey, pal, I'll take a shish kebab and an Adana kebab!"

"Hey, mister, I want three doner sandwiches, three urfa kebabs, and..." I shouted, jostling for space—until I recognized the unique sound of the other customer's voice. The high-pitched, coquettish voice and rising nasal inflection...

"A-Argo?!"

"Oh, it's you, Kii-boy," said Argo the Rat, whisker-painted cheeks breaking into a grin when she saw me. "Ah, yer already at Murutsuki, huh? That was quick."

"Y-you're gonna talk to me about being quick?! I thought it was gonna take five hours to get through the cave of the fourth area..."

The bearded cook shouted "Food's up!" and we received our dishes in short order. Argo could carry her two skewers in her hands, but I had three round sandwiches of seared meat and three skewers on the counter, so it required some cradling and delicate pinching between fingers to get them all.

"H-hey...you wanna sit down at that table over there?" I suggested, glancing at one of the open-seating spots in front of the business. But the info dealer scowled and shook her head.

"I don't think we've got the time."

"Huh...? Why?"

"Because if I'm here, that means..."

At last, I picked up on her implication. If Argo had just arrived at Murutsuki during her chase of Theano, that meant...

"Ugh...so Theano—that's the NPC with the golden cube—already passed through this village...?!"

"I checked with the guide NPC at the entrance, and they said a woman went through here on her own about thirty minutes ago."

"...Thirty minutes..." I repeated, pulling up a mental map of the fifth area.

Murutsuki was in the center of the fan-shaped area. The labyrinth tower in the northeast corner was about a kilometer away. But going along the twisting path made the journey over twice as long. If we walked quickly, it was still less than two hours—and even shorter at a run. We should assume that Theano had a healthy head start on us.

"...Where are the ALS and DKB?"

"They should be on their way, but they said they were gonna stop in Goskai and resupply first...I'd bet they're about thirty minutes behind."

"Hrmm..."

Somehow, I had to think through the delicious smell of the doner kebabs cradled in my left arm and the even-better-smelling urfa kebabs in my right.

The reason for Theano's actions was still unclear. But if she was heading for the labyrinth tower, it was quite possible that her final destination was the boss chamber. If Asuna, Myia, Argo, and I chased after Theano and had to fight the boss by ourselves, it would be nearly impossible to win. We would all die. The right decision was to wait for the big group to arrive in Murutsuki.

...But.

Now the "Curse of Stachion" quest was completely off the original rails. Theano was most likely acting on what you might consider her own will. She was going to end up choosing some action that ultimately cost her her life. It would mean the loss of both parents for Myia, who trusted us enough to follow us around.

In no more than three seconds, I had made up my mind. I ushered Argo away from the kebab shop. At the north end of the oasis area, the two girls were petting the three-humped camel. I called out, "Hey! We're heading out soon!"

Asuna wasn't happy about the idea of eating as we walked—make that *trotted*—but only until she heard what Argo had to report. As soon as she knew Theano was still ahead of us, she eliminated the food in her hands as quickly—and gracefully—as possible.

"You said she passed through the village thirty minutes ahead of us, but what about the field boss?" she asked the info dealer.

"Theano might be tough, but that's a monster that you can't beat on your own, surely."

"That's true…but lookit this," said Argo, who had finished her two kebabs as fast as me. She went to her window and pulled out an odd-looking thing. It was a greenish-brown object about twenty centimeters across in all directions.

"There were tons of these scattered across the ground by the time I showed up to the field boss's lair."

"What is that…?" I asked. Argo tossed it to me without warning. I caught it, alarmed, and was stunned again when I got a good look at it. It felt like balsa wood, and there was a fine fibrous pattern on its surface.

"Wait, is this…the carnivorous plant's body?"

"Prob'ly. When she charged into the fight against the centipede boss in the fourth area, that Theano lady broke down its armor into cubes the same size. It was only the armor, not what was underneath, but its defense plummeted, so the FRs beat it easy with an all-out attack. The centipede—it was called Basalt Morpha—didn't have normal plates of armor but damn tough rock. Maybe that cube Theano had can break down any kind of mineral or plant…?"

True to her reputation, the info dealer's conjecture seemed very accurate. In my head, I was looking at distant Stachion, the main town of the floor.

Every building in that place was built with blocks of rock or wood. To this point, I just assumed the golden cube, sign of the town lord, was merely the standard to which all the construction blocks were made. In fact, that was how it was explained in the beta. But maybe that wasn't actually the case. Maybe, like Argo said, the cube had the power to turn all minerals and plants into blocks, and it was responsible for the hundreds of thousands, if not millions of blocks in Stachion…

"Hey, Asuna, how many blocks do you think there are total making up all of Stachion?" I asked, pausing my thought process.

The fencer frowned and said, "Is that something we need to know right now?"

"I…I think so."

"Well…to break it down *exactly*, the town was two thousand feet from north to south, and one thousand feet from east to west. So divide twenty-four thousand by eight to get three thousand, then multiply by fifteen hundred for a total of four and a half million."

"Uh…thanks…"

Asuna then jabbed my arm, and Argo snorted with annoyance on the other side of me. Up ahead, Myia nimbly turned around while running with a half-eaten sandwich and skewer in her hands. "Kirito, that is only the number of stones forming the ground. But the buildings rise up above the ground, so…"

"Oh, r-right. Um…" I stammered, starting to envision all of Stachion.

Asuna got the point quicker. "Look, why don't we just estimate that it's three times the base total? So that would be somewhere around thirteen and a half million blocks."

"Ooh, thanks a million," I said, but Asuna didn't seem satisfied yet.

"So what do you need that number *for*?" she pressed.

"Oh…I was just thinking, what if the wood and stone blocks that make up Stachion weren't cut individually with saws and chisels, but they were broken down from nearby mountains and forests with the power of that golden cube…?"

"Ah, I see…Well, I just came here after witnessin' a whole pile of blocks dropped by the carnivorous plant boss, so yer crazy idea's got some real legs to it." Argo grinned. But just as quickly, she looked pensive.

We'd long ago left Murutsuki behind and were back on the desert path. The sun had set entirely by now, and though the desert dust clouds blocked the moonlight, there was fortunately a pale-blue environmental light that glowed against the slopes of the dunes. At this rate, we could have rented some camels in Murutsuki and enjoyed a nighttime trek through the desert…if only we had the time, and if only I knew where exactly on a three-humped camel to sit.

In the chilly night air, Argo's voice was more serious than earlier. "You know…if that's true, we might have some trouble on our hands."

"What do you mean?"

"If she can break down all kinds of rock and wood, couldn't she jus' bust through all the walls of the dungeon? Make a straight run all the way ta the boss, forget all the traps an' tricks. The ALS and DKB probably think it was Theano's power that broke up the centipede's armor. But if they find out it was the cube that did it, they'll be on the hunt for it."

"Oh…good point…"

A little imagination pointed out that the golden cube's uses went far beyond dungeon shortcuts. Aincrad was full of plant monsters like treants and nepenthes, and stone-based monsters like golems and gargoyles, which could theoretically be dissolved into blocks in an instant. If you could get experience points for that? You'd be able to level at incredible speed. The guild flag in my inventory had nothing on this cube when it came to potential game-breaking effects.

If the "Curse of Stachion" questline proceeded ordinarily, Cylon would have survived and reformed, the cube would be buried in Pithagrus's grave again, and the player would never know its true power, much less actually possess it. But the night that Morte and the dagger wielder killed Cylon, the quest began to shift dramatically. I had a feeling that we *could* seize the cube if Theano were killed, too…

"…I think that Argo is correct," said Myia, who had finished her food and put the gas mask back on. Argo, who thought of her as a simple quest NPC, blinked in mild surprise.

The girl continued in a very natural manner, "My mother told me once that Stachion is a town 'built of magic and curse.' She didn't tell me what that meant when I asked…but perhaps it was because she knew that the golden cube had a terrible power within it."

"Y-you mean Theano is heading for the Pillar of the Heavens to do something with the cube's power?" I prompted.

"We don't know that yet," answered Asuna. "Maybe she's just trying to do something *to* the cube...But for now, we just need to catch up to her."

"Yep, that sounds right," agreed Argo, who looked forward. Like always, the narrow path wove through the sand dunes, but I could sense that a huge structure was approaching through the deep-blue darkness somewhere ahead.

"...Let's hurry," Asuna said, and we picked up our speed once more.

It was worth putting in the effort not to stray off the brick path, as we only ran into monsters a total of four times, but we did not spot Theano while in the desert.

If she wasn't acting in accordance with a script, the monsters should attack her, too, and lizards and snakes weren't trees or rocks, so the cube couldn't deconstruct them. On top of that, this being the last area on the sixth floor, all the monsters were tough. If she could beat them all herself, Theano would be on Kizmel's level—at the very least, far tougher than Cylon, whom Morte easily killed.

With Myia present, all I could do was pray that no matter how things shook out, we wouldn't have to fight Theano.

There was an especially large dune ahead that we raced up, with Asuna and Myia reaching the peak a few seconds before me. There, they came to a stop and stared upward.

When I crested the hill, I saw it too: Just a hundred meters away, a mammoth structure stood darker than the night. It was the labyrinth tower of the sixth floor. Four days after we started this floor on January 1, we had finally reached it.

The normal plan, prioritizing safety, would call for the full help of the front-line group in mapping out the interior of the tower, taking a day or two to discover the boss chamber, another day to scout out and strategize against that boss, and one more day for the battle itself. But in this case (as in others before), we couldn't sit back and take our time. Like the fifth floor, where we needed to complete the tower and beat the boss in a single day, this was one where we'd need to rush through it, careful mapping be damned.

"...We didn't catch up to Theano after all, and the ALS and DKB didn't catch up to us..." I murmured, looking over my shoulder from the top of the dune.

"The tower is one thing, but I don't know if I like us heading to the boss chamber with a group this small," Asuna said, her tone worried. "Let's just hope that's not where Theano's going."

"Yeah...but there's usually not much else to do in a labyrinth..."

"Then we just gotta catch up before the boss chamber," said Argo. I turned back, and she tossed long, thin bottles to both Asuna and me. I caught mine, popped the lid off, and put it to my lips. Chilled lime flavor with a hint of carbonation refreshed my tongue. It didn't seem to be a type of potion, but it tasted great after a run across the dry, dusty desert. Myia was drinking one, too, holding it with both hands.

Refreshed by Argo's gifts, we rushed down the last sand dune toward the tower. The layout of the sixth-floor tower was not circular, or square, but pentagonal. It was so huge, however, that it was difficult to tell just from looking up at it; I recalled only figuring it out in the beta once I went inside to map it. At the time, there was debate among the testers as to whether or not the five-sided shape meant something, but we never arrived at a satisfactory consensus.

The blackish stone walls of the tower, once seen up close, were indeed run through with lines every twenty centimeters, like the buildings in Stachion. The huge doors at the front of the ground floor were closed tight, and there didn't seem to be another soul around. We were only assuming that Theano was coming here, so there was always the possibility that we were completely off the mark, but I had to trust my gut on this one.

"...Let's open it up."

With that warning, I placed my hands on the bronze doors and pushed hard. They rumbled heavily as they parted to the side, and a gust of cold air rushed out of the structure past me.

Once the doors were completely open, I beckoned the other three into the tower. Like the other towers, it wasn't completely darkened; pale-blue lights high above cast down a faint glow to see by. If the layout was the same as in the beta, there would be a large triangular hall beyond the entrance, with one door on each side wall...

"Oh, look up there!" said Myia, who apparently had better eyesight than the three players she accompanied. She was pointing ahead and to the left. When I saw it, I gasped awkwardly, "*Uwha...*"

The metal door was in the place I remembered, but there was now a huge hole in the stone wall just to the right of it. It wasn't split or smashed open; it looked like the cohesive force of the blocks that made up the tower had been lost, causing them to collapse.

I walked up to the hole, lifted one of the stone blocks, and said, "So...Theano used the golden cube to break down the wall...I suppose."

"But why didn't she go through the door...?" Asuna asked. "Is it locked?"

I glanced farther into the room and said, "See how there are stone pillars growing up from the floor there? You're supposed to solve the puzzles on the pillars, then beat the monsters that appear...I'm pretty sure," I said, trying my best not to be too suspicious with information around Myia.

The fencer seemed satisfied and nodded. "Ah, so she just cut out that step. Then if we follow the path she's taken, we won't have to do the puzzles, either..."

"Probably not. But we'll still have normal wimpy monsters to deal with," I said, tossing the stone block aside. Just then, as if drawn by the sound of the stone—in fact, it almost certainly was—there was a hissing roar from beyond the hole.

"Here it comes!"

I drew my sword and had the other three back away. Asuna and Myia removed their rapiers, and Argo readied the claws that were attached to the back of her hands.

Seconds later, a humanoid creature emerged from the hole with a wide, thin reptilian head like a cobra's, a long, slender torso, and human limbs. It was an ophidian, one of the snake-men that appeared all throughout this tower. It was similar to the lizard-like reptoids and fishy ichthyoids we'd fought already, but with its long arms and spear, it had a fearsome range, as well as poison fangs, if you could get past its reach. And it wasn't just one—here came a second…and a third.

I realized that we should have activated the Meditation buff before entering the tower, but it was too late for that now. Fortunately, the ophidians' fangs were damaging poison, not the paralyzing kind, so we could handle the effects.

"They'll poison you if they bite! Don't rush in; aim for the arms and make them drop the spears! Argo, team up with Myia!" I commanded.

They reacted quickly. Without Kizmel, the highest level in our party actually belonged to Myia, but she was a child and had a very short reach. Argo had the same problem—due to her weapon, not size—so I thought it best for them to team up and wreak confusion.

Of the three ophidians, two had spears, and the third used a glaive. Based on the armor ornamentation, I judged the glaive user to be the leader and charged at it.

"*Shrrrrl!*" hissed the creature, flickering its tongue and jabbing with the glaive. I sidestepped it, struck a shallow blow to the arm holding the spear, and withdrew. Asuna, Argo, and Myia took their own targets and spread out across the spacious room.

That reminds me. I guess Asuna's not using that lance anymore…?

Taking advantage of my moment of distraction, the leader snake used the sword skill Swift Lunge. It was a simple, single thrust, but being at the very fastest level of all the sword skills

234 Sword Art Online: Progressive 6

in the game, it was very tricky to deal with. If you didn't sidestep the moment you saw the visual light effect, you wouldn't avoid it in time.

Instead, I stood my ground. I'd ordered the others to focus on disarming, but accumulating damage bit by bit on the scaled arms of the snakemen took time. We needed to catch up to Theano; we couldn't stop and drag out the very first fight in the tower.

I focused hard on the shining crimson tip of the spear, preparing a Vertical skill with precise aim, angle, and timing, like I was threading a needle. I wanted the body of the sword to press against the spear as it dropped; if the angle was too weak, I couldn't push aside the skill, and if it went too deep, it would block the attack but knock my sword back, too. Only when I scraped the spear at the optimal angle would it change the thrust angle and still strike my target—the Counter Parry technique.

The ophidian's glaive nicked the left side of my chest as it passed me, and my Vertical smashed the hand holding the spear. Triangular scales flew into the air, and the snake arm fell clean off and shattered.

"*Jyashhh!*" the snakeman snarled, trying to counterattack with its other hand. But held with only one arm, the heavy glaive was much slower. It had only just pulled back the spear for full momentum when I recovered from my skill delay. I stepped farther forward, putting myself into its poison fang range.

The ophidian curled its head back, going into the biting motion as if it were hoping for this.

But I'd done it on purpose. As the cobra head swooped forward, I gave it a three-part Sharp Nail skill.

The large fanged head of the ophidian was its greatest weapon and weakness in one. The three slanting slashes all hit the snakeman's snout. It curled back abruptly, froze in place, then exploded into pieces. I rushed through the expanding particles, saving my fist pump for later, and plunged toward the side of the ophidian Asuna was fighting.

* * *

We finished our fight against the three powerful ophidians in a bit over two minutes, made sure we applied the Meditation buff this time, then leaped through the hole in the wall. Asuna told me to face away while we did it, and Argo, ever the business-woman, offered to buy the info about the skill. I told her "Later!" because we were in a hurry.

Soon, we found more and more holes Theano made in walls, but we never seemed to be any closer to her. She had to be fighting the ophidians alone—and the golden cube's effect shouldn't work on the snakemen—but she was clearing them out faster than our party of four could.

I remembered that the ophidians in the tower took about five minutes to re-pop, so if we stopped seeing monsters along the route, we could assume we were within five minutes of catching up to Theano. Yet, the ophidians, beetles, and magical monsters kept coming strong. Within two or three battles, my other party members got the hang of combat in this dungeon, and we started winning our fights within a minute or less, but the fact that we didn't seem to be getting any closer was proof that Theano was very powerful, with or without the cube.

Between her and Kysarah, who had taken all of our keys, if we were going to see more and more ultrapowerful and freethinking (at least in appearance) NPCs in the future, then, for better or for worse, they were going to play a major role in getting through this deadly game. They could be powerful allies or terrifying enemies—though not that this was anything new.

At any rate, thanks to Theano providing us with a minimum-length route skipping all the puzzles and traps, we were racing up the one hundred meter tower with incredible speed. On the fifth floor, the midpoint of the dungeon, there was supposed to be an ophidian boss and some underlings, but when I peered into the chamber, all I saw was a scattering of various loot items. For a moment, I was terrified that some of Theano's belongings would be among them, but the far door was wide open, so I assumed she had passed through safely.

"...At this rate, she might just beat the floor boss while she's at it," murmured Asuna as she stared at the mountain of treasure. Argo gulped down her potion and said wryly, "In that case, maybe she could go on up the stairs and unlock the next floor, too...Still, even I couldn't see all'a this comin'. How's this Theano so tough?"

Theano's own daughter answered her. "My mother never ever skipped on her daily training, and sometimes she would go out of town by herself in the middle of the night and come home all bruised in the morning. I think she was fighting monsters in the woods to the south."

"But...why would she do that...?" Asuna asked.

The girl in the gas mask shook her head. "I asked her many times, but she wouldn't tell me. But...now I wonder if all of that was in preparation for this day."

"Now that's just ridiculous!" I wanted to shout. The "Curse of Stachion" quest had gone off the rails because Morte had killed Cylon. If it weren't for that unpredictable event, it would have proceeded like in the beta: Theano would rescue us from our paralysis, we'd sneak into the mansion and convince Cylon, recover the golden cube from the basement dungeon, calm the vengeful ghost of Pithagrus, and finish the quest.

Theano wasn't weak when I fought alongside her in the beta, but her level and stats weren't far off from mine, and definitely not enough that she could blaze through the labyrinth tower solo like this. If Myia was to be believed, the official release version of Theano had been leveling up for ten years, long before Cylon was killed, for a different purpose than what I saw during the beta.

"Welp, let's loot this stuff and get goin'," said Argo, bringing me back to my senses.

I glanced at the items lying around. "Huh...? We're going to loot this?"

"Well, it's either gonna go bad just sittin' around, or the other guilds are gonna snatch it up when they get here."

"I guess…but it was Theano who beat the mid-boss," I said, trapped between courtesy and desire.

Myia looked at me, perplexed. "Mother left these behind because she just couldn't carry them, I think. If you use your Mystic Scribing art to collect them, I'm sure she would appreciate it."

"Ah, g-good point…I'll do that, then…"

I promptly opened my window and tossed the weapons, armor, materials, and other sundry items into my inventory. Argo picked up the slack quickly, and even Asuna hesitantly joined in.

In less than a minute, we'd cleared out all the loot, and our HP was back to full. "Okay, let's…"

"*Go*," I was going to say, but Asuna stuck her index finger against my lips.

"Wait. I just heard something."

"Huh…?"

I shut my mouth and focused on my ears. It did seem like I was hearing very faint yelling and clanging. But it was from below, not above.

"…Sounds like Lin-Kiba are catchin' up…" whispered Argo. She listened two more seconds, then added, "But they're still far off. We're only hearin' the sounds of combat because of all the huge holes in the walls. It's gonna take 'em a good ten minutes or so to get here…Whaddaya think? Should we wait?"

"No, let's go," I said promptly. "Catching up to Theano is a higher priority than grouping up with the rest of them."

"I agree," said Asuna.

Myia lowered her head. "I just…I don't know what to say…"

I placed my hands on her shoulders and spun her around. "You can figure that out once everything is settled. C'mon, let's run!"

"…Okay!"

The group headed for the open door. In the second half of the labyrinth, the level of the random enemies rose noticeably, but checking the mid-boss's loot as we ran, I found an excellent rapier (if not as good as the Chivalric Rapier) and a set of claws that was

+5 to agility, which I gave to Myia and Argo, respectively. We continued upward at about the same speed as we had through the lower half of the dungeon.

The next thing I knew, it was after eight o'clock, but oddly, the crushing exhaustion I felt on the shore of Lake Talpha did not return. I was certain that the *next* time it happened I wouldn't be able to recover, but for now, all I could do was keep running. Asuna should have been just as tired, but she wasn't complaining one bit.

"Hey…" she murmured, drawing a glance from me.

"Hmm…?"

"Have you noticed it's been a while since any enemies showed up?"

"Oh, now that you mention it…"

She was right. The ophidians and other monsters that had persistently shown up even past the mid-boss chamber had been rather quiet the last five minutes. Not because their pop pattern had changed, but because someone ahead of us was clearing them out, and they hadn't re-popped yet. We were within five minutes' distance of Theano.

Our present location was in the middle of the tower's eighth floor, and the boss chamber was on the tenth. At our current pace, we might still be a bit too late to catch her before she reached the chamber.

"This is a gamble…but I think we should throw caution to the wind and just sprint," I suggested. Asuna agreed, and even Argo and Myia looked back at us and nodded.

Before, we had been carefully monitoring for the growls or shuffling of monsters, or the glimpse of red cursors out of the corner of the eyes, but now I jumped ahead at full speed. I often conserved my top speed while working with the front-line group, but I had the lowest agility of the four present, and now I raced with all of my ability. The textures and joints of the walls and floor turned to a blur, and dry air buffeted my face.

When sprinting within a dungeon, your ability to turn—your

cornering, if this were a racing game—was crucial. Without shoes with excellent grip or a high proficiency in the Sprint skill, you might fail to rotate your momentum and crash into the far wall on a turn. So I gave up on ordinary turning and went back to Wall-Running for a few steps first, like I'd done when Asuna and I raced down the stairs at the inn in Stachion.

Asuna and Argo had mastered this style of turning, too, so I went to a Wall-Run on the next left turn. Only when I dropped back to the floor did I mentally kick myself. We had Myia the NPC with us. There was no way she could pick up this sort of outside-the-box hack that defied common logic.

I glanced over my shoulder as I slowed down—and found that I was worried for nothing. Myia, who was in front of Asuna, nimbly ran five steps along the wall, as though gravity meant nothing to her, before transitioning back to the floor. I had to face forward and speed up, lest she overtake me. Apparently, swordfighting wasn't the only thing Theano had taught her daughter.

Knowing that there was no point to going slower now, I went back to the spring and Wall-Ran around the next turn. Obviously, we had to stop and determine the direction when it came to T-intersections and crossroads, and we always chose the route that did not suggest the presence of monsters or that had loot strewn across the floor. At a dead-end, we found yet another hole in the wall, through which there was a staircase on the right. We took it at full speed.

The tenth floor of the labyrinth was almost entirely taken up by the boss chamber, so the ninth was the last floor of actual dungeon. Normally, this was an extremely dangerous place with vicious monsters blocking the way, but Theano's path left behind nothing but treasure—not even a single scarab scurrying along. We didn't have time to stop and inspect the ordinary monsters' loot, but Argo keenly identified just the rare goods as we ran, hooking them with her claws and tossing them into her window. Even I couldn't mimic that kind of dexterity and opportunism.

After three minutes of running down hallways and through

giant holes, skipping all the terrain and gimmicks of the dungeon's ninth floor, we came to an elevated walkway with a stately design, leading to a huge set of stairs. Those would lead to the tenth floor, but there was no one on the walkway or the stairs yet.

I bit my lip. It seemed like Theano must have already gone into the boss chamber...

"Mother...!" Myia wailed, lifting her gas mask and racing past me.

"H-hey!" I shouted, going after her, until I noticed something. There were faint footsteps approaching from ahead, though the person making them was unseen. There were two sets of stairs that met in a landing in the middle before turning back around. Someone—no, definitely Theano—was climbing the stairs after the turnaround, where we couldn't see. She was less than thirty meters away, but the boss chamber was just above us.

Myia crossed the elevated walkway with a speed even Argo couldn't match and flew up the left-hand set of stairs. At this rate, Theano and Myia might jump into the chamber alone and cause the door to shut behind them. I had no other choice but to draw my sword and rest it on my shoulder.

"Nwaaah!" I shouted, launching off the floor with the Sonic Leap sword skill, zooming across the other half of the walkway to the stairs, and intentionally missing the landing. I lost a few pixels of HP, but it kept me rolling directly up the stairs to the landing, where I caught up to Myia.

My skill delay wore off while I was tumbling, so I kicked back off the wall toward the second flight of stairs, looking up to a figure rushing up the steps ahead. It was a woman with golden blond hair, rapier in her right hand and a large cube in her left. The yellow cursor hanging above her head said THEANO.

"Theano!!"

"Mother!!"

But the woman took three or four more steps and only stopped one stair before the tenth floor. She spun around, ponytail and long deep-green skirt whirling. She looked down on us with ash-green eyes the same shade as Myia's.

This wasn't my first time facing Theano, even in the official release. When we got the quest from Cylon at the mansion in Stachion, the first person we went to talk to was Theano the former servant. But she was dressed in a plain apron dress and looked like any other housewife NPC. Now she was dressed in gleaming, fine leather armor and held a rapier. She looked like a veteran swordfighter.

Her regal beauty softened somewhat, and in a soft but clear voice, she said, "Myia...Kirito. I expected that you would follow after me, but I did not think you would catch up."

"Mother..." Myia repeated, unable to do anything but clutch the handle of her rapier with both hands.

Instead, I spoke for the both of us, choosing my words carefully. "Theano, I don't know what you're trying to do. But please don't charge ahead alone. Stay here and talk with us first...with Myia."

Just then, Asuna and Argo caught up and stood to our sides. Theano looked at all four of us in turn and spoke to her daughter again.

"You've gotten so strong, Myia. I'm sorry for disappearing without a word...but this is my role. As long as this cube exists, the cursed puzzles of Stachion will never disappear, and the bloody battle over the inheritance will continue. With Cylon dead, there is no one to hold back the curse...It must be destroyed."

"But how...?!" I asked her desperately. "What are you going to do with it?!"

Theano's response was to stare right at me. "The cube cannot be destroyed in this state. But if returned to the place where it originally belonged, the power that protects it will vanish."

"The place where it belonged...?" Asuna mumbled. She leaned forward a few centimeters. "Is that the boss chamber...the room where the guardian of the Pillar of the Heavens resides?"

"Not quite, Asuna," Theano said, perfectly recalling and pronouncing the name of the fencer whom she'd only briefly met three days earlier. "The place where it belongs is not in the room but in the creature itself. This cube was originally part of the guardian. Long, long ago, Master Pithagrus pulled it out himself and brought it back to Stachion...Well, at the time, it was just a nameless little village. It was the cube's power that helped the town grow into the splendid form it has today, but it was never meant to fall into human hands..."

Theano paused there, then gazed at the golden cube in her left hand.

That's a part of the boss's body? And the previous lord, Pithagrus, separated it from the boss and used its power to create the town of Stachion...?

I struggled to digest this new information that I had never learned in the beta.

The boss of the sixth floor in the beta was a large cube with each face split into three-by-three sections of red, blue, yellow, green, white, and black—essentially a giant Rubik's Cube with hands and feet. If you struck the edges with your weapons, they rotated ninety degrees in that direction. As you repeated it and matched up the colors, the little cubes would scatter and spill off, revealing a core that could be damaged—but I didn't remember any golden cube.

Then again, it wasn't rare at all for the floor bosses to have been altered between the beta test and the official release. In fact, all of them from the first to fifth floor had been updated in some way, large or small, so the sixth could easily be different, too. The question was, what effect would it have to return the golden cube that Pithagrus removed? The first possibility that popped into my mind was that it would recover its original power, i.e. become superpowered. We had to beat the boss and move on to the seventh floor, so that was something to be avoided.

"Listen, Theano," said the info dealer, who never broke character. "The name's Argo—I'm tight with Kirito and Asuna. I was hopin' you might tell me something. What exactly happens if you return that cube to the guardian beast's body? You don't think it might get so super-tough, even you can't defeat it, do ya?"

Will she understand what the term tight with *means?* I wondered, my mind straying. Theano didn't seem bothered by it, though.

"You adventurers are hoping to defeat the guardian in battle to move on to the next floor, I presume…I don't know the full details, but I am certain that returning the cube will cause the guardian to move and attack. But this is not a bad thing for you. While the cube is out of the guardian's body, the guardian is protected by an unseen power that makes it impossible to harm."

""Whaaaa—?!"" Argo and I exclaimed in unison. We looked at each other, then Theano, then each other again.

If what she said was true, the golden cube was absolutely necessary to beating the floor boss at all. But where had that ever been hinted at…?

And yet, I had to remind myself: The "proper" route for the "Curse of Stachion" test was just what I knew from the beta test. Cylon's death certainly twisted its path, but if it had passed normally, there could certainly have been some information relating to the floor boss at the end—and a hint that the cube would be key to the battle.

"…Meaning that when the cube is put back, and the guardian moves again, we can attack it, and beating it will destroy the cube?" Asuna asked. Theano said nothing but nodded firmly.

"Then, Mother—!" Myia cried, breaking her long silence. "Let me help you! I know the guardian beast is terribly dangerous, and I know you are worried about me…but if you go into the chamber alone and never come back, I won't be able to survive on my own!"

I didn't miss the powerful look of conflict and indecision on Theano's features. This wasn't just some pre-written story event—Myia and Theano had their own independent personalities and were acting in ways perfectly faithful to them.

Seconds later, Theano clenched her eyes shut, thought a moment, then opened them again. She put the rapier from her hand into its sheath on her left side and smiled. "All right, Myia.

You've become so, so much stronger than I ever realized...I taught you the sword so you could survive on your own, even without me around, but that was all my own selfish idea. Thank you...please lend me your strength, Myia."

"I will!" Myia exclaimed, casting aside the strangely grown-up air she'd always worn and leaping up the steps to embrace her mother. Theano brushed her daughter's head and looked at us.

"Kirito, Asuna, Argo, I'm grateful to you for protecting my child."

It was your child who was protecting us, I thought, nodding back to her. The three of us ascended the steps and stood at the entrance to the tenth floor with Theano. With her left arm around her daughter, Theano extended a silent hand toward us, which we shook in turn. A fifth HP bar appeared in my view. Hesitantly, I checked the level: 32.

Hrrmm...? I wondered, taking a quick step back. It was a high number, especially to me, a newly made level-21 swordsman. But it didn't seem so high that she should have been able to destroy monsters on her own that much faster than the party of me, Asuna, Argo, and level-23 Myia. Her gear was fine, to be sure, but nothing fancier than what was sold at the stores.

But there was no use second-guessing Theano's power now. If we waited a few minutes, the main body of the front-line group would reach us, too. Surely Theano would agree to fight with the rest of them, knowing it would make Myia safer.

I whispered a request to Asuna to explain the situation to them. She gave me a glance that said *Honestly? Good grief...*before approaching Theano. I exhaled and looked around.

A menacingly decorated hallway continued on from our position for about ten meters, ending in a massive set of bronze double doors. I took a few steps closer to examine them and saw a decorative relief modeled after the exterior of the tower—or of Stachion itself—in a nine-by-nine grid of squares. Beyond this point, the sixth-floor boss awaited, its name and form still unclear.

Normally, you would want at least three trips for scouting, but according to Theano's explanation, you couldn't attack the boss until the golden cube was placed back into it, and it probably couldn't be removed twice, once it was there again. I had a suspicion, based on that activation trick, that the doors to the boss chamber would stay closed until the fight was over.

But in any case, we were here. It had been a string of unexpected developments, but…this wasn't a single-player RPG, it was a VRMMO with eight thousand players trapped inside. There would surely be more and more unexpected things happening to us, and we had to solve and overcome them as we made our way upward. Up to that far-distant hundredth floor.

I spun around forcefully and returned to my party members' side.

Fifteen minutes later, the rest of the player group charged noisily up the stairs—and got an awkward smile in greeting from me. With the help of Asuna and Argo, I gave the skeptical Lind and Kibaou as much of an explanation of why we were here as was possible.

"Oh, so that NPC was with y'all, then?" grumbled Kibaou, but when we told them that the golden cube was a necessary item to beat the boss, there was no more bickering from the two guilds.

After a meeting and cooldown period, we got down to arranging the raid party for the boss fight. Teams A, B, and C went to the three parties of Kibaou's Aincrad Liberation Squad. Teams D, E, and F were made up of Lind's Dragon Knights Brigade. Team G was Asuna, Argo, Myia, Theano, and me. Sadly, members of Agil's Bro Squad were all low in agility and not suited for long sprints, so they hadn't taken part in the chase.

So we were a bit low on the tank quotient, but we'd have to make up for it with mobility, I thought as I leaned against the wall a distance away from the rest of the group. Just to be certain, I scanned the faces of the ALS and DKB present. There were a few new members in the mix, but again, I didn't see Morte or Joe.

That was a good thing, of course, but it also meant we hadn't solved the question of what the man in the black poncho and his friends were doing, allying themselves with the fallen elves. Was it to get the Spines of Shmargor, those paralyzing throwing needles? They were very powerful weapons, but would they really kidnap the members of Qusack and force them to poison the spirit tree for something as minor as getting a good weapon?

"...I wonder if they'll try something else this time," said a voice next to me. It was Asuna, staring down the stairs with a hard expression. She'd been on the same train of thought.

"Hmm...If they are, I don't think Morte and Joe alone could climb this tower to do it. If they've got some plans in mind, it'll be from the seventh floor, right?"

"I...I suppose," she said, but the note of unease was still there in her profile. Between nearly dying along with Cylon and the attack on Castle Galey, the PK gang had us on the defensive all throughout this floor. I understood why she didn't want to let her guard down, lest it happen again.

I glanced around, hesitated, then worked up the courage to move my left hand to the side. My fingers searched for Asuna's hand, and...didn't grab it entirely, but I did squeeze the joints of our pinkies. Her delicate hand twitched, but she didn't yell at me or pull it away. A few seconds later, Asuna's hand moved in return, enveloping my fingertip in her palm with an awkwardly reserved pressure.

It was nine PM on January 4, 2023.

The raid party, all preparations complete, lined up in front of the double doors. At the front, Kibaou barked a short but forceful encouragement to the group and pushed the doors open.

14

IT WAS HUGE.

The tenth floor of the labyrinth tower was almost entirely taken up by the boss chamber, so that wasn't a surprise in and of itself, but my first impression upon seeing the sixth-floor boss room for the first time in four and a half months was that it was just *huge*. The walls, floor, and ceiling were a bluish-gray color, and the weak lighting made the corners of the room look black. There was a huge star drawn on the ceiling high overhead, a reminder that the tower, and this room at the top of it, was actually pentagonal in shape.

Viewed from the desert below, the width of the tower was about half its height. If it was a hundred meters tall, then the diagonal would be about fifty meters, and each side...

"Hey, Asuna, what's the ratio of the side of a pentagon to a diagonal, again...?" I murmured. The fencer shot me a look that said *Why now?*

"It's one to one plus the root of five over two. That's about one point six one eight."

"One point six one eight..." I repeated. "So if the diagonal was fifty meters, a side would be...about thirty meters?"

"Closer to thirty-one, to be precise, but it probably doesn't matter that much."

"I see..."

The only reason we could chat about unimportant topics like this in the boss chamber was because we were waiting for the ALS and DKB to get set up in position. It seemed like we still had another thirty seconds to go. Asuna turned to me this time and said, "One to one plus the root of five over two is called the Golden Ratio."

"Golden...?"

"It's found in the length-to-width ratio of the Parthenon or in the upper and lower halves of the Venus de Milo...even human faces. The width of the nose and mouth are considered well-balanced if their ratio is 1:1.618, apparently."

"Ohhh," I murmured, staring at Asuna's face in an attempt to see if it was true. She promptly jabbed me in the side, and Argo had to warn us, "Hey, we're in a boss chamber!" Myia giggled.

At last, Kibaou shouted from the other side of the room. "Placements are complete! We're ready to go!"

"Got it!" I shouted, glancing behind me briefly. The double doors, which jutted inward about ten meters from one of those pentagon sides, were still wide open. I prayed silently that they would stay that way and looked over to Theano, who stood next to her daughter.

"Well...go ahead, Theano."

"I will," she said, and the warrior focused on the golden cube in her hands. I saw some kind of expression ripple across her beautiful features like waves on a pond, then vanish. "Then let's begin. Don't go too far forward, Myia," she warned her daughter, beginning to walk toward the center of the chamber.

Where she headed sat a very strange object.

Its shape was quite simple. It was a cube about a half meter to a side. It was as black and unreflective as if carved right out of charcoal, and though the details were hard to make out in the dim lighting, there was a square hole about twenty centimeters across on the side facing us. It was obvious at a glance that the golden cube would fit inside perfectly.

"...Once the cube goes in, it'll be so flush, we won't be able to pull it back out..." I noted idly.

On my right, Argo said, "From my inspection earlier, there's a li'l hole on the opposite side of the cube."

"Oh…so you could shove a stick inside and push it back out…?"

"A stick…or…" Argo started to say, then clammed up. Theano had crouched and stuck the cube into the hollow.

The pitch-black hole accepted the cube as though it was oiled up; there was no scraping or catching whatsoever. The moment the black-and-gold surface became one, the dark bluish floor rumbled briefly.

Suddenly, the black cube began to shine with golden light. Theano quickly retreated, and the raid members readied themselves at a safe distance. Many swords and spears reflected the shining light as the cube silently left the floor and floated into the air.

It came to a stop about three meters off the ground, then began to rotate sideways. It started slow but picked up noticeable speed, becoming one with the gloom. Only the line of the golden cube itself remained visible, creating a ring of light in the air.

Grrrng!

The air shook again. A number of golden cubes appeared, practically out of thin air, and began to spin as well. But in fact, though I couldn't count them directly, I knew exactly how many of the cubes there were: twenty-six.

The golden cubes surrounded the rapidly spinning black cube and began to affix themselves to it. The rotation gradually slowed and came to a stop, revealing one golden block that was three times its previous size—now nearly two meters to a side.

The twenty-six cubes had lined themselves up three by three to connect together, but they were not fused; there was a tiny bit of space left between them. In other words, they formed a gigantic Rubik's Cube.

"It's just like the beta! If you hit the edges with your weapons, they'll rotate to…" I stopped short, noticing something different.

In the beta, the sides were red, blue, green, yellow, white, and black. Here, all the sides were the same golden color. Now there was no way to line them up...Or they were already lined up, I supposed.

With the roar of a combustion engine, the twenty-six smaller cubes began to rotate in all directions at random. When they stopped, there was a bright pattern on the faces of each nine-squared side of the cube, for fifty-four squares in total.

No, that wasn't a pattern. It was more familiar than that, something written...

"N...numbers...?!" Asuna gasped, right as a single-bar HP gauge appeared in the air over the giant Rubik's Cube. Below the bar was the boss's official name, shining in bright English letters: THE IRRATIONAL CUBE.

And as I expected, the double doors boomed shut at that moment.

"Here it comes...!" shouted a voice, most likely Lind's.

In reaction to that call, three of the boss's eight corners emitted pale-gray lines that stabbed at the raid party. I summoned all the lung power I had and bellowed, "Evaaaade!!"

Immediately, red laser beams shot forth, tracing the gray lines. They emitted terrifying swooping, sizzling sounds as small explosions erupted at three places in the chamber. Fortunately, no one took a direct hit, but I did see a few of the many HP bars in my vision dip a little due to local heat damage.

The color and name were different from the beta—it had been the Irritating Cube—but this attack, at least, was very familiar. Aiming lines that were hard to pick up came first, followed a second later by the lasers. It would take a huge chunk of HP from any lightly armored players it struck, but as long as you were calm and observant, it wasn't that hard to dodge them...Assuming you didn't trip or get frozen, of course.

Hoping to get a hint from the boss's English name, I turned to my wiser partner and said rapidly, "What does the word *irrational* mean, Asuna?! In the beta, it was *irritating*, which I looked up later..."

"It's kind of like illogical—or incoherent."

"Illogical…" I repeated. *No kidding!* Even a child could line up the colors, but these numbers…Wait, maybe numbers were the same thing…?

"Are you saying that we have to fill each side with the same number?!" I said, hoping I'd found the solution, but Argo shattered that hope just as quickly as it arrived.

"But the numbers go up ta nine!"

She was right. The glowing Arabic numerals were arranged randomly from one to nine, meaning that it would be impossible to match them up on the six separate sides like a classic Rubik's Cube. I even considered the brainteaser-like option of flipping the nine over to be a six, but that wouldn't be enough, and the six and nine had distinctly separate designs anyway.

As though an NPC was what I really needed for a hint, Theano came back our way. "Theano, what do we do with the numb—?" I started to ask, but the woman just shook her head, looking pensive.

"I don't know, either. The legend around the mansion said only that to destroy the golden cube, it must be returned to the body of the tower's guardian…"

"Oh, okay…"

In the meantime, the boss kept firing its lasers from the center of the room. The raid members weaved and jumped out of the way and struck the floating object with their weapons. Each blow caused the rows or columns of the cube to rotate ninety degrees, but there was no change to its HP at all. It seemed the numbered cube was invincible, and we needed to solve its puzzle to pull the blocks off. But there was nothing we could do without figuring out what kind of puzzle it was.

The unease and frustration that filled the chamber finally sparked, and an orange flash went off near the boss. Someone had used a sword skill on it.

"Don't…!" I shouted on instinct, but it was too late, of course.

A two-part spear strike sent up bright sparks from the face of the Irrational Cube, but it did not a single pixel of damage—and the boss sent out an aiming line as if on cue.

"Dodge!" Kibaou bellowed. A gang of players near the line all leaped at once, except for the spearman, who was still frozen from the skill. The red laser seared him dead-on.

"Aaaah!" shrieked the player, right as I heard a dull explosion. It looked like Schinkenspeck from the ALS. He was blasted off his feet and collapsed to the ground. One of the HP bars from Team C went down into the yellow zone, over halfway to zero. His friends helped move him over to the wall, but it would take some time for him to heal up.

"...Maybe we should retreat for now, Kirito..." Asuna said, sounding tense. I bobbed my head somewhat awkwardly.

It was clearly the right option. The boss was invincible, and we didn't know how to undo it. Letting the battle drag on in this state was inevitably going to lead to disastrous results. But...

I spun around and caught sight of the doors, which were shut tight. Asuna gasped; she hadn't realized they'd closed.

"...We don't know for sure they won't open again," I said, out of hope, if nothing else, and raced for them, crossing the ten meters in the blink of an eye and practically slamming my free hand against the door. The thick bronze metal rattled a tiny bit but did not budge. It was locked...

"...?!"

Suddenly, a series of pale lights flashed across my vision, and I turned away. I held my breath, thinking it was an attack from the boss, but felt nothing. I looked back and gasped again.

Numbers.

There was a grid of light, glowing on the surface of the door, with Arabic numerals in the boxes. They were in the same font as the ones on the boss cube's body...but there were more blank squares here than squares with numbers inside.

I took a step back for a better look, right as Asuna arrived beside me. Together we shouted, ""A sudoku puzzle?!""

There was no doubt about it. The exact same kind of puzzles as in the teleport square of Stachion but filling the entire width of the massive doors.

"So if we solve this, the doors will open?!" said Argo over our shoulders.

"I...I think so?" I said uncertainly. "But...there's just no way..."

It wasn't my style to give up before even trying something, but there was no other option this time. This puzzle had twenty-seven rows and columns of sudoku puzzles, each one in the nine-by-nine format, for a total of 729. That was one more than in the square at Stachion, but the layout was identical.

In my mind, I replayed something Asuna had said four days earlier.

At a glance, these look like maximum difficulty, so even an expert would take a good twenty minutes to solve one. Multiplying that by 728 would be 14,560 minutes...divided by sixty, that makes 242 hours and forty minutes...

Two hundred and forty-two hours. A little over ten whole days. That would be an entire day if split between ten people. And trying to do them while avoiding the boss's attacks the entire time? Impossible.

"I'm guessing even the number layouts are exactly the same as in Stachion's square..." Asuna whispered, her voice hoarse. "We should have solved the puzzles in Stachion, then come to this room by the end of the day. That was the minimum requirement for fighting this boss..."

"But how would we...?"

...know that? I tried to say. But I remembered looking up at these doors from the other side and seeing the grid pattern on the relief. It was a nine-by-nine grid. If I had just made the connection to sudoku, I could have remembered about the teleport square in Stachion.

"......Damn!"

I was about to slam a clenched fist against the cold, glowing puzzle—when I heard a voice behind me.

* * *

"Do we just need to solve the puzzles, Kirito?"

My hand paused in midair. I turned around and saw Myia, her gas mask off, staring at me with big eyes.

"You...you can solve this?"

"Yep!" she chirped, much more appropriately for her age now that her mother was around again. She trotted up to the door and reached for the puzzle in the bottom-right corner. Her finger traced the empty spots with dizzying speed until she settled on one glowing space to tap. When a window appeared with all the digits to choose from, she picked a seven. The other spaces disappeared, replaced by a single large seven. It took her a total of ten seconds.

"Wha...? How...how did you do that so fast...?" I gaped.

Myia spun to face me and beamed. "Well, ever since I was a little girl, I solved these puzzles in the town square with my mother every day."

That explanation didn't cover the speed she exhibited...but then I remembered something. Kizmel had no major connection to puzzles, but she had solved that 15 puzzle in the secret-key dungeon in a matter of seconds. If an AI could solve an NP-high problem that fast, these sudoku puzzles must be no harder than simple arithmetic equations to them.

"I'll help you, too, of course," said Theano, who stepped up next to Myia. I looked from their faces to the puzzle behind me and back.

At ten seconds per puzzle, it would take 7,290 seconds to solve 729 of them. That would be a bit over 120 minutes. With the two of them, that would be sixty minutes—an hour. Maybe there was a chance...

"...Please, Theano and Myia, do your best."

They nodded, set up at the right and left corners, and began solving, their fingers flying. I grabbed the shoulder of my still-stunned partner and said, "Asuna, we've got to go grab that boss's attention. Our assignment is to dodge it for the next hour somehow."

"O…okay, if you say so."

"A-and what should I do?" asked Argo.

"When Myia needs to solve the problems higher on the door, you lift her up!" I shouted, and started to run with Asuna toward the center of the chamber—but hit the brakes just as suddenly.

"Wh-what's the big idea?!"

"Hey, listen," I said, "if you select the right number from a pull-down menu, can't we just go and select every number starting from one?"

The fencer gave me the most annoyed look in our entire personal history together and shoved her face so close to mine, our noses nearly touched. "If they set up the puzzle that way, it's obviously going to fail us as soon as we make a mistake!"

"…Oh. Right."

Chastised, I allowed us to run back to the boss for real this time.

The hour that passed after this point was the longest and hardest hour of all the many I'd spent in Aincrad so far. The boss battles of the second and fifth floors had been tough, but I just focused on fighting the enemy and didn't process the passage of time. Those were fights to win and move on. This was different—we were evading attacks for an entire hour just to *escape* the room.

Watch for the aiming beams from the eight corners of the Irrational Cube, then dodge. That was all it involved, but the finders were hard to see, and their timing and location were nastily designed. Often, it would strike the place you dodged on a time delay. It tried to gather multiple players in one place to collide with one another and sometimes incessantly went after a single individual. Whatever thought process it followed, it didn't seem like a simple algorithm.

When Asuna and I joined the front line of battle, we explained the situation to the ALS and DKB, of course, and it had a slight, if undeniable, effect on overall morale. Until that point, everyone had assumed that if the numbers were rotated enough (however it was supposed to work), they would eventually be able to inflict damage. But the intended numbers were a mystery, and anyone would be disappointed to learn that they needed to dodge for an entire hour just to escape. And if your level of concentration dipped, so did your mobility, making the danger rise.

The next thing I knew, over ten of the thirty-six other raid members were back along the wall after taking direct laser blasts. The Irrational Cube hadn't moved far from the center of the room because that was where the majority of the players were. The more people who retreated to the walls, the sooner the boss would start to target them, too—and the wider its movement range, the more likely it might stray toward the entrance doors, where it could attack Myia and Theano in the act of desperately solving all the sudoku puzzles. That was the one thing we *had* to avoid.

Asuna and I shared thoughts with a single instant of eye contact, and I gave the boss the three-part Sharp Nail sword skill. The HP bar didn't budge, of course, but the hate I built up from the cube caused all three targeting lines to aim for me. By that time, however, Asuna had already lifted me in her arms and raced off with me while my skill delay was still active. There was an explosion behind us, but we suffered no damage, just a little prickle of heat on the back.

Next, Asuna gave the boss the three-part Triangular skill, and it was my turn to move her. That should be enough to keep the enemy focused on the two of us.

Naturally, the algorithm wasn't so simple that it would solely focus on the players with the highest hate quotient, and it occasionally strayed to go after others. But if we could draw half the lasers with our high agility, that would give the other six parties some major breathing room.

"Kirito, ahead to the left!"

I followed Asuna's direction to avoid an aiming beam I couldn't see and dashed in that direction. When applicable, I returned the favor.

After this was repeated enough times, something strange began to happen. Every once in a while, before I even heard Asuna's voice, I felt like I knew which way to go. It happened to her, too. More than once, I called out "Right!" *after* Asuna was already jumping that way. It was as though our minds were connected on some other channel beyond just voice and ears...

It was a painful fight, knowing that it would not end in triumph, but I did feel an undeniable kind of elation as I dodged and wove around the targeting lines. When I had a moment to check my window for the time in the few instants the boss traveled away from me, the minutes crawled agonizingly slowly, but finally, a few minutes after ten in the evening—

"It's the last one, Kirito!" came Myia's young but firm voice from the back of the chamber. I leaped backward on instinct and glanced at the doors. Nearly all the sudoku puzzles on their surface had the correct numbers on them, leaving only the central puzzle, which Theano was in the process of solving now.

She hit the key box, selected a number from the pull-down menu, and it promptly enlarged and began to glow.

As expected, over the course of an hour, they'd solved 729 puzzles. A rumble ran through the doors and the rest of the chamber as well. A line of light appeared through the center of the closed doors, and there was the loud clicking sound of a lock unlatching, telling us that our escape route was opening at last.

"Let's retreat to the hallway! Members undergoing healing, get outside first!" commanded Lind, swinging his scimitar. A dozen-plus players drinking potions along the wall stood up and began to run toward the doors. Even the Irrational Cube, which had been wildly firing its lasers just seconds ago, stopped in seeming recognition of the open door.

At the very least, we wouldn't have to worry about the entire front-line group wiping out. It sucked that we couldn't knock even a single pixel off the boss's HP bar, but that was because we were missing a crucial piece of information. If we went back and cleared out all the quests in Stachion or Murutsuki, we would find out whatever way we were meant to line up the boss's numbers…

"Kirito," Asuna whispered, grabbing my elbow. I saw that she was looking at the doors, which were still closed. She was sensing *something*, but she couldn't yet tell what it was, her body language said.

I stared at the huge double doors twenty meters away, feeling the time gradually lengthen.

729 puzzles had turned into 729 numbers that glowed silently at us.

729…which was twenty-seven squared. Twenty-seven rows and twenty-seven columns.

A three-by-three grid of nine-by-nine number blocks.

I craned my neck, looking back at the floating Irrational Cube in the center of the room, then to the door again. I sucked in as much air as my lungs could handle and screamed, "*Stop!!!*"

The player just a few meters from the door stopped reaching for it and turned in the direction of my voice. The DKB's Shivata was closest to me. He looked aghast. "What's wrong? Aren't we getting out of here?!"

"Wait, I think…those numbers…"

I shot Asuna a look and started running until I had thrust myself in front of the door with my hands out in a sign for everyone to keep back. Then I waited. If my hunch was correct, this puzzle wasn't meant to create an escape route. Clearing it would open the door, but that was probably a trick. If we just waited, I was certain, certain…

The raid party's confusion, irritation, and haste grew thicker and darker by the second. Five, six, seven…When nearly thirty seconds had passed since Theano finished the last puzzle, it finally happened.

The 729 numbers suddenly flashed.

Over half the numbers vanished, as though burned away by

the light. In the various blank spots of the grid, there were faintly glowing boxes. Lastly, four of the grid lines thickened, cutting the entire pattern into nine-by-nine chunks.

"Ah…!" Asuna gasped behind me. To my sides, Myia and Theano were equally shocked.

It wasn't a random and meaningless string of numbers arranged in twenty-seven rows and columns. It was a set of nine new sudoku puzzles.

Gaoooong… A tremendous sound somewhere between a machine and the roar of a living creature shook the room. I spun around and saw that the Irrational Cube was moving again. And not just that… three of its four vertical faces were now growing long arms made of dozens of small cubes. The last face began to glow brightly.

"It's comin'!" bellowed Kibaou from the back, readying his sword. Lind issued a similar order to his followers.

"Retreat canceled! Keep healing if you're damaged, come back and remake formation if you're fine!"

They, too, had sensed that the boss's attacks were going to intensify but that it meant there was now a chance to actually beat it.

"Myia! Theano! Handle these puzzles, too!" I shouted. They sprang into action at the doors and began to slide their palms over the much larger puzzles. Ten seconds later, they pressed key boxes in unison and selected their answers. Those numbers grew larger and shone brighter.

Mother and daughter completed their puzzles at the exact same speed, Theano taking the higher puzzles and Myia going for the low ones. Four, six, eight they completed, leaving just one more to go.

There were fierce blasts and crashes and shouts from behind them, but they did their best to tune it out and focus on the moment. Theano put her hand on the center puzzle and selected a five from the menu. The number expanded to fill the space.

The moment all the puzzles were finished, the doors shone with even more light than the previous time. I took several steps back and memorized the order of the nine mammoth numbers on the door.

"Thank you...We'll handle the rest!" I told them, turning back. I raced toward the raid party and shouted as loud as my throat could handle, "From top left across, it's eight, three, four, one, five, nine, six, seven, two!!"

There was a moment of silence.

Then a dull roar arose from all around. With the numbers we needed revealed, the lowered morale began to rise again. In this situation, the teamwork and coordination of the two major guilds were at their best. Even without the members in the process of healing, they got into a formation that quickly surrounded the boss.

And yet, lining up the numbers instead of colors was much harder than one might imagine. The numbers only had to be arranged on the one face that was lit up, but each blow moved three numbers together. You had to be constantly aware of what numbers were on which face and read several moves ahead of the present arrangement.

Three minutes after combat resumed, my fears turned out to be prescient. The rearranging of the numbers was not moving quickly. They got the first four pretty smoothly, but then moving one caused others to go out of alignment, and irritation began creeping into Lind's and Kibaou's voices. If we whacked at it on a hunch, we'd eventually get it, but the boss's long arms were not to be taken lightly. On top of the lasers, we now had to watch out for slams and swipes from the arms, which steadily ground down the HP of the combat members.

I wasn't sure whether to leap into the front row, or if that would only ruin the teamwork the six parties were using.

"...Okay, I've got it," Asuna said abruptly. She shot me a glance. "Kirito, I'm going to focus on giving orders. Can you handle the boss?"

"Uh...yeah, of course."

We gave each other a nod and moved simultaneously. Asuna

leaped in front of the boss and brandished her rapier. "Knock the lower block to the right!"

"G-got it!" replied Hafner from the DKB. He hoisted his greatsword, circled around the right side of the boss, and swiped sideways. Once again, it did no damage, but the lower block did loudly rotate to the right, as Asuna had instructed.

"Now knock the left blocks down!"

"Roger that!" replied the ALS's Okotan, whose halberd shone. The left column of blocks rotated downward.

At this, the Irrational Cube must have sensed a difference, because it let out a discordant metal shriek. It swung two appendages made of cubes, hurtling them down at Asuna. I promptly leaped forward and activated the sword skill Vertical Arc. That was a two-strike combo of downward and upward slices, and it knocked the two arms away. Behind me, Asuna did not move a single step.

Once she focused solely on the numbers, Asuna's orders were frighteningly precise. With each block rotation, we could sense it growing closer to completion.

But the boss could sense it, too, and it viciously, repeatedly went after Asuna, who was not physically attacking it. I could knock the arms away with sword skills, but the lasers were trickier. Each time the aiming beams swept toward her, I picked her up and jumped out of the way, but that got even harder when it did a delayed combination of lasers and then physical attacks. The raid members looked desperate, but if they tried attacking the boss to draw its attention, the cube formation we'd been working so hard on would be ruined, and if too many tried to surround her for protection, she wouldn't be able to see the numbers.

After yet another backward leap to escape a laser, my back struck a hard, flat surface. Somehow, I'd been pushed against the wall without realizing it. Two arms went into flat swiping motions from my sides, right on cue. I could strike back one of them, but not both…

"I'll get this one, Kirito!" said a voice. I shouted back, "Do it!"

and focused on the arm coming from the left. After I knocked it away with Horizontal, I turned to my right and saw Theano thrusting the other appendage away with her sword.

The strength of a hundred! I marveled silently, preparing for the next attack. Meanwhile, Asuna continued giving orders, which the stout warriors of the raid party faithfully carried out. Occasionally, they made the wrong input, but undoing it was as easy as reversing the last strike.

The damageless assault on the boss lasted for twenty-something moves when Asuna's clear voice called out, "Next one is the last! Strike the center blocks down!"

"We got it!" "Yer on!"

Lind and Kibaou had no intention of letting the other have the honor of the last blow. They charged from either side and slashed at the center-block column with scimitar and longsword together.

Don't push it, Lin-Kiba! I thought, but their aim was true. The center column rumbled and rotated, revealing an order of three, five, seven. The nine numbers on the front face of the boss shone so brightly, I couldn't look directly at them.

"We got it!" someone shouted, which was nearly drowned out by a deafening rumble as the twenty-six cubes and three arms that made up the Irrational Cube's invincible armor crumbled away.

Countless shards melted into thin air, revealing that pitch-black cube, a half meter to a side. In the middle of the side that faced us, we could see a smaller item—the golden cube that Theano put in there.

This time, six new black arms extended from the black cube. They made unpleasant high-frequency ringing sounds as they writhed toward us.

"This is the real battle! Take it slow, an' let's figure out the patterns!" Kibaou boomed. Both the ALS and DKB alike shouted "Yeah!" in response.

It was a fierce battle indeed, but without its spotless armor, the Irrational Cube didn't have the defense to stand up to the elite fighters of the advancement group, and more importantly, the level-32 mother swordswoman, Theano. Its single HP bar fell slowly but surely, past 50 percent, then 30…and in only seven minutes, it was down below 10 percent.

Once everyone knew that the next good shot would end it, the Irrational Cube let out a horrid shriek that sounded like its dying cry and swung its six arms around wildly. All eight of its corners sent out aiming beams.

"It's going wild! Buckle down!" Lind commanded. Everyone went on guard.

Within a moment, all the arms had been deflected, and all the lasers dodged—and as though its batteries had run dry, the boss of the sixth floor of Aincrad fell to the floor with a thud and ceased moving. I relaxed my shoulders, thinking it was finally over…but there was one stubborn pixel remaining on its HP bar.

"Wha…? Hey, what gives?! Izzit gonna self-destruct?!" Kibaou wailed. I wondered the same thing. The raid members nearest to the landing point sprang away and buckled down against an explosion…but nothing happened. The boss, golden cube pointed my direction, was silent.

That reminds me, Argo said something about this, I recalled. *Something about the reverse side of the cube…*

At that moment, someone leaped forward toward the cube. Whoever it was must have assumed there would be no self-destruct and wanted to seize the last attack bonus. He was dressed in silver and blue—the DKB. Lind would probably scold him later, but this would, at last, be the end of the long, long battle…

"Huh…?!" Asuna gasped at my side, and I suddenly realized what she was looking at.

It wasn't a weapon the running player had in his hand. It was a narrow piece of metal only a few centimeters long. A throwing needle…no.

A key.

Time froze as the slender player crouched behind the back of the cube and stuck the key into the keyhole where I couldn't see it. There was a faint click, and the golden cube slid out of the block, tumbling to the floor.

"…!"

Theano let out a sharp breath and jumped forward. I raced after her.

The DKB member stood up. He circled around the block and scooped the cube off the floor.

As she ran, Theano silently drew her rapier.

The DKB member raised the cube high with both hands and shouted.

"Bind!!"

There was a sound of slicing air, and a ring of golden light shot forth from the cube, swallowing Theano and me as it passed us. My feet suddenly stuck to the floor, and I tipped over spectacularly. I thought I was going to tumble, but because my feet were stuck to the ground, I only leaned at an extreme angle before bouncing back upright. Theano was similarly rooted to the spot.

"…?!"

Stunned, I looked down to see translucent cubes growing out of the floor to engulf my feet. On instinct, I checked my HP gauge. To the right of the list of buffs, there was a new icon that hadn't been there a second before. It was an unfamiliar debuff: a human silhouette within a square border.

"*Why?! Why would you do this?!*" I tried to yell, but then I belatedly noticed that I had no voice. My entire body—legs, arms, even fingers—was as heavy as lead.

Even in the midst of this emergency, a part of my mind was occupied with a different question. Theano's level was quite high but not enough to obliterate the monsters of the tower in one hit. She must have used the power of the golden cube to freeze, or Bind, the ophidians.

Suddenly, I realized the boss chamber was filled with silence. I could hear no voices, nor even the scraping of metal armor.

Golden light filled the vast, fifty-meter chamber from corner to corner. Every last raid member must have been bound. I couldn't move my right hand, so I couldn't even open my window. It was the ultimate immobilization debuff, far beyond even the paralyzing poison.

The mystery DKB player slowly lowered the golden cube. He wore a sallet helmet that covered the top of his head, leaving only the mouth visible. The cursor over his head was orange, the criminal color, certainly because of the debuff he'd just used. His name was Buxum. I couldn't recall ever seeing that name in a raid fight before.

Buxum's mouth abruptly curled into a savage grin. The moment I saw it, I knew.

He was with Morte and Joe. He was one of the black poncho's followers. At some point, he had infiltrated the DKB, waiting for this very moment to strike.

If it were Morte, he'd laugh his dry laugh and spout some theatrical lines at this point, but Buxum just leered and said nothing. Instead, he transferred the large cube to one hand so he could draw his longsword.

It was modestly made, but the wet gleam on the thin blade spoke of stats that were no joking matter. The sword dangled from his hand as he strode right toward Theano.

He's going to kill her, I realized instantly.

Whether he was going to kill the entire raid party starting with Theano, or just the NPC on her own, I wasn't sure. But even if the latter, I couldn't passively watch it happen. Myia was behind me. There was no way I could allow a ten-year-old girl to watch the mother she'd just been reunited with be helplessly slaughtered. No way at all…

"………!"

Stressed, silent air escaped my throat in place of a scream. I used every bit of force I could summon. My avatar's muscles quaked and joints creaked. But the invisible shell that surrounded me did not budge.

Buxum came to a stop before Theano. He lifted his sword and aimed carefully at her heart, preparing to finish it all in a single blow.

Move.

Move move move movemovemovemovemove!!

It was the only word in my mind, the boundaries between the start and end blurring into one pattern of sounds, losing meaning. A high-pitched ringing sound rose from deep within me, spreading from fingers to toes...

And then I saw it.

The Bind debuff icon was blinking. A new icon began to flicker next to it. The silhouette of a person in a Zen meditative pose. It was...*not* the Meditation buff. The design was the same, but there was now a golden ring behind the silhouette.

————————*!!*

I thought I heard something break.

My right foot pounced off the floor, instantly launching me over ten meters forward. Drawn by invisible strings, I swung back the Sword of Eventide. Buxum noticed my charge; his eyes widened through the slits of the sallet helm. With remarkable reaction speed, he lifted his sword and took a defensive position.

"Raaaaaahh!!" I bellowed, swinging my sword on a direct line at him.

Pkiiing! It almost sounded like a scream.

Buxum's longsword split just above the hilt—and so did his left arm behind it, nearly to the elbow.

Momentum carried me straight past both Theano and Buxum. As soon as I landed, I spun 180 degrees. It was fast enough that I normally would have tumbled, but it was as if inertia no longer existed.

The twisted smile was gone from Buxum's face, now that he had lost his sword and arm. With his good arm, he lifted the cube again.

"Bi..."

But before the word was out of his mouth, I swung again.

Like the left arm, his right was severed at the elbow, and it vanished pitifully on the spot. Without its support, the golden cube thudded to the floor.

Even for an enemy, I had to admire the quickness with which Buxum reacted after losing both arms. He promptly spun around and raced with tremendous speed for the exit.

"Oh, no, you don't!" I yelled, but the strength had gone out of my legs, and I fell to my knee right on the spot. The icon that resembled the Meditation buff blinked and went away.

I managed to get to my feet, but by that point, Buxum was already at the door. He slammed into it to push it open and vanished into the hallway. There was no way I could catch up to him at that speed.

A few seconds later, one of the HP bars from Team F on the left side of my view neatly disappeared. Struggling against the stifling weight that seemed to be the physical cost of the mystery buff, I surveyed the boss chamber. Theano, Asuna, Argo, Myia, and all the other raid members were still under the effect of the binding spell. Surely it wasn't permanent, but how to undo the paralysis? The answer to that was obvious, however.

I sheathed my sword and scooped the cube up off the ground, then walked over toward the black block. There was still the one pixel of health on the bar hanging in the air over it.

I knelt in front of the boss and gazed at the golden cube, in my hands at last. This object had changed the lives of many people. Cylon, Theano, Myia, Terro the gardener, and probably Pithagrus, too. Now it was time for it to be destroyed.

I stuck the cube against the hole in the block and pushed, and it smoothly slid inside on its own. I waited until the surface was sheer to draw my sword again.

Using the pommel, rather than the well-worn blade edge, I struck the top of the black cube.

That was enough. Cracks spread from the spot, and blue light spilled out from within. At that moment, the Irrational Cube, boss of the sixth floor of Aincrad, was out of HP, and it crumbled into pieces, including the golden cube within it. Only the steel key escaped that fate. It tumbled lightly to the floor.

I plopped down on the seat of my pants as the message proclaiming the LAST ATTACK bonus appeared overhead.

A moment later, the raid members were released from their negative status, and an uproar promptly arose. Some people collapsed to the ground, others flipped over, and Kibaou turned on Lind.

The boss chamber was now light, as though waking from a nightmare, and full of lively sound. I looked up when I heard footsteps approaching and saw Theano coming over.

It wasn't just her. Asuna, Myia, and Argo were all rushing toward me.

Enveloped in an irresistible blanket of fatigue, I could do nothing more than lift my right hand to wave at my beloved companions.

15

"WHEW…WE FINALLY MADE IT BACK…"

Asuna stretched luxuriously as I opened my menu window. But I couldn't even be bothered to keep my hand lifted, and so I let it dangle. It was 12:40 AM on January 5.

I waved my left hand to dispel the window and surveyed my surroundings.

Despite it still being early in the night by online gamer standards, the teleport square of Stachion, main town of the sixth floor, was nearly devoid of people. There were two reasons, by my reckoning: The gate on the seventh floor had been activated, so the tourists were up above, and all the sudoku puzzles that had filled the square were completely gone now.

There was little lingering affection for the puzzles in me, but Theano, who stood on the far side of Asuna, looked out at the blank tiles with a reflective expression. Resting on her back was Myia's adorable sleeping face, with the gas mask sitting atop her head.

Only two hours had passed since the defeat of the Irrational Cube, the sixth-floor boss, and in that time, the trek back through the desert of the fifth area, the passage over Lake Talpha, and the shortcut through the woods of the first area had taken… no time at all, actually. Instead, we climbed the spiral stairs that descended from the ceiling of the boss chamber up to the seventh floor, walked to the main town there, activated the teleporter, and took it back here.

That made Myia and Theano, as far as I was aware, the first quest NPCs to use a teleport gate to travel between floors. In fact, I was even worried that the two might not make it through and would simply be stuck on the seventh floor, but the *SAO* system was more generous than I imagined. Though there was always the chance, like Liten's infinite ore bug, that it would be patched out later.

As for Theano, she had no particular interest in the magical gateway she'd walked through. Instead, she stared at the square and the town in the distance in silence. Eventually, she walked over to Asuna and me and gave us a bow, with Myia still being carried on her back.

"…Kirito, Asuna, you have truly saved me…Not only did you keep Myia safe, but I am certain that I would not have been able to defeat that guardian beast and destroy the golden cube on my own."

Um, you know Myia's a higher level than us, right? I wanted to ask her but wisely refrained. Instead, I shook my head and said, "Please…if you and Myia hadn't solved the puzzles on the door, we would have been trapped inside the chamber and died there."

"He's right," added Asuna. "I think I'm pretty good at those puzzles, but I could never manage one in ten seconds."

Theano smiled weakly. She readjusted her sleeping daughter's position and turned around to view the rising stair-step layout of Stachion. At the end of the main street, the lord's mansion shone in the moonlight. There was no light in the windows, making its lack of a resident clear.

"Um…what's going to happen to the mansion—er, to the entire town?" I asked. I couldn't help it.

In a sense, the town in an RPG was operated by the game system, not by the mayor who lived there, so Cylon's absence shouldn't actually have any effect on the town itself. But I couldn't miss the indescribable sadness in Theano's face as she stared up at the mansion, which prompted my question.

Without turning back to us, she whispered, "I think…nothing will change, except for the puzzles being gone. It was Lord Pithagrus who built up Stachion and saw to its management. He challenged that fearsome guardian beast alone, extracted the golden cube, and used its powers of Break—reducing all stone and plant matter to cubes—and Bind—to stick those cubes together with unbreakable force—to build this great settlement…"

"What…? So Bind was supposed to stick the cubes together?" Asuna asked, startled.

The lady swordfighter looked back and nodded. "That is its intended use. But when a living thing is within its radius, that being will be bound as well. According to Lord Pithagrus, the golden cube was a prototype tool of war fashioned by the mages of the Alliance of the Nine that once existed in the lost lands."

"…"

I looked at Asuna. Kizmel told us the story of Aincrad's creation myth, the Great Separation, but I assumed it was just the elven legend. *Who was this Pithagrus guy anyway?* I wondered, well after the fact, but I wasn't in the mood to dig up the "Curse of Stachion" quest now that we'd finished it. There were plenty of other things to worry about.

For example, the fact that the fallen elf Kysarah had stolen the four sacred keys we collected. And even worse, the mysterious Buxum, who used the golden cube to immobilize us all in the boss chamber and tried to kill Theano at the very least—and possibly the rest of the raid party as well. The ALS and DKB were going to hold an emergency meeting in that chamber, but Asuna and I didn't want Theano and Myia to hear about our death-game predicament, and so we escorted them directly to the seventh floor. The situation couldn't be ignored, however, so I knew that soon I would need to gather the principal members of both guilds and explain everything I knew about the man in the black poncho and his cohorts. After they had witnessed Buxum's deeds for themselves, it shouldn't be hard to convince them that there was a gang of PKers on the loose.

"Ten years it has been since Lord Pithagrus died..." Theano said, picking up where she left off. I had to switch gears to focus on her story. "In that ten years, the mysterious power that protected the cube seeped into the town, bit by bit, growing puzzles on every door in Stachion, just like in the Pillar of the Heavens. I do not know how Lord Pithagrus was holding the power of the cube back, but I always hoped to work with Cylon to discover it, so that we could remove the puzzles that tormented the townsfolk. But..."

She hesitated, darkness blotting her features. In a quieter voice, she continued, "But I could not forgive Cylon for killing Lord Pithagrus in that fit of anger. We had promised to share our future together...which is why I wanted him to admit his sin, to repent, and think about what one must do to truly become the town lord. For ten long years, I waited for the day he would come to visit me..."

As I watched her shake her head, I felt a frequent question come to mind, and without really thinking, I gave voice to it.

"Um, Theano...what was it about Cylon that made you—?"

Asuna elbowed me in the side, which made me realize I'd been asking a potentially rude question. But Theano just smiled wistfully and looked somewhere far off.

"Ever since childhood, he was weak-willed, suspicious, yet proud, and always fighting with the other children..."

Since childhood? They were childhood friends? I wondered, then realized it had to be true. The biggest city on the sixth floor was only six hundred meters north to south and half as wide. Every single child of the same generation would have known one another.

"But really, he was very kind. From early on, it had been arranged for me to serve at Lord Pithagrus's mansion. I was worried, but in order to cheer me up, he said, 'Don't worry, I'll pass Lord Pithagrus's test and become his apprentice. Just hang in there.' He kept his word and dreamed that eventually he would become the next lord of the town, marry me, and we would live in that mansion together. But…when he learned that he would not be chosen, the shock and disappointment must have been great…"

"…Huh? But…" I stammered, glancing briefly at Asuna. "I thought Pithagrus was going to choose you to be the next master of the town. So Cylon shouldn't have been quite so devastated…"

Theano looked bewildered for a moment, then shook her head rapidly. Over her shoulder, Myia murmured in her sleep, and her mother gently rocked her back to a peaceful state. Then she focused on us again and gave another shake of her head.

"No…Lord Pithagrus did teach me, a servant, all about puzzles, but that was more of a game to him. He did not need an heir. Lord Pithagrus was immortal; he had lived for centuries before the town of Stachion was ever built."

"Wh…*what*?!" I yelped, clamping my mouth shut. Once I was sure that Myia hadn't woken up, I resumed in a much quieter voice, "He…he couldn't die…?"

I was beginning to wonder if perhaps Pithagrus hadn't been murdered but was still alive out there somewhere, but Theano made a negative gesture.

"No, I suppose I should say he had everlasting life. He couldn't die of old age. When I came to the mansion, he was already a wizened old man with white hair, but the butler, who was the eldest of all the servants, claimed that Pithagrus already looked that way when *he* was a boy, too."

"…So…when Cylon learned the truth…" Asuna mumbled, and Theano nodded.

"He discovered that Lord Pithagrus would not die of old age, and there would be no handing down of the position…it was the anger, disappointment, and perhaps even fear he felt that drove him to that terrible act. Much like this town itself, Lord Pithagrus was a man unbound by human reason…"

Theano stopped there, a lucid gaze in her eyes, and I sensed that I did not need to pry any further about Cylon. Instead, I felt in my belt pouch for the item I picked up at the end of the boss fight—a dull metal key.

"Um…you should have this, Theano," I said, handing it over. She looked at it for a moment before accepting it. Holding up the key that was once two in the moonlight, she said, "So this key was always meant to be one…Lord Pithagrus gave Cylon and me those keys in the last days of our eighteenth year, but he did not say what they were for. I could never have guessed that they made the key to remove the cube from the guardian beast's body… Why would he give such a thing to us…?"

Neither Asuna nor I had the answer to that question.

At the end of the "Curse of Stachion" quest in the beta, the ghost of Pithagrus bestowed his forgiveness upon Cylon for killing him, told him to work with Theano to protect the town, and vanished. In other words, the Pithagrus of the beta named Cylon and Theano together as his successors.

I wondered if perhaps the same thing would be true of this immortal version of Pithagrus, but I couldn't bring that up.

Instead, Asuna took it upon herself to say, "I am sure that he loved you—and Cylon."

Without a word, Theano looked at the distant mansion again. I felt as though a little glimmer of light may have appeared on the side of her face, but when she turned back to us again after a good long while, all I saw was the same little smile.

"…You might be right."

Theano placed the key inside the collar of her armor, then reached back to stroke her sleeping daughter's head.

She demanded that we come and visit again someday, before taking her daughter out of the square. When their HP bars vanished, a system message appeared in the center of my vision, telling me that a quest had been completed.

Unlike in the beta, we got no col or items, but there were more than enough experience points to make up for it, and both Asuna and I received the level-up effect at the same time. I was level 22 now, and Asuna level 21, but I wasn't in the mood for my usual "Yahoo!" leap.

"The number! And more than just that, but *the number!*" she exclaimed, pounding her hands onto the side of the bed across from where I was lying. I wanted to tell her to save it for tomorrow, but she was too fired up for that, so I managed to roll onto my side and ask, "What number...?"

Asuna leaned over closer, her hazel-brown eyes glittering with excitement. "The door to Pithagrus's secret home in Suribus! Remember the six-digit number on the dial lock? It was driving me crazy that I couldn't figure out what it meant!"

Now that she mentioned it, when I told her the code to undo the lock, she had said something to that effect. That it was familiar to her somehow...

"What was it...six, two, eight, four, nine, six...?" I said, wringing the numbers loose from memory.

She nodded twice. "That's right. That's not just a random string of numbers. They're the first three perfect numbers."

"...P-perfect numbers...?"

It sounded like something I might've learned about in school. Curiosity drove sleep away just enough for me to prop up my head with my left arm. "What's so perfect about them?"

"A perfect number is defined as an integer that is equal to the sum of its proper divisors. See, the factors of six are one, two, and three, right? If you add them up, they make six. And the factors of twenty-eight are one, two, four, seven, and fourteen... which add up to twenty-eight. And four hundred ninety-six is the next one."

"Ohhh...I see..."

It was an interesting discovery but didn't seem like more than a curiosity. It just meant that whoever wrote the story for the "Curse of Stachion" quest picked out the first three perfect numbers on a whim for that lock.

But Asuna already knew what I was thinking. "That's not all of it! So, um...when you did the beta, you saw the cursor for the ghost of Pithagrus, right?"

"Y-yeah, I did."

"What was his name? How was his name spelled?"

"Uh…actually, I think it was just a generic title like Restless Soul, without an individual name attached to it…"

"Ah. So they were hiding it, then," she replied seriously. Then, without warning, Asuna hopped onto the bed. She rolled onto her side next to me and opened her window so I could see. Without showing any recognition of how stunned I was, she went to the MESSAGES tab and used a blank message field as a notepad to type in the Western alphabet.

"You see, I think the proper spelling of Pithagrus's name is probably this. We just never saw it written down this way, only heard it spoken."

"O-okay…?"

I laid my head back down on the pillow to see the window, which contained the following string of letters.

PYTHAGORAS.

"P…Pie…tha…What? Is that how his name is supposed to be spelled?"

"Yes, going by the English spelling. But this might not ring a bell for you yet. You'd be much more familiar with the Japanese pronunciation…or proper Greek."

"The Japanese pronunciation…?"

Truly confused now, I looked at the window again. I tried to sound out the letters in the way that foreign sounds were represented in Japanese.

"Pi…sa…goras? Pisa…Wait, no…should it be a T? Pitagoras?! Wait, is this the famous—?!"

Ninety percent of my sleepiness was gone, shot through with adrenaline.

I wasn't the most attuned student at school, but even I knew this name. In the second semester of my second year of middle school, just before I got trapped in *SAO*, I had learned about Pythagoras, the ancient Greek mathematician whose name was associated with the theorem about the sides of a right triangle. He was the founder of some kind of math club named after himself, too, and discovered a whole bunch of mathematical properties and concepts. So he would have been the one who named them "perfect numbers."

"...So why didn't they just make it clear that he was Pythagoras from the start...?" I grumbled, earning a chuckle from Asuna.

"They probably wanted to put a little distance between the character and the historical figure, and that's why they hid the alphabetical spelling. He would've only been the model for the character, after all..."

"Ah...Was the real Pythagoras good at solving puzzles, too?"

"No, I've never heard anything to that effect. And he's never been called the king of puzzles or whatever. Although, I do think his focus on the harmony and integrity of numbers bears some connection to the concept of puzzles."

"Uh-huh..."

I rolled onto my back and thought back dully on the events of the past four days.

"And the real Pythagoras *was* killed by his own follower," Asuna muttered.

"Huh...he was...?"

"Technically, it was a person who wanted to join his scholastic order, whom Pythagoras rejected. So the man whipped up the people of the town to attack the order out of revenge...Although, I don't remember if his name was Cylon or not..."

"Whipped them up..." I repeated, thinking not of the quest but of the man in the black poncho and his friends. The man named Buxum who infiltrated the DKB and tried to steal the golden cube somehow knew where to use the iron key, when even Theano didn't. And beyond that, he even knew how to utilize the terrible Bind powers of the cube.

How did Buxum get the iron key that Kysarah the fallen elf stole from Myia and me? And how did Buxum and the black-poncho man arrange their relationship with the Fallen in the first place?

The curse quest was over, and we beat the boss of the sixth floor without any casualties, but the mysteries and unaddressed problems were everywhere. If I wanted to solve those issues, and ensure that I could protect Asuna from harm, I had to be stronger. Strong enough to fight Kysarah one-on-one.

"Oh, right, Kirito."

The mention of my name caused my half-closed eyelids to rise again. Asuna sat up and looked straight down at me.

"Wh-what…?"

"Let me see your eyes."

"H-huh…?" I blinked, unsure of what my partner wanted to do.

To my surprise, she said, "In the boss chamber, when you broke through the Bind, I felt like your eyes were shining gold."

"What…really? They were? Are they now?"

"No, they're black."

"Oh…"

Relieved, I relaxed and let my gaze lock with Asuna's hazel-brown eyes. Instantly, I felt something leaving my body and knew that I was really at the limit of my wakefulness now.

Asuna's little smile melted into darkness, and through fading wits, I heard her faint whisper:

"Good night, Kirito."

"*Good night, Asuna*," I said, although I couldn't be sure if it ever left my lips.

(End)

AFTERWORD

Thank you for reading *Sword Art Online Progressive 6*, "Canon of the Golden Rule (End)."

It feels like this one turned out half as long as the first part again, but that's probably just my imagination. Anyway, it scares me to think that, in the planning stage, I thought I could tell a story of this length in one book...I honestly have no idea how it got this long! But that would be the boring version of my thoughts on this story, so instead, I'll jot down some loose reflections.

As symbolized by masterpieces like *Dragon Quest* and *EverQuest*, the concepts of RPG and quest are inseparable. You might say the quest itself is the heart and soul of the RPG. And the format of single-player RPGs always contains your main quest and your subquests.

But when it comes to MMORPGs, I've always felt that the nature of the quest becomes unstable and uncomfortable. As Kirito himself has opined a number of times in the story, you have the same events happening for every player that plays them, the same stories playing out, and this involves some degree of warping the experience—and forcing the narrative to fit the shared world. I've always understood that this was unavoidable but felt it wasn't the ideal way to do things. If there's one quest out there, shouldn't only one player be able to complete it?

I understand that's practically impossible, of course. But what if, instead of a human scenario writer and programmer, an AI acted like the GM of a tabletop RPG, generating infinite quests and adjusting the story to fit the characters' actions? Couldn't the ideal of a story "just for you" become a reality that way? This was a thought I entertained as I wrote this book. I think I managed to stick to my idea of having Kirito and Asuna's quest go further and further from the baseline scenario due to the interference of PKers and NPCs, but next I want to write a player-centric story! In a single volume this time!

If I have any regrets, it's that I wasn't able to use the puzzle theme of the sixth floor more effectively. Originally, I wanted to provide a number of puzzles throughout the story for you readers to tackle, but I didn't like the idea of it turning into the kind of book where the reader can choose one of multiple branching paths. If Bandai Namco ever makes *SAO* into a real VRMMORPG, I'm going to force them to put lots of puzzles in the sixth floor (*laughs*).

Finally, my acknowledgments…To my editors, Miki and Adachi, and my illustrator, abec, for really pushing the schedule with my ballooning page count, I offer my sincerest apologies and gratitude! See you on floor seven in Volume 7!

Reki Kawahara—March 2018